FEATURED WORKS BY DAVID ESTES

THE FATEMARKED EPIC
Fatemarked • Truthmarked • Soulmarked
Deathmarked • Lifemarked

THE KINGFALL HISTORIES
Kingfall • Dragonfall • Magefall • Nightfall • Endfall

THE SLIP TRILOGY
Slip • Grip • Flip

THE DWELLERS SAGA
The Moon Dwellers • The Star Dwellers
The Sun Dwellers • The Earth Dwellers

THE COUNTRY SAGA
Fire Country • Ice Country
Water and Storm Country • The Earth Dwellers

SALEM'S REVENGE
Brew • Boil • Burn

STANDALONE NOVELS
Strings • Star-Born Mage

Fatemarked © 2017 by David Estes
Map © 2017 by David Estes
Interior design © 2022 Robin Sullivan
978-1-943363-24-7 - Limited Edition Hardcover
978-1-943363-25-4 - Regular Hardcover Edition
978-1-943363-26-1 - Trade paperback

Published in the United States by Riyria Enterprises, LLC
Printed in China
Learn more about Michael's writings at michael-j-sullivan.com
To contact David, email him at davidestesbooks@gmail.com

First Edition

2 4 6 8 9 7 5 3 1

Published by
RIYRIA
ENTERPRISES

For all the high-fantasy lovers.

Author's Note

Hello! I'm David Estes, the author of more than thirty fantasy and science fiction novels including the bestselling Fatemarked Epic and my latest series: The Kingfall Histories. With the release of this book, I'm entering a new phase in my writing career—one that has already lasted more a decade.

You see, most independent authors focus on ebooks and many utilize the Kindle Unlimited program—which is essentially Netflix for books, where a monthly subscription gives readers access to tens of thousands of titles and authors are paid based on the number of pages read.

I'm one of those "KU authors," and the Fatemarked books have done extremely well since the first book was release in 2017. Across the series readers have consumed more than 161 million pages! When I add in paid ebook sales, audiobooks, and print on demand paperbacks, there have been more than 330,000 copies sold. That's surreal!

I LOVE being an indie-author. Yes, it's a lot of work, but hard work has never been something I've shied away from. There is one downside to indie-publishing though—and that is the lack of physical books (especially signed copies). Now when it comes to paperbacks, indie authors can utiize print-on-demand production, and I have sold more than 7,000 of those across the Fatemarked Epic. But print-on-demand books have many limitations, the biggest being they can't be sold in retail stores, and they are rarely purchased by libraries.

Why? Several reasons.

The first relates to the high per-unit cost of print-on demand production. Bookstores typically have a 50% margin (in other words they buy the books for half the price they sell them for) and since print-on-demand books typicall cost three to four times more than books that are offset printed, the economics don't add up.

Second, bookstores don't actually "buy books" from publishers; they receive them "on consignment." In other words, they don't have to pay for the books "up front" they receive copies and only pay for those that sell and return unsold copies back to the publisher. But print-on-demand doesn't work that way. Money MUST change hands before the books are produced, and that runs counter to the entire book retailer model.

And lastly, returns are problematic with print-on-demand. This form of production doesn't have "warehousing" and as such there is nowhere to store them (or easy way to get them "back into circulation").

So what's an indie author to do if they want to expand their reach by selling through retail chains and/or directly to readers? Well it requires a lot of infrastructure and a large amount of capital investment.

The first requirement is to do a "print run" where thousands of books are produced. This type of "mass production" drives down the per-book cost, but requires thousands of dollars that must be paid before any books are sold. Then you need somewhere to put all these books and warehouse fees are charged monthly based on how much space your books are taking up. And lastly you need a book distributor, an organization that is already processing sales orders from the retail chain.

Which brings me back to the whole "entering a new phase" aspect to my writing career. The book you hold in your hand was offset printed and the funds to do that were raised through a Kickstarter. For those that aren't familiar with Kickstarters they provide fuel for the entrepreneural spirit. Basically a "creator" decides on a product (or products) to produce, and "backers" pledge funds to pre-order something that doesn't currently exist. For my Kickstarter I produced three different versions of Fatemarked (a) a limited edition faux-leather hardcover, (b) a trade paperback and (c) a regular hardcover with a dust jacket. And because I printed more than just the number required for the Kickstarter, we are warehousing the extra books and making them available in retail chains, online stores, and also sold directly from my website.

While the limited edition copies are only available directly from myself, the regular hardcovers and trade paperbacks will be sold utilizing book distributors, allowing my indie-published titles to appear in bookstores and purchased by libaries. I think just about all authors dream of seeing their books on store shelves, and while that has historically been reserved for only traditionally published authors, the print-run opens the doors to expanded distribution for this book.

So, my eternal thanks goes out to all the supporters of the Kickstarter (many of whom have their names printed in this book in the Kickstarter Backers Section). Not only did you make the Kickstarter a huge succes but non-backer readers will benefit as well. Based on how well this Kickstarter has gone, I hope to be doing more of them for the other books in the series.

Well, I've taken up enough of your time (and maybe talked too much about the publishing business than you wanted to know about), so I'll take my leave. Here's hoping that you'll enjoy Fatemarked, and if you do there are a number of other books based in this world: five books in the Fatemarked Epic and another five in the Kingfall Histories (three currently released and two more coming soon). While you are reading, I'll continue to work hard to keep the stories coming. If you keep reading, I'll keep writing!

David Estes
September 2022

Map

To view a downloadable map online:
http://davidestesbooks.blogspot.com/p/fatemarked-map-of-four-kingdoms.html

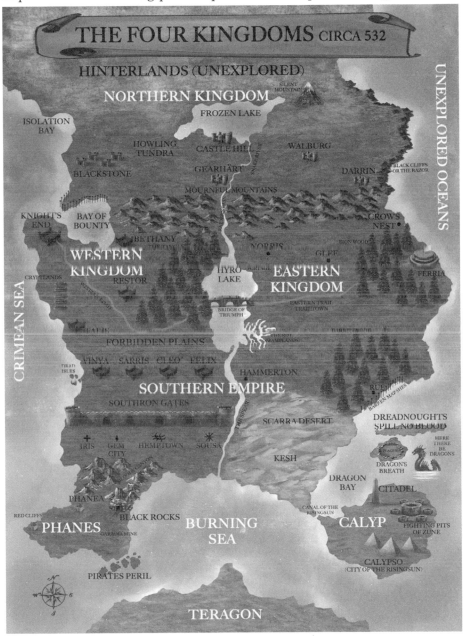

Fatemarked

BOOK ONE OF

The Fatemarked Epic

DAVID ESTES

Prologue

The Northern Kingdom | Silent Mountain

(circa 518)

The newborn babe awoke in an empty cave, lit by a swathe of green moonlight. The weather was cool, but dry, and a warm blanket swaddled his arms and legs. For a moment he did nothing but stare at the point of a stalactite overhead, which stared right back at him. He was hungry, but he did not cry.

Heavy footfalls echoed from an indeterminate distance.

The cave mouth was soon filled by a mountain of a man, near as wide as he was tall, which was saying something considering his eight-foot-tall stature. He'd been called many names in his life, and none of them out of kindness: troll, ogre, beast, monster. *I am all of those things*, he thought.

To his friends, who were few, he was known simply as Bear Blackboots, his birth name lost decades ago, squashed under his thunderous trod and what he had become after his mother had been murdered.

Bear stood over the child, and his long brown beard tickled the nose of the swaddled babe, but the infant didn't smile nor fuss.

In one hand, Bear held a book, its brown leather cover worn, its pages yellow and brittle. In the other he held a torch, which he waved over the child's hairless scalp.

In a blaze of light that sent the shadows running, a mark burst into being, like a single glowing ember in the midst of a dying fire. The mark was a perfect circle, pierced in eight points by four fiery arrows that split the symbol into eight equal portions, like silver scars from an octagonal mace.

The enormous man yanked the torch away from the babe with a gasp, and the mark vanished in an instant, leaving the child's head pale and smooth once more.

So it's true, Bear thought. After over a century of searching, his life extended well beyond that of most mortals, he'd finally found his true purpose, the one his mother had foretold the day before she died.

Because of you, child, the Four Kingdoms shall suffer, Bear thought. *Unless I slit your throat now.*

He raised a meaty hand, thick and strong enough to crush small boulders. The edge of a knife glinted.

After a moment's hesitation, he dropped his hand with a sigh, letting the blade fall from his fingers. "What shall be, shall be," he murmured, his voice grainy and rough from years of disuse.

Who am I to destroy one with such a destiny, and only an infant who will never know his mother's breast? Mother? Are you proud of me? Of course, no one answered. She hadn't answered him for many years.

From one of the many pockets inside his worn leather overcoat, he extracted a milk jug, capped by a drip cloth. "Eat," he said.

The child ate, and for fourteen long years he thrived under the mountain man's surprisingly gentle care. Bear only referred to the boy by one name as he grew:

Bane.

PART I

ROAN • ANNISE • BANE

Sometimes there are those who must die in order for there to be peace.
— THE WESTERN ORACLE

Chapter One

The Southern Empire | Calyp

Fourteen years later (circa 532)

Roan

"Out of the way, cretin!" the horse master shouted as the royal train galloped past, charging for the trio of pyramids in the distance.

Roan barely managed to fall backwards without getting trampled, his lungs filling with fine dust kicked up under dozens of hooves. As he coughed, he used a hand to cover his mouth with the collar of his filthy shirt. The tattered cloth was brown (though at one time it had been white, its true color eternally lost under layers of Calypsian dust) and as stiff as a leather jerkin.

Royals, Roan thought, slumping against the side of the sandstone hut he'd crashed into when he fell. He'd been living on the streets of the City of the Rising Sun ever since he'd run away from his guardian, a large, gruff Dreadnoughter by the name of Markin Swansea, six years earlier. Three years ago, Markin had been murdered. As far as Roan knew, his guardian had gone to his grave still protecting his secrets, something he remembered every day of his life.

"Are you injured?" someone asked, drawing Roan's attention away from the passing cavalcade.

"I'm no worse for wear," Roan grunted, trying to see past the shadows of the stranger's gray hood, which hid his face from the fiery Southron sun. It wasn't unusual garb for a Calypsian, their long cloaks designed to protect against both sun and dust.

The hooded stranger extended a gloved hand and, after a moment's hesitation, Roan took it, allowing the newcomer to pull him to his feet. "Thank you, . . ."

"No one. I am no one," the stranger said, his voice of a timbre that reminded Roan of sand being gritted between teeth.

"Well, No One, thank you all the same. I'm Roan." He *was* genuinely appreciative—in Calypso acts of goodwill were rare and far between. In a gesture that was automatic, if pointless, Roan shook as much of the loose dirt off his clothing as possible. Stubbornly, his shirt remained brown and filthy.

"You can see me?" the stranger asked.

Roan eyed him warily, wondering whether the odd man had been chewing shadeleaf, which was known to cloud the mind. "Yes," he said. "I can see you."

The royal procession continued to thunder past while Roan and the stranger watched it without expression. Throngs of dark-skinned Calypsians lined the streets. Though the plague—a strange flesh-eating disease transmitted by touch—had been running rampart through the city for years, the city dwellers obviously weren't letting it affect their day to day lives. They wore colorful cloaks that stood out against the beige sandstone huts. Some cheered their leaders, but most remained silent. Perhaps they were weighed down by the heat.

Amongst the horses in the cavalcade were several *guanik*, long, reptilian creatures armored with black scales. As they impressively kept stride with the horses, their pink, snake-like tongues flicked between rows of dagger-like teeth. Their riders were the *guanero*, the royal guardians of Calypso.

While Roan watched the guanik and their hooded riders with narrowly disguised disgust, an authoritative voice suddenly shouted, "Halt!" Like appendages attached to a single creature, the line of horses and guanik reared to an abrupt stop, raising yet another cloud of dust.

When the fog cleared, Roan saw a broad-shouldered man wearing leather riding armor slide from his guanik's scaly shoulders. His black hair was spiked in a dozen places, held up by some kind of shiny liquid.

Roan knew exactly who he was, and hated him for it.

The *shiva*, the master of order in Calyp. This man had the authority of House Sandes, the empire's governing family. Roan had once watched him run down a woman in the street for some crime she'd never had the chance to defend herself from.

And now he was walking toward Roan and the hooded man standing beside him.

"Ho, beggar!" the shiva called.

Roan said nothing, but was dimly aware of the way the stranger beside him tensed up, shuffling back a step.

"You are a stranger to these parts, if I'm not mistaken."

"I have not once asked for anything," Roan said. "Therefore I am no beggar. And just because I'm a stranger to you doesn't make me a stranger to Calypso."

Regardless of whether he was or was not a stranger, Roan didn't understand why this man would waste a moment on him. The shiva scowled at Roan. He was garbed from head to toe with leather armor marked with the royal sigil, a silver dragon over a rising red sun. He eyed Roan and the stranger warily, his dark eyes darting between them. "I spoke not to you, but to your companion."

Roan glanced at the hooded stranger. "He is not my companion. We've only just met." And yet Roan found himself stepping in front of the man, blocking him. Defending him?

"Then move aside."

Roan didn't, and he wasn't sure why. *Perhaps because he showed me kindness. Perhaps because he cared.*

The shiva sneered at Roan. "What are you going to do, peasant?"

Nothing, Roan thought. *Choke on dust. Burn up under the sun. Help no one but myself. Live the only life I was ever offered.*

"Oh no. Not again," the stranger murmured behind him. Confused, Roan looked at the man, who had thrown back his hood and was staring at his gloved hand in horror. The gray glove had a slight tear in it, on the heel of his palm, exposing a sliver of white flesh.

Roan was instantly drawn to the man's face, which was much younger than his voice had suggested. His skin was the palest Roan had ever laid eyes on, as white as the eastern clouds or the northern snowfields, a physical trait that was extremely rare in Calyp. His flesh was also parchment thin, doing little to mask the bright blue veins running beneath the surface. But more than any of that, Roan noticed the man's eyes, which were as red as sunrise.

And those red eyes were staring at Roan. "I'm sorry," he said, stumbling backward, throwing his hood back over his head. He turned to run, tripping over his own feet before catching his balance and darting into an alley.

Odd, Roan thought. Then again, he'd met a lot of strange people growing up as an orphan in Calypso.

"Gods be with us," the shiva said, jerking Roan's attention back to the halted procession. The shiva was backing away, scrabbling at his leather breastplate, attempting to yank it over his mouth and nose.

Roan frowned. The rest of the royal guards were backing away, too, the fear obvious in their eyes. "The plague," someone said. Then, louder: "He's afflicted with the plague!"

A woman screamed, high-pitched and piercing.

Roan shook his head. *What are they talking about?*

That's when he felt it. An itch on his cheek. He reached up to scratch his face and noticed something on his hand. A bump, red and puffy. He inhaled sharply, dropping his hand to rest beside the other. Before his very eyes, dozens of fiery bumps rose to the surface of his skin, seeming to jostle for position.

Roan fell to his knees, still staring at his diseased hands. Beyond him, he could see the shiva's black boots standing in the dirt.

For some reason, he crawled forward, reaching for the boots, feeling the need to touch them. *Maybe my hand will go right through them. Maybe this is a dream.* In his heart, however, he knew it wasn't.

The moment before his fingers brushed the shiva's boots, a shadow closed in from the side, swinging a weapon of some kind, which thudded against his skull with a vicious crack.

He collapsed, his cheek pressed to the dust, a set of dark eyes materializing overhead. The shiva vanished from sight as he was pulled away by his guardsmen, who created a human wall around him.

Roan's vision was obliterated as a thick sack was thrown over his eyes.

❧

When Roan awoke it was dark. The sun had long retreated beyond the horizon, and the night held an unnatural chill so foreign to Calypso that he instantly knew he was no longer in the city of his childhood.

But if not Calypso, then where?

Roan tried to think, but it was difficult when his head was pounding. He reached up to feel the side of his scalp, which was bulging and crusted with blood. His ear was badly damaged too, and he wondered if his hearing would be affected. Not that it mattered.

He touched his face to find his once-smooth skin covered in bumps on top of bumps, each filled with heat. He scrubbed at them with the heel of his hand, which was also bumpy and burning. He had the sudden urge to run. To where, he did not know.

As Roan fought weakness and fear to push to his knees, the wind howled over him, and he shivered.

The first strange thing Roan noticed: Even after the breath of wind dissipated, its mournful howling continued like an echo through the night.

The moan was filled with pain, and sadness, and hopelessness.

The nightmarish events rushed back through his mind, pounding away like the throbbing in his skull: the royal procession; the gray-hooded stranger; the unexpected words spoken between he and the shiva; the torn glove; the fear in the eyes of everyone who stared at him.

The plague.

He had the plague, and he knew exactly who had given it to him.

The stranger with the porcelain skin. *Not again,* the man had said.

Something clicked in Roan's mind. The plague had been tormenting Calyp for half a decade. No one truly knew its origin, or whether it could be stopped. Some said it was conjured by the Phanecians, a silent weapon in the ongoing civil war that had ripped through the Southern Empire for twelve long years. Others, however, whispered of the Beggar, whose simple touch supposedly transmitted the disease. The most superstitious believed him to be a wraithlike demon, while others said he was simply a man borne with evil inside of him.

Now, after seeing the sadness in the stranger's eyes, Roan knew the truth: The Beggar was a young man, like him, cursed with something he never asked for. Despite what the stranger had done to him, Roan felt sorry for him.

Something scuffled nearby, and then a heavy force bashed into his side, knocking him off balance. A woman's hot breath splashed against his face. A foul odor filled his nostrils.

"Help me!" the woman cried, her plea punctuated by the howls of her companions, who suddenly surrounded Roan. They appeared to be Calypsians, all of them, their skin as dark as night. One of them held a torch, waving it around like a sword, illuminating grotesque faces that Roan knew would haunt him for the rest of his life.

Their eyes were bulging from their skulls, their tongues lolling from their lips, their mottled skin dripping from their bones.

Even as he thought the word *monsters*, he knew it was not true. For they were merely human victims, like him, transformed by the fast-moving disease.

Gnarled hands reached for Roan, as if to embrace him, but he swatted them away, feeling a burst of energy rush through his blood as something he'd kept hidden for a long time flared from his chest, right over his heart. For there he bore what the southerners referred to as a *tattooya*—a mark of power. In the west they referred to the very same as sinmarks, while in both the east and north they simply called them skinmarks. One of the southern princesses, Fire Sandes, even had one—the firemark. But he'd heard of a half-dozen others, too, spread throughout the Four Kingdoms.

He was one of them.

But perhaps not for long.

The heat spread from his chest to his face to his torso, flowing outward to his limbs like a ripple in a pond.

This time the heat wasn't from the plague. This time it was his own curse, the curse that led to his life as an orphan in a foreign land. For once, his curse felt almost like a blessing.

His body healed as he ran, dodging arms and legs and bodies, each more horrifying than the one before. Bodies littered the ground, most unmoving, and Roan tripped on one, his ankle turning sharply. He cried out, but his yell was cut short when he came face to face with a living skull, its teeth rattling as its jaws opened and closed. What was left of the victim moved slowly, reaching for him.

Roan slashed his elbow across the skeleton's skull, knocking it away.

Should be dead, should be dead, should be dead, he thought, shocked by how long the plague kept its victims alive before eventually turning them to dust. It was unnatural. *Then again, so am I*, he reminded himself as heat rushed to his ankle, healing his stretched tendons.

He was on his feet again a moment later, winding a ragged path through the corpses, sighing in relief as the wails and moans faded into the distance.

What now? Roan wondered, even as he realized exactly where he was. They called it Dragon's Breath, an island off the coast of Citadel, the northernmost city in Calyp. The island, located in the glassy waters of Dragon Bay, was once home to a vicious tribe of cannibals, but the Calypsians had decimated them and rebuilt the land to quarantine all plague victims until the disease finished them off.

According to city gossip, the island was surrounded by an immense wall. Victims were dropped over the sides. They should die from such a fall, but the plague wouldn't let them. The plague held no mercy, only pain and torture to the very end. Roan must've been dropped, too, stumbling feverishly across the terrain to where he ended up. If not for the power of his own tattooya, he'd probably already be too far gone.

Roan wheeled about in a circle—a dark shape surrounded him, rising up toward the red, green, and gold stars. *The wall is real*, Roan thought. Which might mean the other obstacle was real, too, but he chose not to think too hard about that. Not yet. The wall was first, then whatever came next.

Although he could sense the plague all around him, hanging thickly in the fetid air, Roan did *not* have the plague. Not anymore. He'd used his curse to take care of that little problem.

Unfortunately, healing himself had left him feeling drained and ashamed. All of these people were in need of what he could offer, and he selfishly chose to help himself. But there were too many to help. Even if he wanted to, he would collapse from exhaustion before he could heal them all. And then he would die.

He shook his head, trying to focus. His legs felt like lead, but he forced them forward, toward a part of the ground that seemed less littered with bodies.

Dark shapes stumbled across the open terrain, the living dead wandering without purpose.

What felt like hours later, Roan reached the wall, which appeared to stretch all the way to the heavens. All along the base of the wall were bodies in various stages of decay. They formed a pyramid, not unlike the enormous pyramids of Calypso, except constructed of flesh and bone rather than stone and mortar. At its apex, the ramp reached nearly halfway to the wall's summit.

Despite its morbid nature, the human pyramid strategy was an interesting one. Plague victims continued to flock toward the wall, climbing the bodies, eventually succumbing to the disease at the top, becoming new building blocks for future victims to climb. For those afflicted with the plague, climbing the wall would be next to impossible, but perhaps for Roan, who still had his strength . . .

Roan started his ascent, using his hands to steady himself on the unbalanced terrain. His power flared up each time the plague attempted to infiltrate his body, holding the disease at bay. Other climbers noticed his progress, and tried to grab him, their mouths opening to reveal toothless maws. He knocked their disease-weakened arms away and fought onward.

When Roan reached the top of the human pyramid, he was exhausted, his knees trembling, his back sore. Even his bones felt weary, the constant use of his power sapping them of all strength.

Three plague victims were trying to grasp the stone, but their dark skin was slippery with sweat from the fever burning through their bodies. Hearing Roan's approach, they turned, their lips contorted with pain. "Help me," one said, his teeth chattering. "Please," said another. "Please." The third one only reached blindly for Roan; her eyes were milky and unseeing.

"I'm sorry," Roan said, trying to dodge around them.

The largest one, a man who might've once been as tall as Roan before the plague hunched his back and bent his legs, moved far quicker than Roan thought possible. Like him, he might've been a new arrival, not yet fully broken. He grabbed Roan around the neck and slammed him against the wall, his breaths coming hot and quick. Spit flew from his mouth as he demanded, "Give me a boost, boy!"

Roan could feel the plague trying to squirm inside him, the force of his tattooya fighting back valiantly. His vision began to blur from the effort. He had the sudden desire to stop fighting, to give in to the disease, to embrace the darkness and relief it would eventually bring.

His legs wobbled. His heart stuttered. His breath clawed in and out of his throat with ragged gasps.

And then he remembered his mother. Not her, exactly, for he couldn't remember anything about her. Only what his guardian had told him about her, how strong and good she was. How she'd sacrificed everything so he could live.

Could he really throw away her sacrifice so easily?

He couldn't and he wouldn't. "I will help you," he choked out, feeling the sting of the lie in his throat, even as the man released his grip.

The second he was free, he used the wall for leverage and kicked out, knocking the man down the human hill. He smashed into the blind woman, sending her flying as well. The third victim tripped of his own accord, screaming in pain.

Roan's stomach hurt from what he had done, but he forced himself to turn back toward the wall.

He had two choices, die or climb, and that was no choice for a man like Roan.

Mustering what strength he had left, he raised his arms and began to climb.

Thankfully, the wall was hastily constructed and eroded by steady ocean winds, and he had no difficulty finding hand and footholds. Still, with his last reserves nearly depleted, the biting wind threatened to tear him from the wall with each inch he gained. Every time he stared up, the apex seemed farther and farther away, an unreachable goal.

He refused to look down at all the poor souls he had abandoned.

He began to growl with each step up, his feet aching, his hands cracked and bleeding from gripping the rough stone. He was no longer capable of healing himself.

But then, like a rocky coastline disappearing into the sea, the wall ended. He sprawled on the broad windswept surface, unable to hold back a sudden burst of laughter. His chest rose and fell. His hands dripped blood. His muscles spasmed and cramped.

And, despite the gnawing hunger he suddenly felt in the pit of his stomach, Roan drifted off into a deep sleep.

Beneath him, just outside the island's walls, the slumbering dragon's chains rattled as it began to stir.

Chapter Two

The Northern Kingdom | Castle Hill

Annise Gäric

Annise never asked to be a princess.

And yet, no matter how much she wished for a different life, she couldn't change anything. She couldn't change the dark stares of the commoners on her as she watched the finest knights of the kingdom do battle, nor the barricade of guards that surrounded the royal family because of the constant threat of assassination. She couldn't change her face, which was all Gäric with her strong jaw, dimpled chin, and steely gray eyes. The look suited her older brother, Arch, just fine, but not her. Her body was even worse, with too-small bosoms and exceptionally wide hips. Her arms and legs were strong, muscled from spending her days fighting with the lordlings in the training yard, but that didn't stop the colorful nicknames invented by her peers. She'd heard them all: Princess Pear; the Pin-Bodied Princess; Princess Pound-Cake.

Try as she did to ignore them, the words stung each time she heard them.

Now, Annise tried to focus on the tourney, which had moved on from archery to everyone's favorite event—the joust. Well, everyone's favorite except

Annise's. Something about the joust was too practiced, too methodical. The event had no feeling or passion. Every time a knight was unhorsed, it felt cold, just like the never ending winter in Castle Hill.

Hooves pounded the frozen earth. The knights positioned their lances, holding them steady. Wood splintered, metal armor shrieked. Both knights were hit, toppling from their mounts and landing hard. They got up and wrestled in the snow, much to the raucous crowd's delight.

Annise looked away, checking the lineup to see who was next. A white steed pranced forward gracefully. Her brother lifted his faceplate and flashed the brilliant smile that made the girls' squeal with delight. At sixteen, he was the only Gäric who the people seemed to forgive despite their father's constant acts of violence. He had charisma, while Annise only had knotted black curls and an impressive hooked punch that could knock even the toughest lordlings off their feet.

Much to their father's dismay, Arch had tried to teach her to joust on several occasions. They'd conducted the lessons in private, far from the laughter of the castle servants. She was dreadful. Riding had never been her strong suit, but that was only the beginning of the trouble. Getting the unbalanced lance up while attempting to steer her horse in a straight line had proven to be a task as monumentally difficult for Annise as faking a smile to the commoners.

She had given up after only three lessons.

While the two brawlers were cleared from the field, Arch Gäric blew kisses to his adoring fans before dropping his faceplate with a clank. He charged his opponent, his silver shield flashing with each stride.

Compared to Arch, his opponent looked awkward and clumsy, struggling to get his lance up in time. Too late.

Arch speared his own lance into the knight, unhorsing him so violently he did a backflip, landing with a thump.

The crowd cheered and Arch celebrated with them as the unconscious knight was dragged away amidst jeers. Annise closed her eyes and wished it was she they adored.

When she opened her eyes again, she found her mother's stare boring into her. Her mother was everything she was not—beautiful and confident. Her golden hair flowed down her back, braided in three places in the style of the western kingdom. Her features were delicate and soft, befitting a princess of the west rather than a queen of the north. Technically, Sabria Loren Gäric was both. Once a princess of the west, now a queen of the north, her hand given to

Annise's father, Wolfric Gäric, as part of a marriage alliance that lasted all of two years before being shattered by war once more.

Now Queen Gäric was a captive wife, and she seemed to blame her daughter as much as anyone, though Annise had barely been born when her father attacked the west and was named Dread King of the North, a title he seemed to relish more and more with each passing day.

Annise looked away from her mother, unable to hold her crystal blue stare any longer. While the joust continued, she gazed across Frozen Lake, which seemed to stretch into eternity, all the way to the edge of the Hinterlands, the white sun transforming the ice to gold. She dreamed of leaving the castle, walking across Frozen Lake, disappearing into the unexplored territory forever.

Annise shook her head and snapped out of her revelry when the crowd cheered once more. The joust was over. Surprise, surprise—Arch had won.

Down the line of royals, she noticed her Aunt Zelda, a thickset woman who, like Annise, was all Gäric in terms of physical appearance. She'd seen her strange aunt on multiple occasions as a child, but as the years wore on and the king grew more and more violent, Lady Zelda had rarely shown up at court, becoming the butt of many a jape in the castle, earning herself the label of family recluse. It was odd to see her now, almost like a mirage in the snow, when she hadn't seen her aunt in years.

Was it her imagination, or had her aunt just shared a glance with her mother? Annise's eyes darted between the two women, but if they'd made eye contact, it was fleeting. Now both of them were staring without expression at the field below.

Annise scanned the crowd. Despite their poverty and the biting cold, there was a sense of excitement buzzing through the audience. It was like Arch's victory had given them hope. She spotted a young boy no more than nine years old sitting in the snow. His body was shrunken and thin, and his skin was of a ghostly pallor, but he still managed to smile from ear to ear. He was clearly ill. By Annise's reckoning, he wouldn't last through another winter. A sharp pain lanced through her ribs as she was reminded of a childhood friend who'd been stricken by a similar ailment.

Tarin.

He'd been her best friend.

He'd died before his ninth name day.

To this day, Annise still missed Tarin.

It was strange to Annise, the way life seemed to amble along sometimes, slow and unsteady, the days sliding past with all the speed of a spring snail; and other times moving like a falling scythe, slashing through everything in its path. Tarin had been the latter. One day he was a vibrant, energetic boy, running and wrestling and playing with Annise. Only days later he was gone. His body had been so overcome by the disease that his day of mourning required a closed casket. Annise hadn't just lost a friend on that day—she'd lost a piece of her soul.

She blinked away the memory and the dull, lingering pain. Because, finally, it was time for her favorite event, and she couldn't hold back a very real smile. She glanced over to see if her mother had noticed, but the queen was gone. Annise knew slipping away during the penultimate point in the tourney would bring her father's wrath later on, and she feared for her mother, who didn't seem to care anymore. Her mother's actions were not unusual, not lately. It seemed to Annise that, more and more, the queen was behaving recklessly. Usually it meant a few days away from court to allow the bruises to heal.

At the same moment, she noticed Aunt Zelda had departed, too.

A coincidence, she thought. As far as she knew, the two women hadn't spoken in years.

She tried not to think about it as the field was cleared for the final event, the melee. Annise loved the melee. It was an event of true strength and valor, and only the most gallant of knights would come out victorious. She dreamed of marching onto the field of battle, armed with sword and strength, a test of skill or brawn, or, in some cases, both.

Annise wasn't known for her skill, but she'd bested Arch on multiple occasions with both sword and fist using sheer brute strength as her true weapon of choice. She smiled at the memories, especially because of how angry her father had been when he found out she'd shamed the king-to-be on the training grounds.

Annise smirked as Arch trotted up to take a seat—he, of course, wouldn't compete in the melee.

"Scared of getting your pretty hands dirty?" Annise asked innocently.

"I don't see *you* down there," he retorted.

Annise sighed. She would if she could. Other than the rare she-knight, women were disallowed from the tourney entirely.

"Sorry," Arch said, realizing his mistake. "Anyway, I just *won* the joust."

"Really? I must've missed it," Annise joked.

"They cheered louder than ever before."

"And blew you kisses and displayed their bosoms and offered themselves up for your spawn."

"I think you mean *heirs*," Arch said, laughing. "They aren't as bad as you think. Your sharp tongue could learn some manners from my admirers."

"Is that what you call your harem these days?"

"At least they're nice," Arch said, but he was still smiling.

"Then why don't you sit with *them*." Annise knew she was being mean, but she didn't care.

"I would, but then you'd have no one to sit with you," Arch joked, bumping her as he sat down.

Annise squirmed away, refusing to be charmed by her brother the way everyone else was. "Quiet. It's about to start."

Their father stood on the raised platform. He was a large man, tall and strong, his face weathered by cold and storm and battle. He wore a long black robe adorned with the northern sigil, a cracked-but-never-broken golden shield. Annise hated that she could see her own features in his face.

Once he'd been nothing but a prince, the second in the line of northern succession. But then his brother, Helmuth, who had been born with a lame foot, was skipped over by Annise's grandfather, leaving the throne open for her father. Annise had never known her uncle Helmuth, who most people referred to only as the Maimed Prince, as he'd run away from Castle Hill before she'd been born, leaving only a note promising to return seeking vengeance one day. He hadn't been heard from since, and most had long forgotten about him.

Behind the king was his prized pet, the Ice Lord, a tall thin man with razor-sharp features that reminded Annise of a cold blue blade. He was currently the only known northerner bearing a skinmark—in his case, an icy symbol that gave him his power.

The crowd didn't boo, but they didn't cheer either. An awkward wave of applause swept across the commoners. "Has this tournament entertained you?" King Gäric asked. Something about the way he said it sent icicles up Annise's spine. She'd heard enough of her father's speeches to know when he was baiting his people. The Dread King had earned his title a hundred times over, just as her grandfather had earned his own title as the Undefeated King, with his string of dauntless victories over their enemies. She wondered what nickname Arch would bear when he was king. *The Boastful King*, she thought with a smile.

The crowd drew silent—they could sense the change in mood too.

"No? Have you learned nothing? I have vowed time and time again to snuff out traitors like the pools of dripping wax that they are, and yet treason seems to spring up like mounds of horse dirt." The king's booming voice echoed across the snowfields. The crowd didn't dare to move, or even breathe.

Annise's fingernails dug into her palms.

"I demand obedience, or you shall have death! Traitors will be punished! The streets will run red with guilty blood on this very night! So yes, enjoy the melee. Be entertained, for tonight I shall be entertained by my enemies' screams!"

King Gäric slammed his fist down on the balustrade and several icicles broke off, dropping like executioner's scythes, barely missing a young guardsman who was forced to dodge out of the way. His speech finished, Annise's father stormed off, likely to find her absent mother.

"All hail the Dread King of the North," Arch whispered under his breath. Annise was pretty sure he was joking. He might be the golden boy of the kingdom, but she knew he was every bit as scared of their father as she was.

The Ice Lord stepped forward to take his place as tourney master. He stroked his white goatee with long-nailed fingers.

Some members of the crowd attempted to leave the area, but armed soldiers blocked their path. With no other choice, the audience pressed closer to the barrier, watching as the melee participants gathered on the hard-packed snowfield.

Most of them were the usual combatants. An old, grizzled knight named Sir Eldric that Annise had watched a hundred times. Drunk Craig, a red-faced knight who was better known for his love of the drink than his battle prowess. Sir Jonius, a solid swordsman, twice victorious over the last five tourneys. (Jonius had always been kind to Annise, which was somewhat surprising considering the atrocities he carried out on her father's behalf.) Lord Griswold Gäric, her uncle, was notably absent, his spot being taken by his son, Dirk, who was participating in his first melee. (Annise's cousin had never been kind to her, and she secretly hoped he would be shamed with an early elimination.)

There were several newcomers as well, though only two caught her eye. The first was announced as Sir Dietrich of Gearhärt. He appeared of similar age to her brother, and yet more hardened, his jaw set in determination. A long, jagged scar ran from his temple to his chin, and his armor was dented and pocked. Gearhärt was a border city, just north of Raider's Pass along the edge of the Mournful Mountains. The mountains were the main barrier separating the north from both the west and east. Annise wondered whether this young knight had seen true battle or if his scar was the result of some accident. The state of his armor seemed to suggest the former. Despite his scar, he was exceptionally handsome, and something about him made her want to cheer him to victory.

The second newcomer of note was a giant of a man, adorned in all black armor, scrubbed to a pristine shine. He wore black gloves and high black boots. Not a spot of skin was visible, including his face, which was masked by some kind of mesh, with only a slit for his dark eyes. As he raised an enormous black-spiked ball dangling from a long chain, he was announced only as the Armored Knight. Annise's uncle scoffed at the title. "What kind of name is that?" he said. "And what kind of weapon is that?"

Arch agreed. "He'll be the first to fall. All image and no substance."

"Haven't you been reading the tournament streams?" Annise asked.

Streaming had been discovered several decades earlier, by a scholar studying flora and fauna along the Spear. There was a reedy plant that seemed to grow in plenty along the banks of rivers, streams, ponds, and lakes across the Four Kingdoms, almost without exception. The scholar found when she broke the stalk in half, a black, inky substance oozed out. The scholar harvested several of the plants, which were now known as inkreed, to study them later on, and then made her way upstream. Walking along the embankment, she slipped in the mud, tumbling into the river. She clung to a piece of wood, watching as the ink from the broken plants created dark spirals in the current. Then the strangest thing happened: The ink disappeared. At first she thought the ink had just been washed away, but when she experimented with more stalks from her supply, she found the ink would literally vanish each time. When she made her way back downstream to collect more samples, she was astonished to find the water of the river filled with inky spirals, exactly the same as the ones that had disappeared further upstream.

Years later, the process of streaming had been perfected. Although no one really knew why the inkreeds worked the way they did, most scholars conjectured that it had something to do with how all bodies of water were connected, and that plant life naturally wished to return to where it was grown. So now, if the ink from an inkreed harvested from a certain location was used to write a message on parchment, the message could then be dipped into any body of water, where it would vanish, reappearing in the water from where the inkreed originally grew. Furthermore, if a blank piece of parchment was dipped into the water where the message had reappeared, the ink would infuse itself onto the new sheet. Then all the receiver would have to do was dry it out.

Streaming was an amazing communication breakthrough and was now more widely used than messenger birds, with an entire network of inkreeds cultivated at various locations, labelled, and then delivered across the Four Kingdoms to those willing to pay for the luxury.

Annise never missed a chance to read the incoming news streams, especially the ones about the various tournaments held across the northern realm.

Now, Arch just stared at her blankly.

"You know, read? Forming words from letters, sentences from words, entire stories from sentences?"

He yawned. "Sorry, I think I fell asleep for a second. Were you saying something?"

She shook her head, astounded at the heights his ignorance had reached. "Well, if you *had* been reading the tournament streams, you would know the Armored Knight rarely loses. He's been winning tourneys from Darrin to Blackstone and everywhere in between."

"Still, I doubt he'll win the biggest tournament of all," Arch said. "Just look at him, I'll be surprised if he can even swing that odd weapon."

Annise *did* look at him. There was something dangerous about the man. All her experience with such events told her he was one to watch. His weapon was like a mace, but modified, with a chain instead of a club. Arch was right to be skeptical—she'd never seen anyone wield such a device.

"Who are you taking this year?" Arch asked.

"You first," Annise said. Predicting the winner had been a sibling tradition as long as she could remember. At last count they were tied.

"Sir Jonius for the third time in six years," Arch said without hesitation.

It was a good pick, but Annise had a feeling they were in for a surprise. "I'll take the big one," she said. "The Armored Knight."

"The bigger they are . . ." Arch said, grinning.

"The harder they hit," Annise finished.

When the combatants were all announced and in position, the Ice Lord raised his pale hand and squeezed it into a fist. "Warriors!" he said, his voice like a gust of icy wind. "The victor shall claim a position in the King's Defense. Now fight!"

Annise leaned forward eagerly as frozen hell broke loose. Drunk Craig staggered across the uneven terrain and was quickly cut down by Sir Dietrich, who spun with exceptional grace, his sword like an extension of his arm. Drunk Craig dropped his sword and rolled away, shouting, "I submit! A drink! A drink! I need a drink!" Beside her, Arch guffawed loudly.

Toward the far side of the field, the Armored Knight was surrounded by a trio of experienced knights, including Sir Eldric. The gang-up was a common method of eliminating newcomers. All three knights were already members of the King's Defense, and would likely remain allies during the melee until only they were left.

Annise knew she'd chosen poorly; she should've considered such a possibility. She sighed, waiting for the inevitable.

It never came. Instead, the Armored Knight dodged one knight's sword, whipping the chain around with deadly speed. The spiked metal ball crashed into the knight's helmet and he flew back into Sir Eldric. The third knight attacked from behind, but the Armored Knight was ready, thrusting an elbow backwards into the man's jaw. With a roar, he grabbed the knight and slung him down, forcing him to submit.

By then Sir Eldric had regained his feet and, more warily this time, moved forward into position. With perfect form, he slashed his sword in an attacking stroke, but his enormous foe was unimpressed, simply sidestepping and wrapping his weapon's chain around the old knight's throat. Sir Eldric promptly dropped his sword and submitted.

Just like that, the Armored Knight had dispatched three members of the King's Defense.

"Whoa," Arch said. "You weren't wrong about him. He hits hard."

Annise realized she was on her feet now, even if she couldn't remember standing up. Arch followed her lead, motioning across the area.

In the other corner of the field, it was down to Sir Jonius, Cousin Dirk, and Sir Dietrich. Dirk was clearly outmatched by both knights, launching himself with reckless abandon as they easily parried his blows. However, mostly by chance, he found himself behind Sir Jonius as the knight faced off against the newcomer from Gearhärt. Annise's cousin took advantage of the situation, rapping his sword across the previous victor's knees and assuring himself a coveted spot in the final three.

His father, Lord Griswold, howled with delight. Annise gritted her teeth.

"That was a dirty trick," Arch said angrily, his pick having been eliminated. "The day is yours, little sister." Simply to prove that she was in no way 'little', Annise muscled him to the side amidst brotherly protests.

She laughed as he bumped her back. They turned their attention back to the melee, ignoring their uncle's disapproving glare.

As Dirk Gäric and Sir Dietrich circled each other, the Armored Knight waited patiently. Annise wondered why he didn't attack. While they were distracted with each other, he could easily seize victory. And yet, he remained as still as stone, watching, waiting for his turn. Was it a sense of honor and fairness that held him in check? If so, his restraint was immensely appealing to Annise, especially considering the unfair odds he'd already faced. Not to mention the brute strength he'd already exhibited.

Dirk, to Annise's surprise, began to fight brilliantly, almost as if he'd been feigning youth and weakness before. Her uncle laughed and slapped his knees. "That's my boy! Victory! Victory!"

But Sir Dietrich's sword was just as quick, defending against an assault as fierce as a winter storm.

"What in frozen hell?" her uncle muttered, as Sir Dietrich turned defense into offense and drove Dirk back. The eighteen-year-old stumbled and fell, scrabbling for his sword. He froze when Sir Dietrich managed to thrust the tip of his long blade just short of the boy's neck.

"Do you submit?" the knight asked calmly.

The collective crowd held their breath, waiting for Dirk's response.

"Yes," the boy said and the audience exhaled, cheering for the knight. However, the moment Sir Dietrich turned his back to face his final opponent, Dirk swept up his sword, kicked to his feet, and slashed at the knight's legs, much in the way he'd incapacitated Sir Jonius.

"No!" Annise shouted, but Sir Dietrich was already turning, already aware of the attack, already blocking the blow, spinning his sword, flipping the boy's weapon in the air, and catching it in his other hand. It was one of the most brilliantly executed maneuvers Annise had ever seen.

Dirk's eyes widened as both blades pressed up against his chest. "You already submitted," Sir Dietrich said. "Bad form."

Dirk's face was splotched with the red of embarrassment and the white of fear, but he nodded and left the field of battle. When he was clear, Sir Dietrich flung the captured sword in the boy's direction and it landed with a *thunk* in the ground beside him, point down. The boy gritted his teeth as half the crowd laughed at him and the other half cheered in appreciation of the knight's mastery of the sword.

"Good ol' Cousin Dirk," Arch whispered, and Annise was forced to stifle a laugh with her hand.

"That knight is out of control," Lord Griswold said between clenched teeth.

But there was nothing he could do—at least not yet. His son was eliminated and the melee was continuing, with only the two newcomers, Sir Dietrich and the Armored Knight, remaining. Annise could barely restrain herself from cheering for them both. Not for the first or last time, she wished she wasn't forced to maintain the sensibilities required of a princess of the north. She longed to be down there with the commoners, screaming with unbridled glee, just another face in the crowd.

Arch, on the other hand, howled his delight without regard for royal dignity, which only made her more jealous of him than she already was.

"C'mon, Sister," Arch said. "Scream with me."

She wished she could. But if she did, her father would surely hear of it, and then she would have to face his wrath.

The final two warriors squared off across from each other. The Armored Knight began swinging his weapon in a slow arc over his head, gaining momentum with each rotation. Sir Dietrich watched the spiked ball, several times trying to infiltrate its deadly path before being forced to retreat to avoid getting his bones crushed.

On Sir Dietrich's next attempt, the Armored Knight changed the ball's direction, managing to land a glancing blow off the knight's breastplate. When he leapt forward, however, Sir Dietrich launched a counterattack, catching the chain with one hand while sweeping his sword low with the other. With impressive agility for such a large man, the Armored Knight leapt over the blade, twisting rapidly in an attempt to rip his mace free.

Sir Dietrich held tight, and the pair of warriors grappled for ten long seconds, until the knight from Gearhärt thrust aside the chain and whipped his sword back and forth faster than Annise had ever seen in her life. The Armored Knight did his best to block each blow, but he was eventually overcome, losing his grip on the chain and dropping to one knee in submission. "Well fought," he said to Sir Dietrich, who responded in kind.

The crowd roared their approval, and despite her chosen warrior's defeat, Annise could no longer hold her appreciation in. She howled like a wolf while her brother did the same, grinning from ear to ear. Lord Griswold grabbed them both by the collars of their cloaks, and said, "Disgraceful. Wait until your father hears of this."

For once, Annise didn't care about being punished. It was worth it.

Her uncle said, "We'll get to the bottom of this. Ice Lord—with me!"

Annise didn't know what was happening. Yes, Dirk had been shamed, but he'd lost fairly, despite having cheated. Arch leaned in next to her. "I've never seen anyone fight like that. Sir Dietrich must be skinmarked. And if he is and never pledged his power to the crown, he will be executed."

Skinmarked? Annise hadn't considered the possibility. Yes, the knight had fought brilliantly, but surely it was all of his own ability. Right? *They can't execute him.* Even as she thought it, she knew it was a lie. Her father could and would execute anyone he believed had defied him. And it was true, under northern law, not declaring a skinmark was an act of treason.

Lord Griswold reached the field, the Ice Lord a step behind him. Her uncle's thick brown beard was matted with ice and he kicked up snow as he walked. Sir Dietrich dropped to one knee as Lord Griswold approached him. "My lord," he said. "I am honored in victory and stand ready to claim a position in the King's Defense."

"Are you skinmarked?" Lord Griswold asked.

Sir Dietrich tilted his chin up. "No," he said. "Not everyone needs a mark of power to be strong."

"On your feet!" Lord Griswold roared. "Armor off. Underclothes off. You will be searched from head to toe."

Sir Dietrich's expression didn't change. He stood slowly, his sword still in hand. For a moment Annise thought he might attack her uncle. For a moment she wished he would.

But then he dropped his sword in the snow and began to undress. His helmet clanked when it hit the ground, followed closely by each piece of battered armor.

Someone in the crowd protested, stepping forward. Lord Griswold said nothing, merely motioning to the Ice Lord, who strode toward an old man with a bent cane. He was still shouting in anger at the way the melee's victor was being treated.

No, Annise thought. *Not again.* The last time was a pig farmer who had failed to pay a fifth of his production to the crown. That was horrible. This would be worse.

The old man was a tough old coot, and didn't back away, even when the Ice Lord towered over him. "You have been judged and found guilty," he said, with all the authority of the crown. He reached out and touched the man's forehead with a single finger, almost reverently.

At first nothing happened, and Annise dared to hope that something had changed. But no, there it was—a spark of blue.

The Ice Lord turned and walked away as the blue spread along the man's withered body, his veins freezing in blue trails that bulged from his skin. Cracks began to form in his flesh, and then his body broke into chunks, collapsing in a frozen pile.

"Poor ol' chap," Arch said.

Annise looked away. She wanted to scream. She wanted to run down and pound her fists against the Ice Lord's chest.

Instead, she did nothing but watch in horror as Sir Dietrich was stripped naked. Annise bit her lip, relishing the pain, which helped distract her from the battleground that was the knight's battle-hardened flesh. Long scars, short scars, some jagged, some clean, some dark and fresh, others fading away—Sir Dietrich's skin had them all.

Even Lord Griswold seemed shocked by the truth, raising the edge of his lip in a disgusted sneer. "Torch!" he said, and a guard rushed forward. Slowly, he moved the flames across Sir Dietrich's skin.

Annise's heart pounded in her chest. *Please don't be marked, please, please, please . . .*

Scars were illuminated and passed by. A royal barber was called forth to shave the knight's head, which was also scarred in at least a half-dozen places. The job was almost finished when the guard hovered the torch over a large scar on the knight's back, round and black and mottled. Lord Griswold leaned closer to inspect it. "What is this from? The large one."

Sir Dietrich's face didn't so much as flinch. "Three years ago the westerners tried to fight their way through Raider's Pass. I was there. They caught me. They held me down. They stuck a torch to my flesh, much like you're doing now, except they went all the way. They burned me."

Lord Griswold released an inappropriate laugh. "Bastards!" he declared. "Get dressed. You are hereby deemed the winner of the Northern Melee in the year 532 of the Four Kingdoms. You will be sworn into the King's Defense immediately." He turned on his heel and departed without apology. He grabbed his son, Dirk, by the scruff of his collar and dragged him away like a child.

Annise touched a hand to her heart and felt it begin to slow.

"Well, that was close," Arch said. "I have a feeling I'm going to like Sir Dietrich."

Annise was thinking the same thing.

Unfortunately, her thoughts were slashed away when her uncle shouted her name. It was time to face her father.

❧

Her mother wasn't present for their punishment, which wasn't a good sign. The only reason the king wouldn't require his queen's presence was if she wasn't in good enough condition to be seen in public. Annise knew she shouldn't care—her mother never seemed to care what happened to her own daughter—but she did.

King Gäric rested his elbows on the clawed arms of his throne, which was crafted to look like ice. An enormous ice bear's head hung on the wall behind him, just beneath the royal sigil.

Arch was dealt with first. "For behavior inappropriate of a prince of the north while in public, ten lashes with a cane. To be carried out by our new defender, Sir Dietrich."

"But Father, I wasn't trying—" Arch started to protest, but was quickly cut off when the king raised his hand.

"Get out of my sight."

Wisely, Arch left without further discussion. Annise had seen her father double or triple a punishment for simply staring at him for too long or breathing too heavily.

Annise remained kneeling, refusing to look anywhere but at the polished stone floor. Her stomach ached, but not from fear. She was starving, having not had supper yet.

The king spoke. "You want to be a commoner?"

Yes, Annise wanted to say, but she knew it would only make things worse.

"Well?" The king rapped his fingers on the arm of his throne.

"No."

"No what?"

"No, Your Highness."

"Then stop acting like one," he said. "You are a king's daughter, a princess of Castle Hill, of the Northern Kingdom, the most recent generation in a long line of great kings and queens."

But I never asked for any of that, she thought.

"For the same crime as your brother, you will spend a fortnight in the High Tower," the king commanded.

A fortnight? "Father, no!" Annise shouted, unable to hold her tongue. She'd once spent three days in the windowless High Tower, and she'd pledged to never get stuck there again. Of course, her father knew what would hurt her the most.

"No?" he said, cocking his head to the side.

"I won't disappoint you again," Annise said, forcing contrition into her tone. "I promise."

The king met her stare, seeming to consider her plea. Then his eyes narrowed into black spear points. "Your very existence is a disappointment to me," he said.

As the guards dragged her away, she felt like crying, but she didn't let a single tear fall.

ॐ

A sound woke Annise from a light slumber. Her back ached from the hard, unpadded ground, a far cry from the plush bed she always took for granted. Her legs were sore, too, but that was from climbing the tower steps—all one-thousand-and-twenty-two of them. By the time she had reached the top, she'd been wheezing like a hog forced to run laps around its stall. The thought only gave her a fierce craving for bacon.

She'd been forced to go without dinner as part of her punishment, which was almost worse than spending a fortnight in the High Tower.

Annise loved to eat, and she knew it was necessary to sustain the time she spent training with her brother. Though others mocked her for her impressive appetite, she was not ashamed when her strength overmatched the boys in the yard. What she thought was ridiculous was the way the ladies of Castle Hill purposely left half of their plates uneaten at supper. Wasting good food was a sin, in her mind, especially considering there were plenty of commoners starving.

Her stomach growled as she scanned the room.

Although she hadn't been provided a bed, she was given a lumpy straw-filled pillow; however, as soon as the door had closed, she'd ripped it to shreds in a fit of rage, an outburst she was now regretting. Straw and tattered cloth—the remnants of the pillow—were scattered through the small windowless room.

But the worst thing about the tower was the mirrors. They were built into every wall, surrounding her, making the tiny room appear enormous, endless. Hundreds of Annises mimicked her movements as she yawned and stretched.

She hated this place because of the mirrors, a constant reminder of everything she wasn't. Pretty. Slim. Graceful. Everything her mother *was*. It was almost like she was someone else's daughter. *Yes*, she thought. *I am. I am the Dread King's daughter. And I am dreadful.*

Annise rubbed her eyes, wondering what had woken her. Thousands of other Annises wondered the same thing.

A shout. The soldiers were being called to muster. She wished she had a window so she could see what was going on, but then she remembered her father's decree before the melee. It was time to carry out his promise to fill the streets of Castle Hill with the blood of traitors. How he would determine who was loyal to him and who was not was a mystery. In truth, he would probably just choose randomly. The Dread King had always ruled by fear.

She drifted from her thoughts when she heard a voice. It was close, perhaps just outside the door. It was probably Drunk Craig falling asleep on the job again. She was glad it was he who'd been assigned to guard her. If not for fear of additional punishment by her father, she'd consider slipping past him and sneaking out.

Wait. There were two distinct voices: a conversation.

Annise rose to her feet, wondering what was going on.

The door opened.

And the last person Annise ever expected to see in the doorway appeared. Her mother.

Queen Sabria Loren Gäric's lips were pulled into a tight line, almost like a recently strung bowstring, and her face was shiny with exertion from the climb up the staircase. Her sunshine hair was swept up into a makeshift twist atop her head, as if she'd done so as an afterthought. Her red silk dressing gown was wrinkled and clinging to her shoulders, hips and knees. Yet, despite her casual and somewhat harried appearance, her mother was the most stunning woman Annise had ever seen.

"I don't have much time," her mother said, closing the door.

Time for what? Annise wondered. Her mother rarely spoke to her in public, much less in private. And she *never* came to visit her. Confused into silence, Annise simply waited for an explanation.

"Daughter," her mother said. "Annise." Annise's breath was pulled from her lungs. Those two words were spoken with such fervor, the queen's voice low and cracking. Her mother had never spoken to her like this. Never looked at her with such . . . what was that look? Sadness? Caring? Something else, something more?

She could almost mistake the look for love. Almost.

Her mother's eyes watery, she took two steps forward and wrapped her thin arms around Annise, squeezing her daughter into her chest. Annise was so surprised, she didn't do anything at first, her body frozen like an ice sculpture. But then, slowly, tentatively, she hugged her mother back. She could feel her heartbeat, could feel her mother's lips against her neck, the warmth of her tears on her skin.

Could hear her words, whispered briskly in her ear: "I'm sorry I couldn't be there for you. It was the only way I knew how to protect you. I wish I'd been better. Stronger. You are better, you are stronger. And I'm so proud of you."

And then she was gone, releasing Annise and pulling away and slipping out through the door before she could utter a single word in response.

Annise slumped back to the floor, her lips parted in wonder. What had just happened? And why had it happened now, after all this time? The self-doubt in her mother's eyes, in her words, painted a different picture of the woman she looked up to. And if she was wrong about her mother, did that mean she was wrong about herself, too? She stared at herself in the mirrors for a long time, and for the first time in many years, she saw someone else.

Someone different.

Maybe someone better.

≈

Several hours later, Annise was startled awake by a noise. She sat up and blinked away the sleep, the wall sconce casting an orange light across the small space, reflecting off the mirrors.

The sound was more than a scrape. Footsteps approached, heavy and confident, making their way up the stairs.

Drunk Craig must've heard them too, because there was the sound of him bumbling to his feet and he said, "Your Kingship—I mean, Your Highness—I didn't expect—"

"Open the door. I wish to speak to my daughter." The voice was clearly that of the king.

Her father was here? But why? Did he know her mother had come to see her? Would they both be further punished for the queen's visitation during Annise's fortnight of punishment?

Annise rose to her feet and watched the door open. The king marched in, then turned back and said, "Leave us."

"Yes, of course, right away, Sire," Drunk Craig said. He seemed surprisingly sober, albeit exceedingly flustered.

Annise forced herself to one knee. Thousands of sturdy women bowed in turn. All of them were determined to hold her tongue this time.

"You may rise," the Dread King said.

Oh may I? Well, thank you very much, Father, I am oh so appreciative. Annise bit her tongue and kept her thoughts to herself as she stood. "Is something wrong?" she asked. "Your Highness," she remembered to add, stifling a curse with her hand. *What have you done to my mother?* she added in her head.

He waited a moment, admiring several of his reflections in the mirrors. He wasn't afraid of facing himself the way she was. He seemed to relish it. "I know you think I'm a monster, and maybe I am, but this is a dangerous world full of even more dangerous monsters than me. Everything I do is to protect our family, our right to rule."

She said nothing. He could delude himself all he wanted, it wouldn't change anything.

He continued: "When you were born, I was hoping for a son."

She hated the fact that tears threatened to emerge. She blinked rapidly. Why should she care what her father thought of her? Why should she care that he wished she had never been born? He was an evil man, and should be of no concern to her.

"I'm so sorry to disappoint you, Father," Annise said, making no attempt to hide the sarcasm in her voice.

The back of his hand lashed out so unexpectedly she had no time to defend herself. When the blow struck her cheek, her head spun and spit flew from her mouth. Stunned, she raised a hand to her face, feeling a warm trickle of blood seeping from a break in her skin. She'd been hit before. On the practice fields, by fists and wooden swords. By her father when she spoke out of turn or laughed too loudly or chewed in an "unladylike manner."

She set her jaw and turned back to face him.

"You don't disappoint me with your gender," he continued, as if he'd not just hit his own daughter. "You disappoint me with your disposition. With your lack of interest in defending all that we have."

What we have? We have a frozen land full of depressed people who hate you and your taxes and your hellfrozen decrees. She kept her thoughts to herself this time—just because she *could* take a hit better than most boys didn't mean she wanted to.

"Don't disappoint me again," the king added. When she didn't respond, he said, "Do you understand?"

"Yes, Father." *You bloody tyrant.*

"Good. Remember that." With that, her father pushed through the door, slamming it behind him. His footfalls thudded, muffled by the thick door.

And then they stopped and she heard her father say, "What in the frozen hell..."

Curious at what could raise such a reaction from the Dread King, Annise eased open the door and peered out.

Her father was a dozen or so steps beneath her, but turned back toward the tower's apex. However, she couldn't quite see his face. There was something blocking her view, a smoky haze. Through the fog, she saw her father's eyes widen into white orbs, his mouth open. The fog turned to shadow turned to flesh, and she saw a boy, his skin as pale as the Howling Tundra between Castle Hill and Blackstone. His scalp was shaved clean, like the bald peaks of the Mournful Mountains. Something blazed on his head, a circular mark, glowing. The boy turned, saw her, and reached out a set of long bloodless fingers, as if trying to touch her.

Something about his face was eerily familiar.

She shrank back, scared, and he disappeared in the blink of an eye.

Beyond where the boy had just been, her father flailed his arms, lost his balance, and fell backwards down the steps, gaining momentum with each roll. Annise gasped, unable to move as she watched his legs bend unnaturally, then his back. Finally, his head cracked against stone—one, twice, thrice. The staircase curled away and he disappeared from sight.

There was blood smeared on the wall and the steps.

Annise heard her breaths. She heard the beat of her own heart in her chest. She was acutely aware of each and every blink of her eyes, which were stinging.

And then she screamed.

An answering scream flew back up the tower. Not hers. Then a cry. "The king! The king is dead!"

That's when she realized why the strange boy had looked so familiar. Though he was younger, and his face was gaunt and too bony, his features were identical to that of her brother, Arch.

Chapter Three

The Northern Kingdom | Silent Mountain

Bane

"Father," Bane said, reappearing in the protective embrace of the cavern that had been his home for fourteen long years. He dropped to his knees, shaking, feeling bone-weary.

"You cannot call me that any longer," Bear Blackboots said. His beard had long ago turned white and reached his waist. He tugged on it now, a nervous habit he'd only recently acquired.

"Why not, Father?" Bane asked, not understanding. Who but this giant of a man, who had raised him from birth to now, could he call Father? He'd known no other. Even the wandering tribes of nomads appeared as small as black snowflakes on the field of white surrounding Silent Mountain.

"Because it has begun, Kings' Bane," Bear said. It was the first time in years that his father had used his full name, and it sent a shiver through him, though he was not cold.

"What has begun?" Bane said, although he already knew. Bear had often taught him the prophecies of the Western Oracle, though they'd always seemed impossibly distant. He longed for the days before, when he and Bear would hunt along the mountainside, the giant man imparting stories of kings and battles and dragons. He longed to return to the nights of singing beside an open fire, the day's prey crackling and sizzling over the flames.

I hate my fatemark, he thought, though, somewhere in his gut he knew it was a lie.

"You have spilled blood. You have murdered a king. The only father you have now is Death. I have made my choice, and now you must make yours."

"No!" Bane cried. "I didn't mean to do anything. He fell. It was an accident." He couldn't remember what the king had looked like, his mind full only of images of the girl, the king's daughter, who had withered in fear when she saw him.

He didn't even know how he'd moved through space to reach Castle Hill. Or how he'd returned to the cave. All he knew was that the mark on his scalp burned, and that everywhere he looked he saw darkness.

The killing came naturally, even if he didn't want to admit it. It was no accident—he'd shoved the king down the steps.

I am a monster, he thought.

He tried to stand, but his legs wobbled and he toppled over, his body wracked with tremors. "What is . . . happening . . . to me?" he said through chattering teeth.

"You have great power," Bear said.

"I feel so weak."

"My—" Bear cut off sharply. Restarted: "Your creator must've put safeguards in place. When you use your power, you will need time to recover."

My creator. Bear had often spoken to him of the Western Oracle. Of the spell she'd cast across the land almost two centuries ago, of the prophecies that followed, most of which were long forgotten by most. But not all. Not Bear. "Why?" he croaked. Bane felt like he'd been punched in the gut.

"Because else you would kill too quickly. Everything must happen in its own time."

Bane didn't fully understand, but he was too exhausted to think about it. His cheek pressed against the dirt, his eyelids drooping.

Bear waved a torch across his scalp, and though Bane could not see the way his fatemark flared in the dark, he could *feel* how it had changed.

One of the eight sections formed by the arrows had been filled in with blood.

A portion of a prophecy by the Western Oracle repeated itself over and over in his head.

Eight rulers shall die in the name of peace . . .

One ruler was dead. Seven more would follow.

Bane closed his eyes and slept.

Chapter Four

The Southern Empire | Dragon's Breath

Roan

The first time Roan had healed someone it was his guardian, Markin. While slicing meat, Markin had cut the tip of his thick, gray finger clean off. Roan was five at the time, and he'd felt something strange in his chest. A warmth. Instinctively, he'd laid his hand on Markin's arm and felt the warmth drain out of him and into his guardian. Markin had tried to squirm away, but it was too late: already his blood had clotted, his skin growing back, reconstructing his finger. Roan had collapsed, weakness overcoming him. Once he'd recovered, his guardian had taught him of his past, of who he was, how he could never use his power publicly, and never to help anyone but himself.

He taught him how if Roan prevented someone else from dying, it would be *he* who died.

Young Roan had cried for days.

Now, as the dream-memory faded from his mind, Roan's eyes creaked open. At first he couldn't make sense of what he saw. Until it blinked, a massive red eye staring back at him.

His sore muscles protesting, he scrabbled backwards like a crab, watching as the dragon stretched out its neck, its head reaching for the sky, bursting through a low-hanging cloud. The beast's scales were as black as ebony, sparkling in the morning sun. The nearby clouds were bandits, stealing the sky's precious blue hue, their cold breath like plumes of vapor.

The dragon roared.

Roan had never believed the rumors that Dragon's Breath was guarded not only by a giant wall, but by dragons. Now he did.

Could this get any worse? Roan wondered, even as he peered over the exterior half of the wall. A thin stretch of land surrounded the wall. Enormous metal spikes rose up from the rock, each attached to thick linked chains secured to various parts of the dragon.

The dragon was a prisoner, too, forced to spend what remained of its life in this godsforsaken place.

Then things did, in fact, get worse. Much, much worse.

A second head rose up, opening its maw to reveal multiple layers of glistening black teeth. Roan couldn't tell if it was three or four rows of fangs, and he wasn't about to climb inside to count.

Something he'd heard echoed in the back of his mind, about how as dragons aged they grew additional heads, a fact that eventually drove them to madness.

Great, he thought. *The empire sent the crazy dragons to guard Plague Island.*

The second head roared, echoing the first. They were far too close together to have separate bodies. He followed their long sinewy necks down to where they connected to the same muscled torso. Four reptilian legs ended in razor-clawed feet.

Madness.

Roan began to run, although the effort would likely be fruitless. He felt more than heard the flapping of a set of magnificent wings, the displaced air buffeting him like a typhoon, nearly blowing him off the wall. He steadied himself and stopped to look back, immediately wishing he hadn't. Heavy chains clanked as the two-headed dragon rose up, getting as high as the top of the wall before being yanked back by its tether, which groaned from the pressure. Four red eyes seemed to sizzle against the sky, smoke pluming from two sets of dark nostrils. The dragon was working itself up to something, and Roan suspected it involved him and breakfast.

A hopeful thought struck him, far too optimistic for the circumstances. *If I can only get beyond the reach of the dragon's chains . . .*

He turned and bolted, gaining speed when the dragon released a war cry that seemed to cook the air around him. Sweat drained down his back and dripped from his nose and chin. Risking one more glance back, all he saw were two giant caverns filled with blade-like stalactites and stalagmites.

He dove, tumbling across the top of the wall, pain shooting through his leg. Dark scales brushed past, scraping the stone, which cracked under the immense force. The two heads rose up once more, staring down at him from above.

Warmth spread to the wound as he attempted to repair whatever injury he'd sustained. Beneath him, the wall rumbled, as if the earth itself was trying to tear the stone-and-mortar structure apart.

The red-eyed dragon unleashed the fires of hell, a wave of brilliant heat that washed over him like a tide. He screamed as the flames engulfed him, surrounded him, cooking his skin from both outside and in. The pain was beyond anything Roan had ever felt before, and yet he forced his body to react instantaneously, fighting back like it had against the plague, his tattooya pulsing.

For a moment the inferno reached a stalemate with his mark, but was then pushed back bit by bit as the dragon ran out of breath. Roan's skin was scorched, sizzling like bacon on a spit, and he stared at it wondrously, trying to figure out how he was still breathing. On his chest, his mark was bursting with the light of angels through what was left of his burnt shirt—three leaves attached to a single stem. *You bear the lifemark*, his guardian had once told him. No one but his mother and his southern guardian ever knew about it, and they were both dead, taking his secret with them to their graves.

He looked down at his injured leg. A long bloody slash was etched from knee to ankle, tearing through his clothes. The blood was already drying, and his skin was knitting itself back together. Nearby, a dagger-like incisor lay, having broken from the dragon's mouth when it narrowly missed ripping his leg off. Reaching over, he snatched up the black fang. It was oddly shaped and unwieldy, but it was the only weapon he had.

Only a moment or two was left before the dragons would attack again, and he wasn't about to miss his chance. Though weariness threatened to overcome him, he pushed forward, scrabbling across the wall. He wouldn't waste his mother's sacrifice.

The dragon roared once more. Roan fought to his feet, moving as fast as he could, using the fang as a crutch whenever his legs faltered. The wall seemed to rise up as the dragon smashed into its side, crushing stone and mortar. Roan fell, clutching at rectangular blocks that were no longer attached to anything but empty air.

The wall caved in. Several man-sized stones whistled past, nearly bludgeoning him hard enough that even his tattooya wouldn't be able to save him. But luck was with him, and the projectiles missed him by a hairsbreadth. In a strange twist of fate or luck or something else entirely, Roan landed atop the dragon's back. He cried out in pain as the rough muscled skin made for a less than ideal landing, and yet better than the bare, unforgiving rocks below. Somehow he'd managed to hang onto the dragon's tooth in the fall.

The dragon's twin heads wavered above him, searching for their prey. They hadn't felt him land, his miniscule presence no more than that of a gnat to the enormous beast. The wall continued to collapse, and Roan was forced to dodge large chunks of stone. Several small pieces pierced his back and shoulders, but he fought on, making his way toward the slope of the monster's tail.

Without any other choice, he dove forward, beginning a slide toward the ocean that became steeper with each passing second. Halfway down he noticed another problem he hadn't realized until after he'd decided on this unstoppable course of action:

The dragon's tail ended in a barbed mess of spikes long enough to impale him from head to foot and still have room to spare. *Better and better,* he thought, attempting to maneuver his angle of approach to avoid the largest of the spikes.

One spike whipped past, then another. The third caught his shoulder, which flared with pain as blood poured from a long gap between flaps of skin.

And then he was airborne, having reached the end of the tail, which served as a ramp, launching him toward the glassy waters of Dragon Bay, more aptly named than Roan had ever realized until now.

The ocean, which seemed so inviting from the air, smashed into Roan with an icy punch. He plunged into its depths, stopped only when his body glanced off the rocky bottom. The water was clouded by his own blood, but Roan managed to hang onto the fang as it drifted toward the surface. The long, thin incisor was surprisingly buoyant, pulling him upwards, where the place where the water met the air appeared as a sheet of white crystalline light.

He broke the surface, spluttering, feeling the familiar warmth spread through his body, repairing the injury to his shoulder, as well as the battering he took on the underwater rocks. Throbbing aches subsided. Splintering pain disappeared.

Roan was once more pulled under by weariness, and it was all he could do to clutch the fang and hold on as the currents guided him away from the island. His eyes at half-mast, he looked back. There was a huge hole in the wall, and he could see ant-like forms clambering over rock and debris, seeking escape. Plague victims.

The two-headed dragon stood waiting to feast.

Further around the island, Roan saw that the beast wasn't alone. Other multi-headed dragons pulled at their chains, the metallic smell of blood in the air. As one, they roared.

Roan's eyes closed and he slept.

෴

Roan was getting pretty tired of waking up feeling like he'd been in a war. Then again, the alternative—not waking up at all—was far worse.

The sky was different, somehow. Less bright, more gray. The temperature was odd too. He felt . . . cold, a sensation he had very little experience with. Tall grass and broad green ferns tickled his skin as he rocked back and forth against a mossy shore. Ghostly vapors seemed to chase each other across the dark waters.

He didn't know how he'd managed to cling to the tooth while sleeping, but sure enough the obsidian fang was stuffed beneath his armpits, his fingers knitted together around the incisor in the center of his chest, as if collected in prayer.

"Where am I?" He'd spoken the question aloud, although he'd meant to keep the thought in his own head. Even more surprising was the fact that he received an answer to his rhetorical question.

"The Barren Marshes, I'd say," said a man's voice.

Roan whipped his head around, seeking the source. A boat drifted past, several sets of oars dipping idly in the murky water. The boat appeared to be made of . . . metal, rather than wood like the seafaring vessels of the south. Roan found himself wondering how such a heavy craft would stay afloat.

Four stern-looking men sat inside the boat, while a fifth stood at the helm, balancing easily. He wore a gray chest plate, although his arms were bare. He was young, but strong-looking, his muscles as taut as thick shipping rope. He had a handsome face, clean-shaven and free of scars. He was the one who had spoken, an amused sparkle in his chestnut eyes.

Barren Marshes. Although Roan was no scholar of geography or maps, he was certain there were no marshlands in the burnt territories of the Southern Empire. Which meant he must be somewhere in the east. *How could I have drifted so far?* he wondered. But as he inspected the young man standing before him, he knew it must be true, for his armor bore the royal sigil of the Eastern Kingdom, twin crossed swords on a field of black.

"Who are you?" Roan managed to ask.

The young man laughed, pushing a hand through his reddish-brown hair. "Aye, that is a question that deserves an answer first. Halt." As one, the four men churned their oars forwards, stopping the boat's movement and angling it toward Roan.

"What answer?" Roan asked.

"A name for a name," he said, extending an oar in Roan's direction.

"Roan," he said, eyeing the oar with mistrust. These were strangers, and foreigners at that. In this never ending time of war, surely they wouldn't be particularly kind to a southerner.

"Roan With-Only-One-Name," the young man said, laughing again. *His laughter is infectious*, Roan thought, but then just as quickly chided himself. The man pushed the oar closer, nodding at it.

With no other choice, Roan grabbed the tip, and allowed himself to be reeled in. While the young man, who was clearly the leader, watched, two of his men helped pull Roan inside, not unlike the manner in which a fisherman would land a particularly large fish. The leader bent down and scooped up the dragon's tooth, holding it with both hands and examining it.

"This is a strange piece of driftwood," he said.

It wasn't a question, so Roan didn't see reason to answer.

"What is your surname?" the man asked.

"You said a name for a name, not two names," Roan said, delaying

The man, who seemed unflappable, said, "No matter. I am Prince Gareth Ironclad, eldest son of *King* Oren Ironclad, known abroad as the Juggernaut. Which makes me the heir to the eastern throne."

It took all of Roan's effort to appear unsurprised. "If you're a future king, then that's a dragon's tooth," he said, gesturing to the object in Gareth Ironclad's hands. *He does look rather princely*, he thought.

"I didn't say I would *be* a future king, oh Waterlogged One," Gareth said with a smirk. "Only that I am the *heir* to the throne. I plan on dying honorably in battle well before my father reaches death's doorstep. One of my brothers are much more likely to inherit the east. And now, if I'm not mistaken, I've given you many names, so you owe me your last."

Gods. Royalty. He wondered whether he'd escaped the skewer only to end up in the fire. "That's a fine high horse you're resting your royal arse on,

Your Princeliness," Roan said, "but I am known by nothing but Roan, and occasionally 'Born From Dust'."

Gareth's smug expression faltered slightly, but he recovered quickly. "You would think someone relying on the kindness of strangers would be more well-mannered." He turned toward his men. "He's clearly no easterner. Bind him!"

Two of the men raised a rope, but Roan shoved them back. "I wouldn't do that if I were you. I have come from Dragon's Breath, and I have been through hellfire to get here."

"Plague Island?" one of the men said, nearly tripping as he backed away. "He touched me. The diseased fellow touched me." He looked stricken with fear.

Gareth, on the other hand, did not waver. "This man shows no signs of the plague. Rudeness, yes; disease, no."

"I am strong, the toxins move slowly through my blood," Roan said. "Now I'll be on my way. You can keep the dragon's tooth. I'm sure it will fetch a royal price."

He started to climb over the side of the boat, but stopped when the prince said, "The only way you'll survive is if you can outswim my arrow."

When Roan looked back, Gareth had placed the tooth in the boat and nocked an arrow in his bow, pulling the bowstring taut. The bow itself was a work of art, sheathed in metal that curved gracefully at the top and bottom like it had grown that way, rather than been shaped.

Roan chewed his lip nonchalantly. "I'd hate to break a sweat, Your Highness. I'm not much for swimming, but luckily I have a less strenuous manner of escape."

Before the prince realized what he was doing, Roan dove for his legs, hearing the twang of the bow and the whistle of the arrow as it whizzed overhead. Thrown off-balance, Gareth tripped over the side, entering the water with an impressive splash.

The other men cried in protest, but seemed loathe to get too close to Roan, still fearing the plague. Roan took advantage of the opportunity, diving off the opposite side, swimming desperately for shore. "After him!" he heard the prince cry.

Somewhere behind Roan, oars splashed into the water and creaked with the sound of rowing. He reached the marshy shore, grabbing a thick handful of grass to pull himself up. In moments he'd be gone, disappearing into the dense undergrowth. They'd never find him.

But it wasn't meant to be. Just as he was about to plunge into the swamp, strong arms yanked him back, slamming Roan onto his back. A hammer rose above him and his eyes widened.

When it smashed into his skull, he saw stars and then nothing.

❧

The nightmare was, in fact, a memory, one Roan had been forced to relive many times in the last eight years:

He was ten years old. His guardian, Markin, had gone out to buy food in the Calypsian marketplace. Young Roan was looking out the window at the children playing barefoot in the sand, their faces dusty and their long hair windswept. He longed to be out there with them, to join the game they were playing, where they kicked the leather sack through the barrels.

But he knew he could not. You are different, *his guardian told him again and again. Each time the gray-skinned man said it, the words were pounded further and further into his head, like a tent spike driven into hard-packed dirt. "But why?" Roan always asked. "Just because of my pale skin?" "Not just that," his guardian replied. "Your tattooya." Roan still didn't understand. He also didn't understand why he couldn't tell anyone about it. Why he was only allowed to use his talents for himself. "What you have inside you is dangerous," Markin had told him. "Not everyone will understand it. There are those who will harm you if they know what you are, the power you possess. They will try to use you to save themselves, and then you will die."*

Roan wished he'd been born the same as everyone else. Maybe then he could play with the other children. Maybe then he could be happy.

One of the children kicked the sack in front of her, long dark hair trailing behind like royal streamers. Roan had seen her before, and he could never take his eyes off of her. She ran like the wind, outdistancing the defenders. She had an open lane to the barrel, and Roan found himself holding his breath in anticipation of her next kick.

Then he saw the last defender swooping in from the side, tall and muscular and older than the other children. Roan wanted to shout a warning from the window, but his voice lodged in his throat like a whole walnut.

The girl didn't see him coming, not until he crashed into her side, knocking the leather sack away. But Roan wasn't watching where the sack went, his eyes locked on the girl, who flew into the air, her body twisting awkwardly. Strangely, after a full rotation, she landed on one foot, which buckled under her. She cried out in pain, her knee bending in the wrong direction.

Roan was already climbing from his window, sliding down the canvas awning that marked the front of his guardian's home, dropping to the cracked, dusty landscape, and sprinting toward the girl. He hadn't considered the alternative—doing nothing—which is what his guardian would've counselled.

When he reached her, she was clutching her leg and sobbing, tears painting lines in the layer of dust on her smooth cheeks. Most of the kids had continued playing their game, trying to reclaim the ball from the tall boy. However, one child—a boy—huddled around his fallen teammate.

Roan said, "Don't worry," and laid his hands on the girl's leg. He felt heat rush through his body, emanating from a single white-hot point in his chest. The power flowed into the girl, who stopped crying, her eyes flashing open in surprise. Her leg kicked out once and made a popping sound, and then laid still once more.

"Slithering snakes," the boy said.

"Thank you," the girl said, her eyes wide. "But how?"

Roan reached out to touch her sweaty brow, to brush the hair from her eyes, but he was ripped away from her by a strong hand.

In that fateful moment, Markin had returned from the market, and he'd witnessed everything. "Come with me," he growled. At first Roan thought he meant only him, but the girl and boy gathered themselves up and followed along obediently, perhaps stunned by the command in the large man's voice.

"I'm sorry," Roan pleaded. "I was only trying to help her."

"You've risked everything," was all Markin responded, ushering the three children inside.

He marched Roan to his second-floor loft, locking the door and window. Roan didn't know what was happening, but his gut did. His stomach was full of sharp rocks, poking around.

He pounded on the door for a long time, until darkness crept around the gaps in his window frame. Finally, the door opened.

"This is what your disobedience has done," Markin said when he let Roan out. Like all Dreadnoughters, his skin was the color of ash and as rough as untreated wood, and his forehead was broad and flat. An angry vein protruded just above his eyebrow, pulsing with each beat of his heart.

There was an unusual scent in the air, like charred meat. Had his guardian burned their supper?

In the fire pit in the center of the main space were two blackened lumpy forms. Wisps of white smoke curled up from them, rising out through the flue in the leather tent.

"No," Roan whispered, backing away. This wasn't real. He tried to speak, but his stomach heaved. He threw up, and then collapsed. He couldn't stand, couldn't move, couldn't breathe. "You killed them."

"Death is but a change in existence, like rain turning to ice in the north or evaporating to mist in the south."

"You're a monster."

"Maybe so. But I will do what I have to do to protect you. Using your power is dangerous for everyone," his guardian whispered in his ear. "You are too important to risk." He picked Roan up in his strong arms and carried him back to his loft, depositing him onto his hard bed.

This time he left without locking the door.

Roan wept into his hands. "I hate you," he whispered to the night, and he didn't know whether the words were intended for his guardian, or himself. He wasn't sure it mattered.

While his guardian slept, Roan left, refusing to look at the fire pit as he crept past and slipped from their tent.

He never saw his guardian again, vanishing into the enormous sprawl of Calypso, just another nameless street rat; "I am Born From Dust," he liked to mutter when he was alone. But he kept tabs on Markin through other sources, until a few years back when he learned of his guardian's unexplained murder.

Roan never used his power on anyone but himself again.

He also never ate meat again, the smell too much like burning human flesh.

Roan gasped as he awoke, breathing rapidly as the memory faded back into the past, where it belonged. Next, he groaned. His head ached and it hurt to open his eyes, though it was not particularly bright. Despite his efforts, one of his eyes remained stubbornly closed, his flesh puffy around it. Wisely, he chose not to heal himself, for fear of giving away his secret.

With one and a half eyes, he stared at the gray-cloaked sky. Spindly gray branches crisscrossed overhead, borne by chalky tree trunks that appeared more dead than alive. A strange finger-like fog seemed to cling to everything, making visibility poor.

"Why do you both laugh and scream in your sleep?" a voice asked.

Roan tried to get his hands under him to push to his feet, but found them tethered firmly behind his back. Something metal clanked. When he tried to separate his feet, the result was the same.

He sighed. *Royals*, he thought. *Were they the same everywhere?* The irony of the thought made him laugh, despite his pounding skull.

"Did I inadvertently jest?" Prince Gareth asked.

"Everything you say is a jest," Roan muttered, turning his head to find the prince sitting on a log beside a campfire, roasting some kind of meat on a metal stick. A smoky aroma swept into Roan's nostrils and he felt ill. *It's an animal, not human*, he reminded himself, but the thought did little to quell the sick feeling.

Nearby, the other men from the boat were keeping busy—polishing armor, collecting firewood, hauling water from a creek—although he suspected they were listening.

"Like I said before," Gareth said. "Rude. If not for the fact that we found you in the Barren Marshes and you called yourself 'Born From Dust', I would hazard to guess you were a westerner."

Because westerners are rude, Gareth thought. *Ha.* "I've spent my entire life in Calypso," Roan said. *Well, mostly.* It was close enough to the truth that he was able to hide the subtle lie.

"You skin is about a hundred shades too light to be Calypsian."

"And yet, I am."

"Well, despite your appearance, I'm not surprised," Gareth said. "You have the stink of Calypso on you."

"Maybe," Roan said, "or it could be the diseased stench of Dragon's Breath."

"I have to hand it to you, you're able to keep a very straight face when you lie through your teeth. Which makes me wonder whether I can trust a single word from your mouth."

"I'm not lying."

"And this is a dragon's tooth?" The prince smirked, raising the fang over his head with one hand.

"It saved my life," Roan said. *The truth is always easier to speak when everyone thinks it's a lie.*

"How'd you get it?"

"A dragon tried to bite me."

"Where?"

"My leg."

"Which one?"

"Left."

"If a dragon chomped on your leg, you wouldn't have a leg."

"Like I said, it *tried* to bite me. Luckily it was only a glancing blow."

"How long ago?"

Roan had no choice but to lie now. He wouldn't be able to explain his miraculous healing without revealing his secret. "Eons ago. The scar has faded."

"And you carry it around with you everywhere?"

"Wouldn't you?"

The prince shook his head. "No. I would mount it somewhere in my father's royal halls in Ferria. Put it on display."

"How grand," Roan said.

"You should be more mindful of your tongue, you know. Our countries are at war."

Roan nodded. He couldn't argue with that. Then again . . . "There is always war. There was war before the two of us were born, there will be war our entire lives, and there will be war after we are long dead. But regardless of war, we are just two men talking."

The prince laughed his infectious laugh. "And yet one of us is feasting on wild boar"—he took an enormous bite of meat, continuing to talk as he chewed loudly—"and the other is in chains." He tossed Roan a hunk of thick white bread, which hit him in the stomach, rolling to his feet. With no hands to use, Roan was unable to pick it up.

Roan was happy *not* to be feasting on boar, and as hungry as he should be, the smell of cooking meat had stolen his appetite. "And yet they'll stick us both in the ground when we die," he said.

"Bravo," Gareth said. "You have a quick tongue. Regardless, if you're a southerner, why were you so far to the east?"

"I told you—"

"Yes, yes, the plague and all that rot," the prince said.

"Sometimes, Your Majesty," Roan said with mock servitude, "the road beneath our feet is unchangeable."

The prince raised his eyebrows. "That's such a pathetic way of thinking. If I'm on a road I don't care for, I turn around."

If only it were that easy, Roan thought wryly. He felt as if his entire life had been forced upon him, a series of paths paved in regret.

The prince went on. "In any case, it's a good thing we found you first. Had one of my other platoons chanced upon you they might have shot first and asked questions later. Now back to the question that started this interesting conversation. Why were you both laughing and screaming in your sleep? Was it the comedy and tragedy of your situation?"

In truth, Roan had no clue he'd been laughing, and, given all that had transpired in the last day, he could find nothing humorous about his current situation or how he'd managed to flop from the frying pan into the fire. As for the screaming . . . that was certainly due to the nightmarish memory. "A fair maiden was tickling me," he lied. "Then I realized she resembled your mother, so I screamed."

The prince didn't miss a beat. "That's some fetish. My mother has never been called fair considering she has a beard and is stronger than my father!" Gareth roared with laughter, and his men paused what they were doing to join him. With an abruptness that left Roan's head spinning, he stopped and said, "We will find out who you really are, you know that, aye?"

Roan shook his head, which only made it pound harder. Eventually the prince would demand real answers to his questions, particularly the one about Roan's identity. "Look, I truly don't know my surname. I was born a bastard and my father wanted nothing to do with me."

"Aye, that doesn't surprise me," the prince said.

"Which part?"

"Either one." The prince took a bite of an impressively large leg bone, and Roan was forced to look away. "Your father—he must be a westerner. I'm betting that underneath that sun-kissed skin o' yours you're as pale as a western pigeon."

Roan knew he was entering dangerous territory. Easterners reserved a special contempt for westerners, a feeling that was all too mutual. Far too much blood had been spilt along the border at the Spear, and memories were long and passed down for generations.

"I never knew my father," Roan said neutrally.

The prince's eyes narrowed. In the firelight, the edge of his sword, which was propped up on a tree stump, glittered dangerously. Then, as usual, he laughed. "I don't need to be a sorcerer to conjure the full picture in my head," he said. "So your father couldn't resist the seductive beauty of some hip-swaying Southron girl, could he? He took a long tumble in the sand, and months later out popped a squalling bastard named Roan Born-From-Dust, aye?"

"Aye." *Let him think what he wants.*

"There's no shame in that. He won't be the last man to be bewitched by a southern seductress. But leaving you there to be raised by them? Now that is the act of a man without honor. What of your mother?"

Roan paused, but then eventually said, "She died in childbirth." It was near enough to the truth that he felt confident saying it. If not for his birth, she would likely still be alive. One of his heartstrings was plucked and the note was as somber a sound as he had ever heard.

"Ah. I'm sorry, poor lad." It was the closest thing to sincerity Roan had heard in the prince's voice thus far. For a moment he saw a different person, one who might be kind under the right circumstances. Something stirred inside him, but he quickly pushed the feeling down.

Roan couldn't linger on this topic any longer. "Where are we?" he asked, gazing around at the dead trees of the strange forest. It wasn't close to winter yet—the undergrowth should've been thick. Stranger still was the fact that the only sounds were from the crackling fire, the men moving through the trees, and their own voices. No birds sang. No creatures rustled. There wasn't even the slightest breeze to help dry his damp clothes. It was as if the air was frozen in place. This truly was a dead place.

"Barrenwood," one of the men answered. "Past the town of Rue." Roan wondered whether this man was the one who'd cracked his skull with the hammer.

Roan groaned. Why was everything in the east named 'barren'? The answer was obvious. Everything was *dead. Including me, if I don't find a way to escape soon.*

"Why do the trees look like that?" Roan asked.

"You mean, why are they dead?" the prince said. "They've been like this since the savages sailed from the Dreadnoughts and led a battle against the king's army in these woods. It was just after the Dragon Massacre in Ferria. In the Battle of Barrenwood, many died on both sides. After that, the fog came in and never left. Few venture through Barrenwood, as it's believed to be haunted. If I told you of some of the atrocities committed in this place you would not laugh in your sleep ever again."

Of course, Roan had heard of the Dreadnoughts, a long chain of islands in Dragon Bay. It was where his own guardian had come from, a place where it was said that blood could not be spilled on the land, or great horrors would arise. It was another legend he'd never given much credence to. Now, after his run in with the two-headed dragon, he feared the 'spill no blood' legend was just as true.

"How long ago was that?" Roan asked.

"Near on eighty-five years," the prince said, using a bone to pick at his teeth. Roan's stomach curdled. "Don't you know your land's history?"

"I didn't have royal tutors growing up," Roan said. He knew more of the west than he cared to know, but little of the east; except, of course, for the fact that they'd been at war with the west for hundreds of years. He changed the subject quickly. "Where are we going?"

The prince raised a well-manicured eyebrow. He threw his bone at Roan, who had no choice but to let it glance off his chest, joining the chunk of bread at his feet. "Ferria, of course, to my father's eastern stronghold. You're our prisoner, and you'll be tried as a southern spy."

Roan was about to protest that he was no spy when the clip-clop of horse hooves silenced him. A rider was moving fast through the mist, his green cloak billowing behind him, his chestnut mare cutting a path through the white trees. He eased to a trot and then stopped completely when he reached their camp.

"Ho, messenger," Gareth said, standing. "What news bring you?" The prince's men had already formed a staunch barrier around him.

The rider wasted no time, remaining in his saddle as he delivered his news. "I come from Rue, where we've just received tidings from Hammerton." His voice was slightly high pitched.

"What say the barrel-chested men of the smith village?" Gareth asked.

The man threw back his hood, and Roan was surprised to find a young lady hidden beneath the cloak, her hair so silver Roan wouldn't have been surprised to learn it had once been struck by a moonbeam. Her lustrous locks curled around her pointed chin.

Even more surprising was her attire, which was a complete set of polished silver armor, molded so finely it appeared to have grown around her slender form, even forming intricate patterns beneath her mouth, along her delicate jawbone, and swirling past her strangely yellow eyes to her forehead. *She's as spectacular as the prince*, Roan thought. *Maybe more so.*

"We received a stream from our spies in Castle Hill." The young woman paused to let the chain of information sink in. "They're saying the Dread King of the North is dead."

For a moment there was complete and utter silence in the forest. And then the men cheered.

Chapter Five

The Northern Kingdom | Castle Hill

Annise Gäric

Her punishment had been cut short. More than that, her father's orders to flood the streets of Castle Hill with traitors' blood had been halted before it could be carried out.

The death of a king had that sort of effect. Still, it felt odd to Annise that the death of one man could actually save numerous lives.

The news had spread like an ice storm throughout the city, and Annise was certain it would swarm throughout the rest of the Four Kingdoms with equivalent speed as streams were prepared and sent. Soon their enemies would know. They would gain strength from the news.

"They will attack us," Annise said, with certainty.

"Not right away," Arch said. "They'll wait to see what transpires. Even then, our borders at Blackstone, Raider's Pass, and Darrin are strong. We're safe in Castle Hill."

Annise closed her eyes, trying to erase the images of the last several hours. Her father's unexpected appearance in the tower, his typical brutality, the ghostly apparition, and his sudden tumble down the tower steps. Numb with shock, she'd raced down the winding staircase, horrified at how slick the stone was with her father's blood. When she'd reached the bottom, one of the soldiers of the King's Defense was in the process of covering what was left of the king's body with a sheet, but not before Annise had caught a glimpse of his face, which was bruised and bloodied, his skull caved in, so different to the man she'd known her whole life, the man she'd feared and hated with every breath and beat of her heart.

And when she'd seen him like that, so weak, so broken, she'd felt nothing but joy, which scared her a little. Then her brother had arrived, ushering her away to his quarters, where they'd been hunkering down ever since, sitting cross-legged on his bed across from each other, thick as thieves, the way they used to be as children.

As Arch had cleaned the blood from her face from where their dead father had hit her, she'd told him everything the king had said to her, and what had transpired on the staircase afterwards, leaving no detail out. Well, except for the strange spirit who had appeared. The boy who she swore looked like a paler, weaker, younger version of her brother. Clearly, her eyes had played a nasty trick on her, and talk of ghosts would only cause her trouble. Plus, her brother was obviously *not* a ghost, even if he acted ghoulish sometimes.

She'd also left out her mother's unexpected visit. She was still trying to make sense of it herself. Annise could almost feel her mother's arms around her, hear the echo of her whispered words in her mind. *I am proud of you.*

Stark realization hit Annise. "You're the king," she said with a gasp.

"Yes," Arch said. There was no surprise in his voice, as if he'd known it from the moment he'd seen their father's corpse.

That's when something else occurred to Annise. Her brother had lived his entire life with the knowledge that one day he would be king. That understanding had been his constant companion, hidden behind his easy, confident manner, his never ending laughter and jokes, his adolescent nature.

"What will you do?" Annise asked.

Arch laughed, as if the question was an invitation to a party. "What I've been born to do. Rule. Protect the north. Improve the lives of our people."

"You will be a great king," Annise found herself saying, to her surprise. Even more surprising to her was how much she meant it. Despite their everyday childish bickering, she believed in her heart that Arch would be everything her father was not: good, fair, honest, loved.

A knock on the door made her flinch. The door creaked opened and their uncle, Lord Griswold, appeared. Something about his expression unnerved Annise. He almost looked . . . refreshed . . . despite the fact that they'd all been awake for most of the night. His beard was freshly trimmed, his eyes bright and clear, his gray tunic pressed and adorned with the royal sigil.

Sir Dietrich followed him in, offering a slight nod to Annise as he entered. The victor of the melee was even more handsome this close to her, despite the dented armor he continued to wear. Despite his scarred face. She remembered the rest of his body, how many other scars were hidden beneath his armor. He took up a position in the corner, and she pretended not to sneak glances at him.

On the opposite side of Lord Griswold was Sir Jonius, who stared straight ahead. Annise tried to catch his eye, to discern a glimpse of his usual kindness, but he only angled his head further away. It was the side where the top-most portion of his ear was missing, though Annise had never learned the story behind the old wound.

"You were out of your quarters last night," Sir Griswold said.

"I was in the tower," Annise said. "I was being punished."

"Not you," her uncle clarified. "Your brother. His chambermaid confirmed he'd left after nightfall."

"I couldn't sleep," Arch said. "I went for a walk."

"Where?"

"Why are you asking him this?" Annise asked.

Her uncle's voice was like ice. "You will not speak unless spoken to," he said.

Annise opened her mouth to tell him that she was a princess of the north, that he was nothing but a lord, his authority akin to the brightness of the stars, while hers was as powerful as the sun.

Arch placed a hand on her arm, sensing her anger. "Annise. It's fine." Turning back to their uncle, he said, "I went all around the castle. I stopped in the kitchen for a bite to eat. Went by the stables to brush Sampson. Might've met a maiden or two for a tickle."

Annise rolled her eyes. This was the brother she was more accustomed to. Not the man who was so certain he was the king now.

"Did you go to see your sister?" Lord Griswold asked.

"No," Arch and Annise responded at the same time.

"My father came to see me," Annise said. "Not Arch." *Nor a ghost that resembled him*, she added in her head. *My mother, too, but you need not know that.*

"Sir Jonius said he saw you near the tower staircase," Griswold said to Arch.

Annise looked at Arch. Arch ignored her, his eyes never leaving his uncle's. Suddenly this entire conversation felt more like a trial than a series of information-seeking questions. "That doesn't mean anything," Arch said.

"What are you saying? You think Arch killed his own father?" Annise couldn't believe the audacity of this man. "I saw what happened. He fell. It was an accident. If you're going to accuse Arch, you might as well accuse me, too."

"I've spoken to Sir Craig. He said you were in the tower room the entire time. That he was guarding your door. You couldn't have seen or done anything."

Damn that bloody, drunken knight. Annise didn't know if he was trying to protect her, or his own reputation. And yet it was strange that the knight hadn't mentioned her mother's visit. Curious. "Craig wasn't there. My father made him leave. And anyway, he's a drunk," she said. "He probably saw the Southron Empress in the halls tonight, too."

"Silence!" Lord Griswold said, taking one step forward and backhanding Annise across the face. Her head snapped back and she tumbled off the bed, shocked by the attack, which seemed to come out of nowhere. Her cheek felt hot and something wet trickled from the corner of her mouth. Once again, she was bleeding. Like brother, like brother, apparently, her father and uncle cut from the same brutal cloth.

Arch was by her side in an instant. "Sister, are you hurt?" he asked, helping her to her feet.

She glared at her uncle, refusing to cry, although her eyes were stinging. "I barely felt it," she lied.

Lord Griswold seemed to find this amusing.

"Get. Out," Arch said, pointing at the door. When Lord Griswold didn't move, Arch took a step forward and said, "As your *king*, I command you to leave before I see fit to have you hauled to the dungeons."

Lord Griswold smirked. "On the contrary, you are a murderer, and I'll have you in chains. You are hereby accused of killing my brother, King Wolfric Gäric, supreme ruler of the north, the Dread King. Your own father. Apprehend him."

Sir Dietrich stepped forward, his hand moving automatically to his sword hilt. "I'm afraid I can't do that, my lord," he said.

"Why not?" Lord Griswold turned, anger flashing in his eyes.

"Because I am sworn to defend the king. That's him, not you."

"You were also sworn to defend my brother, which you failed miserably at. *Prince* Arch has not yet come of age, and thus I am his lawful regent for the time being."

"And yet not the king," Sir Dietrich said firmly.

Annise wanted to hug him. Well, first slap her uncle, and then hug Sir Dietrich.

"You've made your choice then," Lord Griswold said.

"It was no choice," Sir Dietrich said.

"And yet the consequences will be the same." He snapped his fingers and a third figure slipped through the door, his finger already glowing blue. Sir Dietrich began to unsheathe his blade, but Sir Jonius quickly moved in position to secure his arms while the Ice Lord touched the sword's hilt, which immediately froze, shattering into a dozen icy shards. The knight hissed as some of the magic seeped into his hand, turning it blue. He tried to lift it, but found he could not. His fingers wouldn't move either, as if struck with sudden paralysis.

"Stop it!" Annise cried, rushing forward. Lord Griswold cut her off, grabbing her by the hair and slinging her to the side. She crashed into the bed's footboard, which cracked from the impact. She watched helplessly as her brother tried to intervene but was held by the Ice Lord, who conjured chains of solid ice to bind him.

Dozens of guards marched in, securing Arch and Sir Dietrich, escorting them from the room. Arch glanced back, and for the first time that Annise could remember, he looked scared. In this moment he wasn't a king, but a sixteen-year-old boy accused of murder.

Sir Jonius pushed him into the corridor, still refusing to look at her. Before she could regain her feet, the door slammed behind them, the lock clicking with an ominous finality that left her slumped on the floor.

⊸

All that remained of Sir Dietrich's sword was a puddle on the floor. Annise wondered if his hand would ever heal, or if it would remain dead and useless for the rest of his life. More than that, she wondered how long or short that life might be.

Thinking about Sir Dietrich distracted her from thinking about Arch. *Murder?* It was impossible, regardless of the weird vision she'd had on the staircase. Her brother wasn't able to materialize and disappear like a spirit. He was as human as she was, flesh and blood and bone.

Yes, that was it. Regardless of what Drunk Craig said, she was the *only* witness, and she would attest to her father's death being an accident. He'd tripped and fell. That was all.

But who would believe her? Her father was not a clumsy man. If anything, her denial of Arch's presence in the tower would only implicate her in his death. She was plenty strong enough to have come up behind him and pushed him down the stairs. For a moment she wondered why she hadn't thought of doing that herself.

A knock on the door startled her away from her thoughts. She rolled off the bed, grabbing a large vase on her way to the door. "Yes?" she said.

The door opened and a guard entered. She flung herself at him, bringing the vase down hard on his head. He cried out in surprise and pain, crashing into the wall. Annise trampled over him on her way out, and he grunted from the impact.

Two guards grabbed her arms, and though she managed to break loose from one of them and punch him in the jaw, a third guard appeared and subdued her kicking legs. They tackled her to the ground and dragged her back inside, throwing her on the bed.

"Enough!" one of them shouted, and she realized it was Sir Jonius. "You are only making this worse for yourself, princess." His jet-black hair was disheveled from the tussle and he was breathing heavily.

Her lips curled in disgust. She hated Sir Jonius's two faces. She hated the man who always remembered her name day, giving her small gifts that were exceptionally thoughtful. She hated the man who followed orders without question. She hated the man who seemed to care with one breath and was as cold as an icy blade with the next. "Where is my brother?"

"King Regent Griswold has—"

"Arch is the king."

"He has yet to come of age, and he's been accused—"

"I was there. I *saw* what happened. My oaf of a father tripped. It was an accident!" Annise realized she was gripping the sheets of her brother's bed so hard they'd begun to tear.

Sir Jonius looked at her hands, then back at her face. "Princess, please. There's nothing I can do."

"There's nothing you *will* do. There's a difference." She could see the pain her words had caused the knight, but she didn't care. He was nothing but a pawn. That's all he'd ever been.

Another idea came to her. "I want to see my mother."

"That's impossible."

"Why not?" *What have you done to her?*

Sir Jonius pursed his lips.

"Jonius, it's me. It's Annise." She remembered something he'd once called her, when she was still little and her shape was considered cute. "It's your snow angel."

"Forgive me," he said, ushering in a chambermaid. He left without another word, the other two guards hauling out the man Annise had knocked senseless.

"I'll never forgive you!" Annise screamed, launching a pillow at the door just as it closed. The chambermaid caught the pillow with impressive reflexes.

"Oh, sorry," Annise said. "That wasn't meant for you." She studied the chambermaid, who didn't look familiar. Perhaps her uncle had already sacked all the old servants and brought in new ones. Her face was covered with a shawl, only her dark eyes and smooth pale forehead visible. A few locks of brown hair curled from her brow. She was a solid-looking woman, not unlike Annise's own shape, with broad shoulders, a small chest, and a wide stance. She was decidedly pear-shaped.

She carried a tray with breakfast—two poached and peppered eggs, buttered toast sprinkled with cinnamon, a shiny red apple, and a jug of milk—which she set on the foot of the bed in front of Annise.

"What is your name?" Annise asked.

"You don't recognize your own flesh?" the woman answered, her voice stern and deep.

The voice was familiar, but Annise hadn't heard it in years. "Aunt Zelda?" she said in disbelief.

The woman removed the shawl, and promptly popped one of the eggs into her mouth, struggling to chew. Annise shook her head. She was still coming to terms with seeing her aunt twice in as many days, an event as rare as finding an ice bear that laid eggs.

"What are you doing here?" Annise asked, pulling the tray back as her aunt attempted to snatch another egg.

Zelda eyed the tray with narrowed eyes. "Your mother sent me."

"Mother?" Annise said, frowning. As far as she knew, her mother had never even spoken to Aunt Zelda. The two were as different as summer and winter. Then again, she'd noticed the look they shared at the tourney, the way they'd slipped away, almost synchronized. "When did you speak to my mother? Where is she? Why won't they let me see her?"

Zelda reached for a piece of toast, but Annise swatted her hand away. If she wasn't careful, her aunt would force her to go hungry. "Your mother and I have been friends for a long time," she said. "Secret friends."

Annise was surprised, but she didn't let it show. Her aunt continued.

"Queen Loren"—Annise noticed how she used her mother's maiden name—"is locked in the dungeons, like your brother."

Nothing made sense. Surely neither her father nor uncle would've incarcerated the queen just for missing the end of the tourney. Plus, she'd just seen her mother earlier that night, and though she acted a little strange, she wasn't in chains. "Why?"

"She's being accused of high treason," Zelda said, pulling an apple from a hidden pocket and crunching loudly.

"What treason?" Annise forgot about her breakfast for a moment and Zelda took advantage of her lapse to snag the other egg and take a bite.

Her aunt raised an eyebrow. "Why, the murder of the king, of course."

"That's impossible. She had nothing to do with it." Annise was aware of the way her voice was rising, but she felt powerless to stop it.

"Of course she didn't. Her plan to murder your father was to be executed in a week's time." Zelda finished both the egg and the apple while Annise struggled to form a coherent response.

"You mean, she *was* planning to murder him?" Annise finally said, her appetite gone. She relinquished control of the cinnamon toast.

"Try to keep up, dear," Zelda said. "Your mother was planning to poison him. There is evidence of her attempts to procure darkweed from a most sinister character of the northern black market. "Of course, I was in on it, too, although they'll never link me to the attempted crime."

Though she hated to think of her mother in the cold, dark dungeons, it could only mean one thing: "Then Arch is innocent. They have to release him!"

Her aunt *tsk*ed. "You are so young, child."

"I'm nearly eighteen," Annise protested. "I'm a grown woman."

"In body, yes, but not in experience. Your mother is accused of attempted murder, while Arch of *actual* murder. Your uncle is saying they both wanted your father dead, but Arch just happened to follow through first."

"That's a lie!"

"Of course it is, dear, but the evidence will be stacked heavily against him."

"But I'll have to testify. I know the truth."

"The truth is a snake of many colors, dear, it can change depending on who is charming it."

"No, the truth is *the truth*."

Zelda polished off the toast and waved her words away. "Listen closely. Whatever happens, you must not draw attention to yourself. Be ready."

With that, Zelda covered her face with the shawl, snatched up the empty tray, and left amidst Annise's protests for her to stay.

෴

The wooden execution block had long ago been stained crimson by the blood of those who dared defy the Dread King.

Annise wrapped her arms around herself, her breath misting in the frigid air. She searched the royal viewing box for her aunt, but she was notably absent. The rest of the space was filled by Lord Griswold, his son, Dirk, the Ice Lord, and several members of the King's Defense, including Sir Jonius.

Earlier that day, Sir Jonius had once again entered Arch's room, this time to collect Annise. He refused to look at her or answer her questions. Eventually, she'd given up and allowed herself to be escorted to the box, where she now stood, waiting for something horrible to happen.

The commoners stirred as soldiers marched onto the platform. In the midst of them was Queen Sabria Loren Gäric, guarded by swords as if she might fling herself away at any moment. In that moment, Annise believed her mother had never looked more beautiful or prouder. Despite the fact that her blond hair had lost its luster and hung in knotted vines around her face, despite the smudges of dirt and cinder on her typically pristine white dress, despite the swords aimed at her heart and throat, despite the way the commoners jeered and booed her—as a foreigner with clear disdain for the north, she'd never gained their love—she held her chin high, her expression one of fearlessness.

In that moment, Annise loved her, and wished for her mother's love more than anything. It was an impossible wish, she knew, but then she remembered all that had transpired the night before. Her mother's words to her, the affection in her voice, the regret . . .

Then why, Mother, have you always looked at me with such anger? Why did you hate me for all these years? Why do you refuse, even now, to notice me?

"Mother," Annise whispered under her breath. Her uncle must've heard her, because he grabbed her arm.

"A traitor is the mother of rot and bones and dung. She is not your mother anymore. You have no mother." Annise twisted away from him and said nothing, watching as Queen Gäric was led to a small ladder that ascended to a wooden platform. Above her hung a noose tied to a scaffolding.

Annise wanted to cry out, to plunge herself from the box and onto the platform, to fight through the guards—let them try to stop her—and rescue her mother from this farce of a trial. But her aunt's words from early that morning stopped her. *Whatever happens, you must not draw attention to yourself. Be ready.*

As if sensing her restlessness, her uncle motioned to two guards, who moved to either side of her, blocking her in. *Frozen hell*, Annise thought, *I've already drawn too much attention.*

On the deck, the soldiers stepped aside to allow the executioner to pass. He wore a long, hooded black cloak, boots, and gloves. The hood hung over his forehead, casting his face in shadow. He was a large man, more than capable of moving the platform out from under her mother's feet.

Slowly, ominously, he climbed the ladder. Sabria Loren ignored him, staring straight ahead, even as he fitted the noose around her neck.

Where is the trial? Annise wondered frantically. *Where is the evidence and the witnesses for and against her? This cannot stand! I won't let it! I wo—*

"Queen Sabria Loren Gäric," Lord Griswold announced loudly, "you are charged with treason against the crown and plotting the murder of your own husband, the Dread King of the North. How do you plead?"

Finally—finally—Annise's mother turned her head toward the royal box. But it wasn't Lord Griswold she looked at, but Annise. Annise's breath caught in her lungs and her heart began to pound out a staccato beat. Her mother's lips opened, and for a moment Annise thought she was going to say something to her. But then she said, "Guilty."

The crowd cheered, but Annise didn't hear them. Lord Griswold might've smiled, but Annise didn't see anything but her mother's face, which was stoic and resolute and—

She mouthed something. Three words that forced tears to Annise's eyes: *I . . . love . . . you.*

Lord Griswold's voice carried over all. "You are hereby sentenced to death by hanging. Executioner!"

The black-garbed executioner descended the steps and moved into position.

I love you too, Annise mouthed, unable to speak the words aloud. Her mother's eyes softened and a shadow of a smile crossed her lips. It was the happiest she'd ever looked to Annise.

"Now!" her uncle shouted, and the executioner shoved the platform away.

Her mother's body dropped rapidly, bouncing as the rope went taut, jerking her around like a ragdoll. Her hands went to her throat, and for several long seconds she fought against the inevitable, her body eventually going still, rocking back and forth gently in the breeze.

Tears stung Annise's eyes. Her hands ached from gripping the railing. She whirled around to locate her uncle, but Sir Jonius blocked her view, his face ashen. *Don't*, he warned silently. Annise wanted to scream in his face, to shove him back. She wanted to curse his inconsistency and willingness to let this happen.

Then she recalled the way her mother had looked at the very end. Strong, courageous. She turned away from him, clinging to her mother's last three words, unspoken but heard by Annise's ears louder than a shout.

I love you. I love you. I love you.

Down below, a second platform and scaffolding were moved into position. Her mother's body was cut down, covered with a white cloak, and carried off.

They hauled her away like a sack of oats.

Annise already felt numb, and then Arch and Sir Dietrich were marched onto the platform.

All feeling left her body.

Chapter Six

The Eastern Kingdom | North of Rue

Roan

Roan's hind parts had never been so sore, but there was no relief in sight as the horse galloped beneath him. He dared not heal himself, not when it would be too obvious.

Worse, he was forced to ride behind one of the prince's men, a thick fellow who rarely spoke but grunted often and had an aroma that suggested bathing was not part of his normal routine. Then again, Roan knew he probably didn't smell much better; unfortunately, his lifemark could heal wounds but not body odor.

Although he hated to admit it, he'd rather be riding behind Gareth. Or the silver-clad woman. He couldn't decide.

They'd been riding pell-mell ever since the messenger brought the news of the northern king's demise. Roan hadn't been sad to see Barrenwood fade away behind them, blotted out by the constant fog that seemed to hang over it like a gray blanket.

Now, with each new bruise on his backside, he was hating the eastern plains even more. The terrain was monotonous, the flatland of grass and bush seeming to stretch on to infinity. Somewhere on the edge of the horizon, Roan thought he could see something glinting in the sun, but he couldn't be certain.

"How much further?" he asked, his fingers aching from clutching the thick cantle separating him from the nameless man. Though his hands were still tied, his feet were free, thumping against the horse's ribs on each side.

The man turned his head and offered a grunt.

Prince Gareth Ironclad's horse, a black stallion that never seemed to tire, pulled up beside them, keeping stride. "Ho, plague child!" Gareth called.

Roan pretended not to hear him.

"Drowned rat?" Gareth said.

Roan could see the prince smiling on the edge of his vision. He pretended to only just hear him. "Did you say something?" he asked.

"How are you enjoying the ride?" Gareth asked, slowing his horse's gait to a trot. "Not too sore, are you?" Without being commanded, the rest of his men eased to a halt beside him.

"I'm wonderful," Roan said, trying not to grimace as he slung his leg over the horse's back and attempted to slide off. With his hands tied in front, he wasn't able to steady himself and he ended up sprawling face first into a prickly tuft of grass. The brown mare nuzzled in beside him, munching on the grass.

The men laughed, the prince the loudest, his voice carrying over all.

"I thought we had a spy, but I'm fairly certain we've got a new court jester!" the prince said, much to his men's appreciation.

Roan muttered a curse under his breath and managed to push to his feet. Why were the prettiest ones always the most annoying?

"What was that, jester? Do you have a jape for us?"

Roan did his best to ignore the prince, but it was hard when the young man strode up beside him and clapped him on the back. "Friend, if you tell us the truth about yourself, this will all go much easier."

The truth? Roan was so used to everything but the truth that the truth had almost lost all meaning. "The truth is in front of your face," Roan said. "I was afflicted with the plague, sent to Dragon's Breath, somehow recovered, climbed the wall, fought past a dragon, and was swept by current and fate into your snare."

"Snare? We were but floating along when we happened upon you, battered and broken and clinging to your 'dragon's tooth'." Gareth patted the fang, which hung from his belt. "We most likely saved your life, spy."

"I am no spy."

"You are also no jester," the prince said, "despite the fact that you act like one."

Roan was tiring of this conversation, so he changed the subject. "Who is she?" He gestured to the green-cloaked woman on the chestnut mare, now just a speck of greenish-brown in the distance. Unlike the rest of them, she hadn't stopped when the prince stopped, continuing her feverish gallop across the plains.

The prince tried to hide the grimace, but Roan still noticed it. "So you've noticed her beauty, have you?"

Roan couldn't deny her physical appeal, but that wasn't the focus of his inquiry. There was something strange about her... "She's different than us, isn't she?"

That response seemed to please the prince. "Ha! What gave her away? Was it her yellow ore-cat eyes or steel-silver hair? She is a forest dweller. Her people have lived in the east long before our Crimean ancestors discovered these lands. The king conscripted her as a scout and a messenger because of her stealth and speed as a rider."

"Conscripted? You mean enslaved?" Roan's experience with monarchs was that they always got what they wanted.

"No, I don't mean that at all. In the east, all men and women are free. She could leave the king's service today if she wanted. But she won't. My father is generous to those who remain loyal to him, and she is no exception."

Roan chewed on this information, trying to decide how much to believe. His estimation of the prince was that he was arrogant to a fault, but not a liar. What he was saying was probably true, which surprised Roan. Could the people under the thumb of a monarch ever really be free? He set the question aside to consider later. "But is she . . . human?" he asked. He'd heard of strange creatures in the east.

"Depends on your definition," the prince said. "Mostly, I'd say. But not as human as you or I. Not as flawed."

"What's her name?"

"Gwendolyn Storm. A strong name for a strong woman, don't you think?"

Roan couldn't argue with that, but that wasn't what interested him. "What of her armor? I've never seen anything like it."

"Her . . . kind . . . have power over ore. To them metal isn't a thing, it's part of them, like the air they breathe."

"Her kind?"

"The *Orians*."

Roan wished he'd listened more to his guardian's lessons, but at the time Calypso felt impossibly far from the rest of the Four Kingdoms. He remembered hearing about the forest dwellers of Oria, but that was the extent of his knowledge.

"Will she wait for us?" he asked. Already she was the size of a pinprick, her green cloak nearly lost amongst the never ending plains.

"You're fortunate I'm in a generous mood or I'd cut out your tongue for asking too many questions," the prince said. "I've instructed her to scout ahead. Yes, she will wait. I want to present the good tidings of the northern king's death to my father personally, though he may have heard already through the streams."

"Why do you care about some dead king?" Roan asked. From his experience with royalty, a dead king meant little. There were always heirs, and a king was easily replaced.

"You really don't know much, do you?" the prince said.

"I know survival," Roan said, remembering the night he ran away from his guardian. The first few weeks on the streets of Calypso had been the hardest, especially when he refused to eat the scraps of meat occasionally thrown his way, holding out for moldy bread and cheese discarded by the marketplace vendors. "When you're always searching for your next meal, for your next place to sleep, you care less and lesser about the actions of kings and their offspring."

"You talk of us as if we are a curse on the land." The prince was smiling. He always seemed to be smiling, a fact Roan grudgingly admitted appealed to him.

If only you knew the half of it, Roan thought. "We are all cursed, in our own ways," Roan said.

"How . . . jaded you are," the prince said, tossing him a water skin. "Anyway, drink your fill and then we ride on."

Roan groaned, wishing his hands could be used to rub his sore arse.

❧

Days passed in monotony. Each time the sun set, Roan peered into the distance and swore the glittering *something* he could see was farther away than when they started out. At least his rear end was beginning to build up enough bruises to make the journey slightly more comfortable.

Along the way, Roan remained vigilant, searching for an opportunity to escape. But on the endless plains where a man on horse or foot could be seen for leagues, he wouldn't get far.

So he bided his time, waiting for his chance.

When they stopped to sleep, Roan was given food and water, but not enough to satisfy him. Thankfully, they never offered him meat, so he wasn't forced to explain his unwillingness to eat it. In some ways it was humorous watching the prince taunt him with wild game that provided no temptation.

He'd also been given a white shirt and brown britches, as well as a sturdy pair of boots. "We stole them from a dead man," Gareth had said with a smirk. Roan's tattered clothes and shoes were burned in the campfire, and he wondered whether, despite the prince's nonchalance, his story about the plague and Dragon's Breath had been believed. Probably not. More than likely they were simply taking precautions.

While encamped, twice he tried to talk to the forest dweller, hoping to learn more about the origin of her armor, and twice she ignored him, going so far as to walk away to sit by herself.

Each time, the prince and his men laughed. "Smooth as silk, Sir Born From Dust," the prince said.

"I wasn't trying to be . . ." Roan started to respond, but then shook his head. There was no point in arguing with Gareth.

The third time he spoke to Gwendolyn Storm, she looked right at him, the last dying rays of the eastern sun illuminating her face. In the faux light, her eyes were as golden as the petals of the *lumia*, a desert flower that grew only in the south's arid climate. The lumia was lovely to look at, but when its petals were ground into a paste it became a deadly poison if ingested.

The look she gave him felt kind of like poison.

And then she turned away, saying nothing.

"Why does she hate me?" Roan asked Prince Gareth, who was sitting nearby next to the cook fire, which was crackling happily. Roan had his back against a gnarled tree stump. The rest of the tree was gone.

"It's not that she hates you," the prince said, and, based on the prince's tone, Roan knew immediately his question wasn't being taken seriously. "It's that she can't stand to bear your ugliness for more than a spare moment."

"Now who's the jester?" Roan said.

The prince showed his teeth but didn't laugh. "Sometimes I wonder if that plague of yours ate the small brain you were born with. You're from the south, right?"

Roan nodded slowly, wondering where this was going. "I told you. I grew up in Calypso."

"You think the East-West War has been going on for a long time? Well, compared to our little . . . *disagreement*, the war between the Calypsians and Orians is ancient. They've been doing battle for *thousands* of years, ever since Empress Someone-Or-Other hatched her first dragon and decided she should rule the entire realm. So yeah, she hates you."

Roan shook his head. His entire life he'd been so focused on surviving another day, getting another bite to eat, that he'd never concerned himself with the broader world. After all, despite what his guardian had taught him as a young child, he would never be a part of anything larger than the dusty city in the south. And yet, here he was, cavorting with eastern royalty and their allies.

And now a strange but beautiful woman I've never truly met hates me simply because I grew up in Calypso. No wonder the war will never end . . .

Still . . . "She shouldn't hate me just because of where I'm from. I had no choice in the matter."

"Her father was killed in the Battle of Barrenwood," Gareth said.

Oh. But wait. "You said that was more than eighty years ago. That doesn't make sense."

"I'm feeling more and more like *your* tutor," the prince said. "The Orians live for well in excess of one hundred years. The oldest has been recorded to have survived to her one-hundred-and-ninety-fifth name day."

Blazes. Roan had no idea. "But that would make Gwendolyn . . ." He turned toward where she'd gone and found her standing upright, a silhouette against the darkling sky. She appeared to be looking back at him. She seemed to be holding something, pulling on something. *Aiming something.*

"Don't. Move," Gareth said.

As if he had time. Before the second word was out of the prince's mouth, a thin shadow darted from the gloom and sliced through Roan. He cried out, and when he tried to move his arm, he found it tethered to the tree stump.

The men were laughing. He looked to the side to find a narrow metal shaft protruding from the wood. He felt no pain, so it had missed him. Barely. But it *had* caught a loose bit of fabric hanging from his shirt just beneath his armpit, the impact so powerful it had pinned him to the old tree like a trophy on a board. With his opposite arm, he tried to yank the arrow out, but found it impossible.

"Need a hand?" the prince said, still chuckling. He snapped his fingers and two of his men stepped forward, each grasping part of the shaft, leaning back, and bit by bit, tearing the bolt from the stump.

When Roan was freed, he leapt to his feet and searched the terrain for Gwendolyn Storm. He spied her hunched form sitting cross-legged, facing away from them.

"She could've killed me!" Roan said, taking a step in her direction.

The prince extended a hand to stop him. "If she'd wanted to kill you, she would've. That was nothing more than a message."

Roan frowned. "What message?"

"Stay away from her."

There had to be more to the story of her father's death at Barrenwood. "You said it was the Dreadnoughters who fought your people in the dead forest."

"Actually, I said savages, but aye," the prince said, sitting on a rock by the fire.

"But the Calypsians have nothing to do with the Dreadnoughts. Yes, they are within the bounds of the realm, but the Sandes family does not exercise control over them. So her father's death doesn't explain why she hates me."

There was a sly gleam in Gareth's eye. "I thought you knew nothing about royal politics."

"I don't, really. Just gossip on the street."

"I said the Dreadnought warriors *led* the battle, but they weren't the only Southrons there."

Roan frowned. He was sick of missing crucial details. Why hadn't he asked his guardian more questions before he'd left? Clearly the prince was implying something, and there was only one answer that fit. "The Calypsians?" Roan tried to picture the royal family tree. The Sandes sisters were born of Vin Hoza of Phanes and Sun Sandes of Calypso, before mistrust and deceit ended their marriage and thrust the south into civil war. And Sun Sandes had been the eldest of three daughters of Jak and Riza Sandes. But neither had been of age a hundred years earlier. Who came before them? The answer struck him like a metallic arrow to the brain. "Roan Sandes," he whispered.

The prince nodded. "Gwendolyn's father would've survived if not for the second wave of attack, provided by the Calypsians. *Roan* Sandes was riding a red dragon larger than the trees of Ironwood. They say the beast cooked Boronis Storm alive within his armor. So not only are you from Calypso, but you bear the first name of her father's murderer. Not to mention you claim to be 'born from dust', which isn't far from Sandes. Can you really blame her for remembering the worst day of her life every time she sees you?"

Roan shook his head. He couldn't blame her.

"Just be thankful she sent a message and not an arrow through your eye." The prince laughed.

❧

On the seventh day they reached the place that had been glittering in the sun for days. To Roan's surprise it was another forest. But Roan had never seen a forest like this. Whereas Barrenwood had been dead and dying, the great Ironwood was very much alive. The forest seemed to be in constant motion, growing, changing before his very eyes. Branches stretched and shook out their leaves, which, glinting with metal around the edges, fell across his shoulders.

But that was only the start of the curiosities hidden within the bounds of the forest. The trees were sheathed with iron, which formed intricate patterns on their flanks, much like Gwendolyn Storm's armor. Every time the sun peeked through the clouds, the trees glittered as if studded with diamonds, which explained what they'd seen from afar. Metallic arches and platforms swept overhead, and from time to time Roan saw swift-footed creatures racing across them, moving so quickly he never got more than a glimpse. Above the trees, enormous winged birds swooped and soared. Their wings were as silver as the edges of blades.

"What are they?" Roan asked, watching the silent flyers.

"Orc hawks," Gareth said. "Don't get too close to them. They have a fondness for human scalps, and their beaks are even sharper than their talons."

The prince turned away before Roan could read his expression to tell if he was serious.

The road was wide and well kept, and as their horses marched through the forest, silvery flowers grew and faded before them.

"This is . . . impossible," Roan said. "Metal doesn't . . . grow."

"Do your eyes deceive you then?" a voice said. It wasn't the prince this time, but Gwendolyn Storm, who was waiting for them beside an enormous tree completely encased in iron. The forest dweller had her hood thrown back, her cat-like eyes boring into Roan.

Roan did his best to appear unsurprised that she'd addressed him. "Perhaps it is a dream," he said, dismounting.

Gwendolyn snapped a torch from a nearby sconce. In the moment she brought it near her face, something flashed on her cheek. A symbol of some kind, almost like an X but coming to squares rather than points. She thrust the torch at Roan, and the mark disappeared.

A tattooya, Roan realized. *She's marked. Like me.* Roan wondered what her mark meant—what power it gave her.

"If you are dreaming, then plunge your hand into the flames. It shall not hurt." There was a twinkle in Gwendolyn's eyes, and Roan couldn't tell whether it was because she wanted to watch him burn himself—probably—or if she was merely playing with him like a cat pawing at a trapped mouse—also a distinct possibility.

He'd already felt the pain of all-consuming dragonfire, an agony a thousand times worse than this measly torch, but Roan knew he'd be sorely tempted to heal his burnt hand in front of them. And then his greatest secret would be bared for all to see. As he stared at the flames, he was thankful one of the prince's men had given him a fresh shirt to wear, hiding the lifemark on his chest beneath thick folds of fabric.

"I will burn myself if you will do the same," Roan said.

Gwendolyn blinked.

Behind Roan, Prince Gareth chuckled. "This should be entertaining," he said.

Roan wondered what he meant, but already Gwendolyn had placed the torch back in its fixture on the tree. A moment later she'd unsheathed a sword half as tall as her. Before Roan's eyes the sword transformed, the metal curling and twisting, losing its sharp edges.

Gwendolyn smiled, and Roan couldn't help but to smile back, transfixed.

A moment later he was flat on his back and his entire body felt bruised. She'd moved so fast he'd barely been able to track her with his eyes, much less defend himself. Dazed, he sat up to find her leaning casually against the iron tree.

With that, she mounted her horse and left Roan to nurse his wounds.

Prince Gareth placed a hand on his shoulder. "Don't worry, friend, it's happened to the best of us, myself included. Now come, it's time for you to meet the king."

&

As they traveled along the wide roads through Ironwood, Prince Gareth never seemed to tire of talking about the land of his ancestors. As they walked and talked, Roan slowly, surreptitiously, healed the bruises caused by Gwendolyn's attack.

"In the west they say we conquered the east," Gareth said.

Roan had been told exactly the same thing. In the history he'd been given, the early Crimean settlers who moved eastwards had fought great battles against the natives before claiming the land for their own. Eventually they declared independence from the west, which began the East-West War, an ongoing battle that had raged for hundreds of years.

"You're saying the westerners are lying?" Roan scoffed.

"They weren't here. Just because they would've ridden to the east with war cries and swords doesn't mean we would. In reality, the east conquered us. My forefathers were beguiled by the beauty of this place, and of the forest dwellers who inhabited it. They learned to live *with* the Orians, rather than against them. Of course, there were those on both sides who caused trouble, and there was occasional bloodshed, but we've had peace since the year 150, when our people began to interbond with the foresters."

"Interbond?"

"Bonding is what the Orians call marriage. Most of us have some percentage of Orian in us these days."

"What about Gwendolyn Storm?" Roan asked. She'd moved like the wind. *And* she was fatemarked.

"Give it up, lad. Forget about her. It'll only bring you pain and us laughs." Although the prince tried to keep his tone light, Roan could feel a sharp spike of anger in it. *Why would that be?* Roan wondered. *Does the prince have a history with the Orian woman?*

"I'm not interested in her like that," Roan said quickly. Why would he want someone who hated him? *Because she's beautiful, for one*, he thought. *Just like you.* He stifled the thoughts.

"Then you are not a man."

Roan chose to ignore the quip, mostly because it implied the prince would likely never have interest in him. "But she is of mixed heritage?" he pressed.

"Actually she's one of the few who are descended from a single culture line. She's full forester. Those like her tend to stick to their own kind, which is why you need to forget about her."

The road curved broadly, the metallic trees standing straight and solid on either side, like sentinels. Metal vines grew down from above, curling around Roan's arms and legs, squeezing and releasing.

Roan flinched visibly, and the prince winked at him. "They're only checking you out. Deciding whether you're a threat."

"And if I am?"

"You're not." The prince laughed loudly.

"But what if?"

"They'll wrap around your neck and choke the life out of you," Gareth said casually. He spurred his horse on, and the rest of the men followed behind.

The metal vines lingered on Roan's skin for a few moments longer, before slipping away and rising toward the sky. He breathed a deep sigh of relief, wondering whether or not he *was* a threat to the east. *Probably not*, he decided. *I'm not even supposed to be here.*

Up ahead, Gwendolyn Storm was stopped in the center of the path, waiting. She didn't look at them, instead gazing upon a new part of the forest, different than anything Roan had seen so far.

"The Iron City," Gareth said. "My home. Welcome to Ferria."

Roan stared in awe. If the forest was impossible, Ferria was whatever came after impossible. Unlike Calypso, where everything was stone and sand and dust, the eastern stronghold was iron intermingled with nature. Roan would've expected an iron city to be cold and hard, but this city was anything but. Each structure was a work of art, the metal forming around enormous trees in beautifully unique ways that even the west's best smiths would find difficult to imitate if they had a hundred years to try. Walls were carved with depictions of tree and critter, sword and shield, banner and horse. The crossed swords of the eastern sigil were displayed on each building, etched to perfection.

Dwellings were built within hollowed out trees, so large around that a hundred men could stand arm to arm and still not complete a full circle. Each door and window was independently designed as well, some appearing as wisps of smoke and others as falling leaves. Most of the buildings had spires protruding at odd angles, piercing the gray fabric of the sky, giving them a royal feel, as if Roan were approaching a mystical castle.

As they entered the forest city, many of the townsfolk stopped to gaze at them. Each of them wore metal of some kind, all of it finely crafted. There was a man with a red-painted metal vest with long thin tail feathers. A woman had an iron hat with tiny metallic flowers sprouting from the sides. Another waved as they passed, his hands hidden by metal gloves that seemed almost a part of him.

The prince greeted each person in kind, many of them personally. "Ho, Piper Johns! How are the fish biting?" he said to a man with a metal rod and hook. To another: "Aye, Jam Pepper, you are looking vibrant on this gray afternoon." No one seemed to fear him the way the monarchs of the south were feared. *Is it an act or is it real?* Roan wondered.

Already he'd seen the way Gwendolyn was treated. She made no effort to hide her mark, and, according to the prince, she was free to come and go as she pleased.

For one quarter of one moment, Roan wondered whether this was a place where he could be happy, where he wouldn't have to hide his true self anymore. Where his gift could help rather than hurt those around him.

In the next three-quarters of that same moment, a hundred contradictions presented themselves, and Roan knew he was deluding himself. He was the last person who could find peace in the east.

At least a furlong into the city there was a great marketplace, built within a tree as wide as the Southron pyramids. They passed stands billowing aromatic smoke bearing the scent of broiled hen, smoked trout, and lamb stew, amongst others. One stand even had an entire wild boar roasting over an open fire, the spit turning slowly, fat sizzling and dripping into the flames while street urchins stared longingly at the meat. Roan's stomach turned at the sight of the cooking flesh.

At another stand, children were clamoring at the front, flipping iron coins to the seller and claiming tubs of plum pudding.

"You can eat when you're dead," the prince said, mistaking Roan's interest in the food sellers for hunger. For once, Gareth didn't smile, leaving Roan to wonder whether he was joking. He suspected not. If convicted as a spy, the king would have no choice but to have him executed.

But the threat of death had been Roan's companion for some time, and he did not fear it the way he used to. He swallowed the thought away and went back to gazing around the marketplace. Though the non-meat food was of significant interest to him, the metal workers were what stole most of his attention. They reminded him of Gwendolyn, with their angled faces and strange attire. Each of them were covered from head to toe in metal, which seemed to mold to their bodies, regardless of height, weight, or shape. He'd never seen craftsmanship the likes of what they sold. There were swords that should've been on display rather than used as weapons, shields so pristine they appeared as precious as gemstones shimmering in the daylight, and armor fit for royalty hanging on stands meant to attract normal people.

They stopped at one such stand, and Gwendolyn hailed the owner. A man emerged— Well, Roan thought it was a man, but it was hard to tell. His skin was rough and bark-like, almost like that of a tree. Not just his hands, which ended in stumpy fingers, but the rest of him, too, his face flat and grotesque, his eyes as black as briskets of coal in sunken craters of mottled flesh. There were only three or four spots of pink flesh poking through, including one atop his hairless brown scalp.

"Bark," Gwendolyn said, flashing a smile so lovely that Roan knew it was her real smile, not the fake one she'd offered him earlier just before she knocked him flat on his back. They embraced, and it looked as unusual as if she'd hugged a tree.

"How were your travels, my hero?" the man—Bark—asked. "You've had adventures, I trust." His voice was a watery gurgle, and Roan had to concentrate to understand him.

"Plenty. I'll tell you all about them soon enough. But first, business. The three princes require new armor and a dozen new weapons. Cost is no issue."

"Of course. For you, anything."

The prince said, "And for me?"

"I do it for her, not you," Bark said.

The prince chuckled and mouthed *beguiled* to Roan. Roan shook his head. Insulting royalty in Calypso would earn you a quick trip to the fighting pits if you were lucky; if you weren't so fortunate, you'd be given the opportunity to have your head separated from your neck.

"Meet me at the iron gates once you've concluded business this evening," Gwendolyn went on. "We'll work out the details."

"As you wish, my hero," Bark said, kissing her hand with lips that must've been as rough as the backside of stone.

She cupped his cheek for a moment and then mounted up, leading them further into the city. As they trotted along, she targeted Roan with a sly smile and a devilish look.

"Bark, huh?" Roan said to Gareth.

"She's always treated him better than the rest of us."

"Why?"

"Maybe because he *is* better," the prince said, his lip curling.

Something Bark said to Gwendolyn occurred to Roan. "He called her his 'hero'."

"Is that supposed to be a question?"

"He said it twice. Why?"

"You think too much," the prince said.

Roan daydreamed of the tethers breaking from his hands so he could knock the smile off the prince's beautiful lips.

Maybe his intentions were written all over his face, because his thoughts only made the prince smile broader. "You're as sensitive as an unflowered maiden," Gareth said. "I meant no offense, only that sometimes the answer is all too obvious."

Roan thought about it, realizing his stupidity. "She saved Bark's life."

Gareth nodded. "Once. Now he would retrieve both of the moons for her, if she asked."

"What did she do?"

The prince waved away the question. "Ask him. Or better yet, ask her—that would prove immensely amusing. Now cease with your incessant questions. The iron gate approaches."

Roan turned his attention forward, where a metal wall near as tall as the dragons of Plague Island stood, constructed between natural tree pillars. The metal seemed liquid, rippling just beneath the surface, its face in constant motion. An enormous iron gate bearing the royal sigil blocked the way forward, protected by a retinue of royal guardsmen. Each man must've stood seven feet tall, because even on his toes Roan knew he'd have to angle his head to look any of them in the eye. Standing shoulder to shoulder in full battle armor, they almost looked like a miniature version of the wall they protected.

In the dead center of their formation was an even larger man, who wore a pendant on a long linked chain around his neck. Roan squinted, and was able to make out the design of an armored fist.

"They say he's descended from the mountain men of the north," Gareth said.

"Who?"

"Beorn Stonesledge. The giant you're staring at. By the way, he doesn't like when people stare at him. Especially strangers."

Roan realized the massive guardsman's eyes were narrowed and he was looking right back at him. Roan averted his eyes, pretending to study a speck of dirt on his boot. The prince chortled loudly.

"What is that symbol he bears?" Roan asked. "The one around his neck."

"The ironmark," Gareth said. "It's an imitation of his skinmark. I've seen him use it, too. His foes would've been better off facing one of those dragons you claim to have survived."

It took all of Roan's strength to keep his expression neutral. *Another tattooya?* And again, like Gwendolyn Storm, this man wore his openly, without fear, dangling the symbol of his power around his neck. The very concept was foreign to him.

"Remind me never to challenge him to a grapple then," Roan said, trying to make light of the situation.

"I doubt if you'll ever get the chance anyway," the prince said, once more dancing his horse away and leaving Roan to ponder the subtle threat.

The guardsmen cleared a path for the prince and his men, while Gwendolyn dropped back to escort Roan through the arched gates, which seemed to liquefy and flow into the walls on either side. Inside was a huge courtyard, which curved away in both directions. As soon as the royal convoy was inside, liquid ore poured out from either side of the wall and hardened back into the enormous iron doors. Roan blinked, amazed. "How does that work?" he asked.

Gwen said, "My people channel the ore."

"How?"

She shrugged, managing to make even such a common gesture look graceful. "We just do. I can't explain it in a way you will understand. Ore-channeling isn't something that can be learned. It's either in you, or not." Without another word, she strode away, following the curve of the wall.

Roan scanned his surroundings, which were abuzz with activity, not unlike the rest of the city. To one side troops wearing light armor were being trained in hand-to-hand combat, while another platoon was engaged in target practice, the twang of their bows punctuated by satisfying thwacks as their arrows entered straw dummies. On the opposite side, horses were being watered, rubbed down, and fed. The most interesting thing about the courtyard, however, was that not a single tree had been felled to construct it. Instead, fixtures had been built amongst the nature, almost allowing the forest to guide the construction.

A group of men and women paused in their duties to tend to the prince's horses as they dismounted. "Thank you," Gareth said, handing over his reins.

"This is some setup you have here," Roan said.

"This is nothing," Gareth said, raising his arms over his head so a soldier woman could remove his chest plate. Soon he was wearing only a green shirt, brown britches, and his boots. For a moment, Roan wondered what he looked like beneath the fabric. He shook away the thought—*this man, regardless of how handsome, wants to see you executed*, he reminded himself.

"Wait until you see the rest," Gareth continued. There was something in the prince's eyes that gave Roan pause. Something clicked, a truth he'd been missing from the moment they entered Ironwood. They hadn't blindfolded him once during the trip. They were allowing him to see everything, including the inside of the castle. If they truly believed he was a spy, they wouldn't be so careless unless . . .

His heart skipped a beat.

They were never going to let him leave.

Chapter Seven

The Northern Kingdom | Castle Hill

Annise Gäric

A hush fell over the crowd. Annise knew her brother well enough to see the fear in his eyes, despite his attempt to hide it beneath a stalwart expression. As he walked past the royal box, they made eye contact, and she wanted to scream.

Several commoners expressed their outrage at their beloved prince's situation, but were quickly silenced by the guards, doubling over after being hit in the gut.

Sir Dietrich passed next, his face as calm as ever, like he was just taking a morning stroll, rather than being led to his execution. Both hands were bound, but intact, which meant the icy blue tendrils that had passed into him from the Ice Lord had only had a temporary effect. He even managed to offer her a grim smile.

There were more protests amongst the rabble, this time for the melee champion. More guards moved amongst the crowd to maintain order.

They can't do this, Annise thought. They were empty words, she knew, as hollow as a rotted log. Her uncle could, and would, do whatever it took to assume power in the north now that her father was gone. And with the Ice Lord and the royal guardsmen on his side, there was little anyone could do about it.

The prisoners' footsteps were thunderous on the wooden planks, which creaked slightly under their trod. Guarded by three soldiers, Arch was forced at sword point up the steps to the same gallows his mother had just been cut down from. A fresh noose had been fitted and hung.

Sir Dietrich was sent up to the second platform.

The nooses were wrapped around each man's neck and tightened.

No, Annise thought. *Not men. Arch is only sixteen. He can say he's a man grown, a king now, but he's still my little brother. And now . . .*

She couldn't finish the thought, her eyes burning, her lips beginning to tremble. She was gripping the railing so hard she thought her fingers might break off in the cold.

Arch's breathing was rapid now, his exhalations a ghostly visage before his lips, which opened. "This is a farce of a trial," he said, his voice remarkably strong and clear. He spoke directly to the people, the commoners. The people who adored him. Where was the boy she saw a moment ago? "My mother has just been murdered before your eyes. And now they seek to murder your rightful king, and your most recent melee champion."

"The traitor speaks," Lord Griswold said. "But your voice falls on ears that were loyal to your father. They are deaf to your pleas." Despite his words, a handful of the commoners attempted to charge the platform. The King's Defense formed a barrier, shoving them back. The commoners tried again, and this time the guardsmen used deadly force, killing a man and a woman before the remaining people quieted and backed away. Annise watched as the bodies were removed, too numb to feel anything. It was like her father had been reincarnated in the form of her brother, the reign of the Dread King continuing seamlessly.

For the northerners, this was just another day fraught with fear.

"My words shall be heard," Arch continued. Annise wanted to be proud of her brother's courage, but her stomach hurt too much. Without him . . . "With my father's death, I became the King of the North, Protector of Castle Hill and all who live north of the Mournful Mountains. You, my uncle, are the traitor, and I find you guilty."

Annise managed to pry her eyes away from Arch long enough to look at her uncle's reaction, which was filled with narrowly disguised venom. Spit froze on his lips as he spoke. "You have been found guilty of treason against the very crown you pretend to support. And your so-called 'champion', Sir Dietrich, has disobeyed a direct order from a superior. Both of your crimes are punishable by death."

"No!" several commoners screamed. But this time they were just words without action. Despite their protests, they were unwilling to risk their own lives.

Am I? Annise wondered. There were guards at either elbow, gripping her tightly in the event she made a move to help her brother. She could fight them, surprise them with the strength she knew she had. But would it really help? The odds were stacked impossibly against her.

"Executioner!" her uncle shouted. "Mete out the punishment on these traitors!"

The man in the black cloak stepped forward, assuming a position directly between the two gallows. His head swiveled back and forth, as if trying to decide who should go first. Did it really matter?

He turned then, away from the gallows, his shadowed face aimed at the royal box.

"Executioner! Do your duty!" Annise's uncle shouted.

The executioner threw back his hood to reveal a familiar mesh facemask, dark eyes staring out. *The Armored Knight!* Annise realized a split-second before the large man reached under his cloak and whipped out the chain attached to the spiked ball.

The guards were too slow by half, the melee runner up having already swung his weapon with vicious force. The barbed ball shredded the ropes over Arch's and Sir Dietrich's heads and they collapsed to the wooden platforms. But they didn't stop there, disappearing from sight as if they'd tumbled into a deep snowbank.

What in frozen— Annise watched as the guards tried to apprehend the Armored Knight, but his spiked ball was a whirlwind of fury, smashing armor and splintering spears until the guards were forced to back off. Several of them dropped to a knee and shot arrows, but his armor held strong against the onslaught.

Nearby, Annise's uncle was screaming something—ordering the King's Defense to pursue the prisoners. Jonius and the other guardsmen in the box were clearly distracted.

Be ready, Aunt Zelda had instructed.

She was ready. For what, she didn't know.

With a roar, the Armored Knight swept forward and bludgeoned two of the archers with a single swing of his chain. The rest fled.

He turned and looked right at Annise. The man who'd kicked out the platform beneath her mother's feet. The man she'd chosen to win the melee. The man who'd *killed* her mother and *saved* her brother and Sir Dietrich.

He extended a hand toward her, and she started to climb over the rail.

Be ready.

Two guards grabbed her arms, and though she fought them with all the strength she had, they held firm. Something whizzed past her face. Then another something, and the pressure was gone from her skin. The guards thudded to the floor, arrows protruding from one's neck and the other's eye.

Be ready.

Annise flung herself over the railing as Sir Jonius reached for her. His fingers clamped on the hem of her skirts, but her momentum was too much, the fabric tearing away. She was free!

An arrow zipped past her ear, shot by one of the royal archers who'd retreated to a safer vantage point across the platform. He quickly nocked another arrow to his bowstring. Pulled back. Released.

A dark form sprang in front of her, the arrow plunging into the gap between his gauntlet and vambrace. With a grunt, the Armored Knight scooped her up in one powerful arm and launched himself toward the gallows, clambering up the ladder and diving through a hatch that had opened in the platform floor.

Annise tumbled into darkness, her ankle twisting as she landed awkwardly atop her rescuer, his armor clattering.

"Sister!" Arch said from somewhere in the inky black.

"Allow me, princess," said the voice of Sir Dietrich. Strong fingers grasped her beneath the arms and pulled her to her feet.

"He's injured," was all she could think of to say. "The Armored Knight. An arrow struck him between his plates."

"I'm fine," the knight grunted, his armor clanking as he rose to his feet. "We have to hurry. Go!"

Someone grabbed her hand and pulled her down a black corridor that reeked of . . . filth. Wetness splashed around her legs with each step. "What is this place?" Annise asked, wishing she could see something—anything.

"The royal sewers," Arch answered enthusiastically, like they were off on a grand adventure. "Zelda set the whole thing up. Who knew she was such a rebel?"

"Quiet!" the Armored Knight hissed. "We have company." Even as he said it, Annise's ears picked up the sound of heavy boots landing in water. Shouts echoed behind them.

"We need light," Sir Dietrich said.

"No," the Armored Knight said. "You need me. Now turn right. This way."

Annise was yanked to the right before she could even begin to consider how the knight could navigate in complete darkness. Somewhere behind her, a swathe of flickering light danced on the walls.

"Ten more steps and then left," the Armored Knight instructed.

Annise counted in her head, wondering whether she should add a few steps because surely her strides were shorter than his. In the end, it didn't matter, because Arch tugged her along behind him. "Keep up, sister," he said.

Annise cursed. She was reasonably quick over short distances, but she had a feeling her stamina was about to be pushed to its limits. Her legs were already feeling heavy and she was limp-running because of the throbbing pain coursing through her ankle, radiating up her leg.

Three turns later, she could barely breathe. She tried to say *Stop*, but it came out as a pant. With no other choice, she pried her fingers free of Arch's grip, doubling over and sucking in lungful's of air.

Arch cried out and she could hear his boots splash to a stop. Annise was about to tell him to go on, that she would catch up after a quick rest, but a strong hand grabbed her arm and stifled the words in her throat.

"Going somewhere, princess?" Sir Jonius said, his breath hot on her face. He spoke calmly, his voice low.

"Please," she said. "You know me. Don't you?"

The knight stiffened beside her. "I know nothing," he said.

"You cared once," Annise said, still breathing heavily. "No one has to know. No one. You can come with us. You can be free."

"You don't know what you ask," Jonius said. There was sorrow in his tone. Regret.

"Please," Annise said again, placing her hand atop his. "If you won't come, let us go." One by one, she pried his fingers away. He let her, saying nothing. "Thank you," she whispered as she pulled away.

"Save yourselves," the knight said. "Go east. It's your only hope."

"Thank you," Arch echoed. "For everything." Once more, he found Annise's hand and pulled her into the darkness.

As the distance widened between them and Sir Jonius, she heard more shouts and then the faithful knight said, "There's nothing but a dead end this way. We should go back and find another passage."

The sounds of their pursuers drifted away.

※

The sky was gray and full of snowfall when, hours later, they finally pushed aside a barrier of dead foliage and emerged from the wet darkness of the sewers. A filthy creek burbled nearby, fed by the sewers and, in the summer, snowmelt.

Annise blinked against the snow-reflected brightness as her eyes tried to adjust to daylight once more.

Her legs were cramping, her lungs aching. But she was alive, and so was Arch, which was what mattered the most.

"We cannot linger here," Arch said. "They will know the sewer's tributaries. They'll be searching them all."

"Not this one," the Armored Knight said. "It was secret to all but the king and queen. A last resort in the event there was ever a coup and they were sent to the gallows."

"Then how do you know about it?" Annise said, glaring at the knight under the hand she was using to shield the light. She didn't know this man. Yes, he saved them, but to what end? Where was he leading them?

"Your . . . mother told me," he said.

"My *mother?*" Annise said, her voice rising. Icy tendrils crept into her blood, but they had the opposite effect, heating her skin rather than chilling her. "Don't you dare—"

"Annise," Arch said, cutting her off. "We don't have time for this. We have to keep moving."

"Arch, he killed—" Her voice vanished in a sob, which arose so suddenly she couldn't stifle it. "She's dead. Mother is dead."

"I know," he said, placing a gentle hand on her arm. Her anger faded and she shivered. "She did it for us. It's what she wanted."

No, Annise wanted to say, but she knew it was true. She remembered the way her mother had looked at her. At the way she'd said *Guilty* with such conviction and courage. It was the first time Annise had seen her mother look anything but angry or sad. It was the first time she'd looked truly alive.

"I'm sorry for your loss," the Armored Knight said. His voice was low and gravelly and . . . sincere. Annise wondered how the man who had kicked out the platform could even begin to apologize for what he'd done.

"Stuff your rotting apology," Annise said. "Just get us somewhere safe and warm."

She knew it was a rare moment when she sounded like a spoiled-brat princess, but she didn't care. Her status was the only armor she had left against the weight of grief pressing on her chest.

Heavy snow filled in their footprints as they trudged away from Castle Hill, which shone through the gale like a beacon in a storm.

꩜

Despite her knee-high sheepskin boots, Annise couldn't feel her toes when they finally took shelter within a copse of pine trees. The fallen nettles made for a soft cushion, and she gladly settled onto them, pulling off her footwear, which were sheathed in frozen snow.

Arch settled beside her, shucking off his own boots and massaging his feet.

Sir Dietrich traipsed through the trees, collecting firewood, while the Armored Knight stood sentry, his eyes probing through the snowfall. The arrow was still protruding from his arm, but he showed no signs of being affected by it. His dark armor was slick with blood, which looked strangely black.

"Arch," Annise whispered, quiet enough that only her brother would be able to hear her. "We have to get away from these two. They will ransom us. They are strangers who have no other reason for risking their own lives to rescue us. They are—"

"Annise," Arch said.

Something struck her, so obvious now that she thought about. "They knew each other the whole time!" she hissed. "They've been in league since before the melee. They've been planning this from the beginning. They're—"

"Annise," Arch said again. "There's more to the story than you know. Aunt Zelda came to me."

"Me too," Annise said, frustrated. "She spoke of Mother." Annise managed to get the last word out, barely.

"Yes," Arch agreed. "There were more layers to Mother than we ever knew." Arch's gaze traveled down to his pale feet, and Annise followed it. A moment of silence stretched its wings, before flitting away like a snow moth.

"She saved us," Annise said. "But what about the arrows that helped free me? Where did they—"

"Women loyal to Zelda," Arch said.

Annise blinked. "Women?" Women didn't train in archery. Even her own battling with the lordlings in the yard was looked down upon by the lords and ladies of the castle.

"Yes. Zelda has been training them in secret for a long time."

All these years her aunt had not been idle. Annise hoped she'd get the chance to thank her one day. But it still didn't make sense.

"But why did Mother have to die? Couldn't she have dropped into the sewers like we did? Couldn't we all have escaped together? Couldn't we have—" Annise's words had come too fast and she'd forgotten to breathe. She gasped, and Arch's arms closed around her. Her eyes burned with unshed tears, held back by anger alone.

"No," Arch said. "If she had escaped first, then we wouldn't have been able to."

Annise closed her eyes, feeling the truth of his words wash over him. She'd died so they could live. In the end, she had loved them more than herself, a thought which made Annise unbearably sad. "But how could"—the memory of the platform being kicked out by the Armored Knight, her mother's body dropping, and the struggle that ensued, seared through her mind—"*he* have done such a thing?"

She glared at the Armored Knight, wishing she could rip off his mask and smash her fist against his face, again and again and again and ag—

"Because she asked him to," Arch said, snapping the rope between her eyes and the knight.

Sir Dietrich scattered a load of firewood before them, and began angling them upwards in a pyramid shape, meeting at the top in the center. Vapor rose from his skin as his body heat met the frigid air. He never seemed to tire or falter.

"I'll have you warm and toasty soon enough, princess," he said, flashing a handsome smile.

Just his smile was enough to warm Annise's cheeks. "Thank you, Sir," she said.

"You can call me Dietrich," he said, using a flint repeatedly, trying to get a spark. He cupped his hand to block the wind as a bit of kindling began to smoke. "I'm sure Castle Hill will be stripping me of my knighthood soon enough. Arme too." He gestured to the Armored Knight, who'd begun pacing along the edge of the tree line.

"Arme?" Annise said, raising an eyebrow. The smoke turned to flame, creeping up the dry twigs and underbrush, orange and red fingers reaching for the firewood.

"I've traveled with him for weeks, and still he won't tell me his true name," Dietrich said with a shrug. "The Armored Knight is too long, not to mention pretentious, don't you think? So I just call him Arme."

Annise was about to suggest something else less kind they could call him, but Dietrich cut her off.

"If I may be so bold, princess, Arme was only doing his duty, same as the rest of us. He didn't want to do what he did, but protecting you and the prince—rather, I should say *king*—were his first priority. It was what your mother wanted."

"What do you know of my mother?" Annise said, feeling the warmth of the crackling fire begin to seep into her skin and unfreeze her bones.

"Not a lot. I mostly communicated with Lady Zelda. Arme could tell you more, he's known your mother since he was just a little lad."

Annise stood, squirming out of Arch's grasp as he tried to stop her. She marched over to the Armored Knight, who stopped his pacing when he noticed her presence. He was as still as stone, the only evidence of life the white ghosts of his breaths slipping through his mask.

"How do you know my mother?" she demanded.

"Your mother, the queen, knew my mother," he said, his voice a low growl. He sounded dangerous, but Annise didn't care. If he'd wanted to hurt her, he could've let her get hit by the archer's arrow back on the platform. As easily as he'd participated in her mother's death, he'd saved Annise's life, a contradiction she was struggling to make sense of.

"How?"

The question hung in the air like a fine mist, and when Arme didn't answer, she stepped closer. "Take off your mask."

"No," Arme said.

"Why not? Are you missing an eye? Do you have a growth on your chin? Are you the ugliest man in the Four Kingdoms? Whatever it is, I don't care about that. I just want to know why in frozen hell you killed my mother and then saved me and my brother?" Annise snarled the last words, her anger consuming her.

When the Armored Knight remained silent, her emotions boiled over, out of control. She launched herself at him, slamming her shoulder into his midsection—which was protected by thick iron—pummeling her coiled fists into his breastplate—which sent shockwaves through her hands. She didn't care about the pain, or the futility of her attack. She just wanted to feel something different, something that might chase away the hurt and sadness.

With the same skill she'd witnessed during the melee, the knight spun her around and subdued her furious arms. She tried a backwards kick, but he dodged it and eased her to the ground, his strength akin to that of a blacksmith's sledge.

The Armored Knight's mask hovered over her, a dark net that rumbled as he spoke. His eyes bored into her with an intensity matched only by the words that followed. "I loved your mother like my own," he said. There was something more than sadness in his tone. Something desperate, like a plea for her to hear the truth behind his declaration. "What I did I will never forgive myself for. My only hope for redemption is to protect her children. To protect you."

With that, he released her and stalked from the cover of the trees and into the storm. His footprints were dark with blood.

ᚺ

"Shouldn't we go after him?" Annise asked. She was finally warm and dry, and was just finishing an apple. The apple was dessert. She'd already eaten a full serving of salted mutton, two dried pork shanks, and a half-frozen bread roll. Sir Dietrich stared at her the whole time, his mouth opened in awe. She stared right back, crunching into the apple and spraying juices into the fire, which sizzled and spat.

"Better not to poke a sleeping bear," Arch said.

"Don't fear, princess, he'll return before we leave for Blackstone," Dietrich said.

"Blackstone?" Annise said, still chewing. "I thought we were going east. We could hide in one of the small towns near Walburg."

"We're not going to Blackstone," Arch said. "Nor Walburg."

"But your mother said—" Sir Dietrich started.

"My mother isn't here," Arch said, which finally vanquished Annise's appetite. "She saved us, but now we have to do what's right for the kingdom."

"Exactly," Sir Dietrich said. "We need to hide you. Blackstone is the largest city in the north. There you can blend in, just another snowflake in the blizzard. And when you come of age . . ."

"Though you're big enough to have surpassed thirty name days, you're barely two years older than me, Dietrich, so don't act like a wise elder. I don't care about age," Arch said. "I *am* king. Not two years from now. Not tomorrow. Now. And I refuse to hide from my uncle or anyone else."

Annise was prouder of her brother than she'd ever been, but that didn't change the fact that they needed to go east. "We should make for Walburg," she insisted. "Sir Jonius—"

"Sir Jonius is Uncle's lackey," Arch said.

"He saved us."

"We saved ourselves. I was two ticks away from running him through before he let us go and misled the King's Defense."

That made Annise laugh. "You might ride with perfect form, brother, but you don't exactly have the temperament for spilling blood."

"Then I would've handed my knife to you, and you could've done it. The point is, Jonius is *not* our keeper, and if we go east and he has a change of heart . . . the east will be flooded with Uncle's men."

Annise hadn't thought of that. "Then if not east or west, where shall we go?" She closed her eyes, immediately thinking of her daydream about crossing Frozen Lake to the north, disappearing into the Hinterlands forever.

"South, of course," Arch said, snapping her eyes open.

"South? But the only thing south is—"

"Gearhärt, and then Raider's Pass," Sir Dietrich finished. "Absolutely not. It's too dangerous. Your uncle's troops will be everywhere."

"They're not *his* troops—they're *mine*. And I will claim them."

"You don't understand what you're asking, prince—I mean, Your Highness," Dietrich said. "I am from Gearhärt and I've been on the front lines at Raider's Pass. Ever since your father broke his marriage alliance with the west, there has been continuous bloodshed in the armpit of the Mournful Mountains. You'd do well to steer clear of the battle."

"Which is exactly why I can't," Arch said.

"Your mother would've been proud." Arme stepped through the pine branches and into the clearing. His armor was coated in a layer of snow, making him look more like a monster from the Hinterlands than a knight of the northern realm.

"Welcome back," Dietrich said, frowning. "And Queen Loren instructed us to take them west, to Blackstone. Would you defy her last wishes?"

The Armored Knight reached across his body and grasped the arrow still protruding from his arm. With a grunt, he wrenched it out. Black droplets fell from the tip, and a thin river of dark blood drew a line through the snow stuck to his armor. Obviously the strange coloring was a trick of the light, but still, it gave Annise the creeps.

"Her last wish was that her son shall be king. That's exactly what he's doing."

"Thank you," Arch said. "Then I command Sir Dietrich to escort me to Raider's Pass."

"As you wish, my king," Dietrich said. "But I shall do so under protest."

"Noted. And you, Sir Armored Knight, I command you to protect my sister as you travel west, to Blackstone. She'll be safest there."

"What?" Annise exclaimed. "No! I'm going south, with you. We're going *together*."

"I am the king, and you will do as I command." Arch stood, stepping into his boots and pulling his cloak tight around his shoulders.

Annise gained her feet just as quickly. "I am your elder sister, and we will be separated over my dead body."

Arch laughed, and the sound grated on Annise's nerves. "Don't be so dramatic. You are my sister, and I love you," he said. "May we meet again when the kingdom is ours once more. Travel safely."

With that, he turned and marched away, motioning to Sir Dietrich.

Annise gawked at him, but then pulled on her own boots and started to follow. He could make commands all he wanted, but he couldn't actually stop her.

Unfortunately, the Armored Knight could. Still bleeding profusely, he stepped in front of her, blocking her path.

"Get out of my hellfrozen way," Annise demanded.

"Sorry, my lady," Arme rumbled. "I can't do that."

"You can and you will." When he didn't move, Annise dashed to the right, slapping at the knight's arm as he lunged for her. He was too strong, wrapping her up and tackling her to the blanket of pine nettles.

"Release me!" Annise shrieked, pounding on his helmet, his chest. When he still didn't unhand her, she shoved a finger between his armor where the blood was trickling out. He grunted in pain, but his grip didn't diminish.

She swiveled her head around, searching for Arch, but he was gone.

Her brother had left her with the most dangerous knight in the realm.

The man who'd killed her mother loomed over her, closing his gloved fingers around her neck.

PART II

GREASE • BANE • RHEA • ROAN • ANNISE

The deathmark is the most misunderstood of all the marks, for it brings not death, but life.

— THE WESTERN ORACLE

Chapter Eight

The Western Kingdom | Knight's End

Grease Jolly

The rising sun seemed to set the waters of the Bay of Bounty ablaze, chasing away the shadows of night. At the bay's widest point, Grease Jolly could just make out the ramparts of Bethany; and beyond, the fang-like peaks of the western edge of the Mournful Mountains. On the opposite side of the bay's mouth was a wall of spiked sentinels, piercing the sky like massive spearheads. Rising behind them were the numerous towers of Blackstone, stone behemoths that were as much a symbol of the strength of the Northern Kingdom as the golden cracked-but-never-broken shield printed on their banners.

Not that Grease gave two dungheaps about the north. All he cared about right now was getting out of the stocks so he wouldn't be late for his royal rendezvous. After he'd been caught thieving two lousy loaves of bread from the baker, he'd been clamped in the wooden stockades by a power-hungry city guardsman who clearly had at least two sticks shoved between the cheeks of his buttocks. Grease knew he hadn't helped his cause by spitting in the arrogant fellow's face, but the guy had it coming to him.

Then again, staring out across the crystalline waters of Bounty, with Knight's End behind him, Grease could think of plenty of worse places to be stuck in the stocks.

Not that he was staying. Although his legs were starting to cramp and his back felt as crooked as a question mark, Grease couldn't help but to grin at the scheme he'd concocted months ago in the event he ever got caught stealing.

Right on time, Silent Billy appeared. The kid was supposedly fourteen, but was so small and skinny he might've been eleven. He was also extremely nimble and flexible—he'd helped Grease with several tricky jobs already. The boy claimed surviving the stockades would be a snap of the fingers for someone like him.

"Did my man give you your coin?" Grease asked.

Silent Billy nodded.

Grease sighed in relief. Relying on another street rat to handle the money had been the riskiest part of the deal. He'd purposely included extra coin just in case Brawny Johnny skimmed any off the top. Not that Grease would blame the meathead if he did. He'd have done the same thing.

"And the city guardsman?" Grease asked, holding his breath. Bribing a guardsman wasn't the most difficult task, but you never knew when one of them would suddenly turn righteous. Knight's End was nicknamed the Holy City, after all.

Luckily, this wasn't one of those times. Silent Billy scrounged around in his pocket and produced a key.

Grease let out a soft whoop as Silent Billy unlocked the stockades. Having all his savings go toward his escape sucked goose eggs, but it was better than the alternative. Plus, he was always one scheme away from getting rich.

Billy's scrawny arms struggled to push the heavy top half of the stocks off of Grease, but he eventually got the job done, the wooden planks thudding to the side. Grease stood up slowly, feeling his joints pop and his muscles scream at their newfound freedom.

He massaged his shoulders and neck for a few minutes, and then said, "Get in."

The boy looked ready to run, so Grease grabbed him by the scruff and shoved him into the stocks. "A deal's a deal," he said, closing the upper half and relocking it in place. They couldn't leave the stocks empty, or the entire gig would be up. The guard he bribed for the key would face accusations, and he would most certainly point the proverbial finger at Grease, who would then face more than just a few days in the stockades.

"Hey, urchin," a withered old man hissed from down the line. "Get me out of here."

Grease laughed, pocketed the key, and whistled a tune as he walked away from Silent Billy and the other poor souls stuck in the stockades. He had a date, and he wasn't about to miss it.

He traipsed along the streets outside the walls of the castle, watching the city start to come alive with beggars and barterers, monks and crooks, men wearing long robes and longer beards, and women dressed in chaste frocks so large and frumpy they appeared as shapeless as men. For the most part, they wore all white, the color of purity, occasionally trimmed with light blue or green thread. By law, they were all devoted followers of Wrath, their deity. From what Grease had seen in the three years that he'd been here, Wrath was a very mean-spirited god, his righteous anger meted out by the Three Furies and their holy army of *furia*. Although he'd never utter it aloud, Grease thought Wrath was created by the royals as a way of governing by fear. Gods, he hated this city. If he had to choose a deity, he would prefer the varied gods of the south. Not that he was religious. At the moment, his only religion involved worshipping the fairest maiden he'd ever laid eyes on. If not for her, he would've left already, off to find his fortune somewhere else, dragging his sister behind him.

His stomach growling, he snatched a plum and two pears off a vendor's cart as he passed, his fingers so quick that the seller was none the wiser. Yes, Grease Jolly was in top form today.

He munched on the pears as he walked, saving the plum for the girl he was meeting. She'd be delighted, and that would surely earn him a kiss at the least. He'd tell her the plum was stolen, which would only excite her the more.

He knew he was risking his life meeting her—if her father ever found out, Grease's execution would likely be slow and painful—but that just made her more appealing. He couldn't help it, he thrived on risk and adrenaline, which were his drugs of choice in the city where "getting a drink" meant a long pull of rose- or lemon-flavored water.

Grease skirted the southern edge of the castle wall. When he finished eating the pears, he smashed their cores on the stone. The wall came to a ninety-degree angle, and then shot northward. All in all, the castle walls formed a perfect square, a thick, impenetrable barrier to attack from all sides.

But Grease didn't care about that, because he wasn't meeting the princess within the castle walls.

Instead, he hung a left and moved swiftly along the western coastline, the ocean still dark blue, the rising sun blocked by the walls of Knight's End. Somewhere in the distance, Grease could make out the shape of a Crimean merchant vessel, heading for the Bay of Bounty. He wondered whether the ship was looking to sell to the north or the west, and whether there would be a battle over their goods. More and more, the bay had become a warzone as the dueling kingdoms sought to control the largest shipping port in the realm. Grease also wondered whether the Crimeans would ever tire of having their ships sink to the bottom of the harbor.

Probably not, he thought. *Not as long as there was coin to be had.* Grease knew that at the core of all humans was a greed for wealth and power that could never be fully sated.

As he approached the entrance to the Cryptlands, Grease shined the skin of the plum on the bottom of his shirt. When he heard voices, he darted behind the wall of one of the tombs, pausing to listen.

"You've heard the rumors from the north?" a familiar voice said. It was Sir Barrow, a round-faced lamp-chop of a guard who accompanied the princess everywhere she went.

"I give no credence to rumors," a second voice said. *Damn. Sir Cray.* He was a nasty old knight with eyes like a hawk and ears like a royal hunting hound. Grease knew he'd have to be extra cautious today.

"But you've heard them?" Barrow said. "They're official streams, you know?"

"Yes. I've heard them. But official or not, they're still rumors."

"Even the most outlandish of rumors hold a glimmer of the truth," Barrow said. Instead of sounding wise like he surely intended, he came off like a child reciting a line taught by his tutor.

"Not this one," Cray said.

"Then how do you explain it? The Dread King was killed, not by poison or arrow, but by falling down the largest staircase in the kingdom." Grease already knew all of this. Everyone had heard about the northern king's untimely demise. But Barrow wasn't done speaking. "Some are saying it was his own shadow that killed him." Now *that* was a rumor Grease hadn't heard.

"Absurd," Cray replied. "The so-called Dread King was probably drunk on his own power and tripped of his own volition."

"There's been talk of the start of the Kings' Plague," Barrow said, not backing down. "We're being told to be especially vigilant."

"The Kings' Plague is the equivalent of the contents of my chamber pot," Cray said crudely. "One king's death means nothing."

"One out of eight," Barrow said. "Not to mention all the guards who have been dying."

"Coincidence," Cray said. "Nothing more. You should know better than to talk of fairytale prophecies by a woman who was naught but a witch."

Grease almost laughed, but managed to clamp a hand over his mouth. Sometimes the westerners were so stupid he wondered how they'd risen to power in the first place. More than a hundred years had passed since the Western Oracle's prophecy about the one who would come bearing the deathmark, ushering in the Kings' Plague, a time when the Four Kingdoms would be torn apart by the death of eight kings. Despite the efforts of several generations of kings to stamp out talk of the Oracle altogether, there were still fools like Barrow who spoke of her from time to time.

Just because a stupid king fell down the steps of his stupidly high tower and broke his own stupid royal neck didn't mean rot. Grease had also heard about how a castle knight had died each day for the past week, but Cray was right, it was nothing more than coincidence. Each death had been the result of an accident. One knight fell from his post on the castle walls, probably because he'd been craning to look down a peasant girl's billowy frock. Another had choked on a large chunk of beef in his stew—he was obviously eating too fast. And on and on. Grease shook his head and climbed the wall silently, ignoring the rest of the knights' pointless argument.

Atop the crypt, Grease stayed low, scanning the holy burial grounds. Various stone structures—the crypts—dotted the landscape, each protected by a large gray tree, planted to mark where the dead lay. The furia claimed the bigger and stronger the trees grew, the more secure the position of the deceased in the afterlife. After all, it was most everyone's goal to one day reach the seventh heaven and look upon Wrath's face.

But not Grease. He knew that trees were just trees.

His heart did a little jig when he spotted the princess in her usual location, within the walls of her family's crypt. She came once a week to "mourn the dead," which meant, of course, to meet Grease. This was their sixth such meeting, not that Grease was counting. Her father, King Gill Loren probably thought she was the perfect daughter, as holy and pure as the furia themselves. If he only knew her secrets he'd lock her away and melt the key into a puddle of liquid ore . . .

And then he'd rip Grease's head from his neck with his bare hands and mount it on the wall. He swallowed and turned his mind to more pleasant thoughts.

Grease remembered the first time he'd laid eyes on the princess, her sun-dusted hair plaited into a crown on her head, her lips naturally curled into a mischievous smile. She'd been slumming with her guards in the commoner marketplace. Later she confided in Grease that her father only went for it because she'd sold it as an act of charity to the commoners, spending her gold on their fruit and wares. Rhea bought a chaste green dress from a spritely woman with tiny fingers. The woman looked shocked at the weight of the bag of gold the princess had placed in her hands as payment.

Grease had been enchanted by the princess's grace, by her smile, by the way she'd conversed with the commoners so easily, as if she was one of them. He'd followed her through the marketplace as she moved from stall to stall. He swore she looked at him several times, always wearing her sly smile. He tried winking at her, and to his surprise, she winked back. Something about her was different than the other royals he'd seen, who always came across as pompous, looking down on the common sinners like Wrath from above. Rhea, however, had seemed . . . human.

That's when something had happened that almost made Grease a believer in fate. Despite the gang of castle thugs protecting Rhea, a real thug managed to slip between them and grab the princess. His eyes were fully dilated and he had a desperate look about him, a wildness that reeked of a life of bad luck and poor decisions. Before Grease could blink, the man had a knife to the princess's throat, and he was demanding gold in exchange for her life. An impossible trade, considering the man wouldn't get more than a few steps away with his gold before being cut down, but he wasn't thinking clearly. In any event, the castle guards had been wary of getting too close to him for fear the man would do something drastic.

But Grease was a shadow when he wanted to be. He'd slipped amongst the merchant tents, creeping closer, until he was behind the man. The man had already been given three sacks of gold, tossed at his feet by the guards, but he was demanding more. They didn't have any more on hand.

Grease could see the man's white-knuckled hand clutching the handle of the knife. He could sense time running out, like sand slipping through an hourglass. And he moved with the speed of a well-practiced thief, except this time it wouldn't be food he was stealing—but the princess's life from her abductor.

He'd yanked the man's arm back, twisting it so hard he'd dropped the knife. Then Grease had slammed his fist into the man's face. He'd dropped like a sack of rice, his body all floppy. The guards had hauled him away and stepped between Grease and Rhea.

But he had still been able to see her eyes, her slightly parted lips, so full and pink, like blooming flower petals, the way she looked at him—with surprise and a sliver of excitement. And maybe a touch of fear, too. "Thank you," she'd said. "You very well may have saved my life. Your valor has earned you a just reward."

She'd quickly scrawled a note and handed it to one of her guards, who handed it to Grease. She said, "Present this at the castle gates to claim your reward. You will not be disappointed. May Wrath bless you and your family." There was something sly about the smile she gave him before mounting her horse and riding away, back toward the castle.

Grease had waited until she was out of sight before opening the folded note and reading it:

Crypts, sunrise, it read. *Don't let anyone see you arrive.*

He'd smiled from ear to ear. *Just reward indeed*, he'd thought. *The princess is full of surprises.*

They'd been meeting in the Cryptlands once a week ever since.

Now, on the whisper-quiet feet of a natural-born thief, Grease tiptoed along the wall, circling behind her. The tree she stood under was a behemoth, its gray branches as thick around as stone columns, clear evidence that the dead had already ascended to the seventh heaven. Buried beneath the tree were generations of Lorens and their allied counterparts, House Thorne. Here lay Rhea's grandfathers, King Ennis Loren and Lord Grant Thorne, her grandmother, Gertrude Thorne, her uncle, Ty Loren, a sackcloth that represented her eldest brother, who had vanished mysteriously as a boy and was never seen again, and her mother, the controversial Queen Cecilia Thorne Loren, who took her own life shortly after giving birth to twins, Rhea's younger siblings, Bea and Leo.

Rhea looked radiant in her night-dark dress of mourning, which hugged her vivacious curves from hip to waist to breast. The thick shapeless frock she'd surely worn when she left the castle lay in a heap on the ground.

Grease dropped silently behind her, grinning to himself. He swept in from the back, grabbing her around the waist and scooping her up. She gasped, but when he swung her around a smile crept onto her pink lips. "How do you *do* that?" she asked, staring at him in fascination.

Grease was loath to release the princess's hips, but he did so he could produce the plum. "The same way I nicked this gift," he said. "With skill."

She managed to stifle a laugh with her hand, else their stealth meeting be discovered by her protectors guarding the outside of the crypt.

Princess Rhea accepted the fruit and took a big bite, juice dribbling down her chin. *Gods*, Grease thought, *she can make anything look good.* She handed the plum back to him and he took his own bite, wiping away the juice with the back of his hand.

Rhea stepped closer and his heart palpitated. "Don't you feel bad for whomever you stole that from?" she purred. Grease could feel her hot breath on his—it smelled of peppermint tea. *Gods, she's a temptress.*

"No," he answered, trying to maintain his cool façade. "He had a whole cart full of fruit and I had nothing, so he should feel bad for me."

Apparently it was just the answer Rhea was looking for. She closed her hand over his, prying the plum from his fingers and letting it drop to the ground. Her other hand moved to his chest, probing for the skin beneath the shirt he'd taken the time to wash the previous day. This near, she smelled of summer flowers and burning incense, and he found himself aching with desire. *The plum idea had clearly been a good one.*

She pushed forward and he tripped on a root, stepping backward to maintain his balance until he collided with the large gray tree. Rhea's lips fell on the hollow in his neck, full of urgency, tracing a blazing path to his lips, which opened to receive her.

At this point, Grease became incapable of controlling his own body, which seemed to respond to such stimulation of its own accord. Their lips rolled, their tongues danced, and his hands worked their way from her hips to her waist to her ribcage, every touch like getting struck by lightning.

Rhea Loren might only be sixteen, but she was a woman grown in Grease's mind. A creature more seductive than the women in the clandestine and highly illegal pleasure houses not far from the seedy area where he and his sister lived.

In a rush that stole Grease's breath, Rhea pulled away. "Wrath," she said, breathing heavily. "Sometimes I wonder if the ghosts of my bad ideas will come back to haunt me in the still silence of the winter night."

Damn, she has a way with words, Grease thought. He loved hearing her speak even when she was having second thoughts. Again. "You're worried about your father?"

She nodded, biting her bottom lip, a gesture that made Grease's heart race. "Your father knows nothing," Grease said. He wanted her, and the last thing he needed her thinking about was the pious king and his so-called holy laws.

And it didn't matter if her father found out about them anyway, right? Grease would live up to his nickname and slide away with his sister, on to another town, another bribe, another crime. The princess was nothing but an adventure to him anyway. What happened to her after he left was of no concern to him.

He ignored the sting of the lie in his brain, stepping closer, inhaling her scent.

Her lips opened once more. Like him, she was unable to resist the danger inherent in their forbidden relationship. With the grace of a thief, he scooped her up under her lithe legs and dipped her back, kissing her deeply while lowering her to the mossy ground. She made a sound that was half human satisfaction and half animal desire as he pried one of the sleeves of her dress over her shoulder. The flesh there was perfection, supple and smooth. He kissed it again and again and again, peeling the dress further away from her body.

His hand trembled as it ran up her leg. Her tongue rolled over his like crashing waves.

And then he was lost in her, the early dawn hours melting away into passion.

❧

"I want to do that again," Grease said, caressing Rhea's jawline.

Rhea laughed, a sound so perfect it sent warmth through Grease's whole body. A sound so perfect that the next noise that broke the silence was made all the harsher:

—A scream rent the still fabric of dawn in half, and they both froze.

"What in Wrath's name was that?" Rhea said. Her hands were gripping Grease's arms so hard they were stinging.

"Something happened," Grease said, a shred of fear slicing through him. When another sound rang out—a muffled groan—he pulled the princess to her feet, grabbing her dress and helping her pull it over her head. He hurriedly tugged on his own pants and shirt, and together they ran for the entrance to the crypts.

Grease slammed to a stop before the princess opened the wooden doors. "What?" she said, whirling around, her golden hair disheveled.

"I can't go out there. Your guards will see," Grease said.

"I'm scared,' Rhea said, and though they shouldn't have, her words made him long to hold her, to protect her. Why did this—whatever *this* was—have to happen this morning?

"You'll be fine," Grease lied. "It was probably just a wayward drunkard causing your knights trouble. They will protect you."

Rhea grasped his hand. "We could run away, you and I. We could leave the west forever. We could be free to do as we choose."

Her words shocked him. Not because she spoke them with such sincerity, but because for a moment her offer was tempting, despite its insanity. *Leave?* Impossible. For one, he had his sister to care for. For another, she was the bloody *heir to the queenship*, at least until her younger brother married. Her father wouldn't rest until he'd hunted Grease down and dismembered him with a blunt paring knife.

"This is not the right time," Grease said, pulling away. He didn't say the real truth: that there would never be a right time. That this was probably the last morning they'd ever see each other. He reached for the wall, searching for a handhold.

"Don't leave me," she pleaded, her eyes searching his, as if trying to find the soul that wasn't there.

"I'm sorry, Rhea, but this is who I am," he said, spider-like as he clambered to the top of the wall. He looked down to find her sobbing into her hand, watching him. He felt something break inside of him, though he refused to believe it was his heart. More likely just a bit of muscle pain from the speed of his climb. "Stay inside the crypts until someone comes for you," he said, hoping it was the right advice.

She let out another sob but he was already turning away, sprinting along the wall, heading for the corner where the knights had been posted. When he arrived, he peered down, making out three shapes in the gloom. One was bulky and soft, lying in a pool of his own blood on the ground, his throat slit. *Oh gods, Sir Barrow*, Grease realized.

The other two forms seemed to be locked together, grappling for advantage. *No, not grappling.* One was wearing armor—Sir Cray—and was simply clinging to the other, who was clothed in all black. The black-garbed person pulled his arm back, a blade flashing silver against the shadows. Sir Cray crumpled with a final groan, writhing several times before going still.

Grease's mouth was open, his heart thundering. Both knights were dead.

The third person turned and looked right up at Grease. A single eye glowed in the dark. *Wait*, Grease thought. *Not an eye. A bright marking on his head.*

Grease was about to scream when the person—creature, thing, monster—vanished.

He whirled around, racing back along the wall, his eyes scanning the House Loren cryptyard. Seeing nothing. *Where are you?* "Rhea?" he murmured. "Are you there? I came back. I'm sorry, I shouldn't have left you."

No answer. He climbed down the wall, searching the shadowy nooks and crannies.

She was gone. Rhea was gone.

Chapter Nine

The Northern Kingdom | Silent Mountain

Bane

He felt feverish, heat spreading along his hairless scalp. His hand ached from gripping the knife, which felt like it had melded with his skin. It was stained red.

Bear was with him in their cave, but he wouldn't look at Bane. Couldn't look at him. "Who am I?" Bane asked the man who raised him. Firelight danced on the walls and ceiling, making the entire cave appear to be alive.

"You know the answer to that question," Bear said, his words gruff, like they'd gotten caught in his white beard, which seemed to grow longer and bushier every day.

"I don't!" Bane said, throwing the knife across the cavern. It hit the wall and clattered to the ground near the fire pit. All strength left him and he slumped to the floor, his head in his hands. Smoke and shadows seemed to press in on his vision, an all-encompassing weariness that threatened to pull him under its waves of darkness once more. He wanted to cry, could feel the stinging behind his eyes, but, as usual, no tears would fall. He was incapable of crying. After all, how could Death cry?

He hadn't wanted to kill those two knights, not really. Nor the guards he'd killed each night that week. But when he disappeared from the cave and reappeared in the Western Kingdom at Knight's End, something drove him. A compulsion, a need, a desire . . .

To kill.

"I am Kings' Bane . . ." he wheezed.

Bear said nothing, a human monolith.

". . . then why I am killing those who are not kings?"

Bear sighed. Bane looked at him, and the only man he'd ever known opened his mouth to speak, but then closed it just as quickly.

"It's about fear, isn't it?" Bane said, forcing the words out through dry lips. "It's not just about the cleansing of the royals. I'm meant to scare the Four Kingdoms into peace. Is that it?"

Bear turned away, his shadow growing larger on the gray wall. "I am a simple man," Bear said. "I don't pretend to know the meaning of ancient prophecies."

Watching the only person he'd ever truly known turn away from him was almost worse than what he'd done, especially because he could hear the lie in Bear's voice. "Please," he said, using his last threads of energy to fold his hands together. He immediately unclasped them—he wasn't worthy of prayer. "Father—"

"Don't call me that!" Bear snapped, whirling around, his facial muscles twitching, his skin taut and red.

Bane wanted to run from the cave, to throw himself off the cliff, to dash his body against the rocks. But he couldn't. He was too weak; and anyway, his body was not his own.

"I am sorry," Bear said, his face falling. "I didn't mean to . . . I wasn't trying to . . . I'm not your father. It's a lie. Your father is dead." He approached Bane, extending an arm as if to comfort him, but letting it fall before it got too close.

He's afraid of me, too, Bane thought. *The entire kingdom is afraid.*

"My father . . ." Bane said. He shut his eyes tight against the memory. He wanted to scream. Instead he gritted his teeth and growled, "No." In his head he heard *Yes.*

He opened his eyes and looked at Bear, who'd moved back several steps. "Am I evil?"

"I asked myself that same question once. Not about you, about me. But I can't answer for you, any more than someone else could've answered for me. Only you can decide."

"Is that why you let me live all those years ago?"

"I don't know." Memories stacked on top of memories, some brighter than others. One stood out, a shining beacon of light. He'd only been eight years old, and Bear had found several thick sacks left by one of the nomadic tribes as they passed by the mountain. They had holes in them and were no longer of use to their previous owners. But Bear had come up with a purpose for the sacks—a second life. They'd smeared goat's butter on the underside of the sacks, and then used them to coast down the snowy hillside, whooping and laughing from the thrill. They'd ridden them all day, until shadows began to creep in, destroying visibility.

Right now, Bane wanted nothing more than to coast down the mountainside, laughing, forgetting about what he'd done. About what he'd become.

"Why do the westerners call them sinmarks, while you say fatemarks?" he asked, fighting off sleep, forcing his eyelids to remain open. He needed answers, now more than ever.

Bear grunted. "Because they are ignorant fools," he said. "A lifetime ago I lived in Knight's End. I have few fond memories of the capital of the west. There are few who truly understand the nature of the marks. Myself included."

"But mine is the deathmark. You understand that. And you could kill me now," he said. They both knew it was a lie, which made them both laugh.

It was strange, laughing, especially when Bane looked at his hands and saw the bloodstains. It was almost time for the second royal death. He could sense it, like a current running through his veins. Killing the knights was just a warmup for the main event.

Once he'd recovered, King Gill Loren would fall.

And then there would be chaos.

Chapter Ten

The Western Kingdom | Knight's End

Rhea Loren

For once, Rhea didn't need to fake her tears to manipulate her father. No matter how quickly she blinked, her eyes were eternal wells, overflowing down her cheeks.

"There, there, Rhea," King Loren said. "You're safe now."

Rhea's entire body shook as she remembered the blood. She didn't feel safe—might never feel safe again, even within the castle walls. She'd known Sir Barrow her entire life, and, despite his blundering and bumbling, she still considered him a friend. One of her only true friends.

And now he was . . . he was . . .

A fresh wave of grief shuddered through her, matched only by the trembling fear that turned her bones to ice. Sir Barrow, with his slow movements and ill-equipped swordsmanship, wasn't exactly a fearsome adversary, but Sir Cray . . . she'd seen him on the practice fields. He was deadly. Whomever had killed them was a dangerous foe.

They'd found three other guards dead on the same night, and, unlike Barrow and Cray, they were all within the castle walls.

Wrath-damn that coward Grease Jolly, Rhea thought furiously, her tears finally dried up by her anger. *Wrath-damn him and his stolen fruit and his thick dark hair and sun-kissed complexion and smooth words and strong hands and full lips—*

She'd given him her purity and he'd treated her like a common whore.

She pulled away from her father's embrace abruptly, her mind setting an image of Grease Jolly ablaze. Though Rhea was typically of an easygoing nature, she hated being crossed. A year earlier one of the castle courtiers had informed her father that she'd snuck from her chambers at night, implying she'd been up to no good. She hadn't been up to any good, of course, but she'd lied and convinced the king she'd merely gone to the library to retrieve a book. Later she'd bribed a kitchen maid to crush a small amount of jade hemlock into the courtier's evening stew. The fool had been ill for a fortnight before recovering. Even to this day, however, his complexion was a little bit green, a fact that made Rhea laugh every time she saw him.

And now Grease had crossed her in another, even worse, way.

"What is it, princess?" her father asked. "What can I do to help?" His sunbaked eyes were tender and concerned, the polar opposite to how they looked when he was at court, meting out punishment on the guilty sinners throughout Knight's End. If only he knew what her lips had been doing last night before her guards had been brutally murdered . . .

As she looked at the man who spoiled her relentlessly, she considered her father's offer. She remembered the way she'd pleaded with Grease to stay, to not leave her. How she'd poured her heart out to him, going so far as to offering to run away with him. How he'd rejected her so quickly. How he'd scaled the wall and run along its edge, abandoning her to whatever evil roamed the Cryptlands. The fear that had threatened to tear itself from her throat as she hid with the dead in her family's crypt until the sun was long up, until she'd finally mustered the courage to tiptoe out, only to find her guards staring blankly at the blue sky, lying prostrate in a pool of their own blood.

How one of the furia had found her shaking on the ground, unable to speak, barely able to breathe. All because Grease Jolly left her when she needed him. *Wrath-damn my attraction to criminals*, she wanted to scream. He'd saved her once, but that didn't excuse what he'd done the night before.

She wished she could let it go, find a way to cool her fire-breathing temper. But she couldn't, her anger eating her up from the inside out, screaming for revenge. Yes, she was a princess, but that didn't mean her life was all peaches and cream. Her mother was dead. Her brother had vanished mysteriously when she was naught but a child. Her two siblings—the twins—were sniveling brats.

The urge to tell her father everything was strong, but she fought it back. Her father could never know she was anything but the perfect, chaste, Wrath-loving princess that he'd built up in his own mind. "There's a thief," she said instead. "I've seen him in the markets. He's clever and never gets caught. I watched him steal half a dozen items from all different carts."

Her father's eyebrows narrowed and his eyes seemed to darken with righteous indignation in that familiar way she'd seen half a thousand times at court. "Would you be able to identify this criminal?" he growled.

She nodded. "I know it won't bring back Sir Barrow and Sir Cray, but catching him will make Knight's End a safer place."

Her father clamped his hands on her shoulders firmly, his hands warm through her black dress of mourning. "Take as many castle guards and furia as you need. Bring the thief to justice."

"I will, Father," she said, and for the first time since Grease had kissed her, she smiled.

Chapter Eleven

The Western Kingdom | Knight's End

Grease Jolly

Grease was an expert at forgetting. After his parents died when he was eight and his sister five, he forgot all about them. He even forgot his own name and came up with his own, because after all, what difference did it make? No matter how many times his sister tried to remind him of the past, he let the memories slide right off him. He was Grease Jolly, through and through. It was as if his life had been split up into two pieces. He preferred the new piece, so why dwell on the old?

Rhea was now part of the old, so he needed to forget about her. Plus, she was safe, apparently. Though he'd feared the worst when he couldn't find her, the rumors were already swirling through the city. Two more knights were dead, along with three guardsmen. The knights had been guarding the princess, but she was fine, unharmed. *She is fine, unharmed.* Those words had allowed him to breathe again, but he couldn't dwell on them. No, he had more important things to do, like getting the rot out of Knight's End. After seeing that . . . *creature* . . . in the Cryptlands, Grease was convinced it was time to move on, both literally and figuratively.

Then why is it so hard this time? he wondered as he stuffed his dirty clothes into a satchel.

Because of her, his mind echoed. He shook his head. He shouldn't give a rot about her. She was just a girl. Hell, she was a godsdamned princess! It had been fun while it lasted. A new conquest. And it had been all passion, all physical, hadn't it? There was no true attachment. Nothing *real*.

And yet he couldn't stop thinking about her, how betrayed she'd looked when he abandoned her outside the crypt. "Not my rutting problem," he muttered under his breath. He took a bite of moldy bread and stuffed the rest into his sack.

"I'm not leaving," his sister announced, dumping the contents of her own satchel on the floor of their dingy crawlspace under the steps of the pleasure house. Shae placed her hands on her hips and scowled at him. *Gods, when had she become so grown up?* At fourteen, she was becoming more and more stubborn. With her long strawberry-gold hair, she reminded him of someone, but he refused to think about that, the pain still too close to the surface.

"You are. Pack your bag." When she just stared at him, he snatched her satchel and began shoving the spilled contents back inside.

"You can take my things, but you're not taking me," she said.

"I'll carry you kicking and screaming if I have to," Grease said.

"And clawing . . ." Shae muttered.

Grease placed her bag next to his. "Look . . . I told you when we arrived this was only temporary."

"But I *like* it here. I have *friends*. The furia are nice to me."

And this is exactly why we have to move on, Grease thought. *Among other reasons. Like a murderous demon with the glowing mark. Oh, and the fact that I bedded the eldest princess and the king will probably find out and want to execute me several times in several painful ways.*

The furia were the holy female warriors led by the Furics, a trio of righteous women who had the responsibility of enforcing Wrath's laws in the west. They targeted young street girls, like Shae, giving them food and education while grooming them to eventually join their violent ranks.

"It's not safe here anymore," Grease said. *And I won't have you become a furia.*

"Where will we go?" Shae asked.

In truth, Grease didn't know. According to rumors, the north was in turmoil after the death of King Gäric. The East-West War made the borders along the Spear impassable. And going south only meant you had a death wish—

the Phanecians had been sallying out from the Southron Gates, attacking the border towns at Vinya, Sarris, Cleo, and Felix. Word was they were using trained pyzons and vulzures in the attacks. The very thought of giant snakes slithering across the ground and razor-clawed raptors swooping in from the sky made Grease's skin crawl.

"Grey?" his sister said, snapping him away from his dark thoughts.

"Talis," he said definitively. Apart from the fact that it was dangerously close to the Dead Isles, Talis was the furthest from each of the kingdom's borders, and protected to the west by the sea. "We've never been there. I've heard it's nice. And don't call me Grey."

"Sorry, *Grease*," she said. "Or should I call you Sir Jolly?" She laughed.

"It's not funny," Grease said. "Our real names are dangerous." Although his sister refused to change her first name, she'd been willing to take on the surname Jolly, at least while they were in Knight's End.

"They saved us," Shae said, her bottom lip quivering. Grease wished he'd never said anything about his name. "I won't forget Mother and Father, even if you will."

Grease threw an arm around his sister. "I just want you to be safe," he said. It was the reason he did everything he did. Well, *most* everything. His fling with the princess was something completely different.

"I *am* safe. Here. With the furia."

Gods. If only, Grease thought. Unfortunately, the furia and everything in the Holy City was his sister's enemy. "Your mark," he reminded her.

"It doesn't *do* anything," Shae said. "It's not a sinmark. Just a birthmark, or something." Grease hated that she referred to it as a *sin*mark, like everyone else in the west. There was nothing sinful about his sister—as far as he was concerned, she was an innocent flower. He knew she didn't believe her own words, about it being a birthmark, but he wouldn't contradict her. Not when their parents had died because of her mark.

"Still," Grease said now, "people wouldn't rutting understand."

"Don't curse, Grey. The furia will cut out your tongue if they hear you. Listen, if I become one of the furia, I can change the way people think about the marks."

"I said no," Grease said, hefting both packs over his shoulders.

"This isn't fair!" Shae shouted. "I hate you! I wish you had died instead of Mother and Father."

The words stung, but Grease absorbed them the way he absorbed anything bad in his life. Without feeling. He hadn't cried in nine years, and he wasn't about to now. He had to be strong for Shae, even if she hated him for it.

He moved aside the empty barrels that hid their crawlspace, and strode down the street. He didn't look back to see if Shae was following. He didn't have to, because she always did.

A few minutes later she was by his side. "I didn't mean what I said about hating you," she said.

"I know, Shae. I know," Grease said.

"Or about you being dead."

"Forget about it. They were just words. Words disappear the moment you speak them."

Shae was silent for a minute as they walked along. "Maybe they don't disappear," she finally said. Grease was surprised she'd given what he said so much thought. "But maybe you can grab them before they become real."

"Works for me," Grease said. That's when he realized they were heading in the wrong direction. If they'd wanted to head out of the city in the direction of Talls, they should've been going the opposite way. Instead they were walking toward the castle walls.

Her, Grease thought. "Get the rot out of my head," he muttered.

"What did you say?" Shae asked. "Did you curse again?"

"Nothing. And no, I didn't curse." But still Grease refused to turn his path. When they finally reached the castle, he stopped, craning his head back to look up toward the ramparts.

"What are we doing?" Shae asked, but he didn't answer.

"Goodbye," he said. He felt foolish saying goodbye to a wall, or even saying goodbye at all. Sentimentalities were for fools.

Regardless, there was no reason to rush out of Knight's End. Whatever he'd seen that morning wasn't going to stalk him in broad daylight. So instead of turning around, he led Shae toward the edge of the bay, which swept before them in a crystalline arc of sparkling water that met jagged mountains rising like swords into the clear, blue sky. They sat atop a rise, watching the gulls chase each other on the wind.

"Do we have to leave?" Shae asked.

"For now. But maybe we'll come back some day," Grease lied. He squinted as he noticed the merchant ship he'd seen approaching earlier that morning. Its sails had been tucked back in and tied off with ropes, and it was anchored in the bay, preparing smaller landing vessels laden with goods. It appeared as if the boats would be separated, some moving north toward Blackstone and the rest to Knight's End. *The Crimeans are still selling to both sides*, Grease thought wryly. *Smart move.*

"When?" Shae asked.

Grease didn't answer, because he didn't want to lie again. Not to her. Instead he said, "We should go." He turned and headed back toward Knight's End, this time steering them south through the crowded city streets. The familiar cobblestones slapped beneath Grease's trod. Despite himself, he would miss the Holy City. At just under three years, it was the longest they'd stayed in any one place since their parents' deaths.

And he would miss Rhea. Deeply. No matter what he tried to convince himself of, she was more than some conquest, more than a thrill. In another life, she could've been special to him.

She is special to me.

He was tempted to nick a few supplies from the vendors on the way out, but he didn't for two reasons: first, he didn't want to risk getting caught; and second, his sister would never let him hear the end of it. Like cursing, she was against stealing, although Grease was pretty sure she wouldn't care when her stomach started rumbling.

They reached Corizen Corner, which connected the two major city thoroughfares in a large square marketplace. It was where he'd first seen Princess Rhea, where she'd given him the secret note. Though it was only six weeks ago, it felt like a lifetime now that they were leaving.

He tried to focus on the positive fact that even after having an illicit affair with the eldest daughter of the Holy King, his head was still attached to his neck. *Three godsdamned cheers for me*, Grease thought.

They zigzagged through the marketplace, pushing through the crowd, which was as thick as bees in a hive. A few sellers who recognized him fired scowls his way. They'd never caught him thieving from them—well, except for the baker the night before—but in their hearts they knew what he was.

Don't worry, he wanted to tell them. *You'll never see me again.*

Out of Corizen Corner, they picked up speed, the crowds thinning as the street narrowed. The main city gates were just ahead, manned by furia who questioned every trader or traveler who entered Knight's End. Grease acted calm, reminding himself that they were *leaving*. No one would question two street rats departing the city. In fact, the holy sisterhood would likely be glad to see them go.

"That's him," a voice said, rising above the sound of cart wheels rattling across the cobblestones. The voice was familiar somehow. Grease frowned, bobbing his head back and forth. *It can't be. It's impossible.*

But it was. Princess Rhea was lying prone atop a royal litter hefted by four muscular servants. A dozen guards and furia surrounded her. Even in her thick frock, Rhea was a sight, her hair twisted into a crown of golden vines atop her head, not unlike the hairstyle she'd worn when he'd first seen her in the marketplace. When he'd saved her from the lunatic.

She wasn't smiling, her eyes alight with an angry fire Grease had never seen in her before. She was pointing at him. "Thief!" she cried.

Before Grease could even consider running for it, several of the guards had him and Shae in chains. "Grey!" Shae cried, reaching for his hand. He tried to grab her fingers but the guards pried them apart.

There was nothing to say, nothing to do. Princess Rhea had betrayed him. And it was his fault, because he'd betrayed her, too.

Oh, Shae, Grease thought. *I've failed you.*

Chapter Twelve

The Eastern Kingdom | Ferria, Ironwood

Roan

The design of the castle was ingenious. Each circular metal wall had a gate, but they were at different positions, moving from south to north and east to west. If an invading army were ever to breach the first gate, they would be forced to fight their way around the circle, most likely hauling a battering ram, in order to break down the second gate. At that point they would have to once more fight their way around to the third gate, and so on. All told, there were eight gates, and Roan was breathing heavily by the time they'd cleared the final one. *At least I'm not on the horse anymore*, he thought.

The inner circle was significantly smaller than the previous rings, and also less busy. Metallic steps rang out under his feet.

The prince was already at the top, waiting, grinning as Roan struggled to join him. Roan daydreamed of breaking free of his bonds and pushing the prince down the steps. The thought made him smile.

"Have you thought of a jape, jester?" Gareth said as Roan climbed the last step.

"I have," Roan said, trying to control his heavy breathing. "It involves you, your mother, and a hairless donkey. Shall I skip straight to the punch line?"

"That is up to you. It might very well be the last joke you ever tell, just as the hard bread you ate this morning may have been your final meal." The prince spun around and led the way inside a metal-columned circular building with a massive sphere sitting on top.

Again, Roan couldn't tell how much of what the prince had said was in jest. One of Gareth's men nudged him from behind and he had no choice but to follow.

His breath caught when he saw the inside of the palace. The walls were festooned with intricate metalwork that seemed to flow like water across and up and down. Silvery horses ran, their riders working the reins and slashing swords at red-garbed furia warriors. One by one, the furia fell, only to rise again, the battle resetting itself. *How is this possible?* Roan asked himself. Could the magic of the forest dwellers really create such beauty? From what he'd seen so far, he was confident the answer was yes.

Gwendolyn was standing as straight as a sword on the side of a large throne that, like everything else in Ferria, seemed to grow and change continuously. The regal arms morphed from a long creature with snarling fangs to a sword to the point of an arrow. The throne's high back curved with eagle's wings before becoming a bear's head and finally a shield marked with the crossed swords of the Eastern Kingdom.

A large man with a reddish-brown beard sat on the raised throne, his fingers drumming impatiently on the ever-changing arms. His head appeared to be bald, although it was difficult to tell due to the iron crown that hugged his scalp. Spikes protruded along the edges of the sides, forming into crossed swords. He could only be the one known as the Juggernaut, King Oren Ironclad himself. Gareth's father. Besides Beorn Stonecledge, the king was the most enormous man Roan had ever seen, making his nickname almost seem insufficient to describe his size.

Beside him stood Prince Gareth and . . . Prince Gareth? But wait, Prince Gareth was still in front of him, leading him toward the end of the throne room. Roan closed his eyes, shook his head, and then opened them again. The three Gareths remained. One of them stepped forward. "Brother," he said. "What news from the south?"

Roan gaped as they clasped hands. Obviously, they were twins. *No, triplets.* He had the sudden desire to throw himself on a sword. The only thing he could imagine worse than one Prince Gareth was three.

The lie sat on his tongue for a moment before dissolving.

"We defeated a raggedy tribe of nomads who attacked our camp," Gareth said. "But that was all we saw of the Southrons. It seems the infernal Scarra Desert is as much a wall to them as it is to us."

"Pity," the second prince said. "Your *younger* brothers have bested you once more. My squadron managed to cross the Spear to Felix. We claimed it for the east." He pulled up the sleeve of his dark blue tunic, revealing a long slash wound stitched neatly together. "I have the scar to prove it."

The third brother stepped forward. "Prince Guy is bragging again," he said. "According to what I heard, there was hardly anything left of Felix by the time he arrived, because of the Phanecians, and I expect he cut himself shaving his hairy arms. I, on the other hand, made significant progress reconstructing the Bridge of Triumph. The bridge is nearly halfway complete, even though we were harassed by the furia the entire time. I lost an ear from one of their fire arrows." He tilted his head on an angle to show the charred stump of flesh that had once been an ear.

"Thank you, Prince Grian," Guy said, gritting his teeth. "Still, a victory is a victory, and a scar is a scar."

Roan stopped just shy of Prince Gareth. Now that he was closer, he noticed subtle differences between the three brothers. Guy's hair hung a little longer, while Grian's looked messier, not to mention the missing ear. Gareth's auburn hair, on the other hand, was trim and neat.

"Molten ore! Will my sons never stop competing?" King Ironclad said from the throne.

"We compete for you," Gareth said. "And though I cannot match my brothers' scars, that is simply because I am a far better warrior and did not permit my foes to harm me."

Roan couldn't hold back the laugh, nor his own jape. "He did, however, get a little wet in the Barren Marshes. If you sniff closely, you can still smell the stink of fetid water on his clothes."

All heads turned toward him, and to Roan's surprise, Gwendolyn was forced to mask a laugh with a cough. But when he looked at her she fired knives from her eyes.

"Who in the Four Kingdoms are you?" King Ironclad asked.

He didn't hesitate to respond. "Roan the Calypsian, Your Royal Highness, Oh Juggernaut of the East," Roan said grandly. He bowed as deeply as he could. He would've swept his arms out before him had they not been bound.

Gareth cut in. "He thinks he's amusing," he said. "He calls himself 'Born From Dust,' a bastard son of an unnamed westerner, raised by his whoring Southron mother."

Had any of the prince's words been true, Roan might've felt the need to aim a kick at his royal groin, but as it was, there was no need. *He knows nothing of my mother's moral character*, he thought.

The king stroked his beard. "In some kingdoms, insolence such as yours would be met with death," he said.

"I figured death was already a foregone conclusion," Roan said. "Your son has pegged me as a Southron spy."

"And are you?" King Ironclad asked.

"No more than my father is a king," Roan said, continuing to play his dangerous game. Lies and half-truths had kept him alive thus far.

"You don't look like a Southroner," the king noted. "Your hair is too . . . sunny. Too curly too. And your skin is too light by a hundred shades."

"As I told the prince—"

"Your father is a westerner, I heard the first time. Where is your mother?"

"Dead."

"And you don't know your father?"

"I don't want to know him. He abandoned me. And my *whoring* Southron mother." Truth with lies.

"Your tongue is sharper than many of my swords," the king said. He didn't seem particularly angry, Roan noticed. *Probably because he can squash me between two fingers anytime he wants.*

Roan said nothing.

"What information can you give us about the Calypsians?"

"Nothing."

"Then you have no value to me," the king said. He stood. When he rose to his full height, Roan felt like an ant about to be stepped on. "Unless there's something you haven't told us."

Was this what it would come down to then? Roan wondered. His life matched up against a truth he'd kept secret his entire life, a truth his mother had died for, a truth his guardian had killed two innocent children for?

Luckily, Roan had more than one secret, and one might be enough to save his life.

He breathed in and out, considering his words carefully. The king flicked his fingers impatiently. "Take him away. Never let his face see the sun again."

Two of Gareth's men grabbed Roan's arms. "Wait," he said, barely more than a whisper.

Gareth looked at him, an eyebrow raised curiously. The king said, "I wait for no one. Speak or be gone."

On the edge of his vision, Roan could see Gwendolyn leaning in, frowning. He had everyone's attention. He opened his mouth, but the words remained chained inside his throat. "I'm . . ." he said. He faltered. He couldn't do it. They could kill him, but his secret would go with him to the grave.

There was a flash of movement from the side as Gwendolyn launched herself off the podium. With a quick thrust, she shoved her sword, which was sharp and deadly once more, through his gut.

Roan choked out a gasp, the pain and the pressure ripping through his stomach, radiating outwards to every part of his body through his shattered nerve endings. Gwendolyn pulled out the blade, slick with his blood, and he toppled backwards. He clutched his broken flesh, blood bubbling between his bound hands. The Orian stood over him, her face scrunched. She looked puzzled. "Why do you not save yourself?" she asked.

Agony roaring through him, Roan knew his secret would not go with him to his grave, no matter what he did. He gave himself to the heat in his chest, which swarmed to his gut. Knitting, mending, *healing*.

Gwendolyn's lip curled into a smile as she watched his blood stop rushing out, his skin growing together until it was whole once more. Gareth said, "Molten ore. You really are full of surprises, jester."

Roan yawned. "Is there somewhere I can sleep for a while?" Healing life-threatening injuries was exhausting.

King Oren Ironclad, the Juggernaut of the East, said, "You think this changes anything? Execute him."

As one, the three princes laughed.

Chapter Thirteen

The Northern Kingdom | West of Castle Hill

Annise Gäric

Her mother's killer hadn't choked the life out of her. Instead, the Armored Knight had pushed her knotty hair away from her face, and helped her to her feet. She hadn't tried to fight him this time. Not because she didn't want to, but because it was fruitless. Now, as they trudged through the snow, Arme refused to look at Annise, much less speak to her. If she tried to veer from their course west, he would grab her by the arm and manhandle her like a child. Eventually she gave up. She would bide her time, waiting for a ripe moment to escape and flee toward Gearhärt. She would find Arch and persuade him that he needed her. *He does need me*, she thought, trying to convince herself.

Better yet, she would persuade him to flee north, to leave the kingdom forever. After all, what was in Castle Hill but heartache and sorrow? The Dread King was dead, but her father had been replaced by a new tyrant, as it always would be. Nothing would ever change. With her mother dead, she had no reason to stay, so long as she could convince her brother to accompany her to the Hinterlands. Dietrich and Arme could come if they wanted to.

But everything changed when they reached the edge of the Howling Tundra. It was a wild, uninhabited expanse that separated Castle Hill from Blackstone. "This is folly," Annise said. "We cannot cross the tundra and hope to live."

Finally, Arme looked at her and said, "This is the fastest route to Blackstone. And we cannot travel by the roads along the mountains—your uncle will have patrols."

"Yes, and we are two heavy-footed stompers. Our footprints will be deep and easy to track."

He shook his head, but didn't argue. "To go on well-travelled roads is impossible," he said instead.

"Is it better to die on the ice?"

"You will not die."

"The few who have survived the tundra have spoken of ice bears twice the size of men."

"I am no ordinary man," Arme said, staring out across the frozen wasteland. He looked like he was searching for something.

"Herds of wild *mamoothen* travel these plains. They don't care if you are man or rock, they will trample you the same."

"I'm quicker than I look."

So am I, Annise thought, *but that doesn't mean I can stop a beast from stepping on me.* "Not to mention the exposure. We will freeze before we reach Blackstone. Is that what my mother would want?"

As soon as the words left her mouth, Annise wanted them back. Arme flinched visibly, gritted his teeth, and started across the tundra.

Annise stood for a moment, watching him, wondering how long it would take him to notice if she slipped away. She could hide in a snowbank . . . or something.

She sighed, her breath clouding the air. He would catch her. With no other choice, she stomped after him. The wind howled around them, unbroken by the flat terrain. Despite the heavy layers she wore, icy spikes seemed to cut right through her.

On the first day, they saw no signs of life, unless you included the snowfall, which swirled and danced like flocks of butterflies. By the time they stopped, their shadows were long and thin, trailing behind them like silent stalkers.

"We'll make camp here," Arme said, dropping the bag of supplies. It made a heavy thud in the snow.

Annise looked around. "Where? There is nothing but snow and ice. We have no shelter and little hope of a fire. We will die as we sleep." Hope was slipping away. They'd gone so far that even if she could escape, she wasn't sure if she could make it back or even head in the right direction. She'd more likely end up wandering in circles until she became a snack for some wild beast.

"I pledged to your mother that I would protect you, and I will."

Although she was chilled to the bone, hot rage rose up inside her. "You mean like you protected *her*? You kicked out the platform like she was nobody, you let her fall, let her hang there like—" Unbidden, tears burst from Annise's eyes, freezing on her cheeks long before they could complete their path to her jaw. "*You* should be dead, not her!" she sobbed. She flung herself at the knight, adrenaline pumping through her tired legs and arms. Each time she pounded on his armor, pain shot through her hands, but she didn't care—she *relished* it.

He didn't fight back. He merely grabbed her arms, holding back her fists, pulling her toward him, wrapping her in a . . . there was nothing else to call it . . . a hug. She stopped fighting, shocked at the gesture, all strength leaving her limbs. She sank into him, crying, crying, crying.

"Get the frozen hell off of me," she snarled, pushing him away. How dare he use her grief against her. How dare he pretend to *care* about what happened to her mother. She flopped down on the ground, flexing and massaging her face to break off the ice crystals that had formed from her tears.

She refused to look at Arme, but could sense his stare for a few moments, before busying himself setting up camp. She pretended to ignore him, but watched him from the corner of her eye as he began pushing snow into piles. She knew what he was doing, and it was smart. Even in the bitter cold, the snow would provide protection and insulation from the wind.

She waited a few more seconds, and then rose and began helping him. He glanced at her, but didn't say anything. The work was a good distraction from all that had happened over the last two days. Annise threw herself into the work, glad for once that she was built like a small ice bear and able to really help the knight.

By the time the sky grew dark, they had a suitable wall around a small circular space. On the side away from the wind, they'd left a small entrance. Next they set up a tent in the middle. It was a difficult task even with the wall, the winds whipping the thick canvas into a frenzy, causing them to have to pound the stakes deeper and deeper before they held.

When they finished, the tent was almost tall enough for Annise to stand up in, although the Armored Knight's sheer size forced him into a crouch. Length- and width-wise, things were even tighter. "We'll be like fish in a pot," Annise said.

"This is for you," Arme said. "I'll sleep outside, behind the wall."

A tempting offer, Annise thought. But not one she could accept. "No. We'll sleep back to back. It will work." They settled down next to each other to eat, precariously close. Night fell swiftly, and soon they had to work by feel alone, which made for several awkward moments when Annise grabbed Arme's gloved hand by mistake.

Eventually, however, they managed to ration the food and water between them. In the dark, they ate an unsatisfying supper of dried reindeer meat and half-frozen flatbread. Their water supply was solid ice, so they were forced to clamp the skins beneath their armpits and knees for a long time before they could take a few cold sips.

Annise had never felt more unsatisfied in her life, something that made her strangely sad. *The commoners starved and I've never felt the ache of an empty belly until now.*

Still, the snow-insulated tent was surprisingly warm, and getting warmer by the minute, their bodies coming back to life and acting as a fire without flames. That's when Annise remembered the knight's injury. "I need to inspect your wound in the morning. It will need stitches."

"No," Arme said.

"No?"

He didn't repeat himself.

"Why not?" Annise pressed. "I can't have my great protector dying on me, can I?"

"My armor stays on," Arme said.

This again. He wouldn't let her see his face, wouldn't remove his armor—what was he hiding? "You're going to sleep in your armor?"

"Yes."

"Suit yourself," Annise said, stretching out as far as she could and turning away from him. "Just don't bang into me during the night. And don't let that spiked ball of yours poke me. What kind of weapon is that anyway?"

"An effective one," he grunted.

She rolled her eyes, but couldn't argue with that—she'd seen what it could do. "Does it have a name?"

"Morningstar," he said. "At least that was the name the woman who gave it to me called it."

"What woman?"

"No matter. That was a lifetime ago. I was still just a scared little boy."

Annise closed her eyes, trying to imagine the massive man as a smaller person, a boy. She couldn't. She listened as he creaked and groaned in his armor, trying to get comfortable. *Absurd*, she thought. He was the largest man she'd ever seen—there was no way he'd sleep a wink tonight.

Things weren't much better for her. Despite their body warmth, the temperature began to drop significantly. No matter how tightly she wrapped her skins and blankets, the cold pressed in from all sides, burrowing into any gap it could find. In the dark, she shivered. She tried to lock her jaw, but her teeth chattered.

Arme's armor creaked and he said, "Princess?"

"Y-Yes?"

"Are you well?"

No. "Y-Yes."

"Your teeth are chattering. I can hear your bones trembling."

"G-good thing I am a s-solid woman. It will serve to keep me w-warm through the night."

"Must you always mock yourself mercilessly?"

Despite the cold fighting her facial expressions, Annise frowned. "How else would I m-mock myself? I'm the D-D-Dread King's daughter, so mercy d-doesn't exist in my vocabulary."

"You should not mock yourself at all."

"If I d-don't, someone else will." *And why do you care what I do?*

His sigh was so heavy it seemed to fill the entire tent. "You haven't changed at all," he said. Before she could ask him how he knew anything about how she'd changed or not changed, he asked, "Are you sure you're well?"

"I'm f-f-f-f—" She couldn't get the word out, her throat knotted with ropes of cold air.

"What can I do?"

The question was so innocent that Annise forgot for a moment that he was the one who'd kicked out the platform beneath her mother's feet. He was just a person, like her, trying to survive. And he wanted to help her.

She swallowed twice, trying to generate enough saliva to speak. She knew they only had one choice. "We h-have to sh-share body heat." She felt her face flush, and was glad he couldn't see it. It wasn't that she'd never gone for a roll in the snow before. There was dashing Rory Kettlejoy in the hayloft in the stables. She'd been shocked when he'd taken her hand and led her up the ladder. He'd groped clumsily at her round hips and said her body was "wondrous," a word she'd never have used to describe herself. Of course, later when she'd overheard him bragging about his exploits to the other lordlings, he'd compared her to a mamoothen. She'd pretended it was a compliment, because the wild beasts were incredibly strong—like her.

But this was different. She didn't even know this man, and what he'd done to her mother . . . It didn't matter in this moment. This was about survival. Nothing more.

"I—" He paused for a moment, then said, "Yes. I can do that." Creaks and groans. He bumped her twice as he tried to twist around without bringing down the whole tent. Annise froze, as slowly, tentatively, he roped an enormous arm around her, cinching at her waist. Embarrassed by just how much waist she had, she grabbed his hand and moved it higher, to her ribcage, the only spot on her body where things thinned out a little. His armored body was stone-hard against her back.

"This isn't g-going to work," Annise said. "It's l-like sleeping next to a s-suit of armor. You're cold. And all edges and p-plates. You have to l-lose the armor."

She heard him hold his breath for a moment, and then let it out. "I will do it," he finally said. "But you must promise me one thing."

"What?"

"When the light of morning arrives, do not look at me until I've replaced my armor."

Annise was so cold she would've promised to never look at him again, if that's what he wanted. "Yes. I p-promise."

With considerably more shifting and grunting, Arme began removing his armor, which was quite an ordeal. Twice Annise said "Ow!" when he poked her with it, and thrice she simply bit her tongue. After what seemed like half the night, he slipped behind her and resumed the position, remembering to place his arm around her at her ribcage, a gesture she couldn't help but appreciate.

It was all different this time. His body was still huge and muscled, but so much warmer, like she was sleeping within a fire. "Thank you," she sighed.

"You're welcome," he said.

And then they slept in their cocoon.

⸙

Heavy breathing stirred Annise awake. As she stared at the inside of the thick white tent, it took her a few seconds to remember where she was.

Frozen hell, she thought. She could still feel Arme's body knitted behind her. Sometime during the night, they'd seemed to meld together, his knees nestled behind her knees, his chest pressed tightly against her back, his midsection pushing gently against—

She cringed, remembering the way her mother's body bounced as the rope tightened.

She couldn't breathe, couldn't think, couldn't do anything but grab Arme's hand—which was still wrapped around her ribcage—and—

She stopped, sucking in a throat-burning gulp of frigid air.

Steaming pile of mamoothen dung, she thought, staring at the bare skin on the back of his hand. It wasn't pale exactly. More like a window frosted by cold winter air. And on the other side of the window were twisting snakes, as black as ebony, running up his wrist to his arm, vanishing under the sleeve of his knight's tunic.

Veins, Annise's mind labelled them. *Black veins.* She'd seen how dark his blood was the day before as it trickled onto the snow. She'd thought it was a trick of the light, but no.

His blood was black.

Reflexively, her body stiffened.

His hand fluttered and then recoiled, disappearing behind her. She started to turn, but Arme said, "Don't."

She froze.

"You promised not to look at me."

"I didn't mean to, I just awoke and your hand was there and—"

"It's fine. Just let me don my armor. Please."

The plea in his voice gave her pause. How could a man so strong, so fierce in battle, be so afraid of his own skin? *She* was the one afraid of the tower of mirrors.

"I won't look," she said. He grunted and pulled back, and immediately a rush of cool air surrounded her.

Armor clanked as the wind howled and battered the sides of their tent. Annise's mind was racing, and she couldn't get the image of his strange skin and stranger veins out of her head. She opened her mouth twice to speak, but didn't know what to say. Finally, she could hold back no longer. "What is wrong with you?" The second the blunt question spilled from her lips, she thought, *I'm a frozen-headed yak brain.* "I'm sorry, I didn't mean—"

To her surprise, Arme laughed. "To answer that question, it could take years."

"What I meant was, what happened to you? To your skin. To your veins. Were you born with that . . . condition?"

"Don't worry, princess, it's not contagious."

Heat rushed to Annise's cheeks. "I'm not worried about that. Just . . ." She'd heard of the Southron plague, which ate its victims alive from the inside out. And of course she'd read streams about an eastern flesh-eating disease called mottle, which affected the skin in strange and terrifying ways. But she'd never heard of anything like this. "Does it hurt? Is it hurting you?"

He laughed again, and Annise found it to be a surprisingly pleasant sound. "No. And I wasn't born with it."

"Then what happened? Were you cursed somehow?" Arch was always telling Annise that one day she would be cursed by a sorcerer because of her sins, all her swearing and lusting after various knights and lordlings. She'd never believed him, until now.

"Something like that," Arme said. "You may turn."

Slowly, she eased around to find him fully covered again, his mesh facemask and eye slits aimed right at her. He moved closer to her, and she noticed one of his gloves remained off. He slid his hand toward her.

She swallowed, but didn't recoil.

She took his hand in hers, raising it toward her eyes so she could inspect his skin more closely.

"Most people fear me," Arme said. "But you keep attacking me." She could sense a smile behind his facemask.

"When you grow up with the Dread King as your father, there's not much that scares you," Annise said. She ran a finger over his skin, which was as smooth as silk, save for the black veins, protruding like rolling hills. "Tell me what happened. I command it."

"You *command* it?" Again, there was something different in the knight's tone. Something less gruff.

"You swore to protect me," she said. "And I need to know about what happened to you in order to feel . . . protected." Even to her, it sounded weak.

"Once upon a time," the knight started. "I was a little boy named Tarin."

Annise dropped his hand. *Wait. Wait.* That name . . . "I knew a boy called Tarin," Annise whispered. "He was the horsemaster's son. When I was a girl. I played with him. He was my friend. He—he died."

"Close enough," Arme said.

It couldn't be. Could it? When Annise had lost Tarin, she'd punched holes in a bale of hay for three days straight. Then she'd gone to the practice fields for the first time and bested half the young lordlings in combat. The other half had been too scared to face her.

She remembered how she'd found out. Her mother had told her. It was one of the few times her mother had spoken to just her, without others present. She'd seemed so sad, so broken. Then again, her mother had always seemed fragile and broken, save for the very end as she stood on the gallows.

"But I attended your day of mourning. I cried for you. If not you, then who was in the casket?"

"I don't know," Tarin said. "Probably rocks. My parents would've wanted to hide the truth. And anyway, to them I really was dead."

"I don't understand. You didn't die?" His odd words from the night before came to mind: *You haven't changed at all.* He'd known her from when she was a big-boned girl eating everything in sight and knocking the boys into the snow. And yes, mocking herself mercilessly. *I guess I haven't changed much since then,* Annise mused.

"Clearly not," Tarin said.

"Where have you been all these years?"

"On the eastern edge of the kingdom. I trained in Walburg, then later in Darrin. I joined the army."

"But you're barely a year my elder," Annise said.

"We all must fight some time, and I grew up faster than most," Arme said. "I've protected against eastern invasion along the Black Cliffs for three years."

"You fought in the Battle of the Razor?"

He nodded.

"But they say many died," Annise said, still trying to comprehend that the man hunched before her was the scrawny little boy she'd played with as a child.

"Thousands," Tarin said. "But not me."

Annise needed to fill the gap between her childhood and now. She still didn't understand. "My mother said you had a rare bone condition. A defect, she called it. She said there was nothing anyone could do. I saw you lying in bed, unable to walk. I mourned for you."

"She helped me."

Annise stared into his eye slits. "How? Why?"

Tarin paused to pull his glove on and then said, "She found a woman, a sorceress, she—"

"A witch? My mother would never do that." For all her faults, Queen Sabria Loren had been a deeply religious woman, worshipping Wrath like all westerners. In Knight's End, where her mother had been from, they didn't hire witches, they *burned* them.

"She did."

Annise shook her head. Mysteries on top of mysteries.

Tarin continued. "She loved my mother. Your mother was never comfortable in the north. My mother was one of her few friends. The queen visited us often, broke bread with us, laughed with us . . ."

"I didn't know."

"She didn't tell you, and she forbid me to."

"So the witch . . ."

"The woman, she made me drink a dark liquid. It was vile and burned my throat on the way down, but she held my nose and forced me to swallow. It made me feel better. Then my body started changing, transforming."

Any anger and cruel intentions she'd had toward the knight fell away like a discarded cloak, leaving her feeling cold and naked. "I'm so sorry," Annise said.

"Don't be. Your mother saved me."

"Did it hurt. The transformation?"

"No," Tarin said. His response was too quick, and Annise had already seen the grimace, the flicker of a painful memory in his eyes.

She chose not to press the issue. She understood wanting to forget the past. "But now . . ."

"Now there is something evil inside me, something black. I can always feel it, trying to claw its way out, to make me do things I don't want to do. When you cheat death there is always a price to pay."

"But you're not evil," Annise said. He'd saved them. Saved her. She likely would've already perished on the tundra if not for the warmth of his body.

"Like you said, I killed your mother, the same woman who spared my life. A woman I loved as much as my own mother."

"Because she asked you to. In order to save Arch and I." Was she really defending him? Did he really deserve it? *Yes,* she thought. *He does.*

He shook his head, the dark mesh shifting from side to side. "Sometimes I don't know. I thought I was doing what she wanted, but as she hung there, I felt the darkness inside of me squirming. It was excited. It was giddy. It *wanted* me to do it."

"But that's not *why* you did it, right? You did it for my mother."

"I—I don't know. I think I did, but I can't be certain. And it's not the first time I've killed without being sure of the reasons . . . I see them in my sleep. Countless men. Women too. The easterners have both in their armies."

Annise's blood ran cold. Whatever he'd done, he *was* dangerous, if only because of what the witch had put into his body. She didn't know what to say.

"I won't hurt you," Tarin said quickly. "I swear it. I'm ashamed of what I am, and what I've done, but I will do right by you. I will protect you until I am dead."

"I never asked you to do that." Still, the thought of him wanting to be her protector chased away the chill sweeping through her.

"Try to stop me."

Her stomach growled, and Annise chewed on everything he'd said for a minute, wishing his words were food. "When you are ready, I want to see you. The real you—your face."

"I can't do that," Arme—Tarin said. "Unlike you, I do not wear my scars so well, my lady."

Annise frowned, puzzled. "Me? I bear no scars."

"Not on the outside. But your eyes are the windows to your scars."

Annise knew he was right. If the outside of her body was the pampered, well-fed form of a princess, her soul had been sliced to ribbons. Her father's sins were there. Her unfulfilling relationship with her mother, too. The names she'd been called her entire life, even if they'd always been whispered behind cupped hands. And now, her mother's death and her separation from Arch. There was a worse one, too. The long, ragged scar that seemed to eclipse all the others. Her dead brother, taken far too soon. She couldn't lose another brother. She had to find Arch before it was too late.

"I bare no scars, Sir," Annise said again. She rummaged through their supplies and turned away.

Chapter Fourteen

The Eastern Kingdom | Ferria, Ironwood

Roan

Roan's heart skipped a beat.

The three princes continued laughing as the king's decree echoed through the circular hall. *Execute him . . . execute him...execute him . . .*

Then the king himself laughed, a deep-throated "Har-har-har!" that rumbled through Roan's bones. Apparently just the suggestion of his demise was enough to provide a day's worth of entertainment for the king and his sons.

Gwendolyn, her cat-like eyes still boring into him, was the only one not laughing. But she *was* smirking. *Snakes, has the entire Four Kingdoms gone mad?* That's when Roan realized something. "You're jesting," he said.

"This one's as quick as an ore monkey!" the king declared, still guffawing loudly.

"You're not going to kill me," Roan said.

"Not today," Gareth said. "I cannot vouch for tomorrow, however."

This gallows humor was something Roan was not accustomed to. In the south, you said what you meant and meant what you said. If you spoke of someone's death, you were fully prepared to carry it out.

Gwendolyn offered Roan a hand, and he accepted it. As she pulled him to his feet, he marveled at the strength contained within her slender body. Her lips quirked as she released him, stepping back to resume her position beside the metal throne, which was rippling like the surface of a disturbed pond. Roan struggled to hold his head up, his energy sapped.

"Back to business," the king said. "We've been hearing stirrings from the north."

"Wait," Roan said. They'd just watched his lifemark heal him from a fatal sword wound. "What about me?"

The king raised a thick eyebrow. "You bear a skinmark, correct?"

There was clearly no denying it. He nodded. "On my chest."

"Can you heal only yourself, or others too?"

Roan considered lying, but had the sinking feeling they would find a way to uncover the falsehood. They could cut a child wide open and he'd have no choice but to use his power to save her, killing himself in the process. He certainly wouldn't put such an act past Gwendolyn. "I can heal others. But only to a point. Using my mark drains my energy. The more grievous the injury"— he gestured to where the forest dweller had sunk her blade into his flesh—"the more effort it takes." *And if the injury is life-threatening, I shall die in their place.* He held the last part back. They didn't need to know. Not yet.

The king stroked his magnificent beard. "Typically you would be given a choice at this point. Serve the crown, that's me"—he pointed to one of the molded swords atop the crest of his metal helmet—"or live whatever life you choose." He paused, and Roan had the feeling that he wasn't the typical case. "However, you are not from here, so you have no choice. You *will* serve me, or I will display your head on a pike. Does that answer your question?"

This time, there was no humor in his tone, and no one laughed.

Roan nodded.

"Good. Now, we have a battle to plan."

"Battle?" Roan exclaimed. "What battle?"

The king sighed. "Do we have something to seal his lips with?" he asked no one in particular.

"I've been asking the same question all the way from the Barren Marshes," Gareth said.

"Apologies," Roan said, miming the sealing of his lips. "Not another word from me. I'm a fly on the wall, a silent observer, one without a voice box, a mute, the—"

"Village idiot?" Gwendolyn suggested.

Roan shut up.

"Word from the north is that the queen, Sabria Loren Gäric, was executed for high treason," Prince Guy said, running a hand through his long hair.

"Wait," Gareth said. "I heard it was the king who was dead."

"Try to keep up, brother," Guy said. "Streams have been coming in over the last few days. The king was murdered. The queen plotted against him with her son, Prince Archer, who was next in line for the kingship. The king's brother, Lord Griswold, declared himself King Regent, and found them guilty of treason. He had the queen executed, but Archer, the slippery little bugger, managed to escape with his sister, Princess Annise. Apparently two knights escaped with them, a Sir Dietrich of Gearhärt, and a famed warrior known only as the Armored Knight."

"How mysterious," Gareth said.

"Thank you for your valuable comment," Guy said. Roan had to stifle a laugh. He was quite enjoying watching Prince Gareth being bested by his twin. He and Prince Guy Ironclad might just get along.

The king stretched his arms, placing his hands behind the back of his head. "Sons, this is the moment we've waited years for. The north is weak and ripe for a full-scale attack."

"What?" Roan exclaimed, unable to keep his promise to stay quiet. "Why would you risk more lives in a battle with the north?"

The king pressed the heel of his hand against his forehead, as if it had begun to ache.

Gareth said, "The north is as much our enemy as the west. On numerous occasions they've attacked our borders, killing our people, plundering, pillaging, burning our towns. The Dread King might be dead, but who's to say his brother isn't worse?"

Roan shook his head. It was no wonder the Four Kingdoms were forever at war. No one was willing to leave the past where it belonged and look to a peaceful future. "Who's to say he's not better?" Roan countered. "You haven't even spoken to him, haven't even tried to make peace."

The king had had enough of Roan's argument, slamming his fist down on the arm of the throne. "The north killed my brother. Murdered my wife. The north must fall!"

Roan took a step back. He'd heard rumors of Coren Ironclad's death, but nothing about the queen's. As far as he'd known, Queen Henna Ironclad was alive and well. "I didn't know about your wife." He glanced at Gareth, remembering the easygoing way in which the prince had jested about his mother when they were camped in Barrenwood. Now, Gareth stared at his feet. Obviously he'd been trying to cover up the pain he felt, pain that was now laid bare in the tightness of his eyes, the firm set of his jaw. Roan fought back the urge to comfort him. "I'm sorry. How did it happen?"

It was Prince Guy who answered. "Eastern women are as strong as they come," he said. "My mother was never willing to hide in Ferria and let her husband and sons be the only ones in the family to risk their lives. She traveled with the war parties on numerous occasions, offering her skill with bow and sword. Several fortnights ago, our camp was raided in the middle of the night by men bearing the northern sigil. We fought them off, killing most of them, but she didn't . . . she was . . ."

"I'm sorry," Roan said again, though he knew those two words offered little at this particular moment.

"I will avenge Henna's death," the king growled. "Blood for blood. Death for death."

Roan had nothing else to say. Given the anger he could see simmering in the king's eyes, he knew there was nothing he could say to change his mind. War was inevitable.

"Where will we attack?" Gareth asked. "The Black Cliffs? We lost thousands on the Razor the last time."

"No," the king said. "We go for the heart. We aim for Raider's Pass. And this time we have a secret weapon."

Roan almost asked "What?" again but then noticed the way everyone in the room turned to stare at him.

∾

"I'll behave; you really don't have to—" *Slam!* The metal door to his cell shuddered as one of Prince Gareth's men left Roan alone. Torchlight flickered through the small barred window in the door.

Evidently the soft bed he'd ordered had been substituted for a lumpy mattress stained with a reddish-brown substance he really didn't want to think about.

Exhausted, he slumped against the metal wall, sliding to the ground. "Dragons," he muttered. *How did I get here?* he wondered. Not a fortnight past he was just another browbeaten lad on the streets of Calypso, and then . . . the Beggar touched him. He remembered the way the shiva had recoiled as the plague rose from Roan's skin. In a way, seeing that fear in his eyes was almost worth everything he'd gone through. Almost.

The door eased open without so much as a creak, and a shadow slipped inside his cell. Roan started to rise, to defend himself, but then saw who it was and sank back down.

"You don't fear me?" Gwendolyn said. Her golden eyes shimmered in the torchlight, making her look even more wild.

"You've already shot me with an arrow, beaten me senseless, and gutted me. What else can you do?"

"Quite a lot," Gwendolyn said cryptically. A lock of silver hair fell across her eyes and she pushed it away, tucking it behind her ear. "I missed with the arrow on purpose, you were already senseless *before* I beat you, and my sword stroke was a mere flesh wound."

Roan gaped. "A flesh wound? I felt your blade go *through* my back."

Gwendolyn waved his remark away. "If I'd wanted to kill you, I'd have cut off your head or stabbed you through the heart. I'm guessing your mark wouldn't be able to help much with those sorts of injuries." She handed him a metal plate.

Roan was pretty sure she was right, but he wasn't about to test out her theory. He accepted the platter, which contained an enormous smoked fish, its buggy eye staring up at him. His stomach rumbled and clenched at the same time.

He swiftly placed the plate on the floor, pushing it away.

"Not hungry?" Gwendolyn asked.

Instead of answering, Roan asked, "How did you know I bore a tattooya?"

"Tattooya," Gwen scoffed. "What a barbaric word."

"It's as good as any," Roan said. He repeated the question, switching the word for the one more common to the east. "How did you know I bore a *skinmark*?"

"I didn't, but I had my suspicions."

Roan scoffed. "So you risked my life on a suspicion?" He shook his head. He tried to reconcile the strong violent woman standing before him with the sensitive caring girl he'd seen hug the diseased man they called Bark. There was something intriguing about her . . .

"I was right, wasn't I? I've been watching you. How you could barely walk after a day of riding, but seemed a new man the next morning."

"Maybe I got a good night's rest!" Roan protested. Inwardly, he chided himself for using his lifemark during the journey east.

Gwendolyn ignored him. "And then when I attacked you in Ironwood, they should've had to carry you to the castle, but mere moments later you were ripe for walking again."

"I'm a Southroner. I'm tough."

"Not that tough."

"Fine. But how did you know I could heal a grievous wound? You could've given me a scratch and proved the same thing."

She grinned, cat-like in the gloom. "I didn't know. I wanted to give you sufficient motivation to use your gift. Also, it *was* more fun that way, wasn't it?"

Roan kicked the plate further away, the smell of smoked flesh more nauseating than before. "Look, I get that you hate me because I'm from Calypso, but I'm not the ghost of Roan Sandes."

She froze at the name. Her response was a growl. "I know that." Roan started to speak, but she cut him off. "And I don't hate you."

"Gwendolyn—"

"Gwen."

"Gwen. I know nothing about your people, the Orians, but I have nothing against your kind."

Her lips curled. "My kind?"

He blew out a frustrated huff. "Aye, your ancestors. The metal people, or whatever."

"Metal people?" Her eyebrows rose. "We are more than the ore we sow, just as your people are more than dust and sun."

"You believe that?"

She nodded. "Yes. Despite what Gareth might have told you, I don't hate the Southroners because of what happened to my—I despise the empire and what it stands for, but that doesn't mean the fruit are as rotten as the tree."

"Wait, I'm confused, am I the tree or the fruit?" Roan said, grinning.

A flicker of amusement crossed her face, before winking out like a star disappearing behind a cloud.

"You don't come across as a Southroner," she said, furrowing her silver eyebrows.

Roan held his expression steady. "My guardian taught me much of the west. Because of my—"

"Father. Aye. So you've said. But why would your guardian teach you of the west when it was your father who abandoned you?"

Roan was careful with the next words he spoke. "He believed ancestry was important."

"And what do you believe?"

"I don't truly know. I don't feel connected to anywhere. Not the south. Not the west. My home is wherever I happen to be at the moment."

"Your home is a dungeon?"

Roan smiled. "Aye. It's nice and cool, and if I lean just the right way the stones feel like a goose-feather mattress."

Gwen chewed on her lip, staring at Roan for so long he began to feel uncomfortable. Finally, after what felt like an eternity, she said, "Eat. You'll need to keep up your energy for the next couple of days."

"Why? What's happening in two days?"

"As soon as sufficient supplies have been procured and packed, we ride for Raider's Pass."

With that, she slipped out as stealthily as she'd entered.

Roan wrinkled his nose, but it wasn't because of the fishy smell that permeated his cell. By the time the first moon was full in the night sky, he'd be closer to his true home than he'd been since the day he was born.

That's when he finally realized what he had to do. He had to go home and face his real father, once and for all. It was something he'd been avoiding his entire life, something he always knew, in his heart, he'd have to do in order to make his mother's sacrifice worthwhile.

He needed to escape and flee west, even if it forced his father to kill him.

Because doing so could change everything.

ℒ

The next day Roan was permitted to go for two walks to stretch his legs and ensure they didn't atrophy before the long ride ahead of him.

To his surprise, his first escort was Prince Gareth. "If you try to run, I'll stab you through the heart," the prince said when he opened Roan's cell door.

"No, you won't," Roan said, following Gareth out. "Like your father said, my skill will be needed for the battle against the north."

To Roan's delight, Gareth didn't respond. He'd called his bluff, a fact which gave Roan great pleasure.

The dark corridor led to a metal gate, which was opened by an armored guardsman wielding a dual-edged axe. The sharp edges of his lips seemed to mirror the shape of his weapon, and Roan felt uncomfortable until they were well out of his line of sight.

As before, the castle was abuzz with activity. Carts laden with sacks of food were being hauled in one direction by muscled steeds, directed to various parts of the castle by a small man with a wispy goatee and a baritone voice so loud it could be heard over the clash of soldiers' weapons as they trained. Along one edge of the wall, swords were being sharpened, while along the other side armor was being polished to a gleaming shine. Several broad-shouldered women were pumping an iron crank and water was bubbling from the ground—originating from a deep-earth well perhaps. They filled skin after skin with the water, tossing the sealed pouches in another cart, which was already piled high.

They're preparing to ride to battle, Roan thought. Just as Gwendolyn had told him.

"Must you stare at everything?" Gareth said, keeping one arm on Roan's elbow as they strolled along the castle wall, sticking to a line of shade cast by the enormous metal-and-tree barrier.

"Excuse me?" Roan said. He hadn't realized he'd been staring.

"Why? Did you pass wind?"

Roan shook his head and made a greater effort to offer only fleeting glances at the activity around him. Even more impressive than the sheer number of men, women, horses, carts, barrows, weapons, and sacks that he saw, was the level of organization. Everyone involved seemed to know exactly what to do and when, and where to go once they were finished. It was a far cry from the utter chaos of Calypso with which he was so familiar.

They passed through a break in the wall, moving into the second castle ring. It was quieter here, and Roan studied the metal walls, which were formed between enormous, iron-sheathed trees. The surface of the barriers seemed to ripple, almost like water disturbed by raindrops.

"You are like a child," Gareth said. "Everything amazes you."

Roan couldn't deny the fact that he *was* amazed. "In the south, metal is metal. It doesn't move, and can only be shaped by a blacksmith's forge under extreme heat."

"Seems like an awful lot of effort," Gareth said. "We have near on two-hundred Orians in the castle employ. They maintain the walls, transforming them to suit my father's needs. They work in shifts, so there are always at least two score ready to seal the gates if Ferria is attacked. Additional implements can be quickly added to the castle defenses if necessary—spiked walls, higher turrets, slits to shoot arrows from. Whatever we need."

Roan was duly impressed. Somewhere in his memory he recalled something about an attack on Ferria, but he thought it was a long time ago. He ran a finger along the wall, and the metal seemed to feel him back, like it was alive. He remembered: "The Dragon Massacre," he said.

"Yes," Gareth confirmed. "The last attack on Ferria was over eighty years ago. Your people, the Calypsians, came with dragonfire and death, killing thousands of my people. The wall was just a metal wall back then. It was because of the massacre that my grandfather added an army of Orians to maintain the wall."

Roan swallowed thickly. Though he hadn't been born then, and wouldn't have participated in such violence anyway, he still felt ashamed at what his people had done. No one should have to face a dragon in battle—he knew that better than most.

"I'm sorry," Roan said.

Gareth laughed his apology away, as if talk of the massacre of his ancestors was light conversation. "No matter. In a way, it was an Oresend. The attack made us stronger, more prepared. Would you like a demonstration?"

Based on the way the prince's lips were curled up on the side, Roan was pretty sure he should decline, but he was too curious. He nodded.

Gareth craned his head back and gazed at the top of the wall, where a woman stood, her armor reflecting blades of sunlight. The prince raised a hand and flicked his fingers. There was a metallic shriek, like two blades scraping against each other, and something slashed past Roan. He let out a frightened *yip* and dove for the ground. He rolled over and looked up to find a spike protruding from the wall, a scrap of his shirt dangling from the sword-like point.

Gods, he thought. *No invading army would ever stand a chance against such defenses.*

His gaze stretched past the spike to the top of the wall, but the Orian woman was gone.

❧

Back in Roan's cell, the prince said, "Did you enjoy your walk?" Gareth stood just inside the entrance to the shadowy room, leaning against the doorframe. Even in the dim lighting, his face was exquisite, without blemish, like a painting. Roan could criticize a lot about the prince, but his allure was undeniable. From what Roan's guardian had told him, just thinking something like that in the west could get you in trouble with the furia. But it was different in the south, where beauty and attraction were not limited to one gender. He wasn't certain where the east fell on the subject, but he wasn't about to find out.

The prince raised an eyebrow. "Is there something on my face?" He reached up to touch his cheek.

Roan flinched, realizing he'd been staring. "No. Well yes. Your finger."

"Hilarious." The prince turned to go.

"Sorry, it's a habit of mine."

The prince turned back. "What?"

"Jokes, japes, quips. It's easier sometimes."

"Easier than what?"

Roan shrugged. "Facing reality."

Gareth's eyes met his, and for the first time, Roan felt like he saw something behind them. Something more than a spoiled, obnoxious, arrogant prince. Just as quickly, the amused twinkle returned and Gareth said, "I could see that. If I were you I wouldn't want to face reality either." He spun on his heel and left, slamming and locking the door behind him.

Roan sighed. He supposed he got what he deserved for trying to have a serious conversation with a royal.

Gareth had delivered Roan back to his cell just in time for lunch, which consisted of two pieces of bread smashed together with a thin slice of meat of unknown origin. After the prince left, Roan pinched the meat between two fingers and deposited it in the corner of the small space where a hungry mouse might find it. He wiped his fingers on his pants, and then ate the bread slowly, trying not to think about the fact that it had touched cooked meat.

Thankfully, he was able to choke the meal down, chasing it with a few swigs from a waterskin he'd been provided. All in all, he was being treated reasonably well considering he was from the south. He wondered if that would change if they knew he wasn't as useful to them as they previously thought. Also, he'd made no attempt to escape. Yet. When he did, he feared the treatment would be far harsher in the event he was caught.

Which was why he wasn't planning on getting caught.

ॐ

After his meal, Roan dozed for a few hours, until his cell door clanked open once more. This time his escort was Gwen, and she seemed to take no joy in the task, waving him out the door without so much as a single word.

When they'd left the dungeons and moved out into the late afternoon sun, which was already casting long shadows across the castle grounds, Roan said, "Where are we going?"

"I want to show you something."

"I've already seen all of the rings of the castle," Roan said. "The prince was even kind enough to give me a firsthand demonstration of the wall's defenses. Though I was almost impaled in the process."

"You could have healed yourself anyway," Gwen said, smiling slightly at the prospect of him being skewered. "But we're not touring the castle. We'll leave through the western gate, which I've arranged to be opened."

Roan's eyebrows shot up. "The king trusts me outside the castle walls?"

Gwen laughed. "With me? Aye. You are no more dangerous than an ore kitten."

Roan tried to think of a retort, but came up empty. He'd seen the way she could move. Any notion of escape while under her guard was a fool's mission.

As she'd promised, the western gate opened for them, melting and sliding away. Gwen raised a hand in thanks to whomever had controlled it—an Orian, presumably—though Roan couldn't see anyone.

The western gate didn't lead into the town of Ferria; rather, a long metal-lined path led into Ironwood, the branches so thick overhead that it became difficult to see the sky. As they walked, Roan squinted at the trees, which seemed to be . . . there was no other word for it . . . *melting*.

Gwen noticed Roan's gaze. "The liquid ore is pulled from the ground by the trees' roots. It is what sustains them. Sheathes them with armor."

"But I thought it was your people who controlled the ore."

Gwen's eyebrows arched. "Control the ore? No. The ore controls itself. We can only channel it if it allows us to. There is a mutual respect between the forest, the ore, and its inhabitants. If that respect is ever shattered, I fear the ore will destroy us all."

Suddenly, Roan didn't feel so safe in the wood.

"Come," Gwen said, beckoning him forward. They walked, side by side, for a long while. Roan was lost in his thoughts. The east was so different than the south he could hardly believe the two places eventually connected with each other. The land in the south seemed to be in constant war with its people. Relentlessly, the dunes tried to press in on Calypso, piling high on the dwellings, whipping through every crack and crevice. Until arriving in the east, Roan couldn't remember a day without the constant taste of gritty sand on his tongue and between his teeth. Even the sun in the south was different, a hot blade knifing down during the day.

In the east, there was no battle between the land and its people. They were allies, determined to coexist peacefully. It was like a smaller version of what Roan wished the Four Kingdoms could be.

Eventually, Gwen veered to the right and led Roan along a smaller path into an even deeper, darker portion of the woods. Metallic vines hung from the trees, curling like the tentacles of an ancient sea creature. On the edge of his vision, Roan swore he saw the glint of round orbs amongst the foliage, but anytime he tried to look directly at them, they disappeared.

"Did you see something?" Gwen asked. There was the hint of a smile playing on her lips.

"Eyes," Roan said, realizing what they were.

"Just a trick of the light." But, of course, there was very little light this deep in the woods.

They came to a barrier, a metal gate that reached high into the trees. It was split into two halves. One half was a series of swords, soldered together, their points aiming skyward. The other half was of leaf and flower, and words were carved into the metal. Roan started to read the first line—*Night black, day bright*—but Gwen said, "These words are not for your eyes," and steered his gaze away. The gate opened, swinging before them without so much as a creak or groan.

Light bloomed before Roan's eyes, glittering like diamonds on every surface. He blinked, spots dancing across his vision, explosions of orange, white, and yellow. Cupping a hand and using it to shield his face, he cracked his eyelids, still blinking rapidly.

Slowly, slowly, things began to clarify, coming into focus.

They were in a small, circular clearing, spotlighted by the sun, which had a little daylight left before dusk. The ground was metal, but multi-faceted, like a well-cut gemstone. Each facet caught the light on a different angle, which accounted for the sparkling. In the clearing was a single tree, large, but not as enormous as some of the other trees Roan had seen in Ironwood. The tree was also shimmering, and etched with the same edges and angles.

Craning his head back, Roan gazed higher, his eyes adjusting to the brightness of this place. Every part of the tree, from the leaves to the branches to the trunk, were metal, the surface of the armor uninterrupted. It was . . .

"Perfection," Roan said. "What is this place?"

"My home," Gwen said.

"You live here?" Roan couldn't have disguised the awe in his tone if he'd wanted to. For some reason he'd assumed she lived somewhere within the bounds of the castle.

"When I'm not scouting."

"Alone?"

Although he'd meant it as a light jest, her yellow eyes darted to his, reflecting iron. "I like being alone."

"I didn't mean—"

"I know. Yes, I live here alone."

"You could have any man or woman in Ironwood," he said.

At that, she smirked. "Or woman?"

"Why not?"

"I don't . . . I'm not . . ."

Roan laughed. "You prefer men."

"Not that it's any of your business, but yes. I prefer men."

"Good thing I'm a man," Roan said.

"Depends on the definition," Gwen said.

Roan laughed again. The Orian was rather a quick-wit when she wasn't trying to impale him with sharp weapons. "Well met," he said. He cast his eyes about the clearing and tree once more. He realized he'd been so distracted by the beauty of the tree and the interplay of the light amongst its iron, he hadn't noticed the hammock hanging between two of its branches, open to the sky, to the light. "What if it rains?"

Gwen didn't respond, striding forward. Something about her gait was different. She seemed more relaxed in this place. Less . . . serious. Like she'd been carrying around a heavy iron yoke that she'd left at the gate. Roan watched her as she deftly climbed the tree, pulling herself from branch to branch, reaching the hammock quickly. She sat on one side, swinging, looking down. A large leaf grew from one of the branches, providing a canopy. "If it rains, the ore shelters me," she said.

Roan didn't move. Something about this place seemed sacred, and he was afraid that if he trod all over the place he would disturb it. He almost regretted his earlier jokes. "What were those words on the gate?" he asked.

Gwen said nothing, but stopped swinging.

Though he hadn't had the chance to read the second line, something about the way the words ebbed and flowed, like water splashing against a shoreline, made Roan think of a book of poems he'd once read. "Was it your poetry?"

Gwen shook her head, but Roan wasn't sure whether it was an answer. "Do you think you can climb this high?" she asked instead.

Not as fast as you, Roan thought, but he said, "Yes." Something occurred to him. "Isn't the metal hot?" Surely being in the sun all day must've heated the iron to an unbearable temperature, but Gwen hadn't so much as hissed through her teeth as she grasped each branch.

"It's only hot if it wants to be hot," Gwen said.

"Does it want to be hot?"

"Not for me. For you . . . I guess we'll find out."

Roan approached the tree, reaching for the lowest branch. The moment his fingers touched the metal, he flinched back, letting out a cry of pain.

"Funny," Gwen said from above.

"How did you know it was a joke?" Roan asked, once more grasping the branch, which was as cool as a wet stone.

"Because of the idiotic look on your face."

Roan pulled himself up. His fingers were sweaty and slippery, and he had to be quick to avoid losing his grip. "That's just my face," Roan said.

"I'm sorry." She didn't sound sorry.

After about triple the time it had taken Gwen, Roan reached the hammock and eased down on the opposite side. The ground spun beneath him—he was higher up than he'd thought. He closed his eyes, waiting for the world to stop spinning, and then opened them. Better.

He glanced at Gwen, who seemed preoccupied. "Why did you bring me to this place? To your home?" Roan asked.

She hesitated, her gaze drifting away, back toward the gate. "To show you my freedom," she said.

Roan thought he understood. She was marked, like him, and yet free. "What does your skinmark do?" he asked.

"You know, in the west there was once another name for the marks," she said. He was growing somewhat tired of how she dodged his questions, but now she had his interest piqued.

"You mean sinmarks? They still call them that."

"Yes. And they execute anyone born with one," Gwen said. There was anger in her tone. "But that's not the word I meant."

"What other word is there?" He wracked his memory for anything else his
guardian might've taught him. Nothing sprang to mind.

"How long did you live in the west?" she asked. Her abrupt change of
subject made his head spin.

"What?"

"You heard me."

She was trying to trick him, which meant she suspected at least one of his
lies. Maybe all of them. "Never," he said. "I was born in the south, and never
left. Well, until now."

Her eyes narrowed, but instead of further questioning, she said, "*Fate*marks.
They called them fatemarks."

Roan frowned. "Why would they call them that?" *And why have I never
heard that word before?*

"The bigger question is: Why did they *stop* calling them that?"

He had the sudden urge to tell her about his past, about the little girl who'd
broken her leg. What his guardian had done to her. How he'd been unable to
do anything to stop it from happening. How he'd *caused* it. His mouth opened.
Closed. Opened again. "I lost someone once," he started. A huge empty space
opened up in his mind, and he wasn't sure how to fill it. With his mother? His
father? His guardian? Those two poor kids he barely knew?

"You know nothing of loss," Gwen snapped, her eyes darting back to meet
his. Though they were still yellow around the edges, the black centers had
grown, obliterating much of the color. "You are but a child next to the lifetime
I've already lived, the loved ones I've lost."

He knew she meant her father, perhaps her mother, too, but were they the
only ones? Something about the poetry on the gate made him think there was
someone else.

"There are children who know loss better than those on their death beds,"
Roan said. He wasn't angry, just certain. Regardless of what she'd lost, he'd lost
too. Maybe they were more alike than either of them knew.

The world flipped as Gwen rocked the hammock upside down, spilling
him out. His stomach did a somersault as he fell toward the unforgiving metal
ground. Just when he thought he would break every bone in his body, a strong
hand caught his own flailing fingers, stopping his descent. He hung, dangling
in the orange light, staring up at Gwen.

"I shouldn't have brought you here," she said. "It was a mistake."

Roan felt solid ground under his boots, and when he turned his gaze downward, his eyes widened. A platform had risen from the clearing, reaching up to secure him. Gwen released him and the platform descended. Above him, Gwen sank into the hammock, rocking slightly.

Roan left, the gate opening before him. He didn't stop to read the poem carved into the front. Like Gwen had said, it wasn't for him. He didn't stop until it was dark and he arrived back in his cell, which the guard closed behind him.

Chapter Fifteen

The Western Kingdom | Knight's End

Rhea Loren

Oh Wrath, what have I done? Rhea thought when her father told her the news.

The king paced back and forth, his white robe of purity trailing behind him. He wore an expression that was hard to describe, a mixture of concentration and surprise. Her twin younger siblings, Bea and Leo, stood off to one side, practically bouncing with excitement. It wasn't every day that one of the sinmarked was discovered. "Because of *you*, my princess, my daughter, we have captured a major threat to our city," the king said.

Paintings of Wrath's golden eye hung on the stone walls, flanked by banners bearing the royal sigil of the west—the rearing stallion. Wrath's eye seemed to bore into her, reading her mind and her heart, condemning her the same way her father condemned the city's criminals.

There was something stuck in Rhea's throat. As they did with all criminals, the furia had examined Grease Jolly's sister from head to toe under torchlight. To Rhea's surprise, they'd found a mark on her palm.

"What will happen to her?" Rhea asked. Memories of the city gates swarmed through her head. She'd expected to feel good about getting her revenge on Grease Jolly, triumphant even, but instead she'd felt only empty inside as he'd reached for his sister's hands, desperation and fear in his eyes. She didn't even know he *had* a sister. *Would it have changed anything?* she asked herself. She liked to think it would have, but in her heart she knew her anger was a fire that wouldn't have been easily sated.

Her father stopped pacing to look at her. "The law is clear on this matter," he said matter-of-factly, though his expression was weary. Rhea had expected him to look . . . *happier.*

She wanted to argue with him, to point out that Grease's sister was just a child, no more than thirteen or fourteen name days old, but the words wouldn't come. And even if they had, she knew they would mean nothing to her father. To him the sinmarks and those who bore them were an enemy to Wrath, to the holiness of the city. He was doing Wrath's work, and none could convince him otherwise.

Oh Grease, I'm so sorry, she thought.

"Can we watch?" Bea asked, her turquoise eyes sparkling like the waters of Bounty under the light of the morning sun. Her sister was quickly becoming a lovely woman, perhaps even more attractive than Rhea, a fact that made her dislike Bea even more.

"Yes, Father, can we?" Leo echoed, pushing his long golden hair out of his eyes. Lately, her younger brother had become obsessed with learning about the various punishments carried out by the furia.

Rhea's stomach heaved, and she had to take a deep swallow to keep from vomiting.

"You will *all* be present for the burning," King Loren said. "You must learn what it takes to keep the Holy City holy."

"Like when the furia burned down the brothels of the East End with the whores inside?" Leo said, his eyes wide and shining.

The king approached his only son, roping an arm around his shoulders. "Somewhat," he said. "Those brothels were an infected gash on the skin of the Holy City, yes, but they were only the sins of humans. This girl, this demon, is not of our world. Her heart is black and shriveled, and until she is extinguished, none of us can rest easy."

"I hate her," Leo said.

"Me too," mimicked Bea, plucking at one of her blond ringlets. "Don't you, Rhea?"

Rhea had no choice but to nod thinly, bile burning the back of her throat. *What have I done?* she asked herself again.

Chapter Sixteen

The Western Kingdom | Knight's End

Grease Jolly

"Let my sister go," Grease said. "She had nothing to do with any of this."

The two furia standing before him didn't speak, didn't move, didn't blink. Truth be told, they were starting to give him the creeps, even more than the enormous depiction of Wrath's golden eye staring down from the ceiling. The eye was ringed with fire, and seemed to be burning through him with each passing moment.

Ever since Princess Rhea had pointed him out at the city gates, he'd been told nothing. He was separated from his sister and brought to the Temple of Confession, hauled to this cavernous space, where the vaulted stone ceiling hung like a stormy sky, and stripped to his underclothes. The walls were covered in sins, scrawled by the faithful seeking forgiveness.

I bore false words to my wife.

I lusted after the baker's daughter.

I spoke ill of my father.

Some of the truths were written in dark, shaky letters, perhaps smudged with wet ash, while others were red and thin and gave Grease the shivers. Worse still were the words carved directly into the stone, shallow grooves that spoke of violent crimes.

Cut out her filthy throat.

Gutted the nasty child like a pig.

Beat him, beat him, beat him bloody.

Grease shivered.

"I'm cold," he said. "Can I please have my clothes?"

The furia didn't move, didn't react. Grease wondered whether his thoughts had made it to his lips.

"Please," he said, begging now. He'd screwed up, but he couldn't live with himself if anything happened to Shae. "I'm the thief. Punish me. Confine me to the stockades. Just let her—"

One of the furia pushed back her red hood to reveal an expressionless face. He was taken aback by her pristine skin, her piercing eyes, her sunrise-red hair; he had to admit that the woman was almost as eye-pleasing as Princess Rhea. She moved so fast that Grease didn't have a chance to defend himself. Her foot swept behind him, kicking out the back of his legs and bringing him to his knees.

He grunted, squinting through the web of long, tangled hair that fell into his face. The furia who had struck him was back in position as if nothing had happened. He opened his mouth to speak again, and then thought better of it. He pushed the hair away from his eyes and waited.

After a while, his knees began to throb, but when he tried to stand, the other furia glided forward and swung her fist in an arc. Again, he was too slow to block the attack, her knuckles colliding with his jaw, rocking him back.

Half-naked, lying on the cold, hard ground, he rubbed his jaw. He'd been in plenty of street fights, but had never been hit like that. Slowly, shielding his face with his arms, he sat up, returning to kneeling position.

The furia ignored him once more. Eons passed, his bruised face pounding, his knees aching, the confessions of sinners seeming to scream at him from the walls.

Thief!

Fornicator!

Thief!

Fornicator!

Thief Thief THIEF!

And then the wooden door opened and his heart stopped.

They were actually here. Not the foot soldiers, but the generals themselves, the Furies. The moment they entered, the two furia parted to let them pass, closing ranks as soon as their holy masters were clear.

The Three wore no hoods, their hair as red as hungry flames. They were all as attractive as their foot soldiers, but in a harsh way, their jaws angled and strong, their eyes dark and fierce. Grease tried to hold their gaze, but eventually looked away.

"You have been accused," the one in the center said. "Confess your sins!"

Her bark made Grease flinch.

Grease didn't try to deny it—there was no point. All that mattered was his sister. "I am a thief," he said. "I will accept my punishment. Five days in the stocks. Ten? Name it."

The two Furies on the sides laughed. The one in the center did not. "Stupid boy," she said. "Our punishment is not of men, it is of Wrath."

Something about the way she said it made Grease want to punch *himself* in the face. "I will accept it," he said.

"Yes. You will. Which hand do you use to steal with?"

The question took him aback. "What? I don't know. My left usually—"

The third Fury grabbed him by his neck, shoving him to the ground. The second Fury jammed a knee into his chest, pushing all her weight on him until he could hardly breathe.

And the first Fury, the one who had spoken, forced his left arm flush against the cold stone. She raised a hand, gripping a blade, its sharp edge glinting in the colored light refracting through the temple's mosaic windows.

"No!" Grease shouted, but it came out as a squeal, his windpipe pinched.

Her arm came down. Her blade came down.

Grease screamed.

Darkness swept in like a black tide of unconsciousness. A kindness, under the circumstances.

≈

Grease awoke from the nightmare shivering and panting, trying to catch his breath. He felt cold, so cold, and yet sweat pooled on his face, stinging his eyes. *Oh gods, oh gods, oh gods. Shae!* He needed to wake Shae up and get them the hell out of the Holy City. Forget the main gates—he'd take them down the coastline, past the Cryptlands.

He tried to rise, but something held him back. He blinked in the dim lighting, trying to figure out what was happening. Thick leather straps ran across his body, securing his chest, arms, torso, and legs.

"What in Wrath's name?" he said.

Someone sniffled in the dark.

"Who's there?" Grease said.

"Oh, Wrath, I'm sorry," someone whimpered. "I didn't know. I was so angry."

That voice. *That voice.* "Rhea?"

"I didn't know what they would do. I thought they'd lock you up, make you do penance for your crimes. I didn't know . . ."

Oh gods. Grease didn't want to look, but knew he had to. He lifted his right hand high enough so he could see it, flexing his fingers. He cocked his head and tilted his gaze to the left, raising his other—

The stump was wrapped in white cloth, the blood soaking through in several spots.

Bile rose up in Grease's throat, so fast he couldn't swallow it back down. The vomit dribbled down his chin, staining his already filthy shirt.

Not possible. Not real. A wicked nightmare. Had to be. It didn't even *hurt*. A trick. They'd played a trick. A mean, nasty trick to teach him a lesson, one he would pretend to learn and then be on his way, off to another town, his sister in tow.

"Where is Shae?" he asked. Something throbbed along his left wrist, but he ignored it. If he didn't look at it, it wasn't real.

"Is that her name? I swear I didn't know about your sister. Please forgive me," Rhea said. He could just make out her slumped form in the corner of the small room. She was still wearing her black dress of mourning. She'd never looked so vulnerable, so pathetic, a far cry from the seductress he'd always known her to be. She didn't look or sound like a woman grown anymore. She was just a broken girl.

"You're forgiven," Grease said quickly. A rutting lie. He'd never forgive her if something happened to Shae. He was feeling lightheaded, the room starting to spin. Pain lanced up his arm. "Just tell me where my sister is." *Please. Please. Before I pass out. I have to know.*

"You shouldn't have left me in the crypts. I was scared. That scream . . ."

"I know. I was wrong. I'm sorry." Spots flashed before his eyes, blinking like dying gold stars.

"I forgive you, too."

"Princess." He was pleading now. "Tell me. Where is she?"

"They killed her," Rhea said.

Not real not real not real.

"Oh Wrath, I didn't mean your sister," Rhea said. "I'm sorry. I'm sorry. I'm sorry . . ."

I didn't mean your sister. Grease clung to those words like a man adrift in the ocean with only a single wooden plank to keep him afloat. The princess continued to apologize, her voice rising hysterically. "Stop," Grease said, blinking away the spots obscuring his vision. Rhea clamped her mouth shut, her wet eyes locking on his. "Who did they kill?"

"My aunt," Rhea said. "The queen in the north."

Grease blinked. *What?* "How? Why?"

"They blamed her for the Dread King's death. They executed her. They killed her!"

"I'm—I'm sorry," Grease said, not knowing what else to say.

"My father is livid," she went on. "There is talk of revenge. Of war. Everything is falling apart. We should've left together last night. We should've gone away from this horrid city and sailed across the great ocean and found another life. A *better* life."

This was the girl Grease had fallen for. Spontaneous. Half-crazy. Rebellious. But that was over the moment she pointed her accusing finger at him at the city gates and involved his sister. All kindness left his tone. "We didn't leave," Grease said. "Where is my sister?"

Princess Rhea covered her face with her hands. Her body shook silently. A shadow entered Grease's body, twisting and thickening and squeezing around his heart, which seemed to slow in his chest. The world was fading to black again. Blessed, blessed darkness.

"They found it," Rhea said.

No. Gods, no. Anything but that. His denial was gone, torn away by the truth of Rhea's words. *Take my other hand. Take my head. Take me me me me . . .*

"They found her mark," Rhea said, and then she rose and fled from the room, her sobs echoing into eternity.

Chapter Seventeen

The Northern Kingdom | The Howling Tundra

Annise Gäric

Something wasn't right. Well, something besides the fact that Annise was wandering an endless tundra with a witch-cursed knight who'd once been her childhood friend. She couldn't quite put her finger on it, but whatever was eluding her mind kept gnawing away at her as they trudged through the snow, which was up to Annise's knees and Arme's—Tarin's—armored calves.

It wasn't her half-empty stomach either, although that clearly wasn't right. She knew she was in trouble when the snow started to look like icing on an enormous poppy seed cake.

She stopped. Tarin's long strides carried him a bit further before he realized she wasn't beside him anymore. He turned and said, "What is it?"

"We're going back," she said.

"To where? Castle Hill?"

"No. To the edge of this hellfrozen tundra. And then we're heading south for Gearhärt. We're going to find my brother." *And then we can escape north. Together.*

"It's not safe," Tarin said.

"And this is? Do you even know where we are? This is my life, my decision, and we are turning around. Immediately."

"No."

She gritted her teeth. She hated the way he always said things with such finality, like her opinion mattered little and less. She didn't care that they'd shared body warmth, or had a strange moment of truth. She could consider all that later, if at all. Now she had to take matters into her own hands.

"Stop me." She whirled around and sprinted in the opposite direction. Well, more like *slogged*, her boots clomping through the snow. She heard his heavy feet give chase, and she waited until she could sense him almost upon her.

She dropped flat to the snow. Tarin let out a surprised cry and tripped over her, rattling like a tin can dropped down a staircase. Annise was up in an instant, taking advantage of the opportunity. She already had a handful of snow, which she shoved through his eye slit, not caring if she poked his eyes a little in the process. She even added a solid kick to his armored ribs.

He flailed, scrubbing at his eyes, but she didn't stop to watch. She was off and running. She knew he would catch up eventually, but by then she hoped he'd have reconsidered. It was a foolish, desperate plan, but it was all she had.

She hazarded a glance back. Tarin was still down, prying off his helmet. She almost stopped to look—she desperately wanted to see his face—but then remembered how defiant he was when she'd seen just his hand.

Spinning around, she charged onwards.

Just in front of her, an enormous white form rose up from a snowdrift, unleashing a roar that rattled her frozen bones. She tried to stop, but her feet skidded on the ice, kicking out from under her. Gravity did the rest, slamming her down violently on her tailbone.

By then, the massive ice bear loomed over her, rearing up on its hind legs, slicing the air to ribbons with its razor-sharp front claws. Its gaping jaws revealed a row of glistening fang-like teeth. The white-furred monster was twice the size of Tarin, although Annise couldn't help but notice they had a similar disposition.

She tried to scoot back, but slammed into a drift, chunks of frozen snow raining down on her face. Without other options, she rolled just as the bear slammed its paws onto the ice where she'd been a moment earlier.

Leaning back, she kicked out with all her might, connecting solidly with the beast's head.

This seemed only to enrage it even more. It lunged for her, snarling, raking a claw across her face. Heat bloomed like a snowflake flower on her cheek as she was knocked back. She slid along the ice, blood dripping from her chin.

She tried to stand, but her feet slipped again. The bear seemed to have no such problem, its claws digging into the ice as it propelled itself toward her, its black eyes focused on its meal.

Annise finally found her footing, diving to the right, the creature punching her shoulder as it flew past. She grunted and twisted into another fall as graceful as a one-legged woman learning to dance the Northern Jaunt.

It was desperation time, and Annise was always willing to cheat rather than lose a fight. She squatted in the snow, her heart racing, her chest heaving, her shoulder throbbing, her face bleeding. She packed iceballs as tightly as she could, ignoring the pain and fear. When the bear charged, she let loose a barrage, pelting it in the face, in the eyes, in the mouth. All those years growing up in the snowy north with a pack of bratty lordlings as her only companions were finally paying off. Arch would be proud.

The ice bear squealed, rearing up, its forepaws swatting fruitlessly at the air, trying to ward off this new attack that it clearly didn't understand. "Eat ice, bear," Annise screamed through gritted teeth, hitting another bullseye.

The bear shook its head, whipped around, and took off, loping along the frozen ground with long heavy strides. A full retreat. For now, at least.

A moment later, Tarin came running up, his black helmet back on his head, though it was still crusted with hard-packed snow. "What in the frozen hell are you?" he said.

"A princess of the north," Annise said. "Nice of you to show up, *protector*. Now stay the frozen hell out of my way—I'm going back."

She stomped off, soaking up the blood on her face with the snow left in her hand.

❧

"I could tell the story, but no one would ever believe me," Tarin said, walking beside her.

"I don't care," Annise said. Her shoulder was killing her, her face was stinging, and the injury to her tailbone was worse than she'd originally thought, but still . . . she *did* care. She cared that Tarin was finally listening to her, that he wouldn't stop talking about her victory over the ice bear. She cared deeply, but refused to show it. She wasn't sure why.

"I'm sorry," Tarin said.

Her head jerked toward him. She wasn't used to hearing apologies. "For what?"

"For . . . your mother."

Annise sighed, unable to maintain the fire that had raged in her belly since her encounter with the bear. She stayed silent, unsure what to say.

"I hate myself for it," he went on. "She was a wonderful person, inside and out."

Annise could keep silent no longer. "I didn't even know her. To the very end, she was a stranger to me."

"She shouldn't be," Tarin said.

Annise frowned. "Why not? She barely spoke to me." The memory of the last time her mother spoke to her, in the tower of mirrors, played in her mind.

I'm sorry I couldn't be there for you. It was the only way I knew how to protect you. I wish I'd been better. Stronger. You are better, you are stronger. And I'm so proud of you.

"You're wrong," Tarin said. "Your mother isn't a stranger to you. I see so much of her in you."

Annise scoffed. She scraped her knotted black hair through her fingers. "Yes, my hair is looking particularly sunny this time of year. And I think I've shed two stones since we started walking across the tundra." She sashayed her hips like she'd seen other girls do as they walked past the lordlings.

Tarin shook his head. "You have her eyes," he said.

She opened her mouth to contradict him, but he held up a hand. "Not the color, the intensity. When your mother put her mind to something, she did it. Like saving you and your brother. She was determined. And here we are."

Annise wanted to jest, to laugh his words away, but her desire to know more overwhelmed her usual quick tongue. "What else?" she asked.

Though she couldn't see it, she was sure Tarin smiled beneath his mask. "Your stubbornness."

Annise rolled her eyes, but couldn't argue with that. They continued on, and again Annise felt the gnawing, some important truth eluding her.

"You defeated a bear. An *ice* bear," Tarin said after a while. "I still can't believe it."

"It's not like I killed it." Playing it down. Smiling on the inside, grinning through the pain.

He shook his head. "You are something else." It was the most she'd heard him talk, sounding more like the energetic boy she knew growing up. The thought made her incredibly sad.

Nibble nibble. Gnaw gnaw.

It hit her and she slammed to a stop.

This time Tarin was ready, echoing her movements. She let loose a string of imaginative curses and Tarin took a step back, as if afraid he would become her next victim. Or perhaps appalled at her language, which was decidedly unladylike. Then again, she was no lady, something she'd proven time and time again.

Frozen hell. It was no wonder it had taken her so long to realize something so important. Her entire life she'd assumed that by the time the Dread King was dead and gone, Arch would already be of age. The laws were clear: the eldest male son had rights to the throne once he came of age, at eighteen, only after both his parents—the king and queen—were deceased. Eldest daughters be damned. Because her father always seemed invincible, Annise had never considered the possibility that this law could work in her favor, in the event that Wolfric Gäric the First died early. And even then, her mother would've become the ruling monarch in her father's stead.

But that's not what happened, and no one else had given her the slightest consideration, not even her uncle. Because she wasn't of age, either. She was only seventeen when her father died and her mother was executed.

Now, however, she was counting days.

"Princess?" Tarin said.

"Annise," Annise said.

"Annise. What is it? What's wrong?"

Annise's face was starting to hurt from the deepness of her frown amidst the biting cold. She recounted just to make sure, but she came up with the same answer. Today was *the* day. Her eighteenth name day. She was finally of age and both her father and mother were dead.

She closed her eyes.

Her eyes flashed open.

"I am the queen."

෴

"Your uncle will realize the truth soon enough," Tarin said, leagues later. Finally—*finally*—Annise could make out the end of the infernal tundra. She looked forward to the cover of trees and rolling hills, blocking the frigid wind's eternal sting.

"Yes," she agreed.

"He will hunt you down."

"Yes."

"He will try to kill you, or accuse you of the same treason he laid on your brother."

"Yes."

Annise felt numb, and not from the cold. This was never her plan. She never wanted this. She never even wanted to be a princess, much less the Queen of the North.

Annise shook her head. "It doesn't matter. None of it. Not my name day. Not coming of age. Not my claim. Lord Griswold has already usurped power, and I will support Arch as he tries to reclaim the crown." It wasn't what she truly wanted, but it was better than claiming the throne herself.

Tarin's gloved hand slid down her arm to her fingers. She stared at it, wanting to squeeze his fingers so badly, but instead let her hand drop to her side. "Queen, the laws don't work that way," he said.

"Don't you start calling me that. I'm Annise. Not princess. Not queen. Annise."

"How about Bear-Slayer?"

Annise couldn't hold back her smile. "Although I must point out that I didn't actually kill the bear, I will accept that. It's better than Mamoothen Queen of the North."

"Stop," Tarin said. "You are too hard on yourself. You are—you are—"

Annise held her breath, trying to fill in the blank left by his unspoken words. There were so many words she wished he would say—could say—but she knew they were impossible and untrue.

"Strong," he finished, which wasn't the worst word he could've chosen. "You are strong, Bear-Slayer. Like your mother."

"Or I just played Snow Wars too much as a child," Annise said.

"Regardless, the north needs someone strong."

"My uncle *is* strong," Annise pointed out. He was probably already fortifying Blackstone and Raider's Pass, moving soldiers from the Black Cliffs of Darrin.

"But not kind. A monarch needs to be both."

"Have you met my father?"

"Your father is gone. And just because he ruled by fear didn't make him right. You would rule differently. Better."

Annise couldn't take another false compliment, nor another reference to her ruling the realm. She turned away, heading toward the first hill to the south. "The royal tailors wouldn't be able to procure enough material to make my coronation gown," Annise said.

Tarin fell in beside her. "Why do you do that? Always jest about yourself?"

"Because if I don't, someone else will!" Annise said.

Tarin said, "You are more than what stupid lordlings think you are. I have seen more."

"Says the ice bear who called the snowman white."

Tarin sighed. "This isn't about me."

"Well it should be. You hate the way you look so much you cover yourself up. At least I don't hide my face."

"Your face is fine."

"Fine? Oh, I'm so glad it's not boring and plain like I thought."

"More than fine," Tarin said, and something about the way he said it made Annise's breath catch in her throat. *Stop. Just stop.* He continued: "But *my* face . . . people would run. Children would run."

"Yes," Annise said. "You are a monster from the Hinterlands, all right, straight from a nightmare. But I won't run. I won't even scream. You must remember the way I stared down that ice bear."

Tarin laughed. "How could I forget? You've got the claw marks on your face to prove it."

Annise was tiring of this conversation. The tundra fell away behind them as they crested a rise. She couldn't hold back her smile as she took in the landscape, a sweeping vista of snow-covered land and trees rolling out like a royal carpet. A splash of sunlight broke through the clouds, warming her face.

"We will find Arch and I will remind him of my age, and then I will formally relinquish all rights to the crown," Annise said.

"No," Tarin said. "You cannot."

Annise let out a rapid breath, losing patience. "It's not *your* choice."

"Look," Tarin said, pointing downslope. He grabbed her hand and dragged her down the hill into the valley, where several large oaks provided a canopy against the snowfall.

"What?" Annise said, not understanding.

"Here," Tarin said. He crouched, plucking something from the ground. A tiny flower, with rosy-cheeked petals and a long green stem.

"A hope flower, so what?" Annise said. It *was* beautiful, even with the frost forming around the edges.

"Do you know how the hope flower got its name?" Tarin asked, twirling the stem between his thumb and forefinger. Seeing the enormous black-armored knight spinning the tiny flower was almost comedic.

"I didn't know there would be a test," Annise quipped. "No, I can't say that I do."

She could just make out his eyes through the slits in his helmet. In the shadows, they looked black, just like the blood running through his veins. "This flower can grow in even the coldest temperatures, so long as the soil is exceptionally fertile. When the first explorers trekked the land beyond the Mournful Mountains, it was this flower that gave them hope that they could grow crops and survive the harsh winters."

It was a nice story, but didn't change anything. "It's still just a flower."

"As are you, my queen. And you shall give hope to the north when they need it the most. Happy name day, Annise."

He handed her the flower. She paused for a moment, but then took it.

ℒ

Tarin had insisted on keeping the flower, even though Annise said it would only die. She was done arguing—at least until they found her brother and Sir Dietrich. Surely they would understand her point of view and help her talk some sense into the Armored Knight.

The entire situation was stuffed. They were trudging through the valley, still leagues upon leagues away from Gearhärt. They were some pair. A queen who didn't want to be queen travelling with a knight too ashamed to show his face.

And yet Annise felt . . . alive. More alive than she'd felt in a long time. Being cold didn't matter because she was free. Free of making pointless appearances at her father's court, free of curtseying and making small talk with the insipid lords and ladies at Castle Hill, free of thick stone ramparts and groaning metal gates. Despite the fact that she was surely being hunted in every major castle in the north, Annise had never felt a greater sense of freedom, almost as if she *had* escaped across Frozen Lake to the Hinterlands.

"Tell me something," Annise said. "Last I saw you, you were a scrawny pipsqueak with less muscle in your entire body than I had in my little finger."

"Thanks for that colorful description," Tarin said.

"You're welcome. So what happened? Did your training with the royal army really help you that much? I mean, you're huge now."

"A time of growth."

Annise didn't believe him. "The witch's concoction . . . did it change you in any other ways?"

"You mean besides thinning my skin and turning my blood black? Besides the malicious voice in my head that screams for blood?"

"Yes," Annise said. "Besides all that."

Tarin shook his head. "You're unbelievable."

"So I've been told. Now tell me the truth."

"The truth is a moving target," Tarin said. "Sometimes I think my whole life is a lie. That *I* am a lie. But to answer your question: Yes, the witch's potion seemed to . . . enhance me . . . physically. I grew taller and bigger faster than normal children my age. My stamina increased as well, along with the shortness of my temper. That is eventually why I joined the army. It was the only place I thought I might find a normal life."

"Did you?"

He didn't answer for a long time, the only sounds their feet crunching through the snow. The storm had finally abated, the sky a sheet of white, darkening around the edges as the sun dipped precariously toward the horizon.

Annise waited patiently for his response. She was getting more used to the lengthy silences between them. They entered a pine forest, the trees ramrod straight and lined up in perfect rows. This was no natural wood. The trees had clearly been planted. Tarin rested a hand on her arm and stuck a finger to the spot on his mask that covered his lips.

They crept through the tree farm silently, eyes roving from side to side. The trees thinned out as the wood ended, giving way to a stone structure. A barn of some sort, with a wide opening big enough for carts laden with timber to be pulled through. Inside the barn Annise could see stacks of freshly cut wood, ready for transport. The cart, however, stood idle, a horse hooked to the front, stamping its feet in the cold, hot breaths pluming from its mouth and nose.

A small distance from the barn was a matching gray stone house. It had a squat chimney, and smoke was curling from the apex.

Where is the owner? Annise wondered.

The wooden door suddenly banged open and Tarin grabbed Annise, shoving her roughly behind a tree before ducking behind another. Across from each other, they peeked out.

Soldiers.

Annise's heart hammered in her chest. There were four of them, garbed in shiny mail over wool coats, steel swords hanging loosely from hip scabbards. On their chests was emblazoned the royal sigil of the north—the golden cracked-but-not-broken shield.

One of them, a solid man with a thin black beard, shoved a short balding fellow outside. Another of the soldiers had a woman secured by the arm. Neither the man nor the woman were dressed for the cold. In fact, the woman was wearing a smudged white apron, as if she'd been interrupted while cooking a meal.

Food, Annise's stomach grumbled. *Shut up*, Annise thought back at it. *This is not the time.*

"Where are they?" the solid soldier said harshly, pushing the bald, underdressed man. He stumbled and fell. The other soldiers laughed.

"Who?" the man cried. "We live alone."

His wife was forced to her knees beside him. A soldier with thick tufts of reddish-brown hair poking from his helmet slid his sword from his belt. He shoved the tip against her throat. "Last chance. Where are they hiding? In the barn? In the forest? Where?"

The woman started sobbing uncontrollably, the tip of the sword bouncing against her neck and drawing blood. The man clasped his hands together. "Please. No one is hiding. I'm leaving for Gearhärt tomorrow with our next haul. Search everything if you wish, just don't hurt her. Please."

Annise looked at Tarin, who looked back at her. Annise mouthed *Run?* but Tarin shook his head. Once more, she could see his eyes behind his mask, as black as coal. Something glinted in them, like the reflection of sunlight on silver.

He stepped from the trees.

Everything felt like it was moving in slow motion as he strode toward the soldiers, who were too focused on their prey to notice Tarin until he was almost upon them, his Morningstar tracing scathing arcs around his head. One of them turned at the last moment, unloosing a shout just before the spiked steel ball collided with the side of his skull, knocking him to the side. The soldier with the sword was next, trying to raise the blade to block Tarin's next swing, which crashed into him like a thunderbolt. The sword flew from his grasp and

Tarin kicked him in the stomach. One of the other soldiers grabbed Tarin from behind, but he immediately flipped him over his head, slamming him on his back. The fourth and last upright soldier—the dark-bearded leader—tried to flee.

Too slow. Tarin took two long strides and whipped the spiked ball around, catching him in the back of the head with a vicious clang. The soldier went down, his helmet flying off, his head caved in.

Annise was in shock, her hand over her mouth. At some point she must've stepped out from the cover of the trees, but she couldn't remember having moved at all. She scanned the destruction wrought by the knight. The two soldiers who had taken hits to the head weren't moving, and were most likely dead. The soldier Tarin had flipped was also still, although his hand was twitching from time to time. And the red-haired soldier who'd been kicked in the chest was on one knee, trying to fight to his feet.

Tarin stalked him like a wolf circling an injured elk, his Morningstar cutting a long, slow orbit around his head.

"You," the soldier said, glaring at the knight through tendrils of greasy hair. "You're him. The traitor."

"*You're* the traitor," Tarin growled, and before Annise could utter a single word, he flung his weapon, releasing the chain. The man tried to dodge the blow, but didn't make it, the spiked ball hitting him full in the face before rolling away, leaving a ragged trail of blood. The soldier flopped for a few moments before going still, a crimson pool expanding around his body, a fiery contrast to the packed snow.

From behind the knight, the bald man spoke, only he wasn't looking at Tarin. *He's looking at me*, Annise realized. "You're her, aren't you?" the man asked. "One of the ones they were looking for. Princess Annise."

Annise opened her mouth to answer him, to lie, but Tarin lunged for the man, grabbing him by the throat, picking him up like he weighed no more than air.

"No!" Annise cried, running toward him. "Tarin! Wait!"

Tarin cocked his head to look at her, but didn't release the man, who was struggling to breathe, his face turning red and then purple. Annise hurdled the woman, who was still crying, blood dribbling down the pale skin of her neck. Annise skidded to a stop just short of Tarin, whose chest was heaving beneath his black armor.

"Please, Tarin," Annise said, reaching out slowly with one hand. "He's not the enemy. The enemy is down. He is just a tree farmer. Let him go."

Tarin stared at her, but something about the gleam in his dark eyes was so foreign to the boy she once knew and the man she'd gotten to know in their makeshift tent, that it scared the frozen hell out of her. His eyes boring into her, he squeezed harder. An unnatural gurgling sound rose from the man's lips, his face turning as blue as ice at dusk.

Annise stepped forward. She touched his free hand softly, gently. He stiffened, but she didn't withdraw, sliding her fingers up his forearm, his bicep, all the way to his shoulder, and then to the mesh covering his face. Through the mask, she cupped his chin in her hand. "Please," she said. "You are more than this. I need you to let go."

A rough growl tore from his throat, and for a moment Annise thought he would strike her.

But then his shoulders slumped. His fingers unclenched, the bald man unleashing a gasp as he dropped to the cold, hard ground. He lay panting in the snow, clutching at his throat, but Annise wasn't looking at him.

She was staring through the slit in Tarin's mask, where his eyes were full of horror.

"What have I done?" he said.

Chapter Eighteen

The Western Kingdom | Knight's End

Grease Jolly

Grease awoke to a commotion. Shouts. Screams. Metallic clangs. *What is happening?*

It was dark, the night spilling through a high window in whatever prison room he'd been confined to. Not a bad place, really. It was better than the Temple of Confession, that was for godsdamned sure. For one, it was warmer, and he'd been given back his dirty clothing, although he was still strapped to the bed.

His hand—no, his *stump*—was throbbing something fierce.

"Shae," he said aloud, as another cry split the night. *Rutting Princess Rhea,* he thought. He needed to point his anger somewhere, and she was the easiest target. Otherwise he would have to hate himself. He wondered if they'd killed his sister yet. Her mark was her death sentence, and the Furies likely wouldn't waste time in carrying out their punishment. They certainly hadn't with him. With his hand.

Oh Shae, I'm so sorry. Because the truth was, it was his fault and he knew it. When he'd first received that note from the princess, he should've burned it, or eaten it. Maybe laughed about it. But not acted on it. Not met her. Not kissed her, stolen her purity like the thief that he was. Not abandoned her at the crypts.

All my fault. Sorrow welled up inside him and he coughed, choking on his guilt and anger and sadness. In that moment, he wanted to die.

Screams. Something strange about them. Not war cries. Pain cries. Death cries. *Is the city under attack?* According to Rhea, her father had declared war on the north, because they executed his sister, Queen Sabria Loren. But what if the north had expected that, and decided to attack first?

A thought struck him, the first sprig of true hope he'd had since the guards apprehended him: *Maybe they haven't killed Shae yet.*

Before he could truly consider the possibility, the door to his cell flew open and a wide-eyed Rhea burst inside, slamming the barrier behind her. Her chest was heaving and she looked frantic, her hair disheveled, her long white dressing gown hanging from one shoulder, revealing a moonlit sliver of pale skin that, under other circumstances, would've been a magnet for Grease's lips.

"What's happening?" Grease said. "Is the city under attack?"

The princess's face was awash with horror. "Yes. No. I don't know. They're dead. So many are dead. Something. Something is here."

She wasn't making sense. "The northerners? Did their ships make landfall?" Or perhaps they'd entered the west through Raider's Pass, marching around Bethany and straight for Knight's End.

Rhea's breaths were coming faster and faster, whistling through her teeth. She was in no condition to answer questions, and Grease's window of opportunity was quickly closing. "Help me with these straps," he said.

She took a deep breath, and having a task seemed to calm her somewhat. She rushed over, her hands shaking as she pulled and yanked at the leather bindings. More screams rent the night, and Rhea flinched.

"Focus, princess," Grease said. "One strap at a time. Hurry."

She managed to get his right arm free, and then he was able to help her with the chest strap, following by the four others. His left arm was useless, no better than a padded club, the bandages soaked through with blood.

Free, he swung his legs over the sides of the bed and tried to stand. His legs wobbled and he nearly fell, but Rhea steadied him. The room was spinning and his legs felt like raspberry preserves. *Gods, I can't rutting do this.* "You must do this," he hissed to himself. "For Shae."

"Please," Rhea said, her eyes like melted turquoise gemstones. "We have to leave." Screams. Shouts. Clanging metal.

"Not without my sister. Not without Shae."

Rhea closed her eyes. Opened them. Nodded. "I can take you to her."

"Do it."

Clutching each other—Grease for balance, Rhea for emotional support—they hobbled to the door. Grease opened it slowly and peeked out. There were dark lumps on the floor, and something wet glistened in the light cast by the hall lamps. Two guards. Dead. Somehow dead.

"What the rot?"

"Something is here," Rhea breathed. "Oh Wrath, it's going to kill us all."

Grease remembered that night at the crypts. The monster with the marked scalp. The dead knights. It had come to finish the job.

"Hurry," Grease said. "We have to find my sister."

They scurried along the corridor, avoiding as much of the blood as they could. It was everywhere. On the floor, on the walls, splattered on the lamp fixtures. It was even dripping from the ceiling in spots. The bodies were scattered like toy soldiers in a child's game. Guards. Knights. All dead, most having never even drawn their swords. "Where are the furia?" Grease said.

He hadn't really meant it as a question for Rhea, but she answered anyway, hissing under her breath. "They fled the castle. I saw them from my window. When the screams started, they rode out, led by the Three."

The holy sisterhood had abandoned the castle to whatever evil was slaughtering at will. Although it clearly wasn't a positive sign that the most capable warriors in Knight's End had retreated so swiftly, Grease knew it might mean they hadn't had time to deal with his sister.

The thought gave him energy, his legs buoyed up with a new spirit despite the fear that threatened to pull him into a ball. *Hurry, hurry, hurry . . .*

They passed through a royal ballroom, the long wooden table set and ready for breakfast. Thankfully, there were no bodies, the room bright with green and red moonlight, which winked through the large glass windows. Through the kitchens they went, the hearth warm and glowing with molten embers. One of the kitchen hands was huddled against the stonework, sobbing. "Help me," she whispered.

Grease felt bad for the girl, who looked no older than thirteen, but there was nothing he could do for her now. "Stay here," he said. "Find a place to hide. In a crate, beneath the straw."

The girl only cried harder and louder as they left her behind.

"We're close now," Rhea advised.

They turned a corner, but Grease immediately halted and pulled the princess back. "What?" she said. "What is it?"

He could read the fear in her eyes, so deep he knew it could paralyze her if he said the wrong thing. "Nothing," he said. "I just need to catch my breath." The truth was, he'd seen it. The thing. The monster, its mark glowing pale-white in the dim corridor. The creature had pulled a long blade from a knight's chest, letting the man fall before stalking forward.

Grease counted to ten slowly in his head, hoping it was long enough for the monster to have moved on:

One . . . Please pass Shae by, he prayed.

Two . . . Three . . . Oh, Wrath, if you have any mercy left for a sinner like me, please spare her.

Four . . . Five . . . She is good.

Six . . . She is kind.

Seven . . . Her mark was not her choice.

Eight . . . Nine . . . She doesn't even know how to use it . . .

Ten he pulled the princess into the corridor, scanning the length of the hallway, which was littered with bodies and splashed with blood. The killer was gone.

"Oh Wrath," Rhea murmured.

Grease continued his prayer for his sister in his head. He'd never prayed before in his life, and certainly not to Wrath, unless he included the times he pretended to pray in the temple while stealing from the collection tin. Now he would pray to any god under the Four Kingdoms if it might help save his sister.

"Which way?" he asked, looking left and then right. The princess was muttering under her breath, her eyes blank. He grabbed her chin, trying to get her to focus on his eyes. "Rhea. Please. Which way to my sister?"

She looked right, where the corridor was empty and dark. Then left, where the dead guards lay in droves. She pointed toward the corpses, her finger trembling. He grabbed her hand, holding it tightly, trying to calm her. "Not far," she said.

They blazed a winding path down the stone hallway, once more avoiding the dead. Grease tried not to look at them, but couldn't seem to stop. A burly knight's helmet had been cloven in half, his skull shattered. Another had no noticeable wounds, but his face was frozen in a silent scream, stricken with fear. Some were missing limbs. *Like me*, Grease thought darkly.

The corridor felt endless, iron doors passing on both sides. *Cells*, Grease realized. Cells for the worst criminals, those sentenced to death. Finally, Rhea stopped and said, "Here." She motioned to a cell door on the left. "We need the key."

A guard was slumped against the wall. "Help me," Grease said, squatting down and patting along the man's waist.

"I can't," Rhea said. She was frozen in place.

Frustration boiled over. "I only have one godsdamn hand, so please help me find the rutting key!"

Tears poured down Rhea's cheeks, the dam finally bursting. Grease would've felt bad for making her cry, but Shae . . . Thankfully, the princess dropped to her knees and joined the search, sobbing the whole time.

Something jangled. "Pull them out," Grease said, trying not to shout and upset her more. She did as she was told, extracting a keyring with a dozen keys on it. Together they stood up and the princess tried the first key. No good. The second. Nay. The third. Wouldn't even fit. Screams echoed down the corridor. It was taking too long.

The fourth key turned the lock and Rhea actually managed a thin smile of relief. Grease licked his lips and shouldered through the door, shouting, "Shae!" as he entered.

The cell was empty, save for discarded iron manacles chained to the floor, their edges crusted with dried blood.

Shae was gone.

They were too late.

᠄ᢒ

Princess Rhea wouldn't leave him alone, hovering behind Grease as he made his way toward the main entrance leading out of the nightmarish castle. He refused to look at her, refused to listen to her sobs, refused to let her grab his hand—his *only* hand. Shae was gone, and it was both their faults. They'd both wronged each other, and Shae had been caught in the crossfire.

He felt numb, devoid of emotion. He stepped over corpses, splashing through their blood. None of it mattered.

Rhea tripped and lost her shoe, crying out, and when she started to turn back to retrieve it, Grease finally grabbed her hand. "No time," he said, pulling her forward.

He descended a staircase, halting halfway when he saw a shadow blocking the way out. Rhea crashed into him from behind, and he nearly tumbled down the steps, uttering a curse.

The figure wobbled slightly, as if off balance. "Father?" Rhea said, hope in her voice. That's when Grease noticed the golden spikes of the crown atop the shadow's head.

King Gill Loren, the Holy King, slowly turned around.

The king's throat was a crimson smile, sliced open from ear to ear. His head lolled back, flopping grotesquely before tearing from his neck and hitting the floor with a hollow thud. His body followed, crumpling like a poor child's ragdoll.

Rhea screamed, clutching Grease so tightly her nails dug into his arms.

Grease felt hollowed out, but he was aware enough to catch the princess before she toppled down the stairs. With only one hand, he felt awkward and off-kilter, but he managed to clutch her arm with one hand while steadying her with his stump. He forced her to stumble down the steps to the atrium, and then past her father's decapitated corpse, blocking her view with his body.

He pushed out into the night, where it was beginning to rain, a fine mist cleansing the earth. A phrase he'd heard uttered by Sir Darrow in the Cryptlands entered his mind: *Kings' Plague.* The northern king was dead, as was his queen, Rhea's aunt. And now King Loren too. After what he'd seen tonight, Grease didn't believe in coincidences, and monsters were no longer confined to childish dreams.

Huddled against his side, Princess Rhea was babbling nonsensically to herself. "C'mon," he muttered. "Let's get you somewhere safe." She didn't acknowledge that he'd spoken. Didn't even look at him, her eyes glazed over, blinking against the rain.

Not surprisingly, the guards at the castle gates were dead, struck down where they stood. Instead of cranking open the enormous gate, Grease led Rhea through a side door typically used by small troops of guards entering and exiting the castle.

Somehow the rain seemed to come down harder the moment they were outside the walls. But this was his territory now, and Grease didn't falter, even when they were drenched from head to toe in seconds. He headed for the main thoroughfare, counting on the furia to have chosen speed over stealth as they retreated from the castle. He didn't care what happened to him, he needed to know whether they'd killed Shae before they fled. If so, he wanted her body. He needed to bury her himself. Only then could he die.

After the horrors and death inside the castle, it was strange seeing Knight's End so peaceful. A number of townsfolk were milling about the cobblestone streets beneath canvas awnings, speaking in hushed voices. There were no bodies. No lakes of blood. Evidently Death's servant had no interest in the commoners.

Grease marched up to the first familiar face he saw. Jordan Vaughn, a bootmaker. Grease wouldn't call him a friend, but he wasn't an enemy either. He grabbed the thin man's arm. "Did you see the furia?" he asked.

Vaughn's storm-gray eyes flicked from Grease to the princess, widening with realization. "But she's the—that's her—you've got the—"

"She's Princess Rhea, aye," Grease said. "I don't have time to explain. Did the furia pass by or not?"

Vaughn licked his dry lips, still staring at the princess. "A night to remember," he muttered. "I heard their horses first. I'm a light sleeper as it is, and they charged past like a royal battalion chasing the enemy. There were so many. I've never seen so many together at one time, all wearing red. At the front were the Three."

Grease remembered the way the Three had laughed at him in the Temple of Confession. The way they'd held him down. The way the leader had raised the blade . . . "They were headed south?" Grease asked, shaking away the dark memory.

"Wrath, what happened to your hand?" Vaughn said.

Grease held up his stump. "I let someone borrow it. Now please, were they headed south?"

The old man nodded grimly. "I watched 'em go. We all did. Then we heard screams from the castle."

"Was there anyone with them?" Grease held his breath as soon as he asked the question.

Vaughn frowned. "Like who? It was just furia. They were magnificent. Frightening, but magnificent, like Wrath's army charging into battle."

More like retreating. A woman who must've overheard their strange conversation drifted closer. "I saw sumthin'," she said.

"What?"

"One o' the Three was holdin' someone in front of 'er. At first methinks 'twas a sack, but then I saw a face peekin' out. 'Twas the damndest—Wrath, forgive me language—thing. The girl was bundled up in a blanket, 'er hair spillin' out the sides like streamers."

"What color?" Grease asked.

"What're you sayin' now?" the woman said, her eyes narrowing.

"What color was her hair?"

The woman's eyes lit up. "Oh, yes. Lovely hair, that one. Even in the moonlight it 'twas clear as day, like golden strawberries it was."

Shae. You're alive. Oh gods, where are they taking you?

"Thank you," he said to the woman. Turning back to Vaughn, he said, "I'm leaving the city and I need a favor."

"I'll help if I can," the kindly man said.

"Keep her safe." He nudged Princess Rhea toward him.

Finally, something registered in her expression. "Don't leave me," she said. "Take me with you."

It was the second time she'd asked him not to leave. The first time he'd ignored her, and it had cost him his hand and put his sister at risk.

He looked at the shock and sorrow on her face, at her soaked hair dangling from her scalp, at her bloodied, drenched nightclothes clinging to the curves of her body. In another life he could've loved her, could've treated her better. If he was a different person, or if she was born a commoner, or if the stars were aligned perfectly in the night sky, twinkling as the moons kissed at midnight. But he wasn't. He was an orphan and a thief and the brother of a marked girl who needed his help more than Rhea did. And she was a princess of the western kingdom. And the moons and stars? The moons were at opposite ends of the darkness, as far from each other as he'd ever seen them, one green and one red; the stars were scattered throughout the night sky, sparkling like fate's gemstones—ruby, emerald, and topaz. Occasionally the rubies streaked across his vision, while the emeralds seemed to explode again and again and again . . .

"I'm sorry," he said. "I can't." He wrenched her hands from his arm and strode off into the pouring rain, heading for the southern gates. Surprising even himself, he stopped and whirled around, looking back. He could see the hope in her eyes. That he wouldn't leave. That he would rush back to her and hold her in his arms.

"My real name isn't Grease Jolly," he said. "It's Grey. Grey Arris."

Once more, he spun around and raced toward the gates. As he ran, he felt a piece of himself break off and fall away as he heard her sobs, but he didn't look back again.

Chapter Nineteen

The Northern Kingdom | Silent Mountain

Bane

Bane was covered in blood, slumped against the wall of the cave, staring at his hands. His fingers were spinning a knife, and he watched the firelight reflect off the lifeblood of the dozens of men he'd killed in a single night, including the western king himself.

Demon! many of them had cried. Other words as well: monster, beast, creature, *evil*.

He was all of those things. Not that it mattered. *You can't change what you are.* A wolf was a wolf, and would always hunger for fresh prey. Although Bear Blackboots claimed it was his choice whether he was evil or not, Bane knew it wasn't true.

Bear hadn't even bothered to wait for him to return from his killing spree, as if he was afraid to see what Bane had become.

Monster, creature, beast, demon.

Evil.

Some had prayed to their god, Wrath—not that it had changed anything.

He could still hear the beating of their hearts in his head, slowing, slowing, stopping. He pressed a hand to his own chest and felt nothing. Did he even have a heart, or was it an empty chasm roaring with Death's fire? And if he did, why could he not feel its beat? Had it long ago turned black and hard, a lump of compacted obsidian in his chest?

The surface of his head was on fire, and he knew it was because another eighth of his deathmark had been filled with blood. The blood of the western king. He didn't know if the king was a bad man or not, only that he had to die. Bane's carnal instincts had urged him to kill dozens of the knights and guards, too; the fear the massacre would cultivate was somehow important to the cleansing of the Four Kingdoms, the fulfilling of the Western Oracle's prophecy.

He wondered if his skin would ever be clean again.

With an angry snarl he wrenched off his blood-drenched cloak and flung it into the fire. Next was his shirt, his trousers, his socks, his undergarments. His boots he kept; he would try to scrub them clean because they weren't as easily replaced.

Naked, he watched the blood of the west crackle and burn. In the flames, he swore he could see every moment of his life flashing by, one by one. He saw good days, like painting pictures on the cave walls with Bear, and he saw bad ones, like when he'd slipped and fallen, breaking his leg in the process. Each memory was devoured by the fire. Gone. Incinerated.

Once the fire had consumed the sins of the night and the memories of a life he once loved, he had nothing left, tumbling onto his side, spent. His body shook as if struck by lightning bolt after lightning bolt. He lay by the ring of stones and closed his eyes, waiting for his deathmark's next instructions.

A vision blazed through his mind. As he watched the events unfold, he twitched at the sheer violence of men. Of him.

When the images faded away, his eyes flashed open. He knew where he would be called next.

Raider's Pass.

And there would be blood.

Exhaustion took him once more.

PART III

ROAN • ANNISE • GREASE • RHEA

The deathmark and lifemark are the greater of the fatemarks, while the rest are lesser. But that does not diminish their importance, as all who bear marks shall have a role to play in what is to come.

—THE WESTERN ORACLE

Chapter Twenty

The Eastern Kingdom | Ironwood

Roan

Gwendolyn had apologized for dumping him out of her hammock. Roan was surprised, considering she'd never apologized before, not even after she'd stabbed him in the gut.

Women are strange and unpredictable, Roan mused as his horse trotted along beside hers. At least this time around he wasn't tied up, even if he felt the king's men watching him like orc hawks. They'd been traveling through the immensity of Ironwood for hours, heading northwest. *Toward home*, Roan mused, shaking the thought away as quickly as it had sprouted up. *I have no home.*

And yet it was the west where he knew he had to go, a place where his tattooya could get him killed. He remembered what Gwen had said a day earlier, about what westerners had once called the marks. *Fatemarks.* Did that mean there was more to his existence than randomness and chance? *It's just a word*, he reasoned. *And anyway, the westerners would rather slaughter me than speak to me.*

According to the king, who was riding at the head of the column, they were making their way toward Raider's Pass, the neck of the north. "We go for the jugular," the large man had said as he led them through the castle gates. Roan had subconsciously touched the fragile skin of his neck, feeling for a pulse.

Roan and Gwen were well back from the front, but still in the first third of the legion, which was comprised of hundreds of well-armored men and women bearing all manner of weaponry. The three princes rode up and down the column, trading quips with their soldiers, each of whom they seemed to know personally and by name, a fact that didn't fail to impress Roan.

"These trees have been here for thousands of years," Gwen said, gesturing to some of the tallest trees in the forest. They rose majestically toward the sky, sheathed in intricate ironwork. "They are our gods, along with the ore that protects them."

Roan raised an eyebrow. "So, basically, you worship nature." He was unable to keep the mocking from his tone.

Gwen fired daggers from her eyes, and he half-expected her to draw her bow and aim it at his heart. "Are the Southrons all that different?" she said. "They worship gods and goddesses of fire, of stars, of storm, of bird and beast. Are those your gods?"

"I have no gods," Roan said.

"What about Wrath?"

Again, Gwen's dagger-sharp questions seemed calculated. Precise. Probing.

"Wrath is far too angry a god for me," Roan said. "The world is all that we have. After this, there is nothing."

"Then you are empty."

"Emptiness is better than angriness," Roan shot back.

Gwen cocked her head to the side, her silver hair shifting like moonbeams through a lace curtain. "Explain."

Roan tried to find the right words to explain his feelings. His guardian's lectures came back to him. "Why do the westerners hate the easterners?" he asked. "Or the easterners the westerners? The westerners find your lot godless, because you don't believe in *their* god, in Wrath, or the seventh heaven they live their entire life to try to reach. And the easterners believe the westerners are savages for brutally punishing sinners. And do you love the Southrons any more? To you they are heathens, barbarians."

He clamped his mouth shut, fearing he'd said too much. Gwen said, "Go on. And the north? How do you explain them?"

"The northerners care only about avoiding the worst places in the afterlife. So their goal is to seek power and territory, but not cross some razor-thin line that will sentence them to a life of eternal damnation in a hell even colder than the one they already live in."

"What are you saying? That we should all change our beliefs to accommodate each other's? Cast the ancient traditions of our forefathers aside for a fool's chance of peace?"

Roan shook his head. The truth was, he didn't know. All he knew was that the current status quo hadn't worked for hundreds of years, the Four Kingdoms locked in a war that killed thousands each year, leaving the land filled with orphans and widows and sadness. Even as he was trying to communicate the same frustrations he'd argued with his guardian about as a child, he knew he was being hypocritical. Because he didn't believe in anything but *life*, and yet he'd watched men and women die. Men and women he could've helped.

"I don't know," he admitted.

Gwen laughed. "At least my beliefs are clear," she said. "And useful. I speak to the ore, and the ore obeys, Orion's will be done."

He couldn't argue with that. He'd watched her don her armor this morning, before they'd departed Ferria. The ore had moved with the grace of a dancer, swirling up her legs, around her slim waist, upwards to her ribcage and chest, and finally curled around her neck and over her cheeks.

As unpredictable as Gwendolyn was, Prince Gareth was impressively predictable.

The prince wedged his horse in between them, already smirking. "Ho, Roan the Skinmarked! How is your arse on this fine morning?"

Now that he wasn't required to hide his ability, every few leagues Roan allowed a portion of his power to seep into his hind parts. "Excellent, Your Highness," he said. "As supple as cured leather. And yours?" Despite himself, Roan smiled. He hadn't spoken to the prince since he'd shown him around the castle, and, strangely, he missed the pointless banter.

"Riding is but an extension of walking to the easterners," the prince said, spurring his stallion ahead. He veered to the left, forcing Roan's horse to rear up sharply to avoid a collision. Roan tried to cling to the saddle horn, but the angle was too steep, and he tumbled awkwardly to the ground.

The prince circled around while Roan groaned, rethinking whether he'd missed Gareth's presence. Laughter surrounded him from the king's soldiers. "First lesson of horsemanship, Southron," Gareth said. "Always maintain control of your steed."

The prince chuckled and trotted ahead.

"He's right, you know," Gwen said, dismounting and helping Roan to his feet.

"He could've just *told* me the first lesson of horsemanship," Roan griped, reaching out to secure his horse's reins. They remounted and continued on.

"Lessons are learned better from experience," Gwen said.

Roan thought back to all that he'd experienced over the years. He wasn't sure he'd learned a damned thing from any of it, except that the world was full of tragedy and heartache.

As he mused over his past, he saw something streak across the edge of his vision. He jerked his head to the side, searching the trees and undergrowth. "See something?" Gwen asked. There was a twinkle in her golden eyes.

"Something moved. It was fast. I saw something similar when we entered Ironwood the first time."

"Hmm," Gwen mused, although Roan suspected she was playing a wicked game with him.

Leaves rustled and there was a flash of something metallic, there and gone before Roan could lock his eyes on it. "What the hell is that?" he asked. It moved like—well, like Gwendolyn. Faster than the wind. Faster than lightning.

"I thought you didn't believe in Hell." Gwen's eyes sparkled.

If it moved like her, then maybe it was like her. "Someone you know?" he said. "A cousin perhaps?" He thought he was being clever, but then the thing dove from the opposite side, the barest glint of steel on the outermost edge of his vision.

Roan tried to duck, but, compared to the thing, he was as slow as tree sap. He felt claws sink into his flesh and then muscle smash into his chest. Once more, he flew off his mount, the beast landing atop him, its paws pinning him to the metal ground, its eyes angry silver, its mouth full of tiny daggers. It was cat-like in appearance, with black stripes interrupting the gray sheen of its metal armor, but far larger and stronger than the ornery tomcats that roamed the streets of Calypso searching for scraps.

Roan pushed energy into his lifemark, which burned in his chest, healing the scratches and bruises from the attack and subsequent fall; it helped alleviate the pain, but his powers would be useless when the beast bit his head clean off his neck. As if reading his mind, it opened its jaws wide enough to do just that, growling from deep in its throat.

"Ho, Sasha!" Gwen shouted. "Off!"

The cat snarled at him once more, and then bounded away, pushing off from his chest. Roan quickly rolled to the side, fought to his feet, and moved backwards from the creature—which apparently had a name, Sasha?—which stalked back and forth in front of him, like it was working off pent up energy.

Horsemen and horsewomen parted like a river around a stone, mostly ignoring them, although Roan caught a few laughs and smiles. Maybe he *was* supposed to be the jester, as Gareth had suggested.

Gwen slipped from her horse with all the grace of a waterfall. She approached the beast, which stood almost as tall as her, its head reaching her chest. She extended a hand, palm down, and the animal nuzzled its muscular head against it, purring. "He's not the enemy," she said to the wildcat.

Roan noticed she didn't say "friend." Still, he would take "not the enemy" under the circumstances. "What is it?" he asked.

"An ore cat. This one is Sasha. Ironwood is full of them. She didn't recognize your scent, which made her angry."

The ore cat rubbed against Gwendolyn's leg and she laughed. Sasha approached Roan and he took a step back, stiffening. The cat growled. "She senses your fear," Gwendolyn said.

"I'm not scared," Roan lied.

"Let her sniff you."

Roan held out a hand, but recoiled when Sasha snapped at it. The cat prowled closer, and the way she curled her lips almost looked like she was smiling. First she sniffed Roan's borrowed boots, scrunching up her nose at the smell. Then his legs and arms, her disgust seeming to grow with each odor. Finally, she backed away, growling.

"She doesn't like you," Gwen said.

"Oh, good," Roan said.

As quickly as she arrived, the ore cat leapt back into the forest, disappearing beneath the undergrowth with a metallic flash of her tail.

Roan took a deep breath as they mounted up. He ignored Gwendolyn's amused grin. "Are there any other ore creatures I should know about?"

"Well, there are the ore hawks you saw the day you arrived, but as long as you don't look up at them, they should leave you alone."

Roan had no clue whether it was a jest or not, but he refused to rise to the bait and look up. Gwen laughed. "Also, keep your possessions close to you at night, or the ore monkeys might steal them. Come on," she said, spurring her horse forward.

Good thing I have no possessions, Roan thought. Still, he glanced at the trees, peering between the branches. He didn't see anything. Gwen was already moving away rapidly. He encouraged his mare to give chase, but quickly lost sight of the superior rider behind the ranks of mounted soldiers. He rode along the edge of the column, watching the forest warily for any movement that might suggest the presence of another ore cat. Several of the men and women hailed him as he passed. "Aye! Southroner!" they said. Again, these easterners were hard to read—he couldn't tell whether he was being mocked. He offered a raised arm in greeting and rode on.

Eventually, he reached the front, where the royal bannermen held flags bearing the royal sigil, flapping in the wind. The king was directly in the center, his triplet sons riding behind. On one side was Gwendolyn, and on the other Beorn Stonesledge, the ironmarked, his steed a massive armored stallion that was surely the only horse that could bear the giant's weight.

The scene felt like a metaphor for the East-West War. In the west, Gwen, Beorn and Roan would all have been killed the moment their so-called sinmarks were revealed. In the east, they were revered, permitted to ride *with* the king. Two very different reactions to the same situation. And in the north the marked were forced to serve the crown. Southrons were different still, those bearing tattooya almost worshipped like gods.

Even stranger was the character who rode next to Gwendolyn, the man they called Bark, his brown, mottled flesh appearing as rough as sandstone next to the Orian's smooth-as-silk complexion. Evidently his metalwork was so highly valued that he was given a position of prestige amongst the battalion.

Gwendolyn looked back and met Roan's eyes. She gestured for him to join them at the front. Pleasantly surprised, he weaved his way through the ranks and pulled up next to Bark, who was riding a grizzled horse that seemed on its last legs.

The king craned his neck to look over. "Ho, Roan Born-of-Dust. How are you enjoying the ride?"

Well, Your Highness, first your son knocked me from my horse. Then a playful ore cat named Sasha attempted to eat my head. "Very much, Your Highness," he said.

The king smiled broadly, as if reading the unspoken truth directly from his mind. "I heard you met Sasha."

Roan glared at Gwen, who smiled sweetly. "I told the king *everything*," she said.

"Thank you. That will save me the trouble of telling the tale myself."

One of the princes piped up from behind. Roan wasn't sure if it was Guy or Grian. "Tell us, *Roan*, why are you not in the service of the Calypsians? Surely the Sandes would value a man of your . . . rare abilities."

Roan squirmed in his saddle. He wasn't used to talking about his mark with anyone but his guardian. Even then, it had always made him uncomfortable. "No one knew about it."

Gwen arched her thin eyebrows in surprise. "How is that possible? We discovered it so easily."

"Because I rarely used it," Roan admitted.

Gwendolyn narrowed her eyes. "Why not? Is there no suffering in Calypso? Are there not people in need of what you have to offer?"

Shame slithered through him. *I have nothing to offer.* "I—" He couldn't admit the truth, that if he used his power and his father's spies discovered him he'd be a dead man. "I was careful," he said.

"Why? Why hide your true self?" It was Gareth this time. "It's not like you were in the west, where they'd execute you. The Southrons worship power like yours."

"You wouldn't understand," Roan said. "Just drop it. Please."

Gareth started to question him further, but the king cut him off. "The past is no matter. So long as, when the time comes, you do what is necessary for my brave men and women."

Roan didn't respond, his heart thumping in his chest. He stared straight ahead, even as he felt Gwen's scowl smashing into him from the side.

ꙮ

When they finally cleared the edge of Ironwood, Roan found he could breathe easier once more. He wasn't used to being so enclosed; Calypso was an open city, the sky always visible, turquoise and hot in the day, and cool and filled with both moons and a blanket of stars in the night.

It also didn't hurt that he no longer had to worry about ore cats pouncing from the shadows and eating his face, or ore hawks diving from above and tearing off his scalp, or even ore monkeys stealing the shirt off his back or the boots from his feet.

Ahead of the column of men and women soldiers was a land greener than Roan had ever seen, with rolling grasslands broken only by the occasional copse of overgrown trees. Their legion seemed to flow across the land like a silver river making its way to some unknown destination, or to the sea, perhaps.

Roan angled his mare's path toward Gwendolyn. They hadn't spoken in hours, and he was beginning to wonder whether she would ever speak to him again after having admitted he rarely used his tattooya to help anyone in need.

"Ho, forest dweller!" he called, hailing her the way an easterner would.

"Ho, coward!" she called back, and he couldn't help the sting he felt in his chest at her words.

Gareth chuckled, riding beside her.

Roan wished he could show her his memories of his escape from Dragon's Breath. Maybe then she wouldn't be so quick to judge his character. Then again, he had left thousands of the afflicted to rot or die a fiery death, so maybe he was a coward.

Gareth said, "Your cheeks appear sunburned, Sir Dust," which only made Roan's skin grow even hotter.

Gwen looked away. Maybe she was embarrassed for him. He gritted his teeth and let the cool air tame his cheeks. "Tell me," Roan said. "Are all easterners such jesters?"

It was Gwen's turn to smirk. "Only the arrogant ones."

Roan laughed, although her opinion didn't seem to affect Prince Gareth. "There's a fine line between arrogance and confidence," he said. "I prefer to keep one leg on either side, just like riding a horse."

"You must be sore in the area between your legs then," Roan quipped.

"Not at all," the prince said, recovering easily. "Like all things in the east, I'm made of iron where it counts the most."

Despite everything, Roan couldn't help but to appreciate the prince's quick wit.

Prince Guy pulled up alongside his brother. "We shall see the truth in battle, brother," he said. "May the glory go to the fiercest warrior." He raised his sword in the air.

"Then I shall receive the glory," Prince Grian growled from behind. "Though war is not for glory."

Although the darkness that seemed to be constantly in Grian's eyes scared Roan a little, he couldn't help but to agree. "War only brings death," he said.

King Ironclad split his sons in half, his enormous steed like an armored battering ram. "Then we shall bring death to the north," he said. "And you shall bring life to the east with that skinmark of yours."

ꙮ

Days turned to nights turned to days, and Roan soon tired of the constant greenery. To his surprise, he longed to feel a bit of sand beneath his feet, rather than the leather stirrups strapped to his horse. They camped for short stretches, riding long after dark and arising well before the sun peeked over the eastern horizon.

Gwendolyn had less and little to say to him, which left him with only Gareth to talk to. Not that he minded. At least, most of the time. "She's likely to shoot an arrow through your eye if you don't stop staring at her," the prince said one day as they were riding. In truth, Roan hadn't been purposely staring at the Orian. The four hours of sleep had left him exhausted and listless in his saddle, and he had little control where his gaze landed.

"Let her shoot," Roan said. "She's done worse."

The prince tsked. "Your defeatist nature is a drag on my sunny mood."

"So find another riding companion."

"I would, but my father has instructed me to keep both eyes on you."

"Why? Is he afraid I might make a run for it?" The fact that the king and his sons believed they were forcing Roan to ride west made him laugh on the inside. In reality, they were going in the exact direction he wanted to go, more or less.

"No. He's afraid you might die from a broken heart," the prince said, laughing.

Something boiled over inside Roan. "I have done nothing to her, have no romantic interest in her, and her opinion of me is even less important than yours," he snapped.

The prince held up both hands. "Whoa. I did not seek to offend thine soft and furry ego. I fear my words struck closer to the target than I intended. Like many others, you have fallen for an angel as unreachable as the moons, and as fierce as the sun's heat."

Gods, he's impossible, Roan thought. "I have fallen for no one. I suspect it is you that has fallen for her, am I right?"

The prince smiled broadly. "I am human—I want what I cannot have, and I have no interest in that which is mine." Something about the way he said it, about the way he looked at Roan, made him wonder whether they were talking about Gwen anymore.

"Like the eastern throne?"

The prince seemed to find this humorous. "Maybe you have a bigger rock for a brain than I initially believed. The throne is just a throne, while Gwendolyn Storm is molten ore."

"But she will not have you?"

"No more than she'll have you, Southroner."

Roan remembered what Gareth had told him about the long lives Orians lived. "But surely she's had mates. She's been many years in this world, has she not?"

"Yes. At least ninety-five, if my calculations are correct. Supposedly she was once bonded."

I shouldn't have brought you here, Gwen had said a day earlier after he'd persisted in asking about the poetry on the gate to her dwelling.

"Was he a poet by any chance?"

Gareth made a face. "You believe a strong woman like Gwendolyn would take up with an artist? Surely not. From what I've heard, he was a legionnaire."

"Couldn't he be both a poet and a soldier?"

"Why do you persist in this line of questioning? Are you a poet hoping to romance her with fine words and tender prose? Ha!" The prince chortled at his own wit.

"In truth, I would rather kiss you than her," Roan said lightly.

The prince laughed, but Roan could tell it was forced, his cheeks blushing with embarrassment. "You are a fool, you know that? I would rather kiss my horse." And yet he looked away, unable to meet Roan's eyes.

Roan watched him carefully, and then twisted the subject back to Gwen. "What happened to her bondmate?"

"He perished in the Dragon Massacre, like many other legionnaires."

Roan breathed through his nose. She'd lost so much in the war with the south. It was a wonder she spoke to him at all, much less looked at him.

"And was he a pure Orian?"

Gareth squinted and cocked his head, eventually shrugging. "As far as I know. Which means roughshod humans like you and I have as much chance as a worm crawling out of the muck." He laughed loudly, which only made Roan more certain the prince was overcompensating for something. Hearing the laughter, Gwen turned to look at them. The prince offered a wave and a sly smile, which she ignored, turning away.

Something the prince had said earlier had struck a chord on the strings of his soul. "You truly do not desire the eastern throne?" he asked.

Something unrecognizable flashed across Gareth's face, but quickly vanished beneath a smile. "It is not mine to take."

Roan frowned. "But you are the eldest-born son, are you not? Even amongst multiple births, you would have rights."

"Legally, that is true," Gareth said. "But we have our traditions."

"What traditions?"

"You would not understand."

"Try me."

Gareth looked away. Roan had never seen him look so uncomfortable, especially when on horseback. Even Roan's comment about kissing him hadn't unnerved the prince as much. The prince said nothing.

Roan pressed further. "Why won't you take the throne that is rightfully yours?" he asked.

Gareth only shook his head and dug his heels into his steed's sides, spurring it away from Roan. Roan cocked his head to the side, but didn't give chase.

A shadow fell upon him from behind, and he twisted about to find the king's enormous horse sprinting to catch up. The Juggernaut slowed his steed, settling into an easy trot beside him.

"Ho, king," Roan said.

"Ho, healer," the king said. "Well met. What say you?"

"I say I'm ready for a long sleep," Roan said.

The king chuckled. "The dead may sleep, while the living must soldier on."

Roan didn't feel like arguing about kingdoms and war with a man who seemed as disinterested in peace as the Southron emperors and empresses. Instead he asked, "Why is Prince Gareth loath to inherit your crown?"

"He is the Shield," the king said evenly. "As my eldest brother was before him."

"How can a man be a shield?" Roan said, trying to understand.

"By protecting those he loves."

"Meaning . . . ?"

"A life to save a life."

Wait. Roan remembered something the prince had said back at Barrenwood, something cryptic about dying long before he'd have a chance to be king. At the time he'd thought it was just another one of Gareth's flippant remarks. "He wants to die to protect his brothers?"

"*Want* might not be the best word to choose. But yes, he will eventually die to save Prince Guy, who is next in line for the throne. It is his duty as the eldest brother, as the Shield."

Roan squinted, although the sun was not bright. "You mentioned you had an older brother, that he was killed by northerners . . ."

"Coren," the king said. "A year older than me. He was known as Thunder because of his booming voice."

Was. Something clicked and turned, like a key in a lock. "He died to save your life," Roan said.

The king said nothing, just stared ahead, a wistful look barely visible beneath the shadows cast by his thick, dark brows.

It all makes sense now, Roan thought. Gareth's devil-may-care attitude, his gallows sense of humor, his cavalier attitude toward life and a throne he never intended to claim. He was the Shield, destined to die for one of his brothers, so Prince Guy could live on and become King Ironclad. A royal tradition. But—

"Why?" Roan asked. "Why must he die? Why can't the princes protect each other? Why can't they be each other's Shields and allow Gareth to take the throne?"

The king sighed, a deep huff of hot air. "I loved my brother," he said. "Although he was only a year my elder, he seemed years more mature. He would've made a great king."

"Then why didn't he? Why isn't he the king now?"

The king offered him a narrow glance, but then faced forward once more, gazing into the distance, where his sons were racing each other across the grassy plains. Always competing. "It was twelve years ago, during one of a series of battles at the Razor," he started. "My father had taken ill, and thus the command of the eastern legions had fallen to Coren and I. Our scouts had discovered a hidden cave along the shoreline, one that had potential as an avenue through the cliffs. Prince Coren concocted a scheme in which we would split our force in two, with half scaling the Black Cliffs and distracting the northern defenders, while the rest pushed through the mountain, attacking by stealth from behind."

The king paused, licking his lips. Roan could almost see the memories flashing in his eyes, the dark jagged cliffs rising against a gray northern sky, heavy white waves crashing on the rocks. "Coren made the decision to lead the group over the mountains, while he sent me through the caves."

"What happened?" Roan asked, bringing his horse to a stop while the king did the same.

King Oren Ironclad slowly turned to face him. "We made it through, and when we did, the northern army was in disarray. Coren had led his armored battalion directly through the middle of them, cutting them in two. It was a move the north hadn't expected, because it was suicide. He'd left his flanks open on both sides, and allowed the enemy to surround him. They thought they'd won.

"We came upon them from behind, killing at will. We killed thousands that day, while they only managed to end the lives of hundreds of our men and women, most of them from Coren's force.

"When I found my brother, he was still alive, but barely. His horse was lying atop him, dead, while he bled from a dozen wounds. Coren couldn't speak, but the look in his eyes said enough. *I was your Shield. Do not waste my sacrifice. Be the king you were always meant to be. Be strong, mine brother.* We took Darrin later that day, but lost it in a week's time, pushed into a full retreat through the tunnels by northern reinforcements. The Ice Lord was present, as was the Dread King of the North. They sealed the tunnel soon after."

Roan felt his eyes stinging. Not from sadness, but from anger at the pointlessness of it all. Of war. Of killing. "Then your brother's death was for naught," he said.

The king's eyes were sword blades. "Say it again and I shall end you," he said. "My brother's death was *for me*, just as my wife's death was for my sons, for her people, whom she loved. Coren paid the ultimate sacrifice so I would be a good king, so I would always remember what I lost to sit on the ore throne, so I would be honorable and wise and protect my people. Gareth will one day make the same sacrifice, and only then will Guy be able to become the king he was always meant to be."

With that, the king pulled his horse away, returning to his place at the front. A few moments later, Roan did the same, unable to stop thinking about what it would be like growing up knowing your life was not your own.

They rode on, the sun reaching its apex as Roan snoozed in his saddle. He was jerked out of his fog when one of the forward scouts galloped back toward the head of the column, shouting loudly. Roan spurred his horse after Gareth's, who'd moved in the direction of his father.

They reached the king at the same moment the scout did. "Ho! Rider! What news?" the king said.

"It's Glee," the rider said. His horse stamped his feet and panted while several horsemen prepared water and oats for the animal, exhausted from the long sprint.

"What of the town?" the king said.

The rider shook his head, his shoulders slumped. "It's riddled with the pox," he said. "I barely escaped with mine own health."

The king growled out a curse, and Roan knew exactly why. The plan from the beginning had been to ride hard and fast, and thus, they'd purposely kept supplies to a minimum. They'd intended to resupply at the two major towns along the way, first Glee, and then Norris.

"We can divert to Portage," Prince Guy suggested. "If we ride hard, we will make it in three days." Roan squinted, trying to remember the old maps his guardian had showed him from time to time. The eastern and western kingdoms were separated by the Spear and Hyro Lake. He could faintly picture Portage as a border town on the eastern edge of the great lake.

"Our forces will be starving in two," the king said.

"Plus the western legions have been harassing Portage for days," Prince Grian said. "We will be required to stay and fight. The people will see us as saviors and reinforcements."

"What about changing course toward the northeast," Gareth said. "Crow's Nest?" Roan knew much of Crow's Nest, the northernmost city in the eastern kingdom. It was located on the rocky elbow where the Mournful Mountains met the Black Cliffs near the northern castle of Darrin. With the exception of the tale the king told about his brother's death, neither the north nor the east had had much success traversing the razor-sharp cliffs in order to penetrate their enemy's lands.

"We'd be better served retreating to Ironwood," the king muttered. "No. We ride on for Raider's Pass. We will reach Norris almost as fast as we would Portage. We'll begin half-rations when we next make camp."

"What about Glee?" Gwendolyn said, entering the conversation. Roan tried to catch her eye, but she was arrow-focused on the king and his sons.

"Glee is not our concern," the king said.

Gwen narrowed her eyes, and Roan was suddenly glad she *wasn't* looking at him. "You are the king, are you not?" she said. "And they are within the bounds of your kingdom, yes?"

Roan gawked at her nerve. In the south, speaking to a member of the Sandes royal family in such a way would only guarantee that your tongue would be served at their next meal, marinated and fried.

And yet here, in the east, the king only looked amused. "I *am* the king, and this *is* my kingdom. We will send word of Glee's predicament to the Orian healers in Ironwood. That is all we can do."

Gwendolyn wasn't about to be placated by such a response. "The healers will be too late. There will be no one left. The pox spreads like wildfire."

The king sighed, and despite the huge size differential between he and Gwendolyn, for once he almost appeared smaller. "What would you have me do?"

Her eyes were golden steel as she finally turned to face Roan. "You have the ultimate healer riding with you. Send Roan to prove his worth."

Chapter Twenty-One

The Northern Kingdom | Approaching Gearhärt

Annise Gäric

Tarin refused to speak to Annise, or even look at her. Ever since she stopped him from killing the tree farmer, he was like a deaf, mute monolith, responding only in grunts and head nods as he dragged the three dead soldiers into the trees and buried them beneath the snow.

She'd sent the farmer and his wife inside to get warm, and she wanted so badly to follow them, but she wouldn't until Tarin was finished. She was scared to leave him alone with the last soldier, who eased in and out of consciousness like a lake trout slipping above and below dark waters. The soldier occasionally moved his arms, but his legs were like stone, and Annise was pretty sure he was paralyzed from the waist down.

Four soldiers. One Armored Knight. No contest. Despite the exceptional fighting ability she'd seen Tarin display during the melee, she wasn't prepared for the level of violence he'd unleashed on these northern soldiers. It made her unlikely defeat of the ice bear on the Howling Tundra appear nothing more than child's play.

Frozen hell, he was like a man possessed. And that look in his eyes as he choked the farmer . . .

It scared her deep in her gut, where she felt a dark hole open up that was more than just gnawing hunger.

Tarin finished with the dead men, his armor smeared with blood, and then stood over the final soldier, who was, at present, sleeping in the snow, his chest rising and falling. Tarin bent down and slipped a knife from the soldier's belt. Ran a gloved finger along the blade, slowly. Pressed it to the man's throat.

"Wait," Annise said.

Tarin didn't move, a statue once more.

"We should question him."

Tarin paused for a moment, and then gave a slight nod, retracting the blade and standing. He took two big steps back, and gestured for Annise to move forward.

She moved next to the fallen soldier and knelt down. Pinched his leg, hard. He didn't react. *Definitely paralyzed.*

"Oh," she said. He didn't react. He was still breathing, hot vapors escaping his lips, which were beginning to look pale blue. She grabbed him by the top of his breastplate, lifting him up off the ground. He was heavy in all his armor, but Annise had always been strong. She'd once heard one of the lordlings refer to her as being strong as an ox. She'd been confident it wasn't a compliment, so she'd forced him to eat yellow snow.

Annise shook the soldier, but still he slept. She glanced at Tarin, who pretended not to watch. Holding him with one hand, she pulled the other hand back and then swung it in a vicious arc.

The man's eyes shot open when she slapped him, a gasp bursting from his lips. He stared at her, his eyes twitching back and forth. He tried to land a punch, but Annise grabbed his arm and forced it down, pressing a knee to his chest, consolidating her strength into a single point. Without use of his legs and without any leverage, the soldier slumped back, resigned.

"What are you doing out here in the middle of nowhere?" Annise asked gruffly.

"You're her," the soldier said.

"Aye, I get that a lot," Annise said.

"You're Princess Annise." He frowned. "What happened to your face?"

Annise pressed down harder. "I wrestled an ice bear. The bear lost."

The man groaned but shut up. "Are you going to answer my questions?" she asked. He nodded. "Good. What is your mission?" She released some of the pressure so he could speak.

"You're going to kill me," the soldier said.

"Not if you answer my questions."

The man looked at her, but said nothing.

Annise reached a hand toward Tarin, flexing her fingers. He understood her meaning, hesitating only a moment before handing her the confiscated knife. She gripped it tightly, and then shoved the blade toward the soldier's face, stopping a hairsbreadth from his eye.

The soldier's breathing accelerated. "Fine, fine, frozen hell, woman!" he gasped. "I'll talk. We were sent to find you."

"How many men are searching?"

Another pause. Annise slid the knife's edge along his skin, shaving off a ragged portion of his beard and cutting him in the process. "Ah! What are you doing?"

"Sorry, never done that before," Annise said. "Want me to do the rest?"

"I was going to answer! I was just thinking. Three hundred. Griswold hand-selected three hundred soldiers to conduct the search. The grid stretches from Castle Hill to Gearhärt to Walburg. We're hitting all the small towns and settlements within the triangle."

"Not Darrin?"

"King Griswold said it was too far east, that he couldn't spare any men away from the front lines."

Annise frowned, ignoring the false title given to her uncle. "Front lines?"

"I can't feel my legs," the soldier said, his eyes going suddenly wide. "Why can't I feel my legs?"

Annise grabbed his jaw and forced him to focus on her. What was left of the stubble of his beard was rough against her palm. "Where are you supposed to go after you conduct your search?" she asked.

"Half to Raider's Pass, the rest to Blackstone." Tarin had been right. Had they taken the main road along the edge of the Mournful Mountains toward Blackstone they'd most likely have been captured already.

"What is happening at Raider's Pass?" The passage through the mountains was too close to Gearhärt for comfort. Arch was supposed to be at Gearhärt.

"The king received a stream from our scouts in the east. King Ironclad and an entire legion is moving for the Pass."

"It could be a defensive maneuver," Annise said.

"It's not. They are preparing for war." Annise's heart fluttered. She knew she shouldn't be surprised. Her father, the king, was dead. Their enemies would expect the north to be in disarray, especially if they'd heard about Queen Loren's execution and Arch and Annise's escape.

"And what of Blackstone? Surely the west wouldn't risk an assault across the Bay of Bounty?" Blackstone had never been taken, and most considered its seaward defenses to be impenetrable.

The soldier shook his head, and for the first time looked slightly amused. "No," he agreed. "In a week's time we'll launch our own offensive across Bounty."

"What?" Annise couldn't hide the surprise in her tone. Her uncle had barely seized power and already he was attacking one of their major rivals? "Why would Lord Griswold do that?"

"*King* Griswold learned of another royal death, this one in the west."

Annise cocked her head to the side. Impossible. One non-war royal death might be an accident, but two? Impossible. "King Loren is dead?"

"And most of his castle guards, if our spies aren't exaggerating in the streams they sent. Only the furia managed to escape the city."

"How? Escape from what?"

"Some say it was a ghost. Others a demon. There were few survivors to tell the tale, and they were too traumatized to do much more than babble incoherently. We were lucky to learn anything at all. Regardless, Knight's End is ripe for the picking and King Griswold plans to take it."

Annise tried to make sense of the news, but all she could seem to think about was the eerie disappearing boy that had appeared on the tower staircase. The boy who had set everything in motion, including her mother's execution. Was he the ghost, the demon? Had he really killed the western guards and their king?

A week ago the tale would've sounded like idle gossip, but now . . .

"What else can you tell me?"

"Nothing," the soldier said, his teeth beginning to chatter from the cold, or perhaps the shock of his injury. Annise believed him. "Now, please. Can we go inside? I'm hungry."

"That's not going to happen," Annise said.

"You said if I answered your questions, that you'd—"

"I lied," Annise said, remembering the way he'd laughed at the farmer and his wife as he threatened their lives.

"Step aside, princess," Tarin said, finally breaking his silence. He grabbed Annise's arm, but she shrugged him off.

"I'll do it," she said, looking back at him. His eyes burned into her, but then he nodded.

She stared at the knife's razor-sharp edge, glinting in the white sunlight reflecting off the snow. In the shiny silver blade, she saw her mother's eyes just before she dropped from the gallows. As much as she tried to make herself believe she was going to kill this man to avenge her mother, she knew it wasn't true. No, she was doing it because she was scared to see Tarin kill again, scared to see that darkness in his eyes.

"No," the soldier pleaded. "I was only following orders. You can't do this. You can't—"

Annise slid the blade between his ribs, and she was shocked at how easily his skin and muscle parted to allow the blood to flow out of him. *No more difficult than cutting cheese*, she thought.

The man gasped, blood bubbling from his lips. His back arched, his arms twitched, and then he went still.

"You're the queerest princess I've ever met," Tarin murmured.

"You've met many princesses?" Annise said, trying to hide the quiver in her voice as she looked away from the corpse. It was so cold that his blood was already freezing in red streams and crimson ponds.

"Well, no," Tarin said. "But I'm certain none would be like you." Something in his voice made her heart speed up, although she wasn't sure why.

"Take care of the body and then meet me inside," she said. "And try not to scare the poor farmers when you enter."

❧

The soup was thin, but hot and flavorful. Annise tried not to slurp as she ate. She was unsuccessful.

She pretended not to notice the farmer and his wife gawking at her.

"You've never seen a princess eat before?" she finally said, after she'd picked up her bowl and tipped it back to suck down the final dregs.

The woman went beet-red and the man looked away, pretending to fiddle with some kind of tool. "We've never seen a princess at all," the woman said.

"Oh." Annise hadn't thought of that. "Is there enough for another bowl?"

The woman nodded and refilled the dish.

"Thank you," Annise said, accepting the food. She drank this bowl slower, savoring it. Who knew when her next warm meal would be?

The cottage was small, but warm and cozy. A fire blazed in the hearth, which the woman had used to cook the soup. There was a small straw bed in one corner of the room, but other than it and the table and four chairs used to serve supper, the space was empty of furniture. A threadbare rug covered a small portion of the floor, which was constructed of long timber boards, cut and shaved smooth. Iron pots and kettles hung from wooden pegs hammered between the stone blocks that formed the walls. Near the door was a small rack for thick sheepskin coats, hats, and gloves. Snow-caked boots were lined up against the wall, puddles forming as the snow melted. For the first time in her life, Annise realized how good she'd had it in the castle. Hearty meals, soft beds. She hadn't used a chamber pot in days! She almost laughed at the absurdity of her thoughts. She never expected to miss her chamber pot so much.

I've been selfish to wish it all away, she thought, sipping another spoonful of soup.

"We owe the thanks to you," the woman said. "If you hadn't come along, who knows what might've happened." The man grunted, and it didn't sound like agreement.

Annise looked up at her sharply. "It was because of me the soldiers came here in the first place. It's my fault you almost—"

"You can't control the actions of others," the woman said. And then: "I'm Moira. My husband is Killorn."

Annise really looked at the woman for the first time, taking in her storm-gray hair, which hung like curtains on either side of her face, her wrinkled skin, her sky-blue eyes. There was something comforting about her. Something motherly. Annise had the urge to fall into her arms and spill out every emotion she'd felt since the melee.

Instead she said, "Annise Gäric."

"We know," the woman said. "Can I clean the cuts on your face? They're deep and susceptible to infection."

Annise raised a hand and touched her cheeks, which were finally warm again. She could feel the jagged lines where the bear had clawed her. "Yes. Thank you," she said.

Moira busied herself with a kettle of water, which she heated over the hearth. A few moments later, she positioned it on the table next to Annise, and used a clean washrag to dab the warm water on her face. Soon the basin was tinged pink with Annise's blood.

"Shall I bind it?" the woman asked.

Annise considered the offer, but then said, "No. Thank you. It might be better for the air to dry and heal the wounds."

"Then it's time for you to go," the man said. "And your friend."

"Killorn," Moira chided. "The princess is our guest."

"According to the soldiers, she's a wanted criminal, and we're guilty by aiding her."

"She saved our lives!"

"It wasn't me who saved you," Annise said quickly. "It was my . . . friend. The knight. And your husband is right. I put you at great risk. We should go."

"Not until your friend has eaten. We owe him a life debt."

Killorn grunted and moved to shove another log into the fire.

"He didn't mean it," Annise said to the man's back. He stiffened. "He was just trying to protect me. He would never hurt someone innocent, I swear it." The man's shoulders slumped and he turned back. Nodded once. "Eat and then go," he said.

"We will." Annise glanced back at the door. Where was Tarin anyway? He should've been back by now.

"He's standing outside," Moira said. "Shall I let him in?"

Annise shook her head, but it wasn't an answer. Of course Tarin wouldn't come in, not after what he'd done—or almost done. "You can try," she said.

Moira scampered over to the thick oak door and hauled it open. Tarin's massive frame filled the entrance, and Annise chortled when he flinched back. "I've never scared anyone before," Moira said.

"Beg your pardon, ma'am," Tarin said. "You just startled me."

"Well come in before you let in a draft."

"I'd rather not."

Annise shook her head. "Get your muscled arse in here, Sir, your princess commands it!"

Tarin ducked his head and entered, and Moira closed the door behind him. When he didn't move from the entrance, Moira said, "Eat your soup before it gets cold, Sir . . ."

"Arme. You can call me Arme," Tarin said.

Annise thought he looked like a lost giant. She stood and grabbed his arm, dragging him to the table and pulling him into a chair, which creaked under his weight.

Moira pushed a bowl in front of him, filled to the brim. "Can I take your helmet?"

"No!" Tarin said.

Moira raised an eyebrow. "It's going to be awfully hard to eat through your mask."

"Sorry," Annise said. "But can you give us a few minutes alone so he can eat?"

"Gladly," Killorn said, glaring at them and stomping toward the door. "I'll get back to work loading my cart." He left, slamming the door behind him.

"Don't mind him," Moira said. "He has trouble showing appreciation for anything."

"I don't blame him," Tarin said, his voice low.

"I'm going to check on Killorn," Moira said. She moved to the door, and only once she'd pulled the door shut behind her did Tarin reach for the bottom of his mesh face cover.

"Turn away," he said.

"Tarin, I've already seen—"

"Turn away, Annise. Please."

Annise pursed her lips, but obeyed. She didn't hear the clank of his spoon, just the barest hint of someone drinking. Less than a minute later, he said, "We should go."

She spun around to find his bowl empty, licked clean, his face mask once more covering him. "You can have seconds," she said. "I did."

"I'm not hungry," he said. "And we need to move on so we can get closer to Gearhärt before dark."

"Tarin, we should talk about what hap—"

"Annise," Tarin said, cutting her off. "I can't. Not now."

"Then when?"

"Maybe never," he said. He started to get up, but Annise grabbed his shoulder. Tarin's eyes flicked to her hand and then back to her face.

"I'm not your judge, jury, or executioner," she said.

"Then what are you?"

"I was a friend, once. Maybe I can be one again."

"I don't have friends," Tarin said.

"What about Sir Dietrich? You let him defeat you in the melee, did you not?"

"What? No. He bested me with his valor and swordsmansh—"

"I don't doubt his ability," Annise interrupted. "But you didn't fight to your full potential. Not the way you did against those four soldiers."

"Clever," Tarin said. "But you're not getting me to talk about that. Maybe I didn't fight as long or as hard as I could have in the melee, but if I had, I still would've lost. There's more to Sir Dietrich than a quick sword." Annise remembered how her uncle had stripped him naked. She remembered all the scars.

"You lost control, so what?" Annise said. "It happens. I lose control all the time. Once I practically neutered a smug lordling from Darrin who tried to kiss me after complimenting my hind parts."

Though she couldn't see it, Annise could sense Tarin's lips curling into a smile. "I'm walking out that door, and I hope you'll follow me," he said, pushing his chair back and standing.

"Maybe you *are* made from stone," Annise muttered, but if Tarin heard, he pretended not to. However, before he could reach the door, it opened, a gust of snowy wind blasting inwards.

Moira and her husband stepped inside. Moira said, "Killorn has something he wants to tell you."

Killorn grunted and stared at his boots. Moira jabbed him with her elbow and he glared at her. Then he spoke. "Thank ye fer what ye done, savin' the missus an' me." He rubbed his bald head, adding, "An' fer not chokin' me dead."

Moira slapped him in the back of his head and said, "What else?"

He shook his head, and she pinched his arm. "Frozen hell, woman! I'm gettin' to it!"

"Getting to what?" Annise asked.

"An offer. I be headin' to Gearhärt in the morn. Ye may ride along in my cart if ye see fit." With that, he spun around and headed back to the barn.

Moira grinned. "Well? What say ye?"

"We appreciate all your kindness," Tarin said, "but—"

"Aye," Annise said. "We say aye."

Tarin turned around to glare at her, but Annise only offered a huge smile. She was hellfrozen tired of walking.

⁂

"Do you have a nearby stream or river?" Tarin asked suddenly. "Even a creek or pond will do."

Annise frowned at him, wondering when his manners had shriveled up and died. For the last few hours, he'd said nothing, as Moira made small conversation with Annise. The kindly woman had tried to include Tarin, but had given up after he'd provided no more than one-word grunted answers in return, staring broodily at the crackling fire. Killorn wasn't present, having excused himself to prepare the wagon for the following day's journey to Gearhärt.

"Aye," Moira said with a smile. She seemed happy to finally have something to talk to Tarin about. "A pond. Our source o' fresh water."

"Have you ever streamed messages from it?" Tarin asked.

"Course. We get news from the castle from time to time. An' we communicate with our timber buyers 'fore my fool of a husband travels there."

"Would you mind if I use a few Gearhärt inkreeds?"

"Who do you know in Gearhärt?" Annise asked.

"A woman," Tarin said cryptically, glancing at Moira.

"I git the hint," Moira said. "A secret then. Never fear, I will gather a pot of ink from our reeds fer ye."

"Thank you," Tarin said.

When she'd gone, Annise said, "What woman?"

"A friend of your aunt's. She lives in Gearhärt."

"Are you certain she's trustworthy?"

Tarin nodded, but didn't say more as Moira returned with a pot of ink, a long black quill, and a torn sheet of wrinkled parchment. "Sorry, but this'll have to do. Parchment ain't cheap so we reuse it."

"It's perfect. Thank you," Tarin said. He situated the paper and ink before himself on the table, and then gently dipped the business end of the quill into the pot. "What is the known name of your pond's inkreeds?"

Moira said, "Moira's Pond. They use it in Gearhärt. 'Tis the only place we send streams to." When Tarin raised his eyebrows, she added, "Killorn don't know his letters, so I do all the writin'."

"You're a good woman," Annise said.

"That's me," she said. "A real catch." She smiled. "I'll leave ye to it."

Annise watched as Tarin inked a cryptic letter to his contact in Gearhärt—a woman named Netta—about a hope flower blooming in the city the following day. He signed it 'AK' and included 'Moira's Pond' as the return location.

"Are you the blooming hope flower or am I?" Annise asked, her lips curling on each side.

"Do I look like someone who wears pink?" Tarin said.

"Do I?" Annise retorted.

"It's not meant to be taken literally. We came up with the code a while ago, when Zelda was making plans. The hope flower was her idea. Let's go."

Annise felt something warm in her chest at the notion as she followed Tarin to the door. At the same time, she wondered what Archer's code name was.

Outside the cottage, Moira and Killorn were loading up a wagon with timber and supplies. Tarin opened his mouth to speak, but Moira waved him off, pointing down the snowy slope, eastward.

They trudged through the snow in the direction Moira had indicated, until they came to a small iced-over lake. It was easy to spot the small pod of inkreeds growing on the embankment beside the frozen water. Tarin started to bend down by the edge, but Annise stopped him with a hand on his arm.

"Can we talk about what happened earlier?" she asked.

"No." He pulled his arm away, locating a sharp stone, presumably to break the ice with.

"Tarin—"

"What, Annise? Do you want to know about how the thing inside me screamed in my head as I fought? How fires burned through my veins? How my muscles were ready to snap, to choke, to pummel anything and everything nearby? Or how about the cold and the emptiness I felt in my chest when it was over, when the strength and adrenaline left me, when I was all alone again? Is that what you want me to say?"

"Yes," Annise said.

Tarin looked back sharply over his shoulder.

Annise sighed. "Look, I might not be able to understand exactly what it feels like to be you, but I *want* to understand. You don't have to be alone, Tarin. Not anymore."

He began chipping away at the ice, which broke off in chunks. "I will always be alone." He cleared a large enough hole in the ice directly in front of the thatch of inkreeds to fit his message into.

Annise watched him as he worked, how tenderly he handled the sheet of parchment, his giant gloved hands as agile as a seamstress's. She could hardly imagine the man before her was the same man who'd brutalized four soldiers without breaking a sweat.

He dipped the parchment into the cold water, holding it under for a few moments. Slowly, the ink faded away until it vanished completely, leaving the parchment wet and clear. Although Annise had streamed hundreds of messages herself, usually requesting the results of tournaments across the realm, the process still amazed her, how the ink could travel such great distances through water only to reform in the exact letters and words in which it was written. Somewhere in Gearhärt   wherever the ink was harvested from—the message would appear in the water only to be transferred to parchment and delivered to this Netta woman.

"How long do you think it will take her to respond?" Annise asked as Tarin gathered up the wet parchment and laid it out to dry in the snow.

Tarin said, "You're not going to argue about what I said before?"

Annise shrugged. "I can't change your mind. Only you can change your mind. In any case, you're not alone now, even if you think you are."

His eyes met hers, and he shook his head. "I've never met anyone quite like you."

She laughed. "Was that an attempt at a compliment?" Before he could respond, she added, "Anyway, you *have* met someone like me . . . me! About ten years ago, remember? We ran, I rubbed snow in your face, you cried?"

Finally, he laughed, and Annise was acutely aware how much she'd missed that sound, a deep rumble that seemed to originate deep in his chest. "I could never forget you," he said. "Or the snow being rubbed in my face."

She was considering her next jape, when something caught her eye. "Look!" she said, pointing at the hole in the ice.

In the water, words were forming. They were difficult to read as they bounced and churned on the crests of tiny wavelets. Tarin placed the damp paper back in the water, and the ink immediately stuck to it. When he withdrew it, Annise peered over his shoulder. The message was short:

I'll pick some hope flowers tomorrow then.

Come hungry.

Netta.

"Come hungry?" Annise said. "Is that another code for something?"

Tarin laughed. "No, in this case Netta means exactly what she says. She's the best damn cook I know."

Annise's stomach rumbled. Moira's thin soup had done little to sate her appetite.

❧

Despite having been given the lumpy bed and getting the best sleep she'd had since fleeing Castle Hill, Annise had been surprised to find herself missing sharing the little tent with Tarin, feeling his arm tight and warm against her, her body nestled within his gargantuan frame.

Frozen hell, I'm pathetic, she thought as he offered her a hand up onto the timber-laden cart. His face mask was smudged with something ash-dark.

During the night, she'd woken once, in the darkness, and heard a soft sound arising from Tarin's large form. Crying. He'd been crying. She'd listened to his muffled sobs for a few moments, wondering whether she should go to him, to comfort him, but then they'd stopped.

I will always be alone—his words from the pond the day before continued to unsettle her.

She'd rolled over and gone back to sleep.

Now she ignored his hand and used brute strength to haul herself aboard. She turned back and provided her own hand to pull him up beside her. He shook his head. "My lady is in a queer mood this morning."

"*Your lady* got cold last night." It was a lie, but, after a good night's sleep, she was feeling exceptionally bold.

"It was plenty warm next to the fire," he said. Tarin had slept sprawled out like a cat beside the hearth, refusing to remove a single plate of his armor, even when Moira had offered a large blanket to cover him. *What is he saying?* Annise wondered. That she should've joined him beside the fire? She hated that she could never read his expressions because of his damn mask.

He made his way toward the front of the cart, where Killorn had created an empty space within the stacked timber. It would be tight, but they would fit well enough to remain hidden should anyone happen upon the cart on the road to Gearhärt.

Tarin slid in first, squirming to one side so Annise could follow. She dropped inside, propping her back against the rough wood. It would be a long, uncomfortable ride to the castle, but it would be better than traipsing through the thick coat of fresh snow that had fallen overnight.

Killorn's face appeared above them. "If anyone stops us, shut yer traps," he barked. "Once we arrive, I'll find a place fer ye to slip away. Then I ne'er want to see yer faces agin. Ya hear?"

Moira's face appeared next to his, and she said, "What my lovin' husband means is that we 'ppreciate what ye done fer us and this is how we repay our debt."

"Thank you," Annise said. "But your debt is already paid."

"Then why are we haulin' ye to—" Killorn started to say, but was cut off when his wife jabbed his ribs with a finger.

"We're honored to be of service to a princess of the north," Moira said.

Their faces disappeared, and were soon replaced by several wooden boards, which covered the hole, allowing only thin slits of light to peek through. Wind whistled between the timber as Killorn said, "Giddup, lasses!" and the cart lurched forward, hauled by a trio of grizzled gray ponies.

The snowy road was bumpy, and soon Annise was almost regretting her decision to accept a ride. Twice she banged her head on the timber and cursed, and twice Tarin chuckled. "You should wear armor," he said. "Like me."

"To hide my face?" Annise snapped back, rubbing her bruised scalp. A goose egg was already rising from her skin.

Tarin went quiet for a moment, and then said, "Your words wound me, my queen. Maybe you are not what the lordlings of Castle Hill call traditional beauty, but you are beautiful all the same."

Annise practically choked. It was the last thing she expected him to say. The last thing she expected *anyone* to say. She remembered what he'd said before, about her tendency to hide behind self-deprecating japes as a hundred sprang to mind. She chose one of her favorites: "The princess of the north is so robust that if she stretched out she could insulate half of Castle Hill."

"At least you're not scrawny."

"The princess of the north once bested a royal steed with *both* hands bound behind her back. How? you might ask. She sat on him."

"At least you're not weak."

Annise was on a roll and not about to stop now. "The princess of the north once devoured an entire royal feast in one sitting. And then she ate the plates and silverware, not to mention the table and chairs."

"A healthy appetite, by my reckoning," Tarin said.

Annise finally stopped, unable to hold back her laughter. Once the very quips she'd just spoken had wounded her deeply, but now they seemed so unimportant. Such small things. Frozen hell, she'd fought off an ice bear!

"Why do you defend me? Because we knew each other once?"

"No," Tarin said. "Because we know each other now. Because I see the snowstorms in your eyes. Because you were worth it then and you still are, my Queen of the North."

Annise was dead glad to be able to hide in the shadows of their tiny crawlspace, her face turning as red as the rising sun. Before he could embarrass her further, she went on the offensive. "And what of you?" she said. "You hide your true self behind dark armor, making the world believe you're a monster."

"Maybe what they believe is true." His voice sounded like it had descended into a deep pit.

"Why? Because you fight like a champion of the north?"

Tarin said nothing.

"Why were you crying last night?" Annise asked.

Silence for a moment, and then, "I'm sorry you heard me. I'm sorry I disturbed your sleep."

"Sleep be damned, answer my question."

"I was mourning."

"Whom?" Annise asked, but then had a thought. "My mother?"

"Yes."

Fresh anger, as hot and bright as the sun, burst inside her veins. "You don't get to mourn her. Not you."

"I loved her as much as my own mother," Tarin said.

Annise squeezed her fists until her fingernails bit into her palms. The familiar urge to launch herself at him was there. It wasn't fair that he should love a woman she'd always tried to love. Sabria Loren was *her* mother, not his. But the way he'd cried for her, his secret tears spilling through the night like a dark waterfall . . .

The anger shredded itself into ribbons of sorrow. She couldn't imagine what he was feeling. He'd killed someone he'd loved. The order wasn't his, and someone else would've done it if he hadn't, but still. He'd kicked the platform away. He'd been close enough to catch her body before the rope tightened around her neck.

But he hadn't. Tarin had watched her mother die, and then he'd saved Annise and her brother. Sir Dietrich too.

All because it was what the queen commanded him to do.

"I don't expect you to forgive me," Tarin said. "Everything I am is darkness. Even my tears are black."

The ashy smudges on his face mask, she realized. *Dried tears from the night before.* "I'm trying to understand," Annise admitted.

"There's nothing to understand. I'm a dangerous man. But not to you. Never to you."

It was Annise's turn to remain silent, unable to find the words, her tears threatening to cascade like clear waterfalls down pale cliffs.

"I almost killed Killorn," Tarin eventually said. "An innocent man."

"Adrenaline and bloodlust," Annise said. "Nothing more." Was she really defending him? Yes. And maybe he deserved it.

Thin lines of light carved his helmet into pieces as he shook his head. "I lost control. The *thing* inside me was the only voice I could hear."

"And then you heard mine," Annise said.

"And if you hadn't been there?"

"I *was* there."

"But if you weren't I would've killed him. So what does that make me?"

"Imperfect," Annise said. "Human. You can't control everything. You can't control the disease that afflicted you as a child. You can't control that the witch had to curse you to save you. All you can do is take what you've been given and live."

Tarin sighed. "I will if you will."

"I already *am*," Annise insisted. "I'm here. I'm fighting."

"No you're not," Tarin said. "You're off in the Hinterlands hiding from your destiny. That's what you keep talking about, aye?"

"So what? I don't want to be a princess. I don't want to be a queen. I don't want to rule the north. Why can't I choose another path?"

Tarin grasped her hand with his gloved fingers, his grip fierce and firm. "Because that's not who you are."

"What do you know of me? You've been gone for years! As a child I mourned your death! You were *my friend*. And you left me."

"Not by choice."

"You could've said goodbye. You could've told me something, not let my mother lie about what happened to you."

"I was just a child. I was scared of my own skin, of the darkness flowing through my veins. I still am."

Annise knew he was right and that she wasn't being fair. "I'll find Arch and convince him to leave the kingdom forever. Let my uncle tear the north apart in his war with the other three kingdoms. Frozen hell, I don't care if he's victorious and anoints himself King of the entire Four Kingdoms. As long as I don't have to be a prisoner in Castle Hill any longer."

"You don't mean that. And anyway, Arch will never leave the kingdom."

"He will. He must. I lost a brother once, I won't lose another."

"What?" Tarin said, his tone full of surprise. "What brother?"

Annise clamped her mouth shut, annoyed that in the heat of the argument she'd said more than she wanted to. "Nothing. It's not important."

"You had another brother? I've never heard about another prince."

"He died as an infant. It was kept secret from the realm. Dead royals are considered bad luck."

"What was his name?"

The question took Annise by surprise. Why did his name matter? "My parents hadn't decided. He was three days old when he was killed."

"Murdered?"

Annise swallowed a lump in her throat. She'd mourned the loss of her brother for days and months and years. The truth was, she'd never gotten over him, not really.

"When I said I bore no scars, I lied," Annise said.

"Who would kill an infant?"

"Wolves," she said, the word sticking in her throat. Her mouth tasted bitter. "A door to the nursery was left unlocked and ajar, as well as an outer door. My mother had only been gone for a moment, but that was all it took."

Annise realized Tarin's hand was still clutching hers. She pulled away, both from his hand and from the topic of her dead brother. "Help me or not, that is your choice. But I will flee to the Hinterlands."

"If that is truly what you want, I will help you."

The road bumped. The wind whistled through the timber. Annise cursed under her breath. "Damn you for being so gallant all the time."

Tarin chuckled. "I've been called many things, but never gallant."

"A gallant monster," Annise said.

"Sounds like an awful bedtime story," Tarin said.

"Shhh!" Annise hissed.

She'd heard hoof beats and shouts.

Chapter Twenty-Two

The Eastern Kingdom | Approaching Glee

Roan

Apparently Gwendolyn's opinion meant much to the king, because now Roan found himself riding beside her and a dozen scouts, heading for the small waystation called Glee, which had been overrun by the eastern disease known simply as the pox, or occasionally as mottle, a flesh-eating illness that was known to twist the minds of its victims. The king and the princes would not risk coming within a league of the town.

Great, he thought. *My life can be summed up as 'From the Plague to the Pox'.* At least he was fairly certain there would be no dragons, two-headed or otherwise, to contend with.

When the edges of the ramshackle town appeared in the distance, the scouts reigned their horses to a stop. Tendrils of gray smoke curled from the roofs of several of the town's structures. *A good sign,* Roan thought. *At least the people are well enough to build fires in their hearths.*

"Orespeed," one of the scouts said, an eastern wish for good luck and success.

Gwen nodded to Roan and dismounted. "We cannot risk the horses. The disease spares no living creature."

Roan followed her lead, handing his ropes to one of the scouts. Gwen strode forward, ever fearless. Roan scurried after her, nearly tripping on the thick tufts of grass sprouting from the hillside.

Glee was nestled in an emerald valley, a long narrow river snaking down the gradual decline and swooping along the edge of the town. Blades of sunlight snuck past the clouds, which made the flowing waters sparkle like newly forged steel. Roan veered off toward the stream, his mouth suddenly dry. He cupped his hands in the cool, clear water, bringing it up toward his mouth.

"Do not drink," Gwen cautioned. "We do not know where the pox originated. The water may carry the disease."

Roan stopped, and when he looked at the water it now seemed dark and foreboding. He let it spill between his fingers, which he rubbed dry on the grass. "Thank you for the warning."

"I did it for the people of Glee," Gwen said, turning away. "They need what you can offer."

What can I offer? Roan wondered. He didn't truly know what he was capable of. The urge to flee from the town was like a stone wall pushing him back.

Gwen turned and glared at him. "Time is of the essence," she said.

Roan forced one foot after the other, each step feeling more difficult than the one prior. Still, he managed to catch up to the Orian when she slowed. "Will your mark protect you from the pox?" he asked.

She shook her head. "No. But you will."

"What?" A flood of fear washed over him, as if the stream had burst its banks and crashed upon his shoulders. He couldn't let her life be in his hands. "No. Stay here. I will go into the town alone," he said.

"The pox . . . *changes* people." She pointed to her head. "The afflicted see things that aren't there. They're unpredictable and dangerous. You can't protect yourself and help them at the same time. I'm coming."

Her words were as firm and unmoving as the trees of Ironwood, rooted in the metallic ground. When she spoke them, the mark on her cheek blazed to life momentarily, and then flickered out.

"What power does your mark give you?" Roan asked again. *And why would it show itself when you merely spoke?*

"That is not your concern," Gwen said. She started forward once more, the town a mere stone's throw away now.

Again, Roan followed, the smell of smoke growing thicker and more pungent with each step. That's when he saw the flames, bright red and orange tongues licking the tops of several of the wooden structures. What he'd originally thought was smoke from hearth fires was in reality a raging inferno devouring the town.

Roan tried to call out to Gwen to wait, but she had already slipped between the first two buildings on the edge of town. He hustled to catch up, sidling up beside her at the corner of a wooden structure that was, thankfully, not on fire.

What he saw turned his skin to gooseflesh.

A woman ran across what was likely once a thriving marketplace, screaming. Flames swept up her legs, torso, and chest. She was chased by a man brandishing a torch. He caught her, slamming it into her back. She fell, and he landed atop her, the flames sweeping over him in a rush as a stiff gust of wind hit them.

Another man, shirtless, his muscles bulging, wielded a blacksmith's sledge. He was swinging it wildly at anything and anybody that moved. Dead chickens, hogs, and humans lay strewn about him. "Devils!" he roared with each swing. "Devils! Devils! Devils!"

Other afflicted townsfolk were committing equally horrifying atrocities. A flock of children, their mouths contorted in fierce snarls, surrounded a man who seemed remarkably lucid, trying to hold them off with a metal frying pan. The children threw sharp stones, pelting the man's face and body, blood pouring from each wound. "Help!" the man screamed, to no one in particular. If there were any other people not taken by the pox, they were ignorant to his cries.

We're too late, Roan thought.

He began to back away from the carnage, even as Gwen sprang forward. Roan tried to grab her arm, but she was already gone, moving with blinding speed through the square, dodging flames and blunt weapons swung by delirious hands.

Roan was frozen in place, only able to watch as she leapt the circle of stone-throwing children, grabbed the man around the waist, and retreated. The maniacal children gave chase, slinging stones, most of which bounced harmlessly away.

Gwen reached Roan a moment later, laying the man at his feet. The man was still gripping the frying pan tightly, a glazed fearful look in his eyes. He was covered from head to toe in flat red spots. Mottle.

"Heal him," Gwendolyn commanded.

"What about you?" he asked, but she was already gone, off to find another victim who could still be rescued.

Roan looked at the man, who was suddenly staring at him as if he were a monster, his eyes dark, his mouth an angry growl. "Get away from me!" he screamed. With a wicked swing, he slammed the metal pan into Roan's head. Spots danced before Roan's vision as he went down.

The memory crackled through his mind like flames. The girl with the broken leg. Healing her. The smell of burnt flesh. Charred corpses. So small. So heart-wrenchingly small.

His vision cleared and the man screamed again, launching himself toward Roan. Roan tried to roll, but the pox seemed to strengthen his adversary, giving him supernatural speed. He clamped claw-like hands around Roan's throat, digging into his soft flesh. Roan's lifemark flared, healing his skull and his neck simultaneously, sapping his strength. He knew he could help this man, who was clearly not himself.

But all he could see in the man's face were those tiny, charred corpses. All he could smell in the air was burning flesh. He remembered his guardian's warning, that if he healed someone marked for death then he would die in their place. All he could do was heal himself and—

He bucked his body like a wild horse, throwing the man off. He kicked him hard in the face and took off, running through the square, heat rushing through his veins. *WhereissheWhereissheWhereisshe?*

There! He spotted Gwen fighting to wrench a screaming child from the grip of two women who appeared to be trying to rip the little girl's arms off. Behind Gwen, there was another form closing in, waving a torch, lighting houses and people afire with each step.

The crazed torchbearer reached for Gwen.

Roan opened his mouth to warn her, but before he could another figure streaked out from the cover of one of the intact structures, tackling the man with a heavy thump.

Roan raced forward and grabbed one of the women from behind. She kicked and screamed and bit Roan's hand, but he wouldn't let go until he'd dragged her well clear. With only one delirious woman to contend with, Gwen broke the child loose and carried her away, shouting, "Healer! With me! With me!"

Gwen wasn't aware of what had transpired behind her, how close she'd come to death. Roan looked back at the figure who had saved her, a strange creature that was now on fire, swaying and stumbling as he tried to escape the town's boundaries.

It was Bark.

Acting purely on instinct, Roan ran for the man with the rough skin, simultaneously ripping off his own cloak and wrapping it around him. He could feel the heat of the flames through the fabric, but refused to give them air, forcing them to die down to smoke and ash. He slung Bark's wood-like arm over his shoulders, and helped him stagger through the square. Twice they were accosted by pox-afflicted villagers, and twice Roan was forced to throw Bark to the ground to fend them off with well-placed kicks.

And then, abruptly, they were out of the chaos, screams and cries fading behind them.

He found Gwendolyn curled up in a ball beside the child, who was crying. "Hush, child," Gwen kept repeating, even as red spots erupted from her own skin. The Orian's eyes were slowly closing, but flashed open when Roan and Bark staggered and fell beside her.

"Bark? How did you . . . ? What are you . . . ? What happened?"

"He saved your life," Roan gasped, his lifemark staving off the pox. "You didn't see, but he did."

Bark's blackened skin twitched as he tried to speak. "My hero," he rasped. "At long last, my debt is paid." He collapsed, his eyes closing.

"No!" Gwen screamed, which made the little girl cry harder. "Save him. Roan! Save him!"

Roan was exhausted, and he was using his lifemark to stave off the pox, which was slowly draining what little energy he had left. Plus, all three of them were marked for death now.

If he healed any of them, he would die. He hesitated for only the barest of moments. *This is it*, he thought. *This is my purpose. To save these lives. To sacrifice myself for something good.*

"You first," he said to Gwen, determination coursing through him.

"No!" she shouted, grabbing him by the collar. She shook him, commanding him to save Bark, to save the little girl, but nothing she did could stop Roan from using his power on her, a stream of white light arcing from his chest and into her skin.

The red spots faded, and then disappeared entirely. Weariness flooded Roan, and his vision grew fuzzy around the edges. *I'm dying*, he thought. He didn't care, because he'd saved her. He'd done what he couldn't do for that little girl all those years ago.

Gwen slapped Roan, hit him in the chest, and he flinched, his eyes widening. "Not me, you fool!" she screamed. "Bark! Save Bark!"

Roan wondered whether he had enough strength left to save another, to make his death count for even more. His hand shaking, he reached out and touched Bark's burnt flesh, shocked at how hot it still was. His lifemark probed the man, feeling nothing. He was already gone. "I'm sorry," he said, "there's nothing to be done."

Gwen shook her head, tears sparkling in her golden eyes, which were full of anger and regret. "The girl," she growled. "It's not too late."

Roan turned his attention toward the little girl, whose midnight hair was full of natural ringlets. She'd stopped crying and was staring at him, her eyes full of a mix of rage and fear. "Demon," she breathed.

She tried to swing her tiny fist at Roan's face, but he caught it, his lifemark burning up his chest, giving this poor child everything he had left.

When he had nothing left to give, he collapsed and the world faded into nothingness.

≈

Roan awoke with a gasp, the pain in his chest like a burning fist repeatedly punching him. *Where am I? Is this where souls go? Do I even have a soul?*

At first all he saw was a gray, cloud-filled sky, but then—

A pair of big brown eyes, framed by tiny black ringlets of hair.

"Unnnh," he groaned.

"He's alive!" a tiny mouth shrieked.

I am? But how? He'd saved the lives of *two* other people. He should be dead.

"The Southroner must be part ore cat, for he has more lives than good sense," another voice said. Prince Gareth. "First dragons and the plague, then a stab to the gut, and now pox. The Great Orion smiles upon you."

"Of course he's alive," a gruff voice said. King Ironclad. "The royal healer's skills are unmatched."

"I didn't *do* anything," another voice said. The royal healer, presumably.

Roan blinked to find a kindly face pressing in beside the tiny sprite of a girl with the dark ringlets. "Wha—what happened?" he asked.

"You survived the pox, that's what happened," the man said. A healer, the king had said.

Of course I did, Roan wanted to say. The pox was no issue. But how had he survived healing Gwen and the girl? The little girl in front of him looked familiar.

Yes. She'd lunged at him, called him a demon. She'd had the pox, too, and he'd used his mark to heal her.

Images sprang up, unbidden, slashing across his vision like a hot knife. Burning flesh. Wisps of smoke. A pit of ash. "Please," Roan said. "Don't. Don't hurt her."

The healer frowned. "He looks awake, but he appears to be having a waking nightmare. He needs to rest."

"No," Roan said, squinting when Prince Gareth sidled beside the healer, his metal armor reflecting blades of sunlight.

"Good, because we need to move on before the Orian tries to charge into Glee again."

"Gwendolyn?" Roan said. He remembered healing her, but had he done enough to stave off the disease?

"She saved me," the little girl said. "And then you saved me. You're my heroes. I'm Fria and the prince let me water his horse and I ate three bowls of soup. When can I go see my ma and da?"

Roan's head was spinning and he was struggling to keep up with the girl's rapid changes of topic. "Your parents?"

"Come, Fria," the healer said, ushering her away. "Roan needs to rest."

"But I—"

"You can speak to him later."

As she was pushed away, Fria looked back at Roan and grinned. He couldn't help but to mirror her smile. "Where are her parents?" he asked, when she had gone.

"Dead," Prince Gareth said. "Along with her brothers and sisters. She had two of each."

Roan's abdomen constricted. He remembered the horrific scenes from Glee. The violence. The killing. "Survivors?"

Gareth's face was as somber as Roan had ever seen it. "Only Fria. Unless you include you and Gwendolyn."

Roan took a deep breath. He'd saved two people. They were alive. His guardian was dead—he wasn't going to rise from the grave and burn Fria and Gwen. As much as he knew it to be true, he couldn't stop his heart from hammering in his chest.

And he was alive, despite what his guardian had told him. *A lie*, he thought. *My guardian lied to me so I wouldn't use my mark to save anyone.*

Then he remembered one other. "Bark?"

The prince shook his head. "He was badly burned. His body was already weak from his own affliction."

"*He* saved Gwendolyn. Not me."

A flash of silver flared in the corner of his eye. Gwen appeared, her eyes stormier than he'd ever seen them. "Yes. Bark saved me. Yet you wouldn't save him."

"I tried," Roan said, feeling a pang in his chest when he remembered how lifeless the man had been when he'd touched him.

"Not hard enough. Bark bore no mark, had no magic. Yet he came when no one else would."

Roan could hardly bear the anger in the Orian's eyes, but he refused to look away. "He was a hero," Roan said.

Gwendolyn spat in disgust. "That word," she said, "is meaningless. People love to throw it around like a badge of honor. Bark *was* a hero, but that doesn't even begin to describe the man he was. He would've saved the entire town if he could have, even if it meant his own death. You, on the other hand . . ." She shook her head. "You are no hero, no matter what the girl says."

The words were meant to injure, but Roan felt nothing but numbness. He knew he could tell her he thought he would die if he saved her, and yet he did it anyway, but did that make him a hero? *No*, he knew. It made him tired. It made him human. But not a hero. He would never tell her the truth, not even if she tried to torture it out of him. He didn't want credit, not when he'd wasted so many years avoiding the suffering of others. Suffering he could've relieved. "I agree," he said.

Gwen raised the edge of her lip and glared at him one last time. Then she stalked off.

For once, the prince didn't laugh at Roan. "For what it's worth," he said. "I think you did everything you could."

The prince left, and Roan noticed another, larger form lurking nearby. Beorn Stonesledge approached, making no effort to mask his footsteps. "There is great fear in you," the warrior said, casting a shadow across Roan's face. "Why?"

Roan didn't know how to respond, so he asked a question of his own. "Why do you wear a symbol of your mark around your neck?" he asked, eyeing the chain dangling from the man's thick throat.

"Because else none would know I was marked."

The concept of flaunting a mark was so foreign to Roan he was at a loss for words.

Beorn explained: "I am a warrior. A battle is almost always won or lost 'fore it begins. The first volley is fear, and when men see the sign of me mark they piss their britches. I am victorious without ever landing a single blow."

That's why he mentioned the fear he saw in me, Roan realized. *He thinks I'm weak.*

"Where is your mark?" Roan asked.

"On me arse!" Beorn laughed, a sound more akin to a roar than a chuckle. "Me ma about died when she was bathing me in the firelight and saw it blaze forth."

Roan wished he could laugh, but couldn't find it inside himself. Not when he had no memories of his own mother. He used to think he was angry at his mother for abandoning him to the south, for dying so he could live. He used to think his life wasn't worth it if his own mother had to die in his place. But now he knew those feelings were those of a scared little boy. Realization pressed in on all sides. The only way to make his mother's sacrifice worthwhile was for him to live the life he was always meant to. A life that mattered.

"Have you ever feared using your mark?" Roan asked Beorn now.

Beorn raised one dark bushy brow. "Every day," he said, which wasn't the answer Roan had expected. "Sometimes I'm too strong," he explained. "I can hurt someone by accident, when I mean to do something else."

Roan chewed on that for a moment. He understood the feeling all too well. "Have you ever killed someone by mistake?"

"Yes," Beorn said. "Maybe they deserved it, maybe not. But it wasn't for me to decide. Not in this particular case. And once, I drove someone away. Someone I loved."

"Who?"

"A woman," Beorn said. He looked away from Roan, his expression wistful, radiating memories. "A woman I loved."

"What happened?"

"She was special. Ida. A good name. A strong name. For a good, strong woman. We got on well, talked all the time. I was sorely tempted to touch her. She seemed to want the same. But when I wrapped me arms around her, me emotions got the better of me and I squeezed too hard. Broke her ribs. Snapped a couple bones in her back. She never wanted to see me again."

His eyes ratcheted back to meet Roan's stare, his expression dark and steely. "Love's not for me. Not anymore. I'm here for one thing and one thing only: War."

With that said, Beorn Stonesledge lumbered away, one hand playing with his iron necklace.

ॐ

"Wait!" Roan said, urging his horse forward.

When the battalion had started moving again, Roan had sought out the Orian, but Gwen was already well ahead of the column, galloping toward the ever-darkening horizon. Her eyes were focused forward, as if she couldn't bear to look back at the plumes of storm-black smoke erupting from the town of Glee.

They'd burned the entire town to the ground to ensure the disease was eradicated.

Gwen charged forward, away from Roan. He gave chase, his horse's hoof beats like thunder on the road, which had become stony and hard.

To his surprise, he seemed to be gaining on her, though she was a far superior rider and her steed normally ran like the wind. He pulled astride, glancing over.

Her intentions registered a moment too late for him to react.

She threw herself from her horse, slamming her shoulder into his chest. He toppled from his mount, grunting as she landed atop him and all air left his lungs. She pinned him to the ground, needlessly—he couldn't even breathe, much less fight back.

As he wheezed, she said, "They'll call you a hero because you healed that girl. But you're not. Nor am I. She was one soul amongst hundreds of innocents. We *failed* them, you and I. We *failed* Bark. We *failed* ourselves."

Roan tried to respond, but could only issue a ragged wheeze.

Gwen bit her lip and the anger seemed to leave her. Her shoulders slumped and a single tear slipped from her eye, meandering down her cheek. It was liquid silver. She rolled off of him, and for a few moments all he could hear was the sound of her breathing and his own wheezing as he struggled to regain his breath.

When he felt he could speak again, he said, "What happened with you and Bark? Why is he so important to you?"

Gwen's eyes shot to his, and then darted away. "I'm surprised Gareth hasn't told you."

"He said to ask you. He said you saved Bark's life. That's why he always called you his hero."

Gwen laughed without mirth. "I saved Bark's life, yes, but only after he saved a dozen others. Ever since I've known him, he's been a talented blacksmith. Years ago, he had traveled south, to Hammerton, to sell his wares. I was there, gathering information for the king on the war efforts. Not Oren, but his father, Hamworth. At the time, the Phanecians had been pushing across the Spear and attacking Hammerton."

She paused, and Roan sensed she was gathering her thoughts. He waited patiently.

"An attack came, but not from the Phanecians. From the Calypsians, who had managed to sail a fleet of small warships across the Burning Sea and up the Spear, undetected. They set fire to the city, pouring hot oil from the walls, which they had scaled under the cover of night. Flaming arrows fell upon us like falling red stars. Sadly, most of the soldiers fled rather than fought. Later, they faced the king's wrath for cowardice in battle.

"Bark did not flee, though he was not a soldier. He saved many lives— men, women, children. I even saw him carry a hound away from the smoke and flames. And yet, like me, he kept going back to save others. He didn't bear a mark, like me. But that didn't stop him. Eventually I had to pull him away, because there was no one else to save—the others all dead. No one but him, of course. From that day forward he refused to call me anything but a hero. But it was he, not I, who was a hero that day. He who had a choice, and still he risked his life for the sake of another."

When the tale was finished, she looked right at Roan. "You are nothing like him."

Roan felt his cheeks turn red, but it wasn't from embarrassment. It was because the truth was like a hot sun beating down on him, burning his skin. "I never said I was a hero. I'm not. I never will be." The unsteadiness in his voice only served to help make his point.

"Is that the truth? Because you never seem to say what you mean."

Truth swelled on his tongue, but Roan swallowed the words back down. He couldn't say what he wanted to. Didn't know how. He only said, "Yes. It's the truth."

Gwen growled. "How long did you live in the west? Who are you really? I know a lie when I hear one, and your tongue is full of deceit."

Roan wanted to tell her, truly, but he couldn't, for it would mean his death if she passed the information on to King Ironclad.

Gwen spat in the dirt. "I thought you were different. I've never met someone with a mark like yours, like mine. Something used to *help* people. Beorn Stonesledge only uses his ironmark for killing. Then there's the Ice Lord in the north, Fire Sandes and her damn firemark in Calypso, and the Slave King, Vin Hoza, in Phanes. Their marks are used for terror. For power. For control. You could be different. You *should* be different."

But he wasn't. "I'm sorry," Roan said, hating every word crowding inside his mouth. Hating how true they were, how pathetic. "You don't know me. What I've done. I cannot do what you ask of me." He wanted to tell her about the dead girl haunting his dreams in the dark of night, but he knew it would only sound like another excuse, and he was done with excuses.

"And you think you know what I've done?" Gwen said, her voice rising. "What I've lost? You don't know a damn thing about me."

It wasn't the response Roan expected. "Tell me about your bondmate. The poet soldier."

She shook her head, grimacing. She stood up, not bothering to look at him, and remounted her horse, which had stopped when she'd leapt off. She galloped away toward the sunset.

Chapter Twenty-Three

The Western Kingdom | On the road to Talis

Grease Jolly

Grease Jolly stumbled along the southern road. His stump was throbbing something fierce.

No, he thought. *Not my stump. My hand.*

Which made him crazy. Or delirious. Or both. Because he didn't have a second hand. The Furies had made sure of that. And yet . . . he could still *feel* it. He could feel the aching in each individual bone in his hand, his fingers. *My hand hurts.*

"Godsdamn madness," Grease muttered.

But still he staggered onward, because they had his sister, a fact that was far worse and more painful than losing a hand.

One question kept bobbing around in his mind, like a makeshift raft on the open sea. *Why?* Why was Shae still alive, despite being marked, an enemy to the kingdom? Why had the Furies abducted her? And where in the cursed western kingdom were they taking her?

He'd been following the dirt track for hours, long after the sun had breached the horizon's defenses and fought its way into the sky. Though the impressions weren't deep, Grease had no trouble following the hoofprints left by the furia's horses as they'd fled Knight's End.

This is her fault, Grease thought, trying to convince himself once more. He wanted someone to blame, someone to curse, but, try as he might, he couldn't. Princess Rhea's actions had been rash and unjustified, but what he'd done to her had been awful too. Seeing her at the end, so destroyed by her father's death, had nearly wrenched his heart from his chest.

He jammed his bloody stump against his forehead, his mind clearing as pain lanced up his arm. "My fault," he said, the words chasing the princess, who he'd likely never see again, from his mind. He'd promised his parents that he would protect Shae, and now she was in grave danger because of his own stupidity. Which left him with only one choice: get her back or die trying.

Thunder growled in the distance. Grease looked up at the sky, which appeared clear as far as he could see. The thunder continued rolling toward him, getting closer.

Not thunder—horses, he realized. He needed to get off the road. To the left was prairieland and to the right the sea. The road ahead curled around a series of large cliff-facing boulders, disappearing from sight.

The hoofbeats were getting closer. He veered left, tripping twice over his own traitorous feet before diving behind a thick bramble of brittle plants that poked his skin, drawing blood.

Not a moment too soon. The furia burst from behind the boulders, stampeding around the bend and past him, right where he'd been standing. Through the nest of branches, he watched them, their red capes flashing like sunbursts.

Shae, Shae, Shae . . . He pleaded with his eyes to find her, to see her alive and breathing, carried by one of the holy warriors. The last of the furia whipped past and then they were gone, heading back toward Knight's End.

Shae wasn't with them. And there'd only been one of the Three Furies, riding at the front, leading her warriors. The group of furia had seemed too small, like they'd split up, half returning to Knight's End while the remainder made for some other location.

But where?

Energized by the possibility that the rest of the furia—and his sister—might be close, Grease fought to his feet, ignoring the spots of blood welling from his punctured skin, and returned to the road.

He ran. Slowly at first, but then faster, curving around the boulders, weaving right and then left as the road snaked away from him. He cleared the final obstruction and then stopped, his chest heaving, his lungs burning, his hands on his knees.

The coastal road stretched onwards to the south, narrowing as it approached the horizon, and then disappearing entirely.

The road was empty.

Chapter Twenty-Four

The Western Kingdom | Knight's End

Rhea Loren

Her golden hair was greasy and flat, matted against her sweat- and tear-soaked cheeks. Her dressing clothes were filthy, crusted with dried blood and evaporated rainwater, and she was missing a shoe, her naked foot muddy and bloodstained, sticking out like a pale fish. She refused to let the thin old man anywhere near her, even when he offered her clean clothes. "Don't touch me!" she'd screamed as he'd corralled her into his boot shop and up the stairs to his living quarters. She knew she wasn't being fair to the kindly man, but the thought of being touched made her skin crawl with thousands of spiders.

He was back now, and she couldn't help but to shrink against the wall, hugging her knees to her chest.

"Name's Vaughn. Well, Jordan Vaughn, but ever'one jes calls me Vaughn." He crinkled his eyes and tried to smile, but it came out forced. "Your Highness, I mean," he added.

Rhea tried to speak, but all that came out was a croak.

Her father collapsed in her mind, bloody and lifeless. Again and again and again . . .

She hadn't liked him most of the time, but she had loved him. Some called him harsh, some a tyrant, but he'd been a man of principle, as unfaltering in his beliefs as anyone she'd ever met.

Who could've killed so many guards and then him? Rhea wondered. It was impossible. Knight's End was a fortress.

"I brought you some soup," Vaughn said. He stepped forward and Rhea tried to push herself through the wall. "Don' be skeered. I won' hurt you. Won' touch you. Soup's thin, prolly not what yer accustomed to eatin', but it'll help some. Gotta git yer strength back."

Rhea just stared at him, wishing him away. Wishing Grease would come back and hold her, protect her, the way he had as they fled the castle.

He never would. Not after what she had done to him and his sister.

A thought occurred to her: *This is punishment.*

She'd sinned against Wrath and, just like her father and his priestesses had warned her entire life, their god had brought a fist down like a hammer. Her lack of faith, her lies, her sneaking around and fornicating with a boy she barely knew, a boy she desired all the more because he was a sinner, like her. She'd done this. She was sure of it.

Vaughn squatted and placed the bowl on the floor, pushing it toward her. "I'll be back to check on you in a few hours. Already got a few customers awaitin'."

He moved to leave, but she managed to croak out, "Wait."

He stopped, turned, his scraggly eyebrows pushing toward his brow. Waited.

"Thank you," she said. He nodded and left, his boots clomping down the stairs.

She stared at the bowl, the surface of the soup like brown glass. Her decisions had ruined so many things. Grease's hand. His sister's secret. Her father? She should take the scalding hot soup and dump it over her own head. She should find a knife and stab it into her chest. She should—

Tears streaked down her cheeks. She knew she wouldn't do any of those things. It was her emotions that had caused all the trouble in the first place. Staring at the soup, it felt like the most important decision of her life.

And then she reached for it.

৶

"Take me back to the castle," Rhea said. Startled, Vaughn turned to look at her. He was sitting at a wooden desk, stitching several thick folds of leather together. One finished boot already lay on the slab in front of him. The one he was working on would be its pair. Even from across the room, she could tell the workmanship was excellent. "Please," she added, remembering her manners.

He looked her up and down, taking in the ill-fitting, but clean, clothes he'd given her, a white frock of purity that must've belonged to a woman twice her size and half her height. "'Twas my wife's cloak," he said. "Wore it to the temple ever' day."

Rhea didn't want to ask what had happened to his wife. She couldn't take more talk of death. Not now. "Thank you. I will return it as soon as I've had it laundered. Now please escort me back."

"The castle isn't safe," Vaughn said. "You shuld hear the rumors. Ghosts and goblins and e'en worse things that'll make yer spine tingle."

I know. I was there. I saw the worse things. "I have to find my brother. My sister. They'll be scared. I'm the eldest. It's my duty."

She'd never cared about her twin siblings before. The spoiled brats practically ran the castle. She could hide her face with the frock, head south, try to find Grease—Grey. Maybe help him rescue his sister. It was one way she could make up for what she'd done.

But she'd already made a choice. "I'll go on my own if I have to," she said.

Vaughn chewed on his dry lips for a moment. "I'll take ya. Gimme two licks." Without another word, he went back to work on the half-finished boot, his fingers agile and well-practiced as the shoe began to take shape.

Rhea slowly made her way over to him, but kept her distance, watching over his shoulder. He finished a few minutes later and held both boots up next to each other, examining them for defects.

"Perfect," was the only word Rhea could think of to describe them. And they were. The boots had solid black heels, tight tiny stitches securing them to the black-leather sides. Gold stitching formed an ornate depiction of the rearing stallion—the royal sigil—on each boot.

"You like 'em?" Vaughn said, looking at her expectantly.

"Yes. How could I not?" she said.

"They're yers," he said, extending his arms, and the boots, toward her.

She frowned. "But your customer . . ."

"I made 'em fer you."

"But I have—" She stopped and looked down at her feet. She'd lost one slipper in the castle and discarded the other one upstairs. "I will pay you a fair price," she said. "My father—" She swallowed thickly. "The royal treasurer will make sure you receive a royal compensation." She hoped he was still alive.

Vaughn shook his head. "They are a gift."

Rhea shook her head, confused. "They are beautiful, but I can't accept such a gift."

"They're fit fer a princess, don' ya think?"

"Yes, but—"

"And yer a princess, no?"

"Yes, but—"

"Then they're yers, and I won' hear anuther word about it." Vaughn stood and handed her the boots, and this time she didn't back away. She'd never met a man so . . . genuinely kind.

"Thank you. I shall repay you in spades someday."

"Yer smile is repayment enough fer me," he said.

Rhea had to reach up to touch her cheeks to confirm she was actually smiling. Her lips drooped and the smile vanished. "Well, I will send business from the castle your way, all the same."

"After you, Princess," he said, waving her toward his shop door.

As they left, he hung a sign on the door and locked it behind him. Rhea pulled the droopy white hood over her head and around her face.

"Princesses don' need to hide," Vaughn said. "You will be safe with me."

She reached up and grabbed the edge of the hood, but she couldn't do it. Within the cocoon of fabric, she could only see straight ahead. She could focus on the road stretching before her, on her feet marching one in front of the other. But if she pulled it back, too much information would flood in, and then would come the horrors from the night before.

Left foot, right foot, left foot . . . She chanted in her mind, ignoring the greetings hollered at Vaughn as he passed. Ignoring the hustle and bustle of the city, which she used to love. Ignoring the brightly colored fruits on the stands on either side. Focusing on only one thing: walking.

The castle gates loomed ahead, and a slice of fear seemed to open her up from skull to feet, leaving her exposed. Vulnerable.

She stopped. Vaughn said, "Princess?"

She breathed. In and out. In and out. Her heart, her mind, and her gut all urged her to turn, to run, to flee the castle that had once been a haven, a home—now a living nightmare.

Left foot, right foot, she thought, but they wouldn't obey, frozen in place, like stubborn mules overloaded with sacks of potatoes.

"We can go back to my shop," Vaughn said. It was a kind, generous offer, but not one she could accept. The kingdom needed her; and maybe she needed the kingdom, she wasn't sure.

She opened her mouth. Closed it. Opened it again. Spoke, mustering as much strength and courage as she could. "Thank you, Vaughn. For everything. I will see that you are rewarded for your kindness. You are a good man and I know Wrath smiles upon you." It was something she had heard her father say once. She knew she sounded too formal, too rehearsed, but the façade was a shield, protecting her from the emotions welling up inside her. She was a princess.

No.

"I am the queen," she whispered.

"Your Highness?" Vaughn said, tapping a finger to his ear.

"Nothing," Rhea said. "Just . . . thank you. Goodbye."

Though her heart tried to slam through her chest, though her breath stuck in her throat, though her legs felt wobbly and detached from her body, Rhea threw back her oversized hood, lifted her chin, and marched through the gates, which stood wide open and unguarded.

Because the guards are dead, Rhea reminded herself. *But did any survive?*

Inside, there was a flurry of solemn activity. Castle maids rushed hither and thither, carrying pails full of soapy water and brushes. Several were scrubbing at crimson stains on the ground. More than one were sobbing as they worked.

A large wooden cart was piled up with—

Rhea looked away, swallowing bile, her mouth watering, her head pounding. The bodies were stacked like goods about to be unloaded and delivered to the royal kitchens. Dead eyes stared in random directions—she swore several had been looking at her. The castle walls seemed to close in around her as nightmarish images rushed through her head. She bit the inside of her mouth and refused to vomit. She couldn't show weakness, not when the kingdom was broken in half and leaderless.

Wrath, Rhea thought, *give me strength to do my duty.*

She said loudly, "Stop."

At first no one seemed to hear her, still moving, still cleaning, still loading the cart with the dead. But then, at once, everything froze and all eyes moved to her.

"P-Princess Rhea?" one woman, a maid, said, standing. "Is it you? We thought you to be dead." Her cheeks were streaked with moisture.

"Queen Loren," Rhea said, acutely aware of how ridiculous she must look in Vaughn's wife's old purity gown. "And not but Wrath himself could kill me. As you were."

Stunned, the woman didn't seem to understand, but then fumbled her brush, dropped to her knees, and continued her work.

Left foot, right foot . . . Rhea moved forward, toward the entrance to the atrium, where her father had been—

She marched directly over where he'd collapsed, the marble floor already scrubbed to a perfect shine, the king's body removed. Someone rushed from the side and gripped her arm. She flinched visibly and struggled against the force.

"Rhea, it's me. Your cousin. Ennis."

Rhea stopped struggling, taking in the form of her youngest cousin, who was still twenty-five years her elder. His shaggy blond hair had streaks of gray, and his cheeks were covered in rough stubble. Growing up, Ennis, who had been named after their grandfather, King Ennis Loren, had been her favorite of her five cousins, always willing to play with her, or amuse her with silly jokes.

She fell into his arms, relishing the strength and warmth they provided. "Wrath is good," Ennis said, his pale blue eyes fierce. "We thought you—"

"I'm not," Rhea said, pulling back. "I'm here." She rapidly brushed the tears from her cheeks. She couldn't afford them right now.

"Yes, you are," Ennis said, taking in her strange garb but not commenting on it. "I'm sorry. Your father . . ."

"Where did they take him?" Rhea asked.

"You need not concern—"

"Tell me."

Ennis stared at her for a moment, and then nodded. "He's in his chambers. They are preparing his body for its final rest in the crypts. Only then can his soul make its way to the seventh heaven."

"Good. Thank you." Her next question hung on the tip of her tongue, as if afraid to jump off and be asked. "What of Bea and Leo?"

"Wrath, I should've started with news of them. They are fine. Unharmed. Their chamber guards were killed while the prince and princess slumbered."

Strange. It seemed that everyone but the royal guards and the king had been spared. But why? She refocused on her cousin. "And my guards, how many are left?"

Ennis frowned. "Right now you need to rest, to mourn, to—"

"I'm the queen," Rhea said. "I need to hold court. There are decisions to be made. Our forces must be renewed, our defenses strengthened, the north will—"

"Queen?" Ennis interrupted. "Yes, legally you are, but you are only sixteen and have not been anointed."

"And of sufficient age to rule, under western law," Rhea said.

"My brother has already been deemed King Temporanus," Ennis said.

He meant Jove, Rhea knew. Jove was the eldest of her cousins, near on half a century in age. Had his father—Rhea's uncle, Ty Loren—lived a few years longer, Jove would've been king rather than Gill Loren. As it was, Ty died in an unfortunate hunting accident before his father, King Ennis Loren, was taken by Wrath. Thus, the kingship had fallen to Rhea's father, diverting from Jove and his four siblings, of which Ennis the Second was the last.

"By whom?" Rhea said, her eyes narrowing. Like all of the lords and ladies of Knight's End, she'd been educated in western law and royal politics from a young age. It felt good to discuss something technical, something that would take her mind off of everything else.

"The furia," Ennis said.

"The furia are gone," Rhea said. *They took Grease's sister. No,* Grey's *sister. He'd called himself Grey. And he has gone after them.* She shook the thought away, trying to concentrate.

"Some of them returned. Half perhaps. And one of the Three."

Wrath, Rhea thought. This was unexpected. But it didn't change anything. "They don't have the authority to make such a decision."

"With you missing, they did," Ennis said.

"Missing? Did anyone even *look* for me?"

Ennis threw up his hands in mock surrender. "I'm just the messenger."

"But do you think they're right? Should Jove be King Temporanus?" She held her breath, her cousin's opinion important to her.

Ennis seemed to really consider it for a minute, and then laughed. "That arrogant bastard? I'd rather a Southron monkey be king. If you plan to make a bid for the crown, I will support you."

Rhea took a deep breath. Before, she felt it was her duty to return, to rule, to help the west survive whatever was about to come. But now . . .

She had an out. Jove could rule until she was older, when she'd had a chance to sort things out in her mind. Everything could go back to normal, with her a princess of the court, free to do as she wished.

The temptation was so strong she almost grabbed it with both hands. Almost.

"I will be queen," Rhea said.

℘

Cousin Jove was a gruff man with cold blue eyes and a smile that never reached them. No matter the nature of his expression, he always seemed to be calculating something, or trying to determine a weakness in those around him.

Growing up, Rhea had never liked him, and he seemed to view children as something akin to toe fungus.

"Thank Wrath you are alive," Jove said now. Though his words were similar to those of Ennis when he first saw Rhea, there was nothing of substance behind them, and he certainly didn't step down from the throne to embrace her.

"You're in my seat," Rhea said.

Bea, who had refused to leave Rhea's side since they'd been reunited, snickered. Leo howled. For once, the twins seemed to be on her side, worried the castle would be taken away from them.

Cousin Jove, however, did not laugh, his lips trembling in anger. "The furia have—"

"With all due respect, brother," Ennis chimed in, "the furia only have legal authority in the event that the heir to the throne is not of sufficient age." Rhea spared a thankful look to her cousin.

"Thank you, my dear brother, but Rhea is just a child. You cannot possibly support what she is suggesting." He was flanked by his remaining siblings, each somewhere between Jove and Ennis in age. Sai, his chestnut hair neatly trimmed, seemed fully in agreement with his older brother, while Wheaton appeared bored. He kept eyeing the door like he'd rather be anywhere but in court. Gaia, with her piercing green eyes, had her arm linked with Ennis's. The two youngest, they'd always been close, and Rhea was certain she would have her support.

Not that it mattered. She *was* queen, no matter what anyone said.

"I am a woman flowered," Rhea said. "I've been a princess of the court for the last three years. And I am of age."

A sharp voice slashed from the shadows in the corner of the room. "You consorted with a criminal."

Rhea jerked to the side, where one of the three Furies had appeared, almost as if she'd stepped out of the wall. Her crimson dress flowed around her muscled frame like a flickering candle. Her attractiveness was undeniable, but severe, in the same way that a well-forged sword was appealing.

"Not here," Jove said. "This is a private matter." Rhea knew he didn't mean it, and was only pretending to care about her reputation.

"Are the sins of a princess, of a *queen*, private?" the Fury said. "No. Never. Our ruler must be held to Wrath's highest standard, as your father knew too well."

Anger boiled inside of Rhea. "Do not speak of him like you knew him. He was *my* father."

"Do you deny my accusations then?"

Rhea knew she was caught in a trap, and a dangerous one. She tried to meet the Fury's eyes, but found her gaze dancing back to Jove's stern expression. "I am the one who brought the thief to justice, only yesterday. And I uncovered a sinmark born by his sister in the process." *And I hate myself for it*, she added in her own head.

The Fury glided closer, as if carried by the air itself. "Yes, I remember. And yet, something about your story didn't"—she licked her lips—"taste right. It's amazing what a simple threat from Wrath can do to loosen a person's tongue . . ."

Rhea shuddered, trying to hide her fear by saying, "I do not know what you speak of. Now as your queen, I command you—"

"You cannot *command* Wrath!" the Fury growled. "You have been accused by three witnesses, all of whom will swear to your affair with the very same thief you brought to justice. You have—"

"No!" Rhea screamed, but her response was swallowed by the stream of words from the Fury.

"—sinned against your family, your kingdom, and yourself. You *will* confess your sins and be punished. Until Wrath's warriors have found you repentant and contrite, you will be denied the throne. In the meantime, your cousin, Jove, has been appointed King Temporanus and will reign in your stead."

"I'm sorry," Rhea said. "I swear it."

"Too late," the Fury said. "Take her away."

The dam burst and Rhea couldn't hold back the tears any longer. The strength she'd fooled herself into believing that she had ripped apart like wet parchment, and, if not for Ennis's steadying hand on her elbow, she would've collapsed.

Several furia marched into court and grasped Rhea's arms, pulling her away from Ennis. She cried and bucked, but they were too strong, and she was only a girl—a child—just like Jove had said.

I'm sorry, Father, I was weak. I ruined your good name. I failed you.

The thought of her dead father pushed even more tears from her eyes, flooding her vision. Somewhere behind her, she heard Bea and Leo screaming her name, but not because they wanted her to come back, not when it was followed by another word, a word that pierced the very fabric of her soul.

"Whore!" they shouted in unison.

&

Rhea was terrified. She'd been stripped naked by the furia, forced to hug herself against the chill inside the Temple of Confession. "I'm a queen!" she'd screamed as they tore off the white frock, ripping it in several places. They even took her boots, the beautiful gift from Vaughn, leaving her with nothing but her regrets and sadness.

The furia refused to speak to her, and if she tried to stand they roughly knocked her down. She was covered in bruises.

Somewhere without the temple, a deep, booming bell tolled. The royal funeral bell. All of Knight's End was being hailed to mourn her father's death. "Please," she begged. "I have to be there when they inter him. Please."

The six strong, terrifying women wouldn't even look at her.

The door opened and the Fury entered. Rhea stood, but was immediately pushed back down. She laced her hands together in supplication. "Please," she said. "I have sinned. I am sorry. I repented to Wrath and received the warmth of forgiveness."

"You have received nothing," the woman said. In one of her hands, something glinted. A knife, of a kind Rhea had seen many times before. A holy knife, blessed with pure water, untouched by human hands. She stared at it in horror.

That was when she realized exactly what Grease had been through, because of her. Had that same knife been used to amputate his hand?

"Bind her," the Fury commanded.

"Please," Rhea whimpered, her voice that of a weak child. Pathetic. *Whore!* her siblings had cried. Were they right? She'd loved Grease—Grey—hadn't she? She'd wanted to run away with him.

She scurried back, her bare skin scraping against the stone floor.

Furia surrounded her. Fight as she tried, she was nothing against their strength and numbers. They easily bound her with thick rope, so she couldn't move her feet or hands. On each side of her, they held her down.

The holy knife slid toward her face and she screamed.

Chapter Twenty-Five

The Northern Kingdom | Near Gearhärt

Annise Gäric

The knights were from Castle Hill, Annise gathered as she listened through the wood. And, of course, they were searching for her and Tarin, as well as Sir Dietrich and Archer.

What if they intercepted the stream we sent last night? What if they cracked the code? What if they already know we're here?

They were trapped in a mountain of timber with only a man who clearly hated them to keep them safe. The farmer, Killorn, said, "I plan to sell me goods at Gearhärt."

"You're not worried about being so close to Raider's Pass? The war could easily spill into the city."

"A man has got to eat. And I've lived with the threat o' war my whole life. Wars are fer kings, not men like me."

"And you haven't seen anyone on the road?" one of the knights, a man who introduced himself as Sir Vay, asked.

"Nay. Naught but me horse and the ice faeries." He chuckled at his own wit. Ice faeries were the mythological creatures northerners blamed whenever something went wrong.

The knights didn't laugh. "We have to search your wagon," another of the knights said, his voice deeper than the first. Sir McGary he'd called himself.

Annise found Tarin's hand and squeezed it in the dark. Tarin squeezed back, twice. *It's going to be fine*, he seemed to be saying. She remembered the way he'd defeated the four royal guardsmen, brutalizing them in the process. The anger and violence and bloodlust in his eyes as he began to choke the life out of the very man who was now protecting them.

"Search away," Killorn said, almost gleefully, like it was exactly the command he was hoping to hear. *He wants us to get caught*, Annise thought.

Heavy boots crunched in the snow, approaching from the side of the cart. Someone tapped on the wood with something metallic. A sword, most likely.

"Me timber is the finest in the Four Kingdoms," Killorn bragged.

"You've had the chance to compare to Southron timber?" Sir Vay mocked. More tapping, getting closer to where their empty crawlspace was located.

"Nay, but I've heard the southerners build their dwellings from sandstone and mortar," Killorn said. "Their trees are too thin and scraggly to produce true timber."

The knight didn't respond, because he was too busy tapping his sword against the wood. *Tap . . . Tap . . . Tap . . . Toop!* The sword sounded strange when it hit the wood close to them, vibrating through. He tried again, with the same result. "Is this a different sort of wood?" he asked.

Annise held her breath, waiting for the farmer to give them up. He didn't. "Aye. You have a good ear. That there is blue spruce." Annise knew he was lying, because all the trees in the farmer's forest had been the same. He was lying for them. She exhaled slowly, quietly.

"It looks the same as the rest."

"Are you a lumberman now?" Killorn said.

There was a long silence, and Annise just about died not being able to see what was happening, but then Sir Vay laughed loudly and there was the sound of a hand slapping a back. "You could be a court jester," the knight said. "May I see you in frozen hell someday, old man."

With that, the boots crunched away, a horse whinnied, and hoofbeats plodded into the distance. Silence fell, and Annise waited for the farmer to run after the knights, to shout for them to return. Instead she only heard a whisper through the timber. "A close call, aye?" Killorn said.

"Thank you," Tarin said, his deep voice rumbling. "You are a good man."

"Good man? Don't know 'bout that. Me wife's always called me a fool. Mebbe she's right."

"You are no fool," Annise said. "You have proven that."

"Jest don' waste it," Killorn said. "Don' let 'em catch ya."

"I won't," Annise promised.

The wagon lurched to a start and lumbered forward once more.

≈

The next time the wagon stopped was when it reached Gearhärt. Annise had never been to the border castle, because her father refused to let her or her brother leave Castle Hill. A zing of excitement crackled through her, along with a shiver of fear. This wasn't the way she'd hoped to see the world—hidden within a timber cart, on the run from her uncle, her parents both dead.

The boards above them slid away, and an inky gray shadow crept in. Night had fallen over the north, the stars and dueling moons shrouded by clouds pregnant with unreleased snow. It was a typical northern night.

A hand reached into the alcove, and Annise took it. Killorn pulled her up and onto the stacked timber. She towered over the small man, who she could practically fit inside her torso. "Thank you," she said. "And please pass along my thanks to your wife as well."

"Thanks don' feed our hungry mouths," the man said, but Annise could tell he was pleased by her response. He didn't reach down to help Tarin, but the big man easily pulled himself out on his own. He echoed Annise's thanks, but Killorn was already clambering back into his seat and grasping the reins. He glanced back. "Ye don' know my name," he said by way of goodbye.

"No," Annise said. "No, we don't." Tarin had already climbed from the cart, and he reached up to help her. She started to descend the icy lumber, holding one of his hands for support. Her feet began to slide and she got the airy feeling in her stomach of falling, but then Tarin was there, holding her around the waist and slowing her descent.

She landed softly on her feet, his hands on both of her hips. In that moment, she knew how the reedy, lithe castle dancers must feel all the time.

She tried to pull away. "Thank you, Sir," she said.

"My pleasure, princess." His hands hadn't left her hips, though she no longer needed them to steady her. Her face felt warm, despite the cold. The cart rattled away, but she didn't watch it go. Time felt frozen, the clouds unmoving, the wind pausing, her breath lingering in her lungs.

"We must find shelter," Annise said, breaking the spell.

Tarin's hands dropped and he peered down the empty, narrow street Killorn had left them in. It was an alley of sorts, running between tightly packed stone buildings. "We cannot count on the kindness of strangers here," he said.

"Why not?"

"Kindness left this city years ago," Tarin said. "War does that to a place."

It was an awful thing, but Annise had never really thought about the rest of the northern realm. Her entire life, she'd been so focused on how much she hated Castle Hill, with its prison-like walls and shadowy corridors and grumpy lords and ladies, that she'd forgotten how much worse it would be to live in one of the border cities, with the constant threat of invasion from the east or west.

She was a selfish ice-licker.

"You've been here before?"

"Twice," Tarin said, leading her down the side of the alley that appeared slightly darker. "Once to recruit soldiers to help defend the Razor, and once because my captain desired to visit the famed Gearhärt pleasure houses."

"Oh," Annise said, her cheeks on fire. "And did they live up to their reputation?"

Tarin chuckled. "I wouldn't know, princess. My job was to guard the door. All I know is that we had to eventually carry the captain out. He was as drowsy as a hibernating ice bear."

Annise laughed at that, glad for the levity.

Tarin pushed a finger to his mask, cutting her off. The sound of singing and merriment arose, coming closer. They huddled in the shadows, peering out onto a gray road. Several soldiers stumbled past, holding each other up, as well as several ill-clothed women. They sang with voices so slurred and out of tune that they belonged in the deepest depths of frozen hell.

Weeeee drink until we're drunk!
Weeeee sink until we're sunk!
Weeeee think until we've thunk!
Weeeee stink until we've stunk!

On the last word they broke into a gale of laughter and stumbled onwards, pushing through a door and into a tavern. Annise remembered the day her brother had learned the silly song from one of the castle guardsmen. He'd sung it all day long, until she'd finally threatened to beat it out of his head. He'd only laughed and launched into another round.

Despite the way he'd abandoned her to Tarin and the Howling Tundra, she missed him. *Arch, are you here somewhere?*

"Pull your hood around your face," Tarin said. "Follow the main road north until you reach *The Laughing Mamoothen*, it's a tavern owned by a friend of your aunt's."

"Netta?"

"Aye."

"Why are you telling me this?"

"Because you have to go alone."

Annise frowned. "Where will you be?"

"Close. Watching. I can't be seen with you. Not here. We will be too conspicuous as a pair, especially because of . . . how I look."

Annise held back a laugh. "True. You do sort of stick out like a frost-bitten toe. Will Archer be hiding in the tavern?"

"I cannot say for certain," Tarin said. "But if Sir Dietrich passed through Gearhärt, that's where he would've hidden your brother."

Annise frowned. "It's been nigh on seven days since we've seen them. Would they really linger in the city that long?"

"Perhaps. Perhaps not. But the innkeeper will be able to tell us either way."

Annise had little other choice, having no knowledge of Gearhärt or its people. "Fine. You will meet me at the tavern?"

"Yes," Tarin confirmed. "It's not far. Whistle if you need me."

Annise peeked left and then right. The streets were eerily empty, though she could hear the muffled sound of revelry forcing its way through several closed doors. She turned northward, striding with a purpose through the empty streets, pulling her woolen hood tight around her face. Gearhärt wasn't dissimilar from Castle Hill, with its stone structures and snow-packed streets.

An odd thrill ran through her, walking alone in this foreign city, the chilly night air making her feel as alive as she'd ever felt.

The feeling vanished as she saw a shadow ahead, approaching. *Frozen hell*, she thought. What now? Would it be a castle guard? With her luck it would be a knight.

She was wrong on both accounts. It was just a man, his gait slightly off. He held a flask in each hand, alternating them as he took long swigs of whatever poison he'd chosen. Though Annise refused to look directly at him, she could tell when he spotted her, his movements slowing. She ducked her head and veered to the right, trying to put as much space between them as possible.

He mimicked her movement in reverse, angling toward her. Annise immediately thought of Tarin, stalking her movements somewhere else, watching over her. It didn't make her feel safer; it made her scared for this man, who was clearly drunk and not thinking clearly.

"Come here, woman!" the man slurred. "I won't bite!" He cackled and nearly tripped.

"Leave me, sir," Annise said. *Please, Tarin, don't get involved.*

"Sir? Ha! My lady has good manners. Who do you think you are—a princess of the north?" More cackling. He tucked the flasks into a hidden pocket in his thick coat. His hands free, he groped for her, but she squirmed away.

"I said leave me alone," Annise repeated, slapping his outstretched hands away. *Whistle if you need me.* Annise gritted her teeth instead.

"Ah, that's more like it," the man said, undeterred. "I like a little fire in my women. And war is coming, didn't you hear? This could be our last night alive, shouldn't we spend it with each other's company?"

Annise could hear the sound of heavy footsteps racing toward them. *No,* she thought. Impulsively, she grabbed the man by the collar and shoved him back. He stumbled, landing on his arse. "Bitch!" he spat.

"Drunk bastard," she growled in response, kicking him between the ribs. He groaned and rolled over. A moment later he was snoring.

The heavy footfalls slowed to a stop. Annise whirled around to find Tarin staring at her, his fingers curling and uncurling at his sides, his chest heaving.

She turned away and continued on without a word. The drunken fool would wake up the next morning with not more than a headache and a chill, not knowing a runaway princess had saved his miserable, meaningless life.

᧞

The Laughing Mamoothen was impossible to miss. A huge, frosted sign hung over the door, a large depiction of a tusked mamoothen bearing a wide smile displayed beneath the tavern's name. The door swung open as Annise approached, and three women emerged, trading quips about their husbands.

Too caught up in their own conversation, they didn't seem to notice Annise as she slipped past and through the entrance.

The first thing she felt was the warmth, which hit her in the face like a hot wind. Fires crackled in three separate hearths. Ivory tusks were mounted in several places on the walls, the largest above a long stone counter where patrons sat eating, drinking and talking.

The second thing Annise noticed was that every person inside the tavern was female. Before she could consider this strange fact, a voice said, "Clean your feet and come on in." A woman beckoned from behind the bar, waving Annise forward. She wore a furry brown apron and a smile almost as warm as the atmosphere.

Annise obeyed, stomping the snow and ice from her boots and snaking past round tables, most of which were empty, cluttered with used dishes.

Annise sniffed the air. Something smelled good. *Come hungry*, Netta had responded the day before. The hunger monster in her stomach tried to claw its way through her skin.

"Welcome to *The Laughing Mamoothen*," the woman said. "I'm Netta and this is my place." The tavern's proprietor had gray hair piled in a bun atop her head.

"Where are all the men?" Annise asked, unable to stop herself.

"Women only," Netta said. "You want men, try *Deep Freeze*, *Howling Wind*, or *The White Lantern*. You're not from around here?"

Annise concocted a quick lie, just in case the other women in the tavern were untrustworthy. She could pull Netta aside later and explain she was the blooming hope flower Tarin had streamed her about yesterday. "I grew up along the Snake River, east of Castle Hill. My father's a fisherman."

"And your mother?"

She's dead. She was a beautiful queen from the west. "A damn good cook," Annise said.

Netta laughed, and several other women turned to stare. "She must've been an impressive woman," Netta said.

"That she was," Annise said, her heart skipping a beat.

The women at the bar made room and offered an empty stool. "Mamoothen stew?" Netta asked. "It's the house specialty."

"Aye," Annise said. "Thank you."

The woman on her left, a dark-haired bruiser with the shadow of a mustache over her upper lip, said, "You're young."

"Twenty," Annise lied.

The woman on her right, whose lips were as pink as a hope flower in spring, said, "Are you travelling alone?"

"Sort of," she said. "I have a companion, but he's not always around."

"Ah," the women sighed in unison. "A soldier, then. He's gone to Raider's Pass?"

Annise didn't respond, tucking into her stew the moment Netta slid it in front of her. The concoction was thick and hot and hellfrozen delicious. The women watched her as she gobbled it down, wiping her chin with the back of her hand.

"I take it you like it?" Netta said, smiling.

"You made this?" Annise asked.

Netta nodded. The mustached woman beside Annise said, "It's famous. The men of Gearhärt have been trying to sneak inside for years to get some."

Annise pushed her bowl back toward Netta, who refilled it using a deep ladle. "I've never heard of a ladies only tavern," she admitted.

"Probably 'cause I'm the only one," Netta said.

"Doesn't it anger the men?" Annise barely managed to ask before returning to the fresh bowl of stew. She scalded her tongue with the first bite, but she didn't care.

"That's half the fun of it," Netta said. "But they have their roughshod taverns and pleasure houses, so why shouldn't we have a place of our own?"

Annise had never thought of it that way, but it made sense. "What of your husband?" Annise asked between mouthfuls.

"Dead," Netta said bluntly.

"I'm sorry," Annise said. She stopped eating for a moment out of respect.

"Don't be," Netta said. "He was a mean bastard who liked to hit me if his soup got cold. I hope he freezes in hell."

Annise gaped, but then the other women laughed, and she couldn't hold back her own smile. She'd never met women like this—so strong-willed, independent, and confident. They seemed to have much more . . . texture than the sanded-down ladies of Castle Hill.

"Finish your stew and you can have dessert," Netta said. "I just made teakleberry pie today, and there's still a couple of slices left over."

Annise almost fainted. It was like she'd gone to the western kingdom's seventh heaven and these women were angels. She slurped the last morsels out of her spoon and her bowl was whisked away. While she waited for pie, she asked casually, "Do you know a knight named Sir Dietrich?"

Netta's hand froze in place, gooey teakleberry filling dripping from the end of a flat serving spatula. She dropped the utensil and spun around, her eyes suddenly dark. "Who in the frozen hell are you?" she said. The other women pushed off of their stools and surrounded her.

"No one," she said. "I'm just . . ."

"Queen Annise Gäric," a stern voice said. "Once a princess of Castle Hill and now the rightful heir to the northern throne."

Annise knew that voice, and she craned her neck to see past the circle of women, who parted in the center. A cloaked form emerged from a corner table, wreathed in shadows. She threw back her hood and grinned.

"Aunt Zelda?" Annise said.

❧

The first thing her aunt did was steal her pie. The second thing she did was threaten the tavern women with violent dismemberment if any of them so much as breathed a word of Annise's presence outside of the establishment. They all readily agreed to the secret, and Annise could tell they meant to keep the promise.

"I was pleased when Netta received Tarin's stream yesterday afternoon," Zelda said, when the women had departed and the tavern doors were locked. Only Netta remained, busying herself with cleaning the tables and gathering bowls and glasses.

"I thought everyone wanted me to go to Blackstone."

Zelda grinned. "I want you to blaze your own path, as I have always done."

Annise didn't think her brother would agree. Still, he was her kin, and she longed to be reunited with him. "Where is Arch?" she asked.

"He was here," Zelda said, taking a large bite of pie.

"And now?"

"Gone south, to Raider's Pass."

Annise's heart sank. "Why?"

"He felt his best chance at exerting his right to the crown would be with the soldiers closest to the front lines. I agreed."

Annise remembered how her aunt had referred to her as *Queen* Annise Gäric. "You know I have passed my eighteenth name day," she said.

"Yes."

"And yet you let Arch go south? People are saying war is coming."

"Yes, I let him go, because his decisions are not mine to make, no more than yours are. And yes, the front lines have been quiet for several months, but now the streams are saying there's an eastern legion marching north toward the Pass."

"Why didn't you tell him I'm the ruler by law?"

Her aunt didn't answer, asking a question of her own. "What do you plan to say to your brother when you see him?"

After spending only a little time with the strong women patrons of *The Laughing Mamoothen*, she found herself embarrassed to tell her aunt the truth. But she couldn't lie. "I plan to relinquish the crown."

Zelda nodded, as if unsurprised by her response. "You're so much like your mother," she said.

Annise's heart fluttered. The statement was so much like what Tarin had said that it was eerie. "How?"

"Your mother hated the power the most. She hated Castle Hill and all that it stood for. It was her prison, and she longed to escape from it."

"I know she did," Annise said, feeling suddenly cold inside. She had felt the same way about Castle Hill her entire life, though she'd never thought of how that gave her and her mother something in common.

Zelda nodded thoughtfully. "The only thing that kept her going was her children. You. Arch."

Annise shook her head. "No. You're wrong. She hated us because we're Gärics. She hated that our father was in us. She barely looked at me." *At least until the very end, just before she was . . .*

"It was an act. Your father was a bad man. He only knew one way to rule: fear. He ruled his household the same way. His wife—your mother—knew this. He was willing to threaten her into obedience with anything and anyone she cared about."

Wait. Did that mean . . . "She pretended to hate us to protect us?"

Zelda nodded, her pale complexion almost moon-like as the room darkened when Netta began extinguishing the fires in each hearth. "He would've hurt you to hurt Sabria."

It was suddenly all too much for Annise. She stood quickly, her stool clattering to the floor. Her mother's love was all she ever wanted, and then when she finally received it . . .

Gone. It was gone forever. Still . . .

"Thank you for telling me," she said, "but it doesn't change anything. She's still dead. And I still hate the north."

Zelda nodded again. "That's what Sabria said. She wanted a different life for you. For your brother. She asked me to give it to you and I agreed."

"What life?" Annise leaned closer, desperate to learn about the mother she never really knew.

"Away from here, from these lands, from the war. She wanted me to arrange for you to sail to Crimea, where you could start over."

"You said you agreed with her. Then why are we here?"

"Because I lied." Zelda's eyes met Annise's, dark and piercing.

Annise stared right back. "I won't be queen," she said. "And Arch is too young to be king. He's only sixteen. You have to fulfill the promise you made to my mother. You have to help us get to Crimea."

"Is that what you want?"

The question took her by surprise, because she'd never been asked it before. Not by her father or her mother. Or even Arch, who forced her to go with Tarin when she wanted to go with him. "Does it matter what I want?"

"It's the *only* thing that matters," Zelda said, her eyes twinkling.

Chapter Twenty-Six

The Eastern Kingdom | Norris

Roan

Norris was a well-fortified town on the eastern edge of the Snake River, just north of Hyro Lake. The town's double wall was constructed of felled trees from the Tangle, a thick forest across the waters separating the east from the west. The trees were then bound together with metal wire channeled by skilled Orians and transported from Ironwood. There was a wide gap between the two walls—the kill zone—in which invading enemies would be subjected to varied attacks from above: molten ore, boiling water, flaming arrows, and enormous boulders.

All of this was explained to Roan by Prince Gareth as they passed beneath the first gate and before they reached the second. "Norris has been attacked twice," Gareth said. "Once by the west when they managed to paddle upriver from the Bridge of Triumph and make landfall, and once by the north when they broke through Raider's Pass."

At the mention of the west, Roan's heart hammered. He was so close now. But he'd be even closer on the morrow—he needed to be patient for a while longer.

Running his hands along the walls, Roan inspected them for damage, but there was none save the occasional bit of chipped wood. "What happened?"

"The enemy breached the first wall, but then we slaughtered their armies in the kill zone," Gareth said. "They retreated."

Roan couldn't help but to look up at the men and women patrolling the top of the inner wall. None smiled, despite the fact that the current invaders were friends not foes, and each guard had a deadly glint in his or her eye. "You were here for those battles?" Roan asked the prince.

Gareth laughed. "I was still crawling," he said. "But the Juggernaut was here for both, weren't you, Da?"

"Aye," the king said, bringing his muscular horse astride. "Your mother was, too, before we were bonded. She was a Redfern then, not an Ironclad. Ah, you shoulda seen her then, son. She was a sight to behold, clad in body armor, her sword flashing as she felled soldier after soldier. Those were the days. I was but a prince seeking the glory of the kingdom and the eye of a beautiful woman. Mine brother and I fought back to back against a dozen foes and emerged victorious. He wielded this very ore hammer with more skill than any before him." He held up a massive sledge that looked capable of smashing a skull to rock dust. Roan was amazed the king could even lift it, much less swing the blunt weapon. The handle was laced with exquisite metal-work, engraved in a strange language Roan wasn't familiar with. It was a work of art.

Roan remembered the king's story about his brother, Coren "Thunder" Ironclad, and the sacrifice he'd made at the Razor. Seeing Gareth riding beside his brothers made Roan look away. Knowing Gareth would one day sacrifice himself for his brothers wasn't something he wanted to think about.

"The Foehammer is a powerful weapon, indeed," Gwendolyn said, joining the conversation. She didn't look at Roan. "Thunder was a rare warrior."

Her comment seemed to please the king. Something occurred to Roan. "You were there, weren't you?" he asked the Orian. "At the battles at Norris. And at the Razor, too."

Her gaze remained fixed firmly ahead as they rode into a wide swathe of empty space inside the second wall. "Yes," she said. "I have fought many battles and lived many lives. You are but a babe in comparison."

She spurred her horse and galloped ahead. The king leaned toward Roan as he frowned after her. "If it's any consolation, we're all just children next to her years. She will outlive us all!"

For some reason, the thought made Roan sad. Perhaps because the girl with the golden eyes and silver hair had seen so much death and would see more still. She'd lost a bondmate, his memory haunting her like a ghost.

The people of Norris gathered in the open area, many layers thick all the way to the walls. Regardless of age, background, or gender, they all looked hardened, as if layers of sediment had collected on their skin. Even the children had a stony look in their eyes, their lips tight and grim. None were strangers to a life on the front lines of an endless war. It made Roan wonder why any of them stayed in this place. Someone had to, he supposed, or their enemies would march straight through to the next town.

The king halted his horse and, flanked by his sons, addressed the crowd, his voice booming across the village, echoing off the walls. "Long have the people of Norris defended our land from our northern and western foes."

His words were met with silence. No cheers. No smiles. Just flat, determined faces. The silence didn't seem to bother Oren Ironclad, who let it drag on for several long moments until Roan began to feel uncomfortable in his saddle. Finally, he continued. "You may be called into service once again. For we ride for Raider's Pass. For many years the northern bear has tormented our border towns, but now the beast is weak and confused. We shall tickle him under the chin and then slash his throat."

Again, no one cheered, but this time many of the people raised blades in the air, pointing at the sky. Their jaws were locked, and Roan felt like they were on the verge of rushing into battle this very moment.

"We will have our vengeance for what they did to your queen. We will fight for Queen Henna Ironclad, mine departed wife, mine heart, a warrior in this life and in the next!"

"Aye!" the people finally screamed. Roan could see in their eyes what the queen had meant to them.

"Alas, if we are defeated at Raider's Pass," the king said, "the northerners will counter. Norris will be the first line of defense. So now I must ask you, oh defenders of the east, are you prepared for battle?"

"Aye!" a chorus of voices responded, men, women, and children.

"Are you prepared to die for your fellow countrymen, for your brothers and sisters and mothers and fathers and children?"

"Aye!"

"Are you prepared to be a Shield to those you love?"

Gareth spurred his horse forward, riding in a tight circle before the villagers. He raised his sword in the air. "Aye!" he shouted.

"Aye!" the people replied. "Shield! Shield! Shield!"

"Good," the king said. "Now prepare for war."

❧

Prince Gareth had been polishing the same breastplate for so long Roan had managed to water and feed his horse, brush its knotted mane, wash his own soiled skin, and collect plates of rations—some kind of meat and potatoes, he gave his meat to the prince—for the both of them. Yet still the prince polished, his muscles taut, sweat dripping off his chin, splashing on the metal, which gleamed like a red star under the lantern light.

"Ho, Gareth," Roan said, sitting beside him. Prince Gareth was alone, sitting in the grass, well away from any of the night fires. Only a small lantern provided light as he worked.

Still he scrubbed at the metal, his concentration unbroken.

Roan sat beside him, watching. "Eat," Roan said, pushing the plate toward the prince. "I managed to procure double meat rations for you. I said it was because you needed enough for both yourself and your ego."

It was meant as a bit of light banter, but the prince only grunted and continued his work.

"Careful, you might rub a hole through the armor, and then your heart will be unprotected," Roan said.

Gareth shoved the breastplate aside and it clattered against the rest of his armor.

"Sorry, I—" Roan started to say, but the prince held up a hand to silence him.

He reached for the plate. "Thank you," he said. "I know the meat was yours."

Roan said, "I wasn't that hungry."

"You never eat your meat," Gareth said, chewing loudly.

"I'm surprised you noticed," Roan said, spearing a potato.

"I notice a lot of things."

Something about the way the prince said it made Roan pause. "Like what?" Roan asked, waiting for Gareth to make a jest at his expense.

He didn't. "Like how rain can look like tiny crystals when struck directly by sunlight," the prince said. "Like how in the springtime the wind will blow the long grass and you can almost imagine it's dancing. Like how the golden stars remained fixed in formation in the sky, like a well-trained army wearing jeweled armor. Like how my own father refuses to look me in the eye, even now, on the eve of the battle where I will die."

Roan stopped chewing, unable to look away from the prince. "That's not true," he said.

"Which part?" The prince looked up from his plate to meet Roan's stare.

"I don't know about the rain or the stars or the grass, but you're not going to die."

The prince laughed mirthlessly. "I was born to die," he said.

The man sitting beside him was a far cry from the warrior who'd raised his sword in front of the people of Norris. Which version was the real prince? Roan wondered. He couldn't imagine living day to day knowing his fate was sealed the moment he was born. Or could he? In a way, he and the prince weren't that different. He'd borne the weight of a fatemark his entire life, one his guardian had kept secret until the day when "It would be brought forth for all the realm to see." Whatever that meant.

"What if you don't die?" Roan asked.

The prince cocked his head to the side. "I don't understand."

"What if you all live? All three princes. Your father. What if you are victorious tomorrow and avenge your mother?"

The lines in Gareth's forehead deepened. He seemed genuinely puzzled by the question. "Then I shall live to die on another day."

Although Roan knew he meant it as a statement for his own future . . . "That would be true for any man," Roan said.

"It's truer for me," Gareth said.

"What if your father dies and you do not?" Roan asked, changing tact.

"That won't happen," Gareth responded immediately. There was no doubt in his statement.

"Why not?"

"Because I won't let it."

"Why not?"

"Because it's my duty!" the prince shouted, grabbing his plate and throwing it like a saucer, the meat and potatoes flinging off in a spiral of discarded food.

The words felt like knives, penetrating Roan's flesh. *Duty.* He'd never understood that word. Why was it anyone's duty to die? "Sorry," he said. "I didn't mean to . . ." He trailed off, not sure what to say.

"It's fine. You didn't grow up in the east. You can't possibly understand our traditions."

The prince was right. On this point, they would have to agree to disagree. But there was still more that Roan wanted to know, so he changed the subject. "What does Gwendolyn's fatemark do?" he asked.

"She still hasn't told you?" The prince's typical smirk formed on his lips, and Roan was surprised to find himself glad to see it. He much preferred the sarcastic, laid back prince he'd met in the Barren Marshes.

"I haven't asked."

"Why not?" The prince raised an eyebrow.

"Because she generally looks ready to cut out my tongue if I say or ask the wrong thing."

The prince laughed. "That sounds about right."

"But she did say her skinmark was like mine in some way. Is she a healer?" He knew it didn't make sense, but nothing else did either. Clearly she couldn't heal, or she would've healed Bark herself. And she moved like the wind, but was that her mark or simply because she was a pure Orian?

"Not exactly," Gareth said. "She bears the heromark. Once she told me that it forces her into dangerous situations. She can't control herself."

Time stopped. That word again. *Hero*. He remembered what Gwendolyn had said about the word: *That word is meaningless.*

Yet she wore a mark that represented it. He squinted into the torchlight, relishing the spots dancing across his vision, clearing his mind. He tried to understand. An arrow was nocked against a bowstring and it all made sense. Why Gwendolyn would rush into a pox-riddled town with little hope of saving anyone. Why the king didn't try to stop her—*couldn't* stop her. Why he didn't reprimand her for being so adamant. "She can't turn away from someone in need?" He said it like a question, but he knew it was true before the prince nodded.

No wonder she thinks me a coward, Roan thought. *She's the bravest person in the Four Kingdoms*. Roan thought back to all the times in his life when he'd turned his back on people who needed his help. People he could've helped. All because of one time when he'd helped a girl with a broken leg and it had gone all wrong. Horribly wrong.

"I'm a fool," Roan said.

"I can't argue with you there," Gareth said.

Despite the prince's jape and the way Gwendolyn had treated him earlier, Roan knew he would miss them both when he escaped. But their war was not his war, and he had the power to stop at least one of the major conflicts tearing the Four Kingdoms apart. Aye, his path was leading in a different direction.

Toward his true home.

Time had run out, and he didn't even know what any of these people meant to him. *Nothing*, he thought. He chuckled at his own lie.

"What?" Gareth said, narrowing his eyes.

Roan didn't know when exactly the prince had gone from being his enemy to his friend, but in this moment he felt like he could be even more. "In another world perhaps," Roan said to himself.

"Have your senses dulled?" the prince asked. Roan couldn't look away from the amused curl to his lips, the sparkle in his eyes, the way his hair fell across his forehead.

He leaned forward, hoping against hope that he wasn't being the fool the prince thought him to be. Gareth stiffened, but didn't pull back, even as his lips met Roan's, even as Roan reached up to touch his chin, which was as smooth as polished armor. Roan breathed him in, and the prince seemed to do the same, until—

"What the hell?" Gareth said, jerking back, scrubbing at his lips with the back of his hand. He glared at Roan.

"I—I'm sorry, I thought—"

Gareth stood up, grabbing his armor. "I don't know what is acceptable conduct in the south, but I'm a man, not some tender-gloved boy."

Something felt strange about the prince's reaction, like he was forcing it. He *had* let the kiss linger for a moment, hadn't he? Roan could still feel his heart galloping, his nerves firing. Their kiss, no matter how short lived, had not rang false.

"Our customs are different in the south," Roan said.

"Clearly," Gareth said. He stomped away, almost forcing the grace out of his usual stride.

Roan watched him go, wondering whether he would ever see him again.

Chapter Twenty-Seven

The Northern Kingdom | Gearhärt

Annise Gäric

Tarin was waiting for Annise and Zelda upstairs, where four beds had been made up in a single room with a peaked ceiling. The only window was open, a chill wind drifting through, blowing a lacy white curtain around like a marauding poltergeist.

"You made it," Annise said by way of greeting. The glow of the wall sconces gave Tarin's armor the appearance of being filled with sunlight.

"So did you."

"I thought men weren't allowed in *The Laughing Mamoothen*."

"Shall I leave?"

Annise laughed. "You'll have to take it up with Netta."

Netta appeared right on cue, hefting a pail of steaming water, which she poured into a large iron tub. "Take what up with me?"

"He's a man," Annise pointed out.

"He could be anything beneath all that metal," she said. "Plus men are only barred from using the front door. Through the window is fine." There was a mischievous gleam in her eye as she moved to slam the window shut against the cold. She turned back to face them. "Anyway, you are my only guests tonight, so we can make an exception, as we already have for Lady Zelda's escort."

"Aunt?" Annise said, turning to Zelda, who had made herself comfortable on one of the beds. "You have a man with you?"

"My husband," Zelda said. She punched her pillow three times, creating a nest in the center for her head.

Annise's mouth hung open. "You're married?"

"Not openly," Zelda said. "It was a small, private ceremony."

"Did my father know?"

"Not exactly. That would've ruined everything."

Annise blinked. She was clearly missing something important. Before she could consider what, footsteps approached from the staircase. A familiar ruddy face appeared in the doorway and Annise almost fainted.

"Sir Drunk—I mean, Sir Craig?"

The knight offered a half-grin and tipped back a tin flask, swallowing twice. He pushed it toward Annise. "Thirsty?" he said.

Frozen hell. My aunt is married to this drunkard? "Thank you, but no. I prefer to have my wits about me." She remembered the last two times she'd seen him, first in the melee when he'd made a fool of himself, and then just before her father fell to his death. On both occasions he'd been drunk, which was no surprise.

"Try it," Zelda said.

Annise turned toward her aunt, unable to hold back an angry frown. "I'll pass. I am no lush."

"Neither is my husband," Zelda said, smiling.

Annise looked back at the man she'd always known as Drunk Craig or simply, Sir Drunk. His eyes were as clear as blown glass, his stance steady and somehow taller than usual. His words were equally crisp as he said, "It's only water," once more offering her the flask.

She took it, shaking her head. "Aye, and I bear half a dozen skinmarks," she said. She sniffed the flask's mouth. To her surprise, it was odorless. She spilled a few drops onto her fingers, studying the clear liquid. Licked her fingers clean. The substance was basically tasteless, like water. "Taking a break from the drink?" she asked Sir Craig.

"I've never had a drink in my life," Craig said.

Annise was about to bring up numerous times in the past where the knight was obviously inebriated, but Zelda spoke first. "It's true. He may not be a drunkard, but he is a damn good actor."

Annise didn't know what to say, what to think. "Why?" was all she could manage to splutter out.

"He is my castle spy," Zelda said.

Annise's gaze travelled from Craig to her aunt and back again. Craig shrugged. "Men have loose tongues when they believe they speak to drunken ears," he said.

She was dumbfounded, more surprised than if Tarin had declared himself a wooly yak and stripped off his armor to prove it. "Then I have sorely misjudged you," she said. "For that I am sorry."

He shrugged again. "It was my deception, not yours."

"Still, I have given you less credit than you likely deserved. I laughed with the rest when you stumbled through each tournament in last place."

Craig laughed. "I am no warrior. Feigning drunkenness was as good excuse as any to avoid combat. In battle, I might as well be drunk, for I am a clumsy man. Even my knighthood was gained by accident. Thankfully, your aunt saw something more in me than a witless fool."

"Yes. A courageous spy and gentle lover," she said.

Annise looked at Tarin. "Don't look at me," he said. "I knew of many secrets, but not this. This was well-kept."

Netta returned with another pail of steaming water. She poured it into the tub, which was almost full. "It is late. I thought you might enjoy a bath before bed."

She would, but . . . "Here?" The tub was in the center of the small room, the four beds lined up like seats for spectators. Annise was confident the show would be both a comedy *and* tragedy.

"The others will not peek," Netta promised. She offered a glare at both Craig and Tarin. "Will they?"

Tarin immediately closed his eyes and blundered toward the far bed, nearly tripping on the foot post, which was low to the ground.

"You don't have to close your eyes yet," Annise said.

"Oh," he said, his eyes twinkling when he opened them. He eased onto the bed, his metal armor causing quite a ruckus. Annise shook her head. She still couldn't believe he was able to sleep in full battle armor.

Craig settled in beside Zelda, covering his face with a pillow.

"See?" Netta said. "Can I help you undress?"

"No!" Annise said, too quickly. "I mean, thank you, but I will be fine. Even in Castle Hill I wouldn't allow the maidservants to fuss over me." *Nor see me naked.*

"As you wish." She placed a towel beside the tub, along with a dressing gown. "Call if you need anything. I will not sleep on this night."

"Thank you." Annise watched her go, waiting until the door had closed behind her. She scanned her companions, who seemed too random to be anything but real. Zelda was already snoring, her blanket tucked up under her chin. Annise had so many questions she still needed to ask her aunt, but they would have to wait until morning. Craig's breathing was heavy, a mountain of pillows blocking his view even if he were to open his eyes. Despite his lifelong deception, she felt inclined to trust his honor. Then there was Tarin, lying on his back, his feet hanging well over the edge of the bed. She wondered whether there was a bed in the entire northern kingdom that could fit him. She couldn't tell if he was awake, so she made her way over to him, waving a hand across his eye slits.

"I can't see you, but I can hear you," he said.

Annise peeled up a corner of the blanket and stuffed it inside his mask's eye slit. "Thank you," Tarin said. "That will help with the temptation to steal a peek."

Annise had the urge to hit him, but feared the sound of her fist banging his armor would wake the other two. She settled for stuffing the blanket in further.

"I feel as if I have cotton in my eyes," Tarin said.

"Good," Annise retorted. "Now sleep, you big buffoon, or I'll be forced to hurt you."

Before she'd removed a single layer of clothing, Annise already felt naked and exposed. Now, as she pulled off her woolen overcoat, cotton under-layer, thick britches, wool-insulated boots, double-layered socks, and, finally, underclothing, Annise was acutely aware that Tarin could easily pull the blanket out of his eye slits, open his eyes, and see the real her, pale and muscular and curvy and ill-at-ease in her own skin.

The thought made her practically dive into the steaming water, the level rising precariously, nearly sloshing over the sides.

She peeked out to find her trio of companions in the same positions she'd left them. Taking a deep breath, she gave herself over to the steam and warm water, which chased away the chill that had settled deep in her bones for days.

She fumbled along the bottom of the tub until she found a sponge and a bar of soap, using them to clean her body from head to toe. When she was finished, she felt human again.

As she climbed from the tub, toweled off, donned the dressing gown, and slipped into bed, she wondered how long the feeling would last.

৵

The next day dawned bright, cold and eager.

Annise yawned, pulling the blankets over her head as white light streamed through the window. Armor creaked nearby. Hushed voices spoke.

With a sigh, Annise threw off the covers and sat up. Tarin was helping Netta empty the washing tub—for each pail she carried, he hefted four, two in each hand. Zelda and Sir Craig sat on the edge of one of the beds, conferring softly. They seemed to be arguing.

"Morning," Annise said, to no one in particular.

"That's what they call it when the sun rises," Tarin said. His eyes met hers just before he turned away, hauling the pails to wherever Netta had asked him to

Sir Craig stood and offered a half-bow. "Queen Gäric," he said, and then left before Annise could argue the formal title.

Zelda watched him go, and then stood. She approached Annise, sitting next to her. It was so strange being with her aunt in any capacity. Like with Sir Craig, she'd judged Zelda wrongly in so many ways, succumbing to the rumors that she was a strange recluse who'd completely separated herself from reality. A recluse maybe, and certainly strange, but Aunt Zelda's eyes were sharp and clear and focused. Frozen hell, she'd had her husband pretending to be a drunk in order to spy on the king!

"I want to clear Arch's name," Annise said, the words springing to her lips before she could consider their origin. Why did it matter what the kingdom thought of her brother? She wanted to flee to the Hinterlands with him anyway. Or perhaps to Crimea, like her mother had wanted.

Because he will never leave the northern kingdom, she realized. It was a truth she'd been hiding from for a while, using her dream of carving a life elsewhere as a shield. And if Arch was determined to be king, to rule the north, the people would need to trust him, or at the least respect him. *Or fear him*, she thought, like they had her father.

Zelda shook her head. "Your brother's name doesn't need to be cleared," she said.

"I was *there*," Annise argued. "I saw my father die. It wasn't Arch. It was something . . . I can't explain." *A ghost that looked like another version of Arch.*

"The truth doesn't matter," Zelda said. "The people already love your brother. Thinking he killed the Dread King of the North will only make them love him more."

Annise frowned. She hadn't considered that the northerners might be happy about her father's death. He'd ruled with fear for so many years . . . it made sense. She remembered what had happened at the execution, the way the spectators had reacted when Arch was brought out in chains. Appalled. Shocked.

"Fine. So we let them believe he was guilty of treason. That doesn't change the fact that he's being hunted by your brother's soldiers. Trust me, they'll do anything to find him. To find me. We need to locate Arch before Lord Griswold does."

Zelda nodded. "There's something else you need to know, although Sir Craig thinks it's too soon to tell you."

What else could there be? Annise wondered. It was like the secrets kept pouring from her aunt's mouth in a steady stream. "What? Tell me, I cannot bear to be in the dark any longer."

"Your brother is alive," Zelda said.

"How can you be certain? You haven't seen Arch in—"

"Not Arch," Zelda said.

Annise licked her lips. Surely she didn't mean . . .

Annise stood up, her hand rising automatically to comb her hair, still damp from her bath the night before. "I saw the blood," she said. "I was the one—I was so excited to meet him—to have a baby brother—I went to his crib—there was blood on the sheets—I screamed—I—"

She bit her own hand, fighting back the nightmare that had haunted her sleep for years. Though Annise had only been four years old, the memory was as vivid as any other. There had been gray fur everywhere, stuck to the blood. The wolves had killed her baby brother and dragged him away. Mired in grief, Annise had been sworn to secrecy by her parents. The realm couldn't know that a prince of the north had been killed by wild animals, and within the castle at that.

"Cow's blood," Zelda said now.

Annise shook her head. "It wasn't. I saw the fur. The wolves—"

"I scattered the fur myself. I drained the blood from a water skin. I took your brother from his bed."

A tremor ran through Annise's body. Her legs faltered, buckling under her. Her aunt's hand shot out to steady her, but she flinched away, losing her balance. She collapsed in a heap, cradling her head in her hands. Sobbing. These lies were too much, and if they weren't lies . . .

She couldn't dare to hope.

Her aunt spoke. "I delivered the child to a man known as Bear Blackboots, an old friend of mine who I could trust, who would be the boy's keeper, his guardian, his protector, until he came of age. Bear was the perfect choice—he had no family left, no ties, and, like me, he hated my brother with a passion."

Annise couldn't process any of it, shaking her head back and forth again and again in denial.

"I'm sorry," Zelda said. "I had no choice, under the circumstances."

Annise swiveled her head around and stared at her aunt, her moist eyes flashing with anger. "What circumstances?"

"Your brother bore a skinmark," she said. "He bears a skinmark."

"What? Where?"

"On his scalp. A circle broken into eighths by Death's arrows."

"How do you know this?"

"I saw it. Your mother did, too." Zelda sighed. "Sabria had reason to believe one of her children would bear a mark. She received information once. A prophecy of sorts. The details aren't important, save for the fact that your mother believed it. I didn't put much stock in legend and faith, but I agreed to help her. We secretly inspected each of you after you were born. Once we saw the mark on your brother, we agreed he had to be taken away from your father."

"My *mother* knew?" Annise's teeth were clenched together so hard she thought they might crack under the pressure.

"Yes."

A single word, like a dart to the heart.

"I don't understand." Her father would've loved him all the more for having a mark. The marks were power, and power was the only thing her father had worshipped.

"It was the deathmark," Zelda said. "Your brother bears the deathmark. He is responsible for your father's death."

രു

Annise sat on the horse-drawn cart, which rumbled beneath her. She was numb, not from the cold, but from her conversation with Zelda. The apparition she'd seen in the tower had been her lost brother, somehow. And he'd killed his own father, making it appear to be an unfortunate tumble down the tower steps, creating a chain of events that led to her mother's murder and their current situation.

"It was the only way to stop your father," Zelda had explained. Apparently all the time she'd spent away from the castle had been to study the prophecies of some strange witch who'd lived in the west more than a century ago. She'd once been known as the Western Oracle. Evidently her writings included information on the skinmarks, which she referred to as fatemarks. When her sister-in-law had given birth to the babe and they'd shone the torchlight over his tiny scalp, they'd instantly known what the mark meant.

Death. Something called the Kings' Plague, which, according to the Oracle's prophecies, would result in the deaths of eight rulers, which would somehow bring peace to the Four Kingdoms. It was all very confusing to Annise, who was trying to catch up to her aunt's vast knowledge of the skinmarks.

Even then, Zelda had known her brother, the king, was evil. Queen Sabria Loren Gäric had known the same thing. They'd plotted against him, removing the babe from where the king might be able to hurt the boy, hoping that one day the child would return to murder his own father.

But when years passed and the boy didn't return as a young man, and the Dread King continued to reign terror upon the north, her mother and aunt had taken matters into their own hands, plotting to assassinate him.

Annise knew what her father had been capable of. If he'd believed his own son was a threat to his throne, he would've killed him without remorse. As much as she hated losing her brother, she couldn't deny they'd likely saved his life. However, in the end, all their plotting and scheming had cost her mother her life.

"What is his name?" she'd asked, picturing the eerie boy who had appeared on the staircase. The way he'd looked at her, his face so similar to her brother's that she couldn't deny the resemblance.

"Bear calls him Bane," Zelda had replied.

Kings' Bane, Annise had immediately understood.

They'd been interrupted by Netta, who'd brought breakfast, before Annise could ask anything more. But it didn't matter. She might not be a scholar of fatemark lore, but now she knew enough to understand what was happening.

Bane had killed her father—his father—and then apparently killed King Loren in the west, too, as well as most of his royal guards. Two dead rulers—six to go.

Not Arch, she thought now, staring at the snowcapped peaks of the Mournful Mountains getting closer and closer, but not really seeing them. *Please. Not Arch.*

Surely the eastern king would be next. Or perhaps one of the Southron rulers, Empress Sun Sandes or Emperor Vin Hoza. Arch still had time to establish himself in the north, to build up his defenses, didn't he? And anyway, her uncle had declared himself king in the north, so wouldn't he be Bane's next target? In her heart of hearts, she knew he wouldn't, because he wasn't the true king.

"Why didn't you stop Arch from leaving Gearhärt?" Annise muttered to herself. The question was meant for Zelda, but her aunt was on a different cart, trailing behind them, laden with foodstuffs for the troops at Raider's Pass.

Annise was riding on a cart with Tarin, piled high with gleaming weapons and armor. The carts were escorted by a company of four-score soldiers, who were evidently loyal to Lady Zelda and who had agreed to be the first of Arch's army, joining however many soldiers he could recruit at Raider's Pass. They'd come from the east, and were more than ready for a new king. A true king.

Tarin had asked her thrice whether she was alright, and thrice she had simply nodded and waved away the question. He'd eventually given up, and settled in for the short ride south to the Pass, where the streams spoke of an eastern legion bearing royal sigils having made camp in the shadows south of the Mournful Mountains.

Annise wondered what they would find when they arrived.

Chapter Twenty-Eight

The Eastern Kingdom | South of Raider's Pass

Roan

They'd left the defenses at Norris intact, riding out before dawn, mere shadows on a darkened landscape.

No one spoke, not even Gareth, who seemed fresh out of jokes at Roan's expense. In fact, the prince wouldn't even look at him, his eyes dancing away whenever Roan tried to meet them. *I've ruined our friendship*, he thought. *All for that one ill-advised kiss.* And yet the memory of it, as short-lived as it was, warmed his heart.

Gwendolyn took on the role of scout, riding well ahead of the front with two other Orians, both male. From a distance, he could see them laughing and talking. He didn't feel jealous of them, only sad. Sad that any friendship he might've had with Gwen kept slipping further and further away.

Am I destined to be alone, devoid of friends and love? he wondered.

He gritted his teeth and rode onwards, trying to remind himself that such thoughts were childish considering they were riding to war, and he would soon be leaving both of them anyway.

They reached the Snake River at midday, the waters fresh and clean, riding high from the snowmelt to the north. The current was strong, and Roan wondered whether he'd even be able to ford the river when the time came. He was a strong swimmer, but there were dozens of places where a body could be smashed along the rocky shoreline on either side. Across the river was the Tangle, an immense forest that had a reputation for being nearly impenetrable due to the dense foliage full of vines, roots, and spiky plants known to carry poison that caused fever and night chills.

And yet, despite the dangers, the forest was alluring, the first time Roan had laid eyes on the west since he was a baby. All of the answers to his questions about why his mother had to die so he could live, and whether his father knew exactly what she'd done were there, just ready to be discovered. He could almost see them in the shifting branches, in the fluttering leaves. The answer to Roan's biggest question of all—*Can I make a difference in the course of the Hundred Years' War?*—felt close enough to touch.

Nearby, Guy Ironclad spat in the dirt. "An awful place, aye?" he said, noticing Roan's gaze toward the west. "If their god, Wrath, was wise, he would let the west sink into the sea."

"Aye," Roan said. Maybe it was better that no one spoke to him. "An awful place."

For now, Roan would continue riding directly north with the war party, biding his time until he could slip away.

Paused by the river, they watered their horses, ate a light lunch, and moved out across the plains, which were flat and packed hard.

The weather began to change as the mountains loomed larger in the distance. First it was a cold breeze slipping through gaps in his clothing, but swiftly became an icy wind, blowing hard enough to make him shiver. He pulled the cloak that was tied to his reins free and wrapped it around his shoulders.

Snow began to fall. The edges of the river were frozen. Then the middle, the entire body of water crusted with ice that looked thick enough to walk upon. Roan licked his lips, eyeing the river. Would it really be that simple? Could he just walk across? Even the forest looked less . . . tangled, with wide gaps between the trees.

Gareth cruised over to him, smiling. His eyes met Roan's and there was no awkwardness there. *Thank the gods*, Roan thought. "The northerners must be mad to live in a place like this," he said. "Their skin must be thicker than ours, don't you think?" Roan couldn't help but to agree. Though he was pleased to see the easygoing smile back in its place on the prince's face, something about it wasn't quite right, like he'd used a quill and some ink to draw it on.

"The Southroners would've already retreated," Roan said. "They are not built for such weather." *And neither am I, which is one of many reasons I'll be going west.*

"You speak of the southerners as if you are not one of them," Gareth noted.

"As I've said, I'm only half-Southroner," Roan said, mentally berating himself for his loose tongue.

"Hmm, I remember now. Something about a western father, right?"

Roan froze, pretending the question meant nothing to him, that he was simply mesmerized by the sheer size of the monstrous peaks rising before them. The mountains were a mix of black, green, and white. The green was at the bottom, the black in the middle, and only white at their heights, capped with snow. He was cold now—he couldn't imagine what the temperature must feel like atop the cliffs.

"Impressive, aye?" Gareth said, noticing his wide eyes. Roan was glad the prince had changed the subject.

"Raider's Pass cuts *between* the mountains, right?" Roan asked.

"Aye. The river has created a thin canyon. There's a path along the river, but it's rocky and difficult. Years ago, when the north and the west were still willing to trade, the pass was ruled by bands of raiders who ransacked the numerous caravans and barges that made the trek between the kingdoms."

"Hence the name," Roan said.

"Hence. Now the Pass is the front lines in the Hundred Years' War. It's the only geographical point where the western, eastern, and northern kingdoms meet. Much blood has been spilt between the shoulders of the Mournful Mountains."

And much more will be spilt, Roan thought, *but I won't be around to see it.*

The king and his retinue had stopped up ahead. The battalion formed ranks behind him. Regardless of what Roan thought of their traditions and intentions, he couldn't deny the quality of the eastern training. The soldiers, whether male or female, Orian or human, were obedient and well-organized.

Before the sun fell beneath the horizon, the camp was erected, the horses tended and shielded from the wind, fires made, supper cooked, and water barrels filled. Gareth disappeared into a secret meeting with his father and brothers. The only other attendee was Beorn Stonesledge with his ironmark.

Roan lounged by one of the larger fires, internally chuckling at the three soldiers who pretended not to watch him, but who he knew had been assigned to guard him. Without being bound or jailed, he was a prisoner just the same. But not for long.

To his surprise, a slim figure stepped into the firelight and sat down beside him. In the moon and firelight, her silvery hair almost appeared as white as the snow on the mountains. Gwendolyn spoke without looking at him, staring into the flames. "Thank you for saving my life. And the girl's. I should've said it before, but all I could feel was anger and sadness."

"I tried to save Bark's life, too," Roan said. "I swear it."

"I know. I have trouble with failure. I think those with marks feel it more."

He remembered swinging from her hammock. "How do you know the westerners once called them fatemarks?" Roan asked.

"My father told me. He told me about the Western Oracle. He said she'd prophesied about the fatemarks, about how they could one day bring peace to the Four Kingdoms."

"How?"

"Why are you so interested in the west all of a sudden?"

"Gwen, I can't tell you everything. I want to, but I can't."

She chewed on this for a while, and then sighed with resignation. "I don't know what he meant about the fatemarks, but I'm not certain he did either. Twice he mentioned rumors of a Peacemaker, one of the marked. According to the Oracle, this was the one who would unify the kingdoms and bring peace. But no one seems to know for certain. Most of the Oracle's teachings were lost. No one knows what happened to her. Some say she died, executed by the western king. Some say she just ceased to exist. And others believe she's still alive, hiding somewhere, waiting for peace to return."

"What do you believe?"

"That there's always hope for a better world."

She's lost so much, and still she has hope. "Because of your heromark?"

Her eyes darted to his, surprised, but then moved back to the fire. "I don't know. Perhaps. It's like I can feel the souls of the dead crying out to me."

Roan's heart skipped a beat. "I understand."

"Do you?" There was frustration in her voice. Not anger—not yet—but resentment.

He'd heard the same cries. The girl he'd healed so long ago. The boy who'd been unlucky enough to be with her at the time. And since then, so many more—people he could've helped, but didn't. An entire island of souls on Dragon's Breath alone.

And now the village of Glee.

But one cry seemed to rise above all others, louder and stronger than he'd ever felt before.

His mother's. Now, this close to the west, this close to his birthplace, Roan needed more than ever to understand what had happened to set his life on this course.

Roan shook his head, the horrific images burning through his mind. "Yes. I understand. But at least I have a choice."

Gwendolyn muttered a curse under her breath.

Roan frowned. Had he said something wrong? He was about to ask, when Gwen said, "I've lied about my mark my entire life." Roan had no idea what she meant, or how to respond, so he just waited for her to continue, which she did. "Everyone believes my mark forces me into dangerous situations, but in truth, it doesn't."

"Then what does it do?" Memories bloomed in Roan's head: Gwen moving like the wind, as strong as a man twice her size, dragging a small girl to safety.

"You don't know?"

He did know. His mouth cracked open with realization. The only force compelling Gwen to rush to save the lives of others was herself. All her life, she'd been hiding the truth. Because . . . because why? *Because she doesn't want to be given credit for her selfless acts*, Roan realized. "You are a true hero," he said. "And not because of your heromark."

Gwen cast her eyes downwards. "Perhaps I just don't want to waste the power I've been given."

It's not what Roan wanted to hear, because it implied his own failings. Not to mention his future failings if he were to run from the impending battle before it started. How many would die because of his choice? "You never asked for your mark. Neither did I," he said.

Gwendolyn suddenly grabbed his arm, and her fingers were so hot they practically burned his skin. But still, he didn't flinch away, his heart an entire battalion of thundering hoofbeats in his chest.

"So what?" Gwendolyn said. "Do you think anyone asks for what they're born with? Do you think I asked for the speed and strength to save some, but not all? Do you think I wanted to outlive most of my friends, to see death and life alternate like the changing of the seasons?"

She gripped his arm tighter still, and Roan could feel the beat of his heart in his veins beneath her fingertips.

"It's not what you start with, it's what you do with what you've been given," Gwen said.

Seeing the passion on her face, feeling the heat from her fingertips on his skin, this heroic woman had never looked more beautiful. She smelled of jasmine and steel, leather and talc. He wanted to taste her passion, to feel her warmth flowing through him, to discover whether his heart galloped when he kissed her as it had when he'd kissed Gareth.

He remembered Gareth's rejection, the anger in his eyes.

He didn't move, as frozen as the mountains.

Gwen's fingers lingered a moment longer, and then she released his arm, which continued to burn, stood up, and strode into the darkness.

Roan blinked, looking around to see if anyone else had observed their exchange. To his surprise, the three soldiers assigned to watch him had been reduced to one, and the last man was asleep, snoring loudly.

This was exactly the chance he'd been waiting for. Like a wraith, he would slip away. He had nothing left to stay for. Whatever he felt for Gwendolyn, for Gareth, was clearly not reciprocated. They would not miss him, would not care. Away from them, his life would be his own again, and this time he would make it count. Even Gwen's last words to him seemed to agree with his decision to leave, to set out on his own and make a difference in this world. His past was the key to the future, he just had to turn it in the lock of his present. He would tell no one of her secret.

He stood, creeping away quietly, heading for the frozen river. The embankment was rocky, but not particularly steep, and there was even a slice of red moonlight penetrating the clouds to light his way. For once, fate seemed to be on his side. In his chest, his lifemark seemed to pulse in agreement. *My fatemark*, he thought, remembering the word Gwen had introduced him to.

Reaching the river, he took a tentative step onto the ice. He pressed half his weight, then all of his weight. Nothing. The ice was thick and strong and didn't so much as crack or groan. He would literally be able to stroll across to the west. From there he could follow the mountain range all the way to the Bay of Bounty, eating snow to sustain him. If necessary, he would stop in Bethany and beg for scraps. From there it was presumably less than a week's journey to Knight's End. The thought made him feel a slash of something in his chest. Was it excitement or fear? He wasn't sure.

He was halfway across when he thought of Gareth. His feet stopped, almost of their own accord. Though he'd never intended it, the prince had become his reluctant friend, at the least. The prince believed he would die in the next day or so, somewhere between here and Raider's Pass. *Not my problem*, Roan thought desperately.

Right?

What if I turn back and die in the battle? he thought. What if he never had the chance to return home, to face his father, to learn about the truth of his mother's death? What then? Gwen herself had pointed out that he had a responsibility to use the power he'd been given, and between his lifemark and his lineage, he could make a difference more than anyone else, if he was only courageous enough to try.

He took another step forward and stopped again. Took a deep breath, holding the icy air in his lungs, relishing the distraction provided by the burn in his chest. Released it, watching the white vapors escape into the frigid night air.

But Gareth. But Gwendolyn. But King Ironclad and Beorn Stonesledge and all of the other easterners who were standing up for the death of their queen, a strong woman they respected so much they were willing to give their lives for her memory.

It's not my fight. My fight is elsewhere.

Roan took two more steps forward, listening to the scrape of his boots on the ice.

And then he made a decision that surprised even him.

He turned around.

He had a battle to stop.

⁂

The war council was over, the princes and Beorn Stonesledge having gone to bed. The rest of the soldiers slumbered, too, and Roan was able to slip back into camp. He was surprised to find King Oren Ironclad still sitting by the main campfire, which had been reduced to a pile of glowing embers. Roan eased down beside him.

"You have made your choice?" the large man said, staring into the dying fire.

He knows, Roan thought. "I didn't know I had a choice," he said.

The king offered a half-smile, but didn't make eye contact. "There is always a choice, and I wasn't about to deny you yours."

Roan was dumbfounded. "You allowed me to escape?"

The king stroked his thick beard thoughtfully. "We have built our monarchy around the idea of choice. Our soldiers are free, as are our servants. They are paid well. We treat them as they are."

"And what are they?"

"People." Now the king looked up. "Tell me, Roan. Why did you come back?"

Roan wasn't sure the king would like the answer, but it was a moment of honesty between them, and he wouldn't lie. "To stop the battle."

The king nodded, as if he'd guessed as much. "And how do you plan to do that?"

"By speaking with you. Man to man."

The king laughed, a deep-throated chuckle, his eyes reflecting orange embers. "And what would you say to me? Man to man." There was mocking in his tone.

"That this war is folly. Defend your lands, aye, but do not go on the offensive. Countless lives can still be saved, including your own son's."

The king's smile faded into the firelight. "Do not speak to me of saving lives, boy," he snarled. "I cradled Henna's head as life faded from her eyes. She'd been stabbed through the gut as she'd slept, left by our enemies to die a slow, miserable death."

"I'm sorr—"

"You don't get to be sorry!" The king stood, towering over Roan, his fists clenched at his sides, anger seeming to pulse from every angle of his body. Beneath his shining, bald head, his face was awash with red light, his eyes burning with something Roan had trouble identifying at first. There was a mania in his expression that Roan had not seen before. It was a mixture of anger and unspent violence and something else. Roan suddenly realized what it was:

Pain.

Grief.

Anger so deep and fiery it was an unquenchable inferno burning beneath the surface of his skin.

This man, who was typically so in control, had become a slave to his pain, which seemed to be eating him alive from the inside out. "She's dead. My blood cries for vengeance, and I will have it! Blood for blood. Death for death. If the Dread King is dead, then it falls to his wife. If she is dead, it falls to their children. If the children are dead, it shall be every northerner who stands in my way!"

He bent down and grabbed the Foehammer, which had been resting beside him. With a roar, he raised it over his head and brought it down in the center of the fire, scattering blazing embers like splinters of a shattered torch. One such ember landed in Roan's lap. He sprang to his feet, brushing the ember from his trousers, which had already begun to smolder.

When he looked up, the king was gone, leaving what was left of the fire to burn itself out, along with Roan's hopes of stopping the battle.

Chapter Twenty-Nine

The Northern Kingdom | Raider's Pass

Annise Gäric

At Raider's Pass, the northern forces were preparing for battle. Men donned battle-scarred armor, sharpened swords, battle axes, and mace, and drank from water skins. One company was beating their chests and shouting angrily at each other, as if trying to work themselves up to violence. Another company was huddled in a circle, and seemed to be praying. To what god, Annise didn't know.

Peeking out from under the edge of the tarp, she was so close to Tarin it was like they were joined at the hip. Zelda had stopped their caravan a while back to hide them beneath the sheets of thick canvas. Although Annise's aunt was confident they would have even more allies at the Pass, she didn't want to risk her niece being identified until she was certain it was safe. Despite the cold, Annise was sweating beneath her layers.

The northern edge of Raider's Pass was a rocky outcropping nestled between two enormous boulders perched at the base of the Mournful Mountains. The Snake River flowed swiftly downstream—though you couldn't tell because of the thick layer of ice on its surface—cutting a narrow canyon between the white cliffs. Eventually the river would flow into Hyro Lake, which fed the Spear, finally emptying into the Burning Sea many leagues south.

Annise scanned the camp's activity for her brother, but all the men were too tall, too broad, and too grizzled by years of war to be Arch. *Where are you?* she wondered.

That's when Tarin whispered, "Sir Dietrich." His head was angled to the left, and Annise followed his gaze excitedly, zeroing in on the tall, handsome knight immediately. The master swordsman stood sentry outside a large tent, his armor more dented and dinged than ever, almost like he'd purposely banged it against a sharp rock.

Evidently, Zelda and her escorts had spotted him, too, because the carts and soldiers diverted their path toward the tent, stopping nearby, the horses stamping their hooves in the cold. Sir Dietrich approached warily, his eyes narrowed.

"Who goes there?" he demanded, grabbing the edge of the tarp and thrusting it back with a flourish. The snow that had gathered on top flew in the air and landed on Annise's head.

"Frozen hell," she growled, "we're supposed to be in hiding." She grabbed the tarp and struggled to pull it back down as Sir Dietrich's eyes widened.

"Princess Annise?" he said, dumbfounded.

"Queen Annise, actually," she said. "Who were you expecting? An ice monster from the Hinterlands?"

"Queen . . ." he said, trailing off as if the word was spoken in a foreign language.

"She had a name day," Tarin explained.

"Arme," Sir Dietrich said. "She's supposed to be at Blackstone."

"Tell *her* that," he muttered.

Annise was no longer listening, because she'd become aware of the fact that dozens of soldiers had stopped what they were doing to watch the commotion. They crowded around the cart, a dozen men thick.

"The princess has arrived," one of them said.

Annise's breath caught in her chest. All the hiding, all the fighting, was for naught.

"Princess Annise," another said.

The men were so close they could clamber onto the cart in half a moment. Even warriors like Tarin and Sir Dietrich would be unable to stop more than a small portion of them if they wanted to take her, to drag her back to her uncle at Castle Hill. Still, Tarin's hand shot to his Morningstar, which he uncoiled with the clanking of chains.

"All hail, Annise Gäric, Princess of the North!" a man said and a cheer went up.

"What?" Annise said.

Sir Dietrich laughed loudly. "You have nothing to fear here," he said. "Raider's Pass is ours."

While Annise tried to process the idea of being safe amongst so many northern soldiers, another voice inserted itself into the conversation. Though Annise recognized the voice as if it were her own, there was something different about it, something powerful. "Sister?" the voice said.

Annise turned. Her brother stood outside the large tent wearing a full suit of silver armor, missing only the helmet. Though he seemed exceptionally surprised at her presence, Annise could tell from his expression that he was pleased to see her.

She leapt from the cart, landing in a crouch, and then barreled toward him. She was planning on tackling him and wailing on him like she always did growing up when he'd done something stupid. He seemed to think the same thing, because he put his hands up and began backing away. At the last moment, however, she pulled up, wrapping him in an embrace, squeezing extra hard.

"If you *ever* run from me again, I will pop you like a grape," she hissed in his ear.

"Nice to see you, too, sister," he said.

Behind them, the men cheered and pounded their chests.

Annise released her brother when Aunt Zelda approached and said, "Come inside. We have much to discuss."

꒰

"Those men who supported Lord Griswold have fled toward either Blackstone or the Razor. Those who survived, that is." Sir Dietrich said the latter with satisfaction, as if he'd killed half of them himself, and chased the rest away with his sword held high.

They were gathered in Arch's royal tent—Annise, Arch, Lady Zelda, Sir Craig, Sir Dietrich, and Tarin, who had to duck his head to avoid hitting it on the ceiling.

Annise shook her head, still trying to come to terms with the fact that her brother had managed to secure himself an army, albeit a rather small one.

Arch seemed able to read her mind. "It didn't take much convincing," he said. "Most of these men have never even met Lord Griswold, and owe him no allegiance. They are tired of fighting to secure the Pass, tired of treading water in the armpit of the north. I brought them something they haven't had in a while."

Annise raised her eyebrows in question.

"Hope," Arch explained. "Change."

"What change?"

"An end to the war," he said. "I have promised them that if they can hang on a little longer, if they will help me restore the north to its true heir, that I will initiate peace talks with the west."

Annise opened her mouth to speak, to inform him of what everyone had seemed to have forgotten: That Arch was not of age, and now Annise was. The true heir he spoke of so confidently was her, not him.

But Zelda placed a hand on her shoulder and stopped her with a sharp glance and barely perceptible shake of her head. "Peace with the west may be impossible now," Zelda said. "The news of your mother's death was not taken well. She was their princess, after all."

"That was Uncle's decision, not mine," Arch said. "He tried to kill me, too. I can explain that to the Lorens. I will *make* them understand."

Zelda nodded. "I have no doubt you will try," she said. "Have you received word of whether the line of succession has been determined?"

Arch bit his lip, an expression that finally made him look his age. Then he spoke and the boy he'd once been gave way to the man he'd become. "We received a stream two days prior. Rhea Loren is of age, but has been accused of fornication under western law."

Annise knew the west was strict on many things, but surely taking a lover wouldn't preclude the princess from inheriting the throne.

"The work of the furia, no doubt," Zelda said, sighing. "This is unfortunate news. Rhea might've been an easy ally. I assume her eldest cousin, Jove, has assumed the crown as King Temporanus?"

"Correct," Arch said. "We streamed him a message only yesterday explaining the situation in the north, though his spies have likely already informed him. We will defend the Pass while we await his reply."

"What did you ask of him?" Zelda said. "The west is in turmoil. They are in no position to offer assistance to our cause."

"I did not ask for assistance, nor do I need it," Arch said calmly. He sounded like a king. Not like her father, full of anger and fearmongering, but strong and willful. "I simply warned him of Lord Griswold's illegal seizure of the throne and his gathering of forces at Blackstone. In the event that I can defeat my uncle, I requested that we negotiate peace under new terms. *Our* terms, not those of our elders."

Zelda smiled thinly. "You have done well."

"There is something else we must discuss," Sir Dietrich said.

Annise glanced at Lady Zelda sharply, knowing immediately what the knight was about to bring up. Her name day. Northern law. After hearing her brother speak, she didn't want him to know the truth. He was always meant to be the king, anyway, not her. Already he'd shown his ability to rule, to make hard, fast decisions. And she'd thrown snowballs at an ice bear, defeated a lusty drunkard, and hidden amongst timber and swords. If all that made her worthy of being a queen, then she would leap atop a wild mamoothen and storm Castle Hill herself.

Zelda seemed to feel the same way, because she once more interjected, cutting Sir Dietrich off. "Yes, we must discuss the strategy for the impending battle. I assume preparations are complete?"

Sir Dietrich frowned but seemed to take the hint, clamping his mouth shut. Annise exhaled slowly. She would talk to the knight later, try to convince him that the truth was better kept from her brother, at least for now.

Before Arch could respond to Zelda's question, Sir Craig said, "Wait. Shouldn't we first consider whether we *should* defend the Pass?"

Sir Dietrich's frown deepened. "What are you suggesting—that we let the easterners march right through, free to enter our lands unmolested?"

Sir Craig raised a placating hand. "Why not? They will help our cause in the short term. If they make it to Castle Hill they may even overthrow Lord Griswold. Why should we defend the usurper king?"

Sir Dietrich opened his mouth to speak again, but Arch cut him off. "It's an interesting proposal, but why should we replace one unlawful king with another? Either way, we'll still have a rebellion to carry out."

"We could reason with King Ironclad afterwards," Sir Craig went on. "He might listen, especially if we made certain promises of peace."

Though she was against the proposal, Annise was pleased to see Arch well and truly consider the idea—something her father never would've done. After a moment of reflection, Arch said, "Sister, what do you think?"

Annise was surprised but honored that her brother was interested in what she had to say. He really was becoming a wise king, a fact that made the weight of her secret even harder to bear. "I wish we could avoid violence at the Pass," she said, "but we cannot allow our anger at our uncle dictate our decisions. We are northerners, and if the east would invade our lands, we have no choice but to defend it, to the death if necessary. We have no reason to believe the Ironclads would be open to peace negotiations, not after all the bloodshed between our kingdoms."

Arch nodded vehemently, as if her opinion had solidified his own. "I agree with my sister's wisdom. Other opinions?"

There were none, and Sir Craig backed down. Arch moved on to the battle strategy. Evidently the eastern king, Oren Ironclad the Juggernaut, had decided the north was ripe for defeat. He'd led a large battalion of soldiers from his stronghold in Ferria to Raider's Pass. Given the poor weather conditions, he was expected to mount an attack through the Pass soon, perhaps as early as on the morrow. Preparations had been made for just such an assault. When the Pass was once dominated by the raiders of old, numerous fortifications had been built directly into the cliffs, manmade caves offering a strong position from above. Arch had sent half of his forces to each of these outposts, hauling timber and heavy stone. These men included his best archers. The goal was to send as many of the easterners into the frozen river as possible before they could traverse the narrow pass and reach northern territory.

However, if any of the enemy did make it through, Arch had planned accordingly. Enormous ice slings had been constructed, and were prepared to bombard any who emerged from the pass. Furthermore, his most capable swordsmen, including Sir Dietrich, as well as those with experience in hand to hand combat, would provide a final line of defense.

The goal was victory with as few casualties as possible—they would need a heavy force to march on Castle Hill and take back the throne.

Annise once more marveled at the change in her brother. He was all business, a far cry from the boy who always had a quip at her expense on his tongue. He was born to be king, and she wouldn't try to convince him otherwise. Once this was over, she would flee to the north, or possibly Crimea, but she wouldn't try to convince him to go with her. No, she couldn't ask that of him.

❦

"Explain yourself," Sir Dietrich said, grabbing Annise's arm as he caught up to her.

"I don't have to explain anything to you," she spat back.

Tarin stepped up, moving chest to chest with the knight who'd defeated him in the melee, an event that now felt like a lifetime ago to Annise. "Remove your hand, Sir," Tarin said.

Sir Dietrich raised his eyebrows. "I see you two have...*bonded* out on the tundra," he said, laughing. Still, he released his grip and pulled his hand back.

"You know nothing," Annise said.

"Really? I know that you are legally a queen now. That it is you and not Arch who should be making a claim for the throne. Regardless of your intentions, you must tell him the truth."

"I will," Annise growled. "After the battle. And I will relinquish my rights to him. He is the king; no name day can change that."

"It can if you want it to," Sir Dietrich said.

"I don't," Annise said quickly.

The knight moved closer once more, as if daring Tarin to stop him. "What are you afraid of, Annise?" he said, his voice husky. "Of being adored? Of being cheered? Of being strong?"

Annise shoved him away. "I already *am* strong, and adoration is for pretty princes with big smiles and arrogant demeanors." She walked away, toward the tent Arch had provided for her, while Tarin stopped Sir Dietrich from following.

"If you don't tell him, I will," Sir Dietrich called after her.

❦

Annise had been trying to sleep for a long time. The camp was quiet and dark and, strangely, peaceful. *The calm before the storm*, she mused, rubbing her eyes.

Faintly, she could hear Tarin's snores from without her tent. Though they'd shared a much smaller tent than this one, he refused to sleep inside, preferring to guard the entrance. "That was survival," he'd said when she'd offered. "Now, it wouldn't be proper."

Proper, she thought now. She hated that word, more so because it always seemed to follow her around like a chaperone. *Don't cheer too loud at the melee, princess, it wouldn't be proper. Don't eat too much or too fast or too loudly, it's not proper. Don't fight with the boys or play Snow Wars or do anything that could possibly be construed as fun, it's just not proper.*

"You can take your proper and shove it up your—" she muttered, but stopped when she heard voices outside.

"Yes. Of course." Tarin's deep voice, sleepy but alert.

The tent flap opened and Annise sat up. Her brother's face appeared. He was still in his armor. For once, Tarin wouldn't be the only one passing the night in full body armor, his weapon at the ready. Two thoughts crossed Annise's mind in an instant: Sir Dietrich had made good on his promise and told Arch the truth; and, the enemy has attacked.

"Have the easterners begun their march through the pass?" Annise asked quickly. She almost wished they would. The waiting seemed worse, somehow.

"No. Did I wake you?" He closed the tent behind him, the wind whistling in his wake.

She shook her head, searching his expression. "I couldn't sleep if I was knocked unconscious," she said.

Arch laughed, and he wasn't a king anymore. He was just her brother. "Me either."

"Why are you here?" *Did you talk to Sir Dietrich?*

"Do I need an excuse to visit my elder sister, who I haven't seen in a fortnight?" he said.

"You're the king," Annise said. "You don't need an excuse for anything. Father certainly didn't."

"Good point. But still, I keep going back and forth on every decision I've made, second-guessing myself. Did I word my letter to Jove Loren correctly? Was it too strong? Too weak? Should I let the east invade the north uncontested, like Sir Craig suggested, and allow them to defeat Uncle for me? Is my battle strategy sound? Am I just a child playing a game where I pretend to be a king?"

Annise laughed. "Back in your war tent I never would've guessed you had so many doubts."

"I'm good at hiding them. Just like the joust."

"You always won the joust," Annise pointed out. "You always looked like you *knew* you would win."

"All an act," Arch said.

Annise raised her eyebrows. "Why didn't you ever tell me?"

Arch sighed. "Because you were always so strong. I wanted to impress you. I wanted to impress my eldest sister." He went silent for a minute, looking thoughtful. "I'm glad you're here," he finally said.

"I thought you wanted me to hide in the hustle and bustle of Blackstone," she said.

"See?" Arch said. "That was a mistake. Perhaps all of my decisions are mistakes."

"Perhaps," Annise said, smirking.

"Frozen hell!" Arch protested. "You're supposed to make me feel better."

Annise knew this was the perfect, light-hearted moment to admit the truth and simultaneously relinquish her rights to the northern throne, but she didn't want to spoil what might be her last time alone with her brother. Plus, she didn't want to do anything else to shake his confidence. Instead she said, "Arch, you were meant to be king, I believe that. I trust all of the decisions you've made so far, even the one concerning me and my safety."

"So you're not angry?"

"I'm not angry, but that doesn't mean when this is all over that I won't rub snow in your face, for old time's sake."

"I wouldn't have it any other way," Arch said, smiling. "Now we should both try to get some rest. By morning there could be war."

With that, he left. Just before the tent was sealed shut once more, Annise caught a glimpse of Tarin's dark eyes peering in. For half a moment she considered commanding him to come inside, but then thought better of it.

She lay back down, and this time she fell right to sleep. After all, the attack likely wouldn't begin until morning.

Unfortunately, King Ironclad had other plans.

PART IV

RHEA • GREY • ROAN • ANNISE • BANE

There are those who are not fatemarked who may influence the events that transpire; whether for good or evil is still to be determined.
— THE WESTERN ORACLE

Chapter Thirty

The Western Kingdom | Knight's End

Rhea Loren

Rhea wanted to die. The next best thing, however, was closing her eyes and never opening them again.

After passing out from the pain, she'd awakened in a room full of mirrors. Everywhere she'd turned was another looking glass, spitting her horrid reflection back at her. She'd screamed and curled into the fetal position, her disfigured face smashed against her hands, her skin throbbing with pain.

She used to relish the time in the morning spent in front of the broad mirror over her dressing table. Staring at the big turquoise eyes her mother had blessed her with, the flawless skin, the sly smile, the silky sun-kissed hair. She loved the way she looked, loved how—even garbed in her cloak of purity—every male head would turn when she passed. She loved how Grease had stared at her with smoldering desire every time he'd met her in secret.

No, she thought bitterly, her teeth grinding together. *Not secret. Someone knew.* And now her sins had been used against her, her only talent—seduction—stripped away by the holy knife of the Fury whose image would forever haunt her nightmares, dwarfed only by her own face screaming back at her from the looking glass.

She'd been carved from temple to chin on both sides, perfectly symmetrical, the work of a master butcher. From each end of her chin, two additional, shorter slashes had been cut, angling along the edges of her lips and connecting in a point beneath her nose. Her perfect nose. Her perfect lips. Her perfect face.

Now that of a monster.

The symbol was unmistakable—a 'W' for Whore, a mark that would forever label her as a fornicator, a sinner, unclean. She'd seen similar markings on prostitutes caught working the streets in Knight's End. She'd always pitied them. Though she was certain many of the women had once been fair, she'd never been able to see past their disfigured faces.

And now she was one of them.

Her parents were dead. Her younger siblings hated her. Her cousin had usurped the throne that was rightfully hers. Grease—*no, Grey*, she remembered—the only boy she'd ever loved, was gone, not that she blamed him. No man would ever look upon her with desire again.

She squeezed her eyes shut tighter, tears leaking out, the salt burning the deep cuts in her flesh.

The door creaked open, but still she wouldn't look, afraid of seeing her own reflection. "Oh, Rhea," a voice said. "Wrath save us all."

She knew the voice, which only made her tuck her head further into her hands, her entire body wracked with thunderous sobs.

Strong arms wrapped around her, and Ennis said, "I'm here, dear cousin. You are safe."

Rhea hated how much she believed him, although his words were nothing more than a kind lie.

"The furia have gone mad. They're patrolling Knight's End day and night, punishing sinners. My brother ordered it. Jove said the city needs to be cleansed, that your father was too lenient and that is why we are being punished."

Rhea sniffled, taking it all in. Her father was the strictest man she'd ever met, even if he was too trusting of his own daughter to realize what she was up to half the time.

Ennis continued. "The furia are spreading rumors about you. That you lay with a man. A thief with a sinmarked sister."

They aren't rumors, she thought. Still, it was all she could take. Yes, she'd bedded Grey. And so what? She loved him. She wanted him. And yet, if not for having met him, she would still be beautiful.

She squirmed away, unfolding her arms, her eyes flashing open. "Where were you when they did *this* to me?" she spat. Dozens of grotesque Rheas mimicked her accusation.

Ennis tried to hide the shock in his eyes, but failed miserably. "Oh, Wrath."

"No," Rhea said. "Wrath is not here, if he ever was. Knight's End died when my father died."

"You don't mean that." Ennis's gaze was locked on her face, and she knew he couldn't bring himself to look away from her disfigurement.

"I do," Rhea said, hot tears streaking down her cheeks. "I want this city to burn, along with everyone in it."

Ennis stood up and held out a hand. "Come. You're permitted to leave now. A good rest and some food will help. I will have your handmaiden attend to your face. The wounds will heal. The scars will fade."

Oh, Wrath, Rhea thought. She wanted to believe her cousin's words so badly it hurt deep in her chest. But she knew his words were hollow, as false as a fire without heat. The Fury had used a holy blade, blessed by Wrath. Her scars would remain deep and jagged forever.

However, his offer did give her an idea, a dark thought that would've made her cringe with disgust just a few days earlier.

It was a wicked idea, and yet it was exactly what she needed in order to go on. She clung to it as she stood, allowing her kindly cousin to escort her from the room of mirrors and to her bedroom

She would have her revenge, or she would die in the process.

Chapter Thirty-One

The Western Kingdom | Talis

Grey Arris (Formerly Grease Jolly)

Grease Jolly was dead. Grey knew that. After all, Grease Jolly had been a slick operator, his left hand faster than a striking cobra. The master thief had died when his hand had been cut off.

"I'm Grey Arris," he said aloud, his true name sounding strange on his tongue after so many years of disuse. He was on the outskirts of a walled city he assumed was Talis, though he'd never been there before. It had taken him three days to travel from Knight's End to Talis on foot. On day two, the heavens had smiled upon him, letting loose a light rain that he'd collected in his hands, licking the moisture from his skin. He'd scavenged for berries twice, and though his stomach was still mostly empty, the tiny fruits had been enough to sustain him.

Now his muscles were aching, and he longed to rest. But he wouldn't, not until he found Shae. Though the furia had a head start and were on horseback, surely they'd have to stop sometime. Once he found them, he would use his stealth to determine what had happened to his sister. Then he would do everything in his power to help her escape.

Even more concerning, however, was his stump. It was leaking thick pus, greenish-brown and occasionally spotted with blood. He knew it was infected, but chose not to think too much about it, leaving the wound covered and out of sight.

The city walls were far too tall to climb, and anyway, climbing walls was something Grease would've done. No, one-handed Grey Arris would enter the city the conventional way, through the front gates. The road curved around the outside of the city, toward the sea, which was frothing with angry whitecaps. A trio of gulls chased each other, cawing the news of Grey's arrival.

When he rounded the edge of the wall, he pulled up short, gaping. The front gate faced the sea, trailing a snaking staircase that descended to one of the largest ports he'd ever seen, nearly as bustling as the docks at Knight's End. Half a dozen ships were anchored, hordes of seamen crawling across the decks, unloading crates and barrels. Small horses stood waiting on the docks, waiting to be loaded. *Not horses*, Grey realized. *Donkeys.* Several of the sure-footed animals were climbing the steep steps, driven by their masters, who used long sticks to encourage them forward. Each donkey carried an impressive load, their heads down, their backs bent.

Grey could relate. Though not physical in nature, the load he carried at this very moment weighed heavily on his shoulders.

Shaking away the thought, he continued along the path toward Talis's front gate, watching the commotion on the docks. The ships were large and flew the yellow crescent flags of Crimea, their sides bristling with long oars to ensure safe passage even when the winds disappeared. He wondered if the north was aware that the Crimeans were diverting a portion of their merchant fleet south to Talis. Probably not.

He reached the city gates just behind several of the donkeys and their masters. Following behind them, he marveled at the fact that the city entrance was unprotected during the daytime. He marched through without question, though his clothing was filthy and bloody.

If the Phanecians ever manage to break through the border cities and cross the Forbidden Plains, Grey thought, *Talis will fall quickly.* Which would leave Knight's End unprotected from the south. Caught between the Southroners and the northerners, the western stronghold would be squashed like a grape under a well-placed boot.

For some reason that thought made Grey frown. *Why should I care what happens to the kingdom that has done nothing but hurt me and my family?* Grey wondered to himself.

Because of her. Because of Rhea.

She was likely queen now, and any turmoil for the kingdom would affect her. *Gods, I'm a fool*, Grey thought, wishing he could wipe his feelings for Rhea away as easily as a smudge of dirt from his face.

His thoughts *were*, however, wiped away when he passed a marketplace and saw the glares fired his way by the owners of each cart and stall.

At first, he ignored them, trying to figure out what their problems were. Was it his disheveled appearance? Surely they'd seen travelers before. He'd already passed several beggars—he was no worse for wear than they were.

It dawned on him: his stump. Sure enough, he saw the sellers' eyes flick from his face to his missing hand and back again, their angry frowns deepening. His stump was like having a tattoo across his forehead that read THIEF.

Don't worry! he wanted to scream. *Grease Jolly is dead!*

Still, he would need to get food one way or another, and he had no coin to purchase it. Pretending not to notice the way one of the traders was staring at him, Grey sidled up to his stall. "I'm looking for a girl," he said to the owner, a plump middle-aged woman with gray hair. He described Shae in detail, while she just stared at him. Then he said, "She was taken by the furia."

The woman flinched and seemed to lose her composure. "Ain't seen nothin'," she said. When Grey tried to force the issue, she quickly stepped back and swung a wooden gate closed across the front of her stall. Though she'd been unwilling to talk, Grey knew her fearful reaction was enough to confirm that the furia had been through the city recently—maybe were still here.

He tried the next stall, but the owner had already shuttered the sides of his store. Grey could barely make out a pair of eyes staring at him from inside. *Yes*, he thought. *I am close.* After similar experiences with several more merchants, Grey knew a different tactic was necessary.

He strode up to a stall further down the line, before the owner closed his gate or shutters. "Nothing is for sale," the man said immediately, blocking Grey's view of the fresh fruits and vegetables, which only made his mouth water more.

"No?" Grey said, raising his eyebrows. "That's good, because I'm not looking to buy anything."

The man was old, his flesh sagging under his arms and eyes. "You best be moving on," he said. "The furia are in the city. They're likely to take your other hand if you're not careful."

Grey's heart palpitated at the confirmation of what he already believed. "Where are they?" he asked. "The furia."

"Why should I tell you?"

Something broke inside Grey. He stepped up to the man and grabbed his collar with one hand, shoving him hard against the cart. Several apples shook free from the pile and bounced to the ground. "Listen up, old man, I'm tired and hungry and I'm trying to find my younger sister. I don't give two shites about you and your fruit. So if you don't tell me where they've gone, I swear to Wrath that I'll make you wish you had." Grey was shocked by his own actions, but it was like his temper had a mind of its own. Was this who Grey was? Violence and threats?

Someone said from nearby. "Hey, Briar, is there a problem?"

Grey ignored the newcomer, his eyes boring into the old man named Briar.

Briar opened his mouth slowly and said, "Everything's fine. I'm just giving this fellow directions."

Grey released the man, using his one hand to brush the dirty fingerprints from his shirt.

"Thank you."

The man nodded. "I don't want any trouble. The furia arrived two days ago. They even have two Furies with them. The city's been on its best behavior, but the holy warriors aren't here to enforce Wrath's will. No, they've been waiting."

Grey frowned. "Waiting for what?"

"The ships," Briar said. "Soon as the ships made port this morning, they headed for the docks. Seems they're looking to take a voyage."

Grey shook his head. "A voyage to where?"

"I don't know. Sorry."

"Was there a young girl with them?" Grey asked, holding his breath.

"You mean, like an acolyte?"

Grey hadn't considered the fact that the furia might be traveling with acolytes, the young girls training to be full-fledged holy warriors one day. Typically, the acolytes wore cloaks that were half red, half white to distinguish them from the ordained members of the holy sisterhood. *Would they have disguised Shae as an acolyte?* Grey wondered. "I don't know. Maybe."

The man chewed his lip and considered it. "Yes. They had an acolyte with them. Just one."

Grey had to fight to control the emotions that swirled through him. *Was it you, Shae? Are you alive?* "Thank you," he said again. "I'm sorry I threatened you."

"I understand," the old man said. "I had a sister, once. I would've done anything to protect her." He lowered his voice. "And between you and me, I wouldn't want her in the sisterhood either."

Grey nodded and turned away, heading back the way he'd come. It appeared his stay in Talis would be a short one. He had a ship to catch.

"Hey!" the man called out from behind him.

Grey half-turned, anxious to be on his way. The man tossed him one of the dusty green apples that had tumbled from his cart when Grey had assaulted him. "Take care now," he said as Grey caught the fruit.

Grey pursed his lips, found a clean spot on his shirt, and shined the apple. He took a big bite and raised it in appreciation, but the man had already started talking to another customer, haggling over prices. Grey turned and ran.

As he hustled past the marketplace, he took small bites of the apple, immediately feeling the effects of the bittersweet fruit. He galloped through the front gates and began making his way down the steep staircase, dodging the piles of dung buzzing with flies. He passed several donkeys and their masters, but they didn't give him more than a sideways glance before urging their beasts onward.

The sun beat down on Grey's face and his mouth went dry with thirst and anticipation. His sister was so close. If he could find her he was certain he'd find a way to help her escape.

Finally, he reached the bottom of the steps, which gave way to a long wooden platform that extended out into the sea, supported by stone columns that disappeared beneath the surface of the dark blue water. Along the main dock were wooden offshoots to both the left and right. Seaworthy vessels of various shapes and sizes were anchored on each side. He stopped several times, using his hand to shade his eyes so he could scan the ships.

Several of the workers were wearing red, but none of them were women. He continued on until he reached the end of the platform, where one final ship was docked and being unloaded.

A young shirtless man with bulging muscles shining with sweat noticed Grey and said, "Watcha doin'?"

"I'm looking for someone. An acolyte traveling with the furia.

The man squinted, his gaze zeroing in on Grey's missing hand, as if only just noticing it. "The furia, huh? They were 'ere. Word is they chartered a ship all fer 'emselves. Paid a royal price, too, they did. Ya jest missed 'em." He pointed southward, to a stretch of ocean off the coast.

A shadow blotted out the lower portion of the horizon, the ship's sails full with the wind.

Grey closed his eyes and bit his tongue, anger and frustration roiling through him. His fist clenched and then unclenched as he sank to the wooden deck. His stump was throbbing and he could feel the warm trickle of fluid leaking out.

It was over. Shae was gone, probably forever. Darkness closed in around him.

"I know where they went," the man said.

Grey opened his eyes and the darkness lifted. He blinked. "Where?"

"Ever'one's bin talkin''bout it. They're headed fer the Dead Isles," he said.

Grey's heart sank. The Dead Isles were a place of, well, death. Few lived to tell nightmarish tales about the island where it was said the dead remained alive, haunting the stone cliffs. "How do I get there?" he asked.

"Our ship's goin' back to Crimea to pick up another load. You can try Smithers ol' wreck. He sometimes makes the trek south, though most think he's a fool fer doin' so. An' he's always lookin' fer new crew on account of payin' so poorly."

"Where?" Grey said quickly.

The man pointed down the row. "Sixth vessel on the left. *The Jewel*." Grey counted and locked in on the ship, though its name was generous. *The Junker* was a much more appropriate title.

"Thank you," Grey said, and started back the way he'd come.

He reached the boat, which was covered in barnacles and a mess of chipped paint. The bow was ornamented with a rusted statue of a woman, her bulging chest naked, descending to a lower half that had a long fish-like tail rather than legs and feet. THE JEWEL was scrawled onto the side in chipped blue paint.

"Admiring me wife, are ye?" a man said, staring down from the deck. He was an old coot, with patchy gray whiskers and curly gray hair. He was leaning on one of the few sections of railing that wasn't cracked or missing entirely.

"She's a real beaut'," Grey lied. He wasn't sure whether the man meant the boat or the naked statue.

"Bloody right she is. What can I do ye fer?" he asked.

"Are you Smithers?"

"In the flesh. This here's my lovely lady."

So he'd meant the boat when he referred to his 'wife' earlier. "I heard you're heading south . . ."

"Ye heard right. All the way to Phanes. Mebbe even Calyp, if the winds are right."

"Seems I'm going that way myself."

"How far?"

It was a tricky question. If he lied and said he was heading for Phanes, too, the man would be skeptical. Westerners were not welcome in the south. "The Dead Isles."

Smithers blinked. Raised his eyebrows. And then laughed, the railing creaking as he slapped it with the heels of his palms. "Ye had me goin' there fer a second. The Dead Isles. What a hoot!"

Grey waited until the moment of frivolity had worn off, and then said, "It was no jape."

"Son, did ye lose yer mind when ye lost that hand o' yers? Naught but one with a death wish would set foot on the Dead Isles. Well, 'cept fer the furia, and that's jest another reason not to go there."

Grey was willing to die for his sister if that's what it took to save her. "All the same, that's where I'm headed."

Smithers shook his head, but it wasn't an answer. "We'll pass near the isles, but we won't git too close, on account of the bad luck carried on the wind. You'd hafta swim the rest o' the way." He glanced at Grey's missing hand again. "Can ye swim?"

Grey had learned to swim back in Restor, which had several large ponds. It would be significantly more difficult without his left hand, but he'd find a way. He had to. "I can swim," he promised.

"You ever worked on a boat?"

"No, but I'm willing to learn."

"We can't pay ye. All ye git in return fer yer labors is a one-way voyage to the gates of hell."

"Deal," Grey said. He made his way to the gangplank and clambered aboard the rickety vessel.

Shae, I'm coming.

I'm coming.

Chapter Thirty-Two

The Western Kingdom | Knight's End

Rhea Loren

Rhea was clean and perfumed, dressed in a chaste blue dress that swept around her ankles. By western law, she'd never be permitted to wear white again, her purity oath forsaken when she sinned with Grey.

Though Ennis had insisted on having her handmaiden assist her, Rhea had refused. She didn't want anyone to see her. Not now. Not like this. For the first time in her privileged life, she'd bathed and dressed on her own. Unexpectedly, there was something liberating about it.

She'd avoided her mirror the entire time, until now. She approached cautiously, her eyes downcast. Ennis had left a jar of healing salve on her dressing table. She reached for it, still refusing to raise her gaze to the looking glass she had once loved.

Taking a deep breath, she lifted her chin. Disgust coiled through her like a snake. Her eyes took pity on her and filled with tears, blurring her vision. She dabbed a finger in the gooey salve and pressed it to her face. The effect was instantaneous, cooling and numbing her shredded flesh. Shaking, she traced a path along the wound, from left temple to chin, up the edge of her lips to her nose, down the right side of her lips, and angling up to her right temple.

Finished, she blinked furiously, watching her face take shape once more. Her saliva tasted bitter on her tongue as she glared at herself. "I hate you," she breathed. The words were meant for many: for her cousin, Jove, for taking what was rightfully hers and so much more; for her self-righteous siblings, Bea and Leo; for her father for dying; for Grey Arris for stealing her heart and her purity; for the furia with their red cloaks and violence; for Wrath himself, the god of purity and punishment; and lastly, for herself, for being ugly and weak and young and stupid.

Rhea grabbed the jar of salve from the dressing table and whipped it at the mirror, which shattered upon impact, jagged shards tinkling to the table and floor.

Someone pounded on her door, shouting through the timber. Ennis. Worried about her. He must've been outside her chamber the whole time, waiting. He was a good man, unlike his horrid brother.

Slowly, Rhea bent down and selected one of the glass shards, a long spike ending in a vicious point. Careful not to cut herself, she plucked it from the floor between two fingers, using one of her silk scarves to wrap it up. She tucked it beneath the folds of her dress and picked her way past the rubble to open the door.

Ennis practically fell inside. "Princess! Are you—are you hurt? I heard a loud sound." He scanned the room, immediately noticing the destroyed mirror.

Rhea felt anger and fury and something darker throbbing inside of her— something she never knew she had. But she held all of that back and said with a meek whimper, "I'm sorry—I couldn't—I couldn't look at—I didn't want to see . . ." She covered her face with her hands and squeezed tears from her eyes. This time, it was her choice to cry, for her own purposes and not out of sorrow.

"Oh, Rhea. Oh, Wrath," Ennis said. "You need not worry. Your chambermaid will see to the mess. The mirror will not be replaced."

"Thank you, cousin," Rhea said. "For everything."

He nodded, his eyes full of pity. She almost felt bad deceiving him. Then again, he'd let her be taken away by the furia just like everyone else. "Shall I leave you?"

"No," she said. "Wrath, I'm a blubbering mess. Wait one moment." Rhea retrieved a handkerchief and used it to wipe away her tears and clear her nose. She selected a pale blue hat with a matching veil, which she draped over her face. She'd always hated the western clothing she was forced to wear. But now it was a Wrathsend. None would be able to see her face.

When she turned around, a shiver ran through her from head to toe. It wasn't fear—it was anticipation. For the first time since that night when Grey abandoned her in the crypts she felt in control of her own life.

"Take me to your brother, King Jove Loren," she said. "I want to pledge him my support and beg his forgiveness."

Ennis's eyes widened in surprise, but he didn't object. "As you wish, princess."

He led her into the corridor, and Rhea patted her side, relishing the feel of the shard of mirror hidden beneath the cloth.

They'd taken everything from her, and now she had nothing left to lose.

⁂

Jove was sitting on Rhea's throne, wearing *her* crown. Though seeing him like that, with his smug expression and pious pity, made her want to scream, she forced herself to appear repentant and broken.

The false king was alone, save for three guards who'd either managed to survive the attack that killed her father, or who'd been recently added to the castle cortege.

"Thank you for seeing me, Your Highness," Rhea said, her head bowed toward the stone floor. She kneeled in what she knew would appear to be reverence and fealty, a pose she'd seen countless others strike while groveling before her father.

"Yes, well, you have paid for your sins, and I am not an unmerciful king."

You are not a king at all, Rhea thought. "I would prefer to do this alone, with only Wrath as my witness," she said.

"My lady?" Ennis said from behind her. *Yes, cousin, I mean you should leave. Especially you.*

"Leave us, brother," Jove said. "You can escort her back to her chambers once we are finished."

Rhea remained on her knees, though they were throbbing from the hard stone. Pain was nothing now. She had felt pain. Agony was her only friend. She heard Ennis mutter something, but then leave, his footsteps fading away.

"You may rise," Jove said.

"Thank you, Your Highness." *It took you long enough.* "And your guards?"

Through the pale blue lace of her veil, she saw her cousin's eyes narrow ever so slightly. "You would have your new king unprotected?"

Rhea cast her eyes down once more, feigning embarrassment. "Of course not, my king. They would still be guarding the door from intruders, and there is no other way inside the court." *And surely you don't fear a sixteen-year-old scarred girl with a broken spirit, do you?*

The king seemed to consider the truth of her words for a moment, and then flicked his fingers at his trio of protectors, as if he didn't care whether he ever saw them again. *He's already drunk on his power*, Rhea thought as the guards left, closing the door behind them.

Queen Rhea Loren was alone with the false king.

For a moment, her nerve faltered, and she had the urge to truly beg his forgiveness, to ask for a place in his court, so she could go back to the life she'd loved, filled with feasts and dancing and midnight rendezvous with notorious criminals.

But her face made all of that impossible. If the furia and Jove had wanted to create a monster, then they were successful. Rhea would be the monster.

"Well?" Jove said, impatiently drumming his fingers on the throne's armrest.

"May I approach, Your Highness?" she asked. Eyes still down. Broken. Pathetic. Penitent.

"As you wish," he said, like he didn't care whether she did or not—whether she lived or died or faded away into obscurity.

She shuffled forward, lifting her skirts as she mounted the three steps to the raised throne. She felt the shard of mirror shift and her breath left her. *If it falls out, it's over.*

Surreptitiously, she clamped a hand to her side, pinning the dislodged spike against her hip. While she bowed deeply, she clawed her fingers through the material, closing them around the base of the makeshift blade. It was a crude weapon, and even the handle was sharp, pricking her fingers through the silk covering. She relished the warmth of her own blood as it flowed down her palm.

"Your Highness," Rhea said. "I am here to beg your forgiveness and pledge my service and life to you. It's what my father would've wanted."

The king said nothing, still tapping his fingers. Had she misjudged him? She waited for him to proceed with the traditional rite of royal forgiveness. He cleared his throat. Said, "Have you realized the error in your sinful ways?"

He was going to make her work for this. "Yes," she said, trying to keep the angry growl from her voice. Warm blood trickled down the skin of her hand.

"Are you willing to receive the light of Wrath back into your life?"

"Yes."

"Will you accept a political marriage proposal if I arrange one?"

How dare you? she wanted to scream. He was already planning to marry her off to one of the other kingdoms in an effort to form an alliance. He was likely to send her to the north, like her Aunt Sabria. Lord Griswold had to be half a hundred years old! And her aunt had died because of such a marriage.

"Yes," she said, the obedient girl she'd always been.

The king sighed, continuing to drag things out. Finally, he extended his hand toward Rhea. His second finger bore a Loren family heirloom, the ring of kings. An enormous blue diamond sparkled from a thousand facets, fixed within a thick band of pure gold.

All she had to do was kiss the ring, and it would seal the deal. She'd be a happy princess in the good graces of her righteous king.

She kissed the cool gemstone, and he said, "By the power bestowed upon me by Wrath and his holy servants, I absolve you of your sins and accept your pledge of service."

Beneath her veil, Rhea smiled. In one swift motion, she withdrew her hand from her dress, erupted from her lowered stance, and lunged at the king.

Leaning forward so she could kiss the ring, Jove had left himself completely unprotected. She drove the spike into his neck, shocked by the amount of blood that erupted from his skin, a crimson geyser, splattering warmth on her face. He tried to cry out, but all that arose was a wet gurgle.

Rhea backed away, slightly horrified—slightly more excited—by what she'd done, by the power over life and death she'd claimed for her own. Wrapping his hands around the glass shard, his eyes wide with shock and terror, Jove sprawled forward, tumbling down the steps, smearing blood on the stonework.

For a few seconds, Rhea could do nothing more than stare as her cousin twitched, shook, and then went completely still.

She didn't have much time, but still, she approached slowly, imagining Jove rising from the dead, his ghost ready for vengeance. Thankfully, he remained dead, and she managed to roll him over. His mouth was open, his eyes wide, but she didn't bother to close either. Instead, she wrapped her hands in cloth from her dress and wrenched the spike from his neck. More blood bubbled out, adding to the lake.

Rhea forced herself to look at it, until the bitter taste of bile rose from the back of her throat. She vomited. It was all part of the charade.

Spitting out the last of the bitterness from her mouth, she gripped the glass shard, took a deep breath, and raked it across her abdomen, slicing clean through her dress in the process. Pain flared up and blood flowed freely. The cut was deep enough for her ruse, but not so deep as to kill her—at least she hoped not.

She dropped the spike at her feet, collapsed in the puddle of vomit and blood, and screamed at the top of her bloody lungs.

Chapter Thirty-Three

The Eastern Kingdom | Raider's Pass

Roan

Wearing the dark cloak of night, the white cliffs loomed like sentries on either side as the eastern battalion marched into Raider's Pass. In the typical manner of the east, the king led the column, unafraid to die for his brave men and women. Despite the way his conversation with the king had ended the night before, Roan marveled at the courage of Oren Ironclad and his sons, who never once considered sending their soldiers ahead as a shield. It was almost as if the death of the queen had become their armor.

Then again, Gareth *was* the Shield, a fact that reminded Roan why he was still here, marching with an army he had no real connection with.

Am I brave? Roan wondered to himself. After all, he could've left the night before, could've crossed the river, vanished into the Tangle, never to be seen in the east again. After the king had rejected his proposal for peace, he'd once more considered leaving. Instead he'd just shook his head and gone to bed. *No,* he chided himself. *I'm just stupid.*

The thought made him chuckle, despite himself.

The horses had been left behind, the Pass too narrow and steep for their size.

Roan was in the second wave of soldiers, because he was "too valuable to lose during the initial attack." He'd been given a beautiful sword designed and forged by the late Bark, an irony that wasn't lost on Roan. Even in death, the man would protect Roan, though Roan had been unable to save him outside of Glee. Roan had also been assigned a protector, though she accepted the position grudgingly. Gwendolyn ignored several of his glances as she walked beside him.

Once into the wide mouth of the pass, the trail became rocky, gaining in elevation with each step. It narrowed, too, until they were forced to march four astride, then three, then two, and eventually single file. Gwendolyn insisted on going first, though it wasn't clear whether she was just following the king's orders, or if she genuinely cared for his well-being. Roan suspected it was the former.

The trail was treacherous in the dark, forcing the column to slow as the soldiers placed each foot carefully, feeling their way forward. On their right was a steep, snowy incline. On their left was a sheer drop to the frozen river. In Roan's opinion, any advantage gained by a night attack was lost due to the snail-like speed of their approach and the risk of falling to their deaths. Unfortunately, however, the king showed no signs of changing his mind, the front lines moving forward step by step.

Occasionally, armor clanked, but other than that, the only sounds were their muffled footsteps through the snow and their ragged breathing. Also, the Snake River burbled under the ice, masking all. Earlier, Roan had been inspired by his own attempt to cross the ice, and asked whether it would be easier to simply walk along the surface of the iced-over river, but his idea had been quickly shot down. Evidently the ice had already been tested—it could hold the weight of several large men, but not a force of their size. Plus, a well-aimed boulder falling from the cliffs above would send the entire battalion into the deadly waters.

The wind picked up, a gale force that threatened to sweep them all from the trail as it whistled through the canyon. Roan lowered his head, focusing on each step, doing his best to remain as far to the right as possible, hugging the hillside.

Two harsh hours passed without event, other than Roan's toes losing all feeling. He wondered if they'd fallen off, rattling around in his boots. Now there was no going back, the distance to the northern edge of the pass as close as their camp.

The snowfall—which had thus far been nothing more than a few errant flurries—began in earnest, coating their armor and blinding their vision. With the snow on the rarely used trail deepening, the going became even slower, and Roan was forced to stop several times when those ahead of them paused to clear the pass.

It was during one such halt that the first attack came. Initially, Roan couldn't identify the sound, which was nothing more than a *zip* and the displacement of air. Just ahead of him a soldier toppled from the cliff, a feathered arrow protruding from a narrow gap in his faceplate.

A chorus of *zips* filled the air at the same time as someone shouted, "Down!"

Roan reacted too slow, and Gwendolyn hauled him to the rocky trail a half a moment before an arrow whizzed past, landing somewhere below. Several more soldiers fell from the cliffs, their screams lost on the wind, before the only noise was the clank of shields and armor jostling for position, and the plink of arrowheads bouncing off iron.

Gwendolyn's shield was long and narrow, and they huddled behind it, so close that Roan could taste her breath on his tongue. "What do we do?" he asked, regaining his own breath.

"Wait."

Eventually, the archers paused, realizing the surprise of their initial assault had lost its effectiveness. A cry went up from the cliffs, some kind of birdcall, and it travelled down the line, away from them.

"A warning to the northern defenders," Gwendolyn said. "Even if we make it through the pass, they'll be ready for us. The element of surprise is lost."

What am I doing here? Roan asked himself as a second wave of arrows— these ones on fire—rained from above. *I am no warrior. I hate war.*

I'm here so Gareth doesn't have to die, he reminded himself. *I'm here because he doesn't deserve to die.*

A burst of flame ripped past his ear, so close he could feel the heat. He shook his head, rattling the thoughts away. Regardless of why he was in this exact place at this exact time—whether by some twisted stroke of fate, plain bad luck, or because of a random series of foolish choices—it was not the time to be philosophical.

"On my mark we will rise as one," Gwendolyn hissed. "Hold my shield and stay behind its edges." Roan felt like a child, a burden to the true, highly trained warriors within the battalion. Even if he wanted to, he couldn't save anyone from a fall from the cliffs, skinmark or not.

"Now!" Gwendolyn said, bursting to her feet. Roan pushed himself up beside her, keeping his head down and holding the weight of her shield, which was surprisingly light despite its size.

Gwendolyn didn't waste a moment, extracting her bow from where it hung on her back. She fitted arrows to the string in short succession, firing two at a time, a feat Roan had once seen in competition, but never in real life. Then again, he'd never been in the midst of a real battle before.

There were shouts from above, but Roan didn't know whether they were a result of Gwendolyn's shots. Knowing her, she'd probably hit her targets every time.

Down the line, other archers in the company were shooting at the cliffs too, aiming for the flashes of fire each time a flaming arrow was lit by the enemy. "Dead men falling!" someone yelled. Roan risked a peek past the edge of the shield just in time to dodge a corpse that tumbled past, nearly taking off his head. Even dead, their enemies were dangerous from the high ground.

"Forward march!" a voice bellowed, and Roan found himself pleased to recognize the king's gruff tone. Somehow, it invigorated him, sending hope to his cold bones and tired muscles.

The battalion moved forward, quicker now, their eyes fully adjusted to the darkness, assisted by dozens of fire arrows sticking up from the snow, lighting the trail. The occasional arrow still rocketed from above, but they were few and far between. As the trail started to widen once more, Roan began to think it all felt too easy.

That's when the first boulders tumbled down the mountainside.

"Look out!" someone shouted. Everyone craned their heads to look, not that it mattered. The boulder was enormous, bouncing and rolling and gaining momentum as it plunged from above, pushed past the tipping point by the northerners.

Those in its direct path tried to scatter, but there was nowhere to go, hemmed in on both sides by their own allies. And yet it wasn't they who died, because, at the last moment, the boulder split in half, each jagged piece changing direction wildly. Those in its initial direct path were spared, while the soldiers on either side were hit head on. Dozens of men and women, humans and Orians, were crushed.

Roan's heart was in his throat, the horrifying image flashing in his mind in the eerie silence that followed, just before there was the crack of ice and a heavy splash.

And that was only the first boulder. Dozens more rolled down the mountain, splitting and changing direction, eliminating soldiers in a seemingly random fashion. Not knowing what else to do, Roan hunkered down tight against the cliff face. Luckily, the mountainside above him had a cleft in its shoulder. At least two boulders literally flew directly over his head, appearing to move in slow motion.

Gwendolyn was tight beside him, her expression fierce and determined. "It's your turn," she said as another boulder arced past.

Roan stared at her. "Turn to do what?"

"Don't you hear their cries?"

In truth, Roan couldn't hear anything but the roaring of blood through his veins, her voice in his ear, and the occasional crack of stone hitting ice. He cocked his head to the side and listened intently, the sounds slowly coming into focus.

Men and women in agony, pleading for help. Or perhaps to be put out of their misery. "I hear them," he said.

"Will you answer their call?" Gwendolyn asked. "I have made my choice. Have you?" Before he could respond, she was already gone, leaving him with her shield and a decision to make. For Roan, it was no decision at all. Not anymore. He'd made the choice on the frozen river the night before.

Chapter Thirty-Four

The Northern Kingdom | Raider's Pass

Annise Gäric

Annise awoke with a start. She listened intently, initially only hearing her own breathing. Then:

The shriek of a birdcall in the distance, answered by another, then another, rolling down the line until the calls were within their encampment. They were under attack.

She sat up quickly, thrusting the thick blanket away from her. She pushed to her feet, already dressed and ready. The spare armor she'd been fitted with was snug against her thick trousers and greatcoat.

Her tent flap opened and the Armored Knight filled the entrance. In this moment, she could discern none of the boy named Tarin she'd once known. He was truly the monster he believed himself to be, a towering armored warrior with death in his eyes.

Annise reached for the sword by her bedroll, but Tarin said, "Princess, you're to stay here in safety. I will defend you to my death."

Though his intentions were honorable, a spark of anger flared up inside her. "For my mother?" she said, her voice heavy with sarcasm.

"For you," Tarin said huskily.

Frozen hell, Annise thought. She ignored the snow flurries in her stomach and took a step forward.

"I don't need defending," she said. "Either you fight alongside me, or you do not fight at all. Just don't accidentally hit me with your hellfrozen Morningstar."

For a second she thought he was going to hold her hostage in her tent, so she added, "I'm the Bear-Slayer, remember? You said it yourself." She didn't remind him that she had only scared the ice bear away, not killed it.

With a short bob of his head, Tarin moved aside, and Annise strode out into the frozen night. The sword felt unwieldy in her grip, and her hand was already aching from holding the weapon too tightly. She tried to relax, loosening her fingers. She wasn't about to admit she was scared, nor that she was no swordfighter. If it came down to it, she would do what she had to do to survive.

Somewhere in the distance, she could see the occasional flame arc through the darkness, landing in the pass between the mountains. She watched one of the fire arrows the whole way, until it hit something and stopped. There was a brief moment when there was only darkness, like the flame had been snuffed out in a snowdrift, but then flames burst in all directions, taking shape.

The burning shape was that of a human. The victim staggered, stumbled, and then fell, vanishing from sight.

All around her, soldiers were on the move, pushing toward the front lines, preparing to carry out her brother's war plan if necessary.

Beside her, Tarin said, "I would be honored to fight alongside you." He held the chain of his Morningstar in one hand, the steel links curling around his neck, the barbed ball dangling in front of his chest.

"Just don't get in my way," Annise growled, but it was an act. She'd never seen real battle, and the thing with the ice bear was nothing more than adrenaline and dumb luck, both of which she'd need on her side before this night was over. The only man she'd ever killed was the one who Tarin had paralyzed.

As one, they slipped into the stream of soldiers moving into position.

That's when the first of the ice slings unleashed their payloads. At the same time, Annise saw an unearthly burst of light from the pass.

❧ Roan (Moments earlier) ☙

The northerners were rolling barrels that had once been filled with water down the hill. Now, in the cold, they were completely frozen and as deadly as battering rams. Roan had watched one woman a mere arm's length away get hit by one. She hadn't even had time to scream before she was gone. One crashed down from above, and Roan ducked, feeling a whoosh of air as it swept past his head.

A narrow miss, which made Roan wonder for the hundredth time whether he'd made the wrong decision in pressing forward in the direction Gwendolyn had gone. *So much for being my protector*, he thought. Not that he'd ever have the opportunity to inform King Ironclad of his dissatisfaction with her services.

Still, he moved onwards, trying to find someone he could help. The bodies he did find lodged on the trail, however, were unmoving. He checked them one at a time, but there was no life within them. Some were incredibly young—barely more than children—while others were old and grizzled and had likely seen more battles than Roan had seen name days. Several of the dead were Orians, their flawless skin and strangely colored eyes so out of place amongst the carnage and ice.

Roan had just finished checking one such warrior when he heard a new sound. A rumble, almost like thunder, emanating from above. *What new torture is this?* Roan wondered, gazing at the hillside.

Long, dark shapes tumbled down the slope, bouncing and changing direction, scattering hither and thither. *Timber*, Roan realized. Entire tree trunks, stripped of branches and limbs, rolled from high above in an avalanche of wood. Whilst boulders and barrels cut a relatively narrow path of destruction, this new weapon used broad killing strokes and would be nearly impossible to dodge. As if to illustrate his thoughts, one massive log took out a dozen soldiers just ahead of him.

Roan froze, unable to move, bound to the cliff by indecision. He glanced right as another tree barreled down the hill. Unless it changed course drastically, it would land somewhere near him.

He forced his feet to move, charging forwards even as he could feel the log closing in from the side, a dark shape bucking and writhing, creaking and hammering. At the last possible moment, he dove, half-tripping on another soldier, who lay prostrate on the trail.

Pain erupted in his calf as the end of the log clipped his leg, shattering bone and tearing muscle. He moaned, landing on sharp rocks that protruded like lances from the packed snow.

Rolling in agony on the path, he used his lifemark, which began to warm his chest, fingers of healing stretching toward his injury.

Nearby, the soldier he'd assumed was dead, groaned. He or she was still alive.

The blood of innocents cried out to him. Why? Why? Why did you heal me only to let him *burn us alive?*

"No," Roan growled between his teeth. That was long ago and his guardian was long dead. Markin Swansea couldn't hurt Roan anymore. And Roan *had* healed that girl with the pox, back in Glee. She was still alive. In fact, she'd hugged him around the waist before they'd rode out from Norris, where they'd left her with a family, safe and sound. Once more, she'd called him her hero.

Roan shook his head. No, he was not a hero, but that didn't mean he couldn't do something heroic. He could do it again, especially now that he knew his guardian had lied to him about so much.

The soldier groaned once more, and Roan squinted in the darkness until the face clarified. A girl—she appeared young, but it was obvious from her coppery hair and orange eyes that she was Orian, so age was a moving target. Still alive, but barely, her face green in the moonlight, already slick with wet snowmelt.

Roan gritted his teeth and rolled over, growling through the agony that lanced through his ankle. He reached out and touched her.

Light burst from his chest, arcing from him to her, swarming over the metal armor she wore. She gasped, and he could feel what she felt, could feel her injuries, which were deep beneath the surface of her skin. A crushed lung, cracked ribs, a punctured organ. The light knitted her tissue and bones back together, sapping Roan's strength.

The girl breathed in and out, in and out, and then said, "You saved my life."

Roan said nothing. He hadn't done anything. His mark had saved her. He'd done nothing but touched her and made a choice.

And now he felt like sleeping, his eyes closing of their own accord.

"Healer," the girl said, and he felt her cold hands on his cheeks. "Warm yourself. Repair your leg. There is time. The battle has moved away."

Roan couldn't open his eyes, but he had just enough awareness to concentrate on the heat that still lingered in his chest. He let it drift throughout his body, warming his extremities before settling on his devastated leg. The pain throbbed once, twice, and then vanished.

His eyes flashed open and the forest dweller reached down to help him up. Like all the Orians, her small stature hid a remarkable amount of strength— she easily pulled him to his feet. "Thank you," she said. "Be safe." And then she was gone, sprinting along the trail toward the screams. Toward the danger.

Roan marveled at the young warrior. Despite having nearly died, she was willing to risk her life again. Even still, he wanted nothing more than to turn around and flee. He was no soldier. She'd called him a healer, but he wasn't that either. *What am I?* Roan wondered.

"You are . . ." Roan whispered, feeling the words in the mark in his chest. "You are . . ." They were right there, so close he could touch them, taste them, hear them echoing in the dark folds of his mind.

But still, he couldn't say them, couldn't speak the truth. The truth was a dangerous beast, and Roan didn't know what would happen if he uncaged it.

Roan breathed deeply, steeling his nerves, which had been severed in half a dozen places.

And then he started forward once more, testing the limits of his weary body.

⮜ Annise ⮞

The easterners burst from the pass, their armor glinting in the red and green moonlight. Though their numbers had clearly been culled while they ran the gauntlet, there were still hundreds of them, swords raised high. Toward the front was a gargantuan man who could only be King Oren Ironclad, the Juggernaut, his famed Foehammer hefted on his shoulder. He shouted something and his soldiers roared in response.

The ice slings released one final volley, huge chunks of ice arcing through the sky and landing amongst the enemy, who scattered like fallen leaves. Several were crushed, but the rest regained their feet and charged toward the north, now well past where the long-distance ice slings would be effective.

So this is what it has come to, Annise thought. This journey, all started by the death of her father, was on the precipice of fate, and she felt like a single false step could mean the end. Her brother had found his army, and yet his rebellion against their uncle hung in the balance.

"Annise!" a voice cried now, and a hand grabbed her shoulder from behind. Arch stared at her, his eyes wide. "You should not be here."

"I tried to stop her, Your Highness," Tarin said.

"You are my king," she said, "and my brother, and I will not hide behind an army like a weakling."

For a second it almost looked like Arch might laugh, but instead he offered a thin smile. "No, my sister, you are anything but weak." To Annise's surprise, he threw his arms around her and pulled her tight. "Tonight we fight together."

"For the kingdom," she returned, and he kissed her cheek.

"For the kingdom," he echoed.

And then they charged into battle, their cries lost amongst hundreds of others.

❧ Bane ☙

Raider's Pass was already in turmoil when Bane arrived as quietly as a whisper. He could smell death in the air, could hear it in the cries of the warriors who did battle. He sniffed again, and smelled something else.

Royalty. Bloodlust. Barriers to peace. For who could be blamed for the Hundred Years War but the leaders who rallied their troops into battle, drunk on their desire for power and conquest?

His bare scalp burned with need, a fire for death that had to be sated or else he would be consumed. Bane blinked, and he moved, not with his feet but in another, unexplainable way.

Swords clashed around him. An enormous man wearing dark armor from head to toe swung a black chain ending in a spiked ball in a deadly arc. Twice Bane watched as it crashed into the skulls of armored warriors. He could feel their instantaneous deaths deep in his bones, in his marrow, in the black hole that should've been his soul.

Another massive man roared and strode forward to face the armored knight. He was wearing a necklace that bore a strange symbol: an iron fist. *Ahh*, Bane thought. This man is like me. This man is fatemarked. More specifically, *ironmarked*.

Armed with the ironmark, the enormous man fought with the strength of ten men, tossing opponents aside like a child's playthings, closing in on the armored knight. The knight swung his spiked ball at the ironmarked, a heavy stroke so powerful it would kill any man in an instant. But this was no ordinary man. The ironmarked caught the chain in his hand and began to reel the knight toward him.

Bane licked his lips as he watched. To see another who was fatemarked was exhilarating, the raw power intoxicating.

The massive knight dug his heels into the snow and attempted to stop his progress forward, but his feet slid across the ice. He'd have to release his weapon if he were going to survive the encounter. The large knight was stubborn, however, refusing to give up his spiked ball and chain.

The ironmarked grinned as he dragged the knight into his grasp. Bane leaned forward, eager to watch.

At the last second, the knight dropped the chain and drove forward low to the ground, tackling the ironmarked around the waist. The large man went down, his head cracking against the hard ground. The knight was remarkably nimble for his size, pushing quickly to his feet while his opponent's girth caused him to flounder like a turtle on its back. The armored knight snatched up his weapon and whipped it down hard, again and again, on the ironmarked's body, landing blows to his chest, abdomen, legs, and finally his head.

The huge man fought the strikes at first, attempting to block them with his thick forearms, but was eventually overcome, his body going still.

Someone roared and strode forward, his dark eyes burning with anger. He stared at the ironmarked's body, gripping his long, elaborately forged hammer with white-knuckled fingers. The newcomer was of impressive size, too, though not as large as either his fallen man or the knight he now faced.

Bane's deathmark pulsed with excitement. This man was a king. From the description Bear Blackboots had given him, it had to be King Oren Ironclad, Juggernaut of the East. A man who had seen many battles, who had chosen war over peace, following in his father's footsteps. A man who had to die.

The armored knight's weapon cut through the air, battering the king's armor. But, seemingly fueled by anger for his fallen comrade, the Juggernaut pushed forward, grabbing the chain, yanking it back toward him. The armored knight stumbled as the king swung his hammer at his midsection. There was a raucous clangor as the armor held true, the blow glancing off and past the knight.

He swung a huge fist at the king's head, catching him in the temple and dislodging his helmet. The Juggernaut was exposed, but not dead, wrenching his hammer back and bringing it down on the knight's neck. This time the armor dented, and when the king landed an elbow to the knight's face, his facemask and helmet popped off like a cork from a bottle of sparkling wine.

Finally, tired of being merely a spectator, Bane moved in for the kill.

✑ Annise ✑

Annise had lost her sword and her brother somewhere in the fray. She'd used her blade to block a slash from an enemy soldier, and then Tarin's Morningstar had finished him off. No matter where she'd charged, Tarin had been there, his spiked ball protecting her. She'd caught sight of Sir Dietrich several times as well, facing more opponents than should be humanly possible, and yet he always seemed to emerge unscathed, his sword moving with the speed of lightning strikes.

Finally, however, after defeating the largest man Annise had ever seen, Tarin was locked in battle with the eastern king himself, who was also nearly as big as the armored knight. The distraction left Annise on her own. A young easterner burst through the lines and swung at her, but Annise was ready, pretending it was just a wooden sword on the training fields, not a razor-sharp blade of steel. She ducked and threw herself forward, hitting the man in the chest, rocking him backward. She landed on him and he gasped.

Annise took his own sword, which he'd dropped, and stabbed him between his plates of armor. Like the only other man she'd killed, taking his life seemed too easy, a thought which unnerved her.

Still straddling him, she looked up, searching for Tarin.

Her breath left her when she spotted him.

He was face to face with King Ironclad, literally. Both men's helmets had come off and they were staring each other down. The king's head was bald, his dark beard long and thick. But that's not why Annise couldn't breathe.

She could see Tarin's face.

Like his hand, his cheeks were so pale they were almost glowing, his skin as thin as stretched silk. Beneath his flesh were long snakes of black, his veins, which protruded in tangled rivulets.

The king also seemed shocked by his opponent's appearance, his confidence wavering as they circled each other. "What manner of northern devilry are you?" the big man bellowed, holding his mighty hammer in front of him.

Tarin didn't answer, flicking a glance at Annise, who couldn't stop staring at his face. He looked back at the king, but didn't respond, choosing instead to swing his chain over his head, preparing to strike.

Like a cloud of vapor materializing from some unknown netherworld, a form appeared between them.

Annise stood, gaping at the familiar boy, his scalp marked with a circle of fire, a quarter portion of the image as dark as Tarin's blood. Like the first time she'd seen him, on the tower steps the moment before her father fell to his death, the boy's resemblance to Arch was startling.

Tarin's Morningstar slowed and fell harmlessly to his side. He was also staring in wonderment at the boy.

Annise's brother. Now called Bane, according to her aunt. Kings' Bane. Killer of monarchs. Bringer of death.

King Ironclad continued to hold his hammer at the ready, eyeing Bane with narrowed eyes.

A short blade appeared in Bane's hand, materializing the same way that he had. He stepped forward. The king swung his own weapon in a deadly trajectory, but he caught only empty air. Her brother was gone.

No, Annise realized. *There!* He was behind the king, his lips a snarl.

Seemingly from out of nowhere, a form appeared from the side, sliding his sword in front of the king's back, blocking Bane's killing stroke.

At the same moment, Tarin whipped his Morningstar around once more.

There was a vicious *CRUNCH!* as the spiked ball landed squarely on the king's exposed head.

Annise turned away, trying to blink away the awful image. Not even the massive king could rise from a wound like that one.

~ Roan ᔕ

Roan had managed to work his way through the pass, healing several injured easterners as he went. His energy was waning, but he refused to stop until he was unconscious. It was strange, but now that he'd begun using his mark more, his body seemed to grow accustomed to the bouts of fatigue, fighting them off and recovering more swiftly.

With each person he healed, he felt something burning inside of him, a feeling he couldn't quite pinpoint until he emerged from the canyon and onto open land. That's when he realized what it was that he felt:

Purpose.

He moved forward, searching for those who were injured but not dead, allowing his mark's energy to range outwards, further and further, rainbows of white light illuminating the snowfield.

All around him, the battle raged, but he ignored it. Twice a northerner tried to remove his head from his shoulders, but each time he'd managed to duck the blow until an ally moved in to protect him. He had a sword, but it hung from his belt, unused. His purpose did not involve killing.

It involved *saving*.

Cries began to rise up on all sides. "Protect the healer!"

He spotted Gwendolyn, and a swell of airy relief filled his lungs. She was fighting like an ore cat, felling foes like saplings under an axe, alternating between her bow and her sword, a graceful dance of death.

Roan was about to move toward her, just in case she sustained an injury, but then saw Prince Gareth running in the opposite direction. He was screaming at the top of his lungs, his sword pumping beside him.

Tracing a line in front of the prince with his eyes, Roan saw the impossible. The king, his enormous frame wobbling, his enormous Foehammer slipping from lifeless fingers, his caved-in head resting like a rotten pumpkin atop his shoulders.

He fell. The king fell.

Though it was obvious from a distance that even Roan wouldn't be able to save the monarch, he sprinted after Gareth anyway, determination coursing through him. Somewhere in the back of his mind, Roan realized Gareth was now the king, a thought that struck him as exceptionally strange.

Near the king's body, Prince Guy was doing battle with a strange adversary. A boy, unarmored, wearing nothing more than a black cloak, stabbed at the prince with short rapid strikes. Guy was barely able to block them, backpedaling against the ferocious onslaught.

Gareth was closing in, and Roan knew exactly what the new king had in mind. He was planning to protect his brother, not only with his sword, but with his body, becoming the human Shield he was born to be.

Despite all the trouble the prince had caused him, despite all the mockery and the threats and the taunts, despite how he'd rejected his kiss, Roan couldn't let him die. Not today. This was why he was here.

He sprinted, hurdling the dead, dodging those locked in battle.

The boy knocked Prince Guy's sword away. He swung a final blow toward his throat. Gareth tried to dive in front to block the killing stroke, but Guy was already falling, his neck slashed open. The boy tossed him aside and plunged his blade deep into Gareth's chest.

Roan didn't stop, couldn't stop, rushing forward and diving at the prince, who was lying on the cold hard ground, blood bubbling from his armor and his lips. "No," Roan breathed. "You're not dying on me. You're not."

He reached for the prince, but a strong arm grabbed his hand and pulled it back.

The boy, his skin pale and smooth and free of hair, neither stubble nor eyebrow nor lash. "I smell it on you," the boy said, as Roan struggled against his grip, which was like iron. "You are not supposed to be here."

Roan didn't care what the boy smelled, but for once he disagreed with the notion that he shouldn't be in this place at this time. "I am," he said, his mark flaring to life.

The boy released him and cringed, backing away. "No," he said. "Impossible. You can't be both."

"Both what?" Roan said. For the first time since the battle began, he slid his sword from his scabbard. For the first time since the battle began, he considered the fact that he might need to kill in order to save. The light in his chest moved along his arm and into the blade, which sparkled like a sunlit icicle.

"A king *and* the Peacemaker," the boy said, launching himself forward.

Roan blocked the blow with his sword, which pulsed with white light, pushing back against the darkness that seemed to surround the boy and his blade like a shadow.

Roan didn't care who this boy was or what he knew, he wouldn't let him get to Prince Gareth, who was running out of time. He shoved back with all his might and the boy vanished into the cold night air.

Behind him, the prince gurgled, choking on his own blood. Roan whirled around and pressed his hands to Gareth's blood-soaked cheek.

Too late.

The new king was dead, following his father and brother too soon.

Roan looked up, blinking away the tears in his eyes before they froze on his cheeks. So many dead. Lives ended too soon. For what purpose? To what end? *If my fate is to be here, to witness this*, Roan thought, *it is a cruel fate.*

Beyond the dead he saw a strong-looking woman, curvy and muscular, looking his way, watching as he huddled over the fallen kings. There was something about the determined look in her eyes that gave him pause. No, it was something else about her. Her cheekbones, or the slight tilt of her nose. Something familiar. She looked away, her attention drawn to something else.

Roan peered back down at where his hand continued to rest on Gareth's cheek. He felt something pulse, there and gone again, a flash of the very thing that had driven his every act since he entered Raider's Pass:

Life.

The mark on his chest burst forth with what energy he had left.

↝ Bane ↜

Bane's body was buzzing with electricity from his encounter with the Peacemaker. Too soon. The Western Oracle's prophecy allowed for the death of eight rulers before he would do battle with the Peacemaker. And nothing in the prophecy stated the Peacemaker would be a king. But he was—that much was obvious.

Bane reappeared a distance away from the battle, beginning to feel weak from using his mark. His scalp was still hot, and he could feel a fourth section of his deathmark begin to fill with blood; the third was already blood-soaked, from when the Juggernaut had died. Bane wished he'd been the one to kill Oren Ironclad, but dead was dead. At least he'd killed the eldest son of King Ironclad, the one named Gareth. The moment his father had died, he'd become king.

A short-lived reign, to say the least.

Wait. Wait. Somewhere across the killing fields, a brilliant white pulse shot from the ground toward the heavens, a column of pure light. He could feel the death-throb in his scalp begin to subside, his skin cooling rapidly, the blood draining from the fourth section of his mark.

And he knew. He knew.

The King Peacemaker had managed to save King Gareth Ironclad, ruler of the Eastern Kingdom, from death's grip.

Despite the weakness settling into his bones, the night was not over. Not until more royal blood had been spilt. The armored knight with the black blood had killed a king, but Bane had not. King Gareth was out of reach, but another was not, the lawful northern ruler.

He disappeared, and when he emerged from the fabric of life, a young man barely older than he stood before him, staring, his mouth opened slightly.

There was no mistaking the similarity in appearance: the man who thought he was the king was his brother.

❧ Annise ❧

Annise was forced to use her hand to shield her eyes against the light, which was so bright it was as if the sun itself had fallen from the sky and crashed into the earth.

The light came from the man she'd seen staring at her. He was with the easterners, but was so different in appearance from them that she couldn't help but to stare back. He reminded her of the westerners, his sunshine-golden hair long and lustrous. He reminded her of her mother.

The light vanished, and Annise was left blinking away white spots and her foolish thoughts. Why would a westerner be here, now? And no westerner would be caught dead in the company of an eastern army. They hated each other more than the north hated both of them. She had no idea what sort of sorcery the light was, but she didn't particularly care at the moment, not when Bane was still on the loose somewhere.

Bane appeared again, this time in front of Arch. *No*, she thought. *Not him. Not my brothers.*

"Who are you?" Arch said, taking a step forward, his voice full of awe.

"Arch," Annise called out, but he didn't react, unable to tear his gaze away.

"I am Bane," the boy said. "I am your brother." His black pinprick eyes flicked between Arch and Annise, as if speaking to them both.

Annise shuddered as Zelda's tale of her lost brother came back to her. This boy had killed her father, and if he was truly the Kings' Bane, more would fall to him before the prophecy of the Kings' Plague was fulfilled.

Starting with Arch.

Bane strode forward, grabbing Arch by the collar, lifting him effortlessly into the air. Arch struggled against the smaller boy, one brother locked against another—one she knew as well as herself, and one she barely knew at all.

Arch managed to take a swipe at his brother, who merely dodged the blow. "Stop," Bane growled. "Stay out of this. You don't have to die."

Annise took a step forward, cocking her head to the side. Realization swarmed like angry bees. Bane wasn't here for Arch, because Arch wasn't the true king. By northern law, *she* was the ruler. She was the queen.

Her lost brother was here for her.

Arch took another swing at Bane, who blocked it with his blade, slinging his brother to the ground. Breathing heavily, Arch leaped up and fought back with all the skill he could muster.

Her heart hammering, Annise charged toward the duo, praying she'd make it in time.

"I. Don't. Want. To. Kill. You," Bane roared, shoving Arch back once more. Annise was ten steps away, five. With fresh determination, Arch attacked, his blows quick enough to disarm most opponents. But Bane wasn't most opponents.

He blocked each strike and then attacked, his blade sinking into Arch's gut at the same moment Annise bashed into him with her shoulder. They went down in a tangle of arms and legs, his blade swinging wildly, slashing her hip open.

She pinned him to the ground, but he bucked, as strong as an ice bear, throwing her aside like she was a dainty princess and not a broad-shouldered queen. He bared his teeth and leapt upon her and she knew she was dead.

Until an enormous black shape eclipsed everything, standing before her. Tarin, the back of his pale head snaking with dark veins, swung his Morningstar at the Kings' Bane.

Bane dodged the blow and stepped inside its arc, punching the knight's armor with his small fist. The sound was so loud Annise thought the earth itself might be cracking open. Tarin flew backwards, over her, skidding to a stop.

"I'm sorry, sister," Bane said. "I cannot resist it. Not anymore. This land needs a chance to heal, to start over. Father had to die. And now you do, too."

Annise wouldn't fight back. Not against her own brother, no matter what he was. This was the brother she'd mourned as a child. The brother she'd lost. He hadn't chosen his life any more than she'd chosen hers. She didn't know if Arch was dead or not, but if he was alive, he would be king after she was gone, and she knew he'd be a good one.

But Sir Dietrich had other ideas. His armor dented and splattered with blood that Annise suspected was not his own, the knight stepped forward to face her youngest brother.

"Don't hurt him," she pleaded, struggling back to her feet. She didn't know who she was speaking to. Maybe both of them.

Bane ignored her. He sprang forward, his blade moving faster than Annise's eyes could follow. And yet each slash was met with an even faster block by Sir Dietrich, whose sword almost seemed to separate itself from his grip, moving of its own volition.

It was impossible. Even when Bane disappeared and reappeared several times behind the knight, Sir Dietrich managed to whirl and deflect his attacks. No swordsman in the Four Kingdoms was that good. Not naturally, anyway.

Bane took a blow to the shoulder, and he roared, clutching his skin as blood poured between his fingers. He seemed shocked, his mouth agape. Another slash of Sir Dietrich's sword forced the boy back, and he stumbled, falling to the ground. His body was beginning to shake, wracked with tremors. Sir Dietrich stood over her trembling brother, sword held high.

Annise threw herself at the knight, knocking him aside as his sword came down. There was a meaty thump and a cry, and, as she landed, Annise turned her head to look back. Sir Dietrich's sword was stuck in the ground, Bane having rolled away. The knight was glaring at her, dumbfounded. "What was that?" he growled.

"You were going to . . . I couldn't . . . I had to . . ." Annise started and stopped and started again, none of the words sounding quite right in her head.

Beyond the knight, Bane had regained his feet, though his knife was missing and he was swaying from side to side. He was no longer clutching his shoulder, which bled freely. He looked as surprised as Sir Dietrich at what Annise had done. "Why?" he said breathlessly.

"Because you're my brother," Annise said.

Bane's lips parted slightly, and then closed. A moment later he was gone.

This time he didn't reappear, gone to another place, to which, Annise suspected, she could not follow.

Ignoring Sir Dietrich's dark stare, Annise pushed to her feet and ran toward where Tarin had gone down earlier. She found the knight on his back, his eyes closed, his chest plate dented where her brother had punched him.

"Tarin?" she said, ignoring the strangeness of his skin, which was too thin, too . . . stretched. She cupped his chin. "Tarin?" When he didn't respond, she felt beneath his nostrils for breath. She felt something, but didn't know if it was her imagination or the wind or air from the knight's lungs.

"Please, Tarin," she said. "I know I haven't always been the easiest traveling companion, but I—" *I what? What am I trying to say?* The truth whispered through her heart. "I need you. You are my hope flower, and I need you."

His eyes fluttered open and she let out a quick gasp of relief. He smiled, though it was weak. "Have you seen my helmet?" he asked.

Annise laughed and sank back into a drift. For a long time, she stared at the snowfall, which hung like pale stars in the sky.

Chapter Thirty-Five

The Northern Kingdom | Silent Mountain

Bane

He'd tried to kill her, and she'd saved his life.
His sister. The queen.

He'd seen it in her eyes, a miasma of emotions, each trying to gain advantage: regret, hope, sorrow, love, anger.

Anger, yes. That he understood. Sorrow and regret, too, perhaps. Hope? Love? Those were foreign to him, as impossibly distant as the shores of the Burning Sea.

His shoulder was throbbing, his skin slick with blood. But that was only pain, of little concern to the Kings' Bane. Though he'd lost his dagger, he had others. Sitting by the fire, he picked one up and thrust its blade into the flames, which were still crackling happily. Once the blade was sufficiently hot, he pulled it out and touched the broad side to his broken flesh, a flare of agony shooting through his arm as his skin sizzled. A moment later, his wound was sealed.

It would heal, eventually, which was more than he could say about the invisible tears in the fabric of his mind.

Dropping the dagger, he curled and uncurled his fingers, taking deep breaths. He'd grown used to the feeling *after*, though he wouldn't be able to stand if he tried. He lowered his head slowly to the ground, sighing with weariness.

That's when he noticed something: Bear was gone. Not just out—gone. None of the large man's scant possessions remained. Both sets of his boots had been taken. All of his fur-lined clothing. Near the fire, a freshly stacked pile of moist firewood stood, drying in the heat. Six jugs of melting snow were lined up nearby. Recently carved meat hung from the ceiling, slowly being smoked.

Bear was gone. "Father . . ." Bane murmured. "Father, why?" He'd been abandoned. He had no one.

He was Death, and Death was forced to walk paths of shadow and isolation.

He released the last of his energy through his throat, between his lips, his cry of anger and sorrow and pain and utter aloneness roaring from the mouth of the cave, startling a white owl who was perched on a scraggly tree on the mountainside.

When he had no sound left inside him, Bane closed his eyes, still clutching the dagger between bloodstained fingers. He had nothing left but a prophecy. A prophecy about him. *Eight rulers must die. Eight—no more, no less. I cannot fail. This is my purpose. Three dead—five to go.*

Though he didn't trust himself to face his sister in the north again—not this soon—he had no qualms about cleansing the other kingdoms. He'd start as far away from the north as he could get. Not that he had a choice, because he already knew where he would be called to next.

Yes. As soon as he'd recovered, Bane would leave the only home he'd ever known.

The Southern Empire would be the next to fulfill the Oracle's prophecy.

Chapter Thirty-Six

The Eastern Kingdom | South of Raider's Pass

Roan

Over the last few weeks, Roan had awoken in a number of strange places. Now, in darkness, he awoke in chains. He squinted against the light of an approaching torch.

Voices rumbled nearby, but he couldn't understand them, his ears still ringing with the clash of swords and rumble of timber cascading down a mountainside.

He remembered the light, flowing from his chest, splitting the sky in half.

The voices clarified. "How many dead?" one asked. Prince Grian. A memory stirred in Roan's mind: Prince Guy's throat cut wide open as he tumbled to the ground.

"The tally isn't finished," another voice replied. One of the platoon commanders, Hardy Ironclad, a cousin to the three princes. "But the numbers have already stretched over four thousand."

"Our army was only five thousand."

"Yes," Hardy agreed. "The enemy lost only a third of our number. The rest retreated toward Gearhärt."

"The northern force seemed smaller than we expected."

"It was. Our scouts have returned from their northern expedition. They bring word of a girl resembling Annise Gäric riding with the army."

"Annise Gäric? The princess was supposed to be in hiding, along with her brother."

Hardy shook his head. "Apparently not. And the army was small because it was nothing more than a group of rebels who are planning to take back the throne from Lord Griswold."

"We were defeated by a group of *rebels*?" Grian scoffed. "The king was *killed*. My brother was *killed*."

"They were well-prepared," Hardy said. "We lost many through the pass. Also, there was . . ." His lips hung open, unspoken words crowding inside his mouth.

Grian nodded, as if reading the commander's mind. "What was that *thing*?" he asked. Roan immediately knew who—what—he meant. The boy cloaked in shadow. The boy who'd slashed open Guy's throat and stabbed Gareth in the chest.

"Your father—" Hardy started to say.

"My father is *dead*!" Prince Grian snarled.

"You think I don't know that?" Hardy said, glaring at the prince. "He was my uncle, but I loved him like a father, too. My father was the Shield, remember? He saved your father's life once."

Roan peered between half-closed lids at the two, wondering where Gareth was. *He isn't dead*, he reasoned with himself. *I felt the life still inside of him. I poured everything I had left into him.*

But what if it wasn't enough?

The prince and the commander glared at each other for a few long moments before their expressions softened simultaneously. "I can't believe the Juggernaut is dead," Hardy said.

"I thought the old man was invincible," Grian agreed.

"It was that cursed knight," Hardy said. "Did you see his flesh? It looked dead. His blood was black. The northerners are practicing dark magic. Sorcery. He almost killed Stonesledge, too. No human man could've done that."

He *almost* killed Stonesledge. The ironmarked warrior had somehow managed to survive the battle, despite his grievous injuries.

"We will have our revenge," Grian said.

A third person arrived, her slender figure a shadow, backlit by the torchlight. "Ho, Grian. Hardy," Gwendolyn said by way of greeting.

"How is Gareth?" Grian asked.

"You mean the king?"

Grian grimaced. "I am the king. My brother is in no position to rule. It should've been Guy, but instead the responsibility falls to me."

Gwen sighed, as if she was already tired of dealing with the prince. She didn't argue the point. "He is alive, but weak. Roan managed to stave off the worst of Gareth's wounds. But his injuries were grievous, and Roan lost strength before repairing them all. It will take him time to recover, but recover he will. And then he will be king."

Gareth is alive, Roan thought, his eyes flashing open. *I saved him. He was supposed to die and I saved him anyway*. His chains rattled as he tried to lift his arms. "Where is he?" he groaned. "I can heal him the rest of the way. My strength is back. Mostly."

Grian stood over him. There was no kindness in his eyes. Gwen hung back. Roan tried to catch her gaze, but she wouldn't look at him. He'd never seen her look so uncertain.

"Who are you really?" Grian asked. "Not your normal nonsense about not knowing your father and your Southron mother. The truth. Now."

When Roan hesitated, fumbling for a way to explain a long story in just a few words, Grian drew his sword and shoved the tip under Roan's chin.

"Cousin," Hardy cautioned.

Gwen said, "Remember, he saved Gareth."

"Gareth was the Shield. He was not meant to be saved. The wrong brother died."

If Roan wasn't in chains, he might've tried to hit the prince. In the face. Hard. Traditions be damned, no man should have to die simply because he was born first. "Fate disagreed with you," he said instead.

"Your words are as dusty as your lineage. You are the *enemy*," Grian said, glaring at Roan, who was too scared to breathe, fearing the movement might puncture his neck on the blade. Turning toward the Orian, Grian added, "You said it yourself."

"I said nothing," Gwen said. "I merely told you what I overheard the strange boy say."

Hardy pulled on the prince's shoulder, and Grian finally retracted his blade. Roan breathed deeply, his heart thudding in his chest. "My father is . . ." he started to say.

But Gwen cut him off. "Your father is—was—King Gill Loren, ruler of the western kingdom. You have three siblings, Rhea, Bea, and Leo. Your aunt was Sabria Loren, executed by Lord Griswold. Her daughter and son, Annise Gäric and Arch Gäric, lawful heirs to the northern throne, are your cousins. It is said they fought bravely at Raider's Pass, and Annise was seen retreating under her own strength. Arch was injured, but is presumed to be alive."

Roan was stunned. She must've heard what the boy had said and connected the dots. There were a lot of dots to connect, but then again, she'd lived a long time. "I—"

"Which now, under western law, makes you the western king," Hardy said.

"Roan *Loren*. Our sworn enemy," Grian added. "All this time you were right under our thumbs. Marching along beside us, trading quips with Gareth and Gwen. We should kill you now." His blade gleamed in the light, reflecting the deadly glint in his eyes.

"No," Gwen said. "You cannot. He has great value as a ransom." Her eyes caught Roan's, and there was a gleam in them that belied her words. *She's lying*, he realized. And for the first time since he'd met her, he could tell she really saw him.

"You don't give orders," Grian said.

"Your father respected my counsel enough to listen."

Grian's lips went tight, but he didn't argue further. "We will discuss *King* Roan's fate soon enough," the prince said. "Keep an eye on him."

Grian and Hardy left, carrying the torch with them, presumably off to check on Gareth's condition. Roan wanted to follow them, but his chains were secured to a stake driven deep into the ground.

"Gareth is alive," Roan breathed. Under the moon and starlight, he could just make out Gwen's profile in the dark.

"Because of you."

Roan nodded. "Maybe you're rubbing off on me."

Gwen didn't laugh, her eyes dark and serious. "That strange boy called you the Peacemaker."

Roan shook his head, but it wasn't an answer. "Yes, but I don't know what that means."

"You swear it?"

"You know far more than me about the marks. I never even knew about the Western Oracle until you told me."

Gwen chewed on his words for a moment, seeming to contemplate them. She sighed. "My father always believed the marks were of greater importance than most people thought. Not just because of the power they gave the bearers, but because of the role they might play in the fate of the Four Kingdoms. He often searched the eastern libraries for information, but alas, the Ironclads have never been particularly scholarly—the shelves were full of thin volumes with naught more than the occasional reference to the Western Oracle's teachings. I do, however, remember him speaking of the Peacemaker, who would come to save the Four Kingdoms."

Too bad her words are just words, Roan thought. *And I am just a man.* Then again, he was a man who, for the first time in his life, was unafraid of his fate and the mark he bore on his chest. He was no longer a slave to his past—maybe he never was. Something told him his story wasn't over, not yet, and if he'd simply turn the page, the next chapter would begin.

"I am no savior," he said.

"No, you are not," Gwen agreed.

"I am no hero, either."

"Perhaps not. But heroes are not born, they are grown. Each choice is a drop of water, each experience a ray of sunlight. They grow, day by day, until they are the tallest tree in the forest, willing to protect all who live under their shadow."

"I fear I'm naught but a sapling at this point. The wind blows and I bend to the ground."

"And yet I was wrong about you. You are no coward either."

"Thank you. I will remind you of that as oft as I have the opportunity." Before she could respond, he said, "I've been thinking more about the marks. Isn't it strange that those who bear the marks are born in the very places that their particular powers are most suited to? For example, the Ice Lord is in the frozen north. And Fire Sandes was born in the burnt desert of Calyp. Even Beorn Stonesledge's ironmark is suited to your ore-sheathed forests. Nothing is as random as it seems, as if there is a hidden design to it all. There's a *reason* your father taught you the word fatemark, and I want to learn more. I suspect the Western Archives will be more complete than the east's."

"Aye. Surely they weren't all destroyed. But I fear they are well hidden."

"Nothing is hidden from the sight of a king," Roan said.

Finally, Gwen smiled. "You always knew who you really were, didn't you?"

Roan couldn't deny it any longer. "I did. My guardian lied about many things, but not my lineage. Though I never used the surname Loren, it was always there, a part of me. I knew I couldn't hide from it forever."

"And you would be willing to risk your life by returning to the west?"

"I've already risked my life a dozen times in the last fortnight. What's once more?"

"I saw you on the frozen river, the night before last," Gwen said. The abrupt change of subject made Roan flinch.

"You did?" He frowned. He'd thought he'd been stealthy, but it seemed everyone knew of his midnight romp. Everyone except Gareth, perhaps.

Gwen nodded. "I thought for certain you were leaving. I misjudged you."

"Why didn't you say anything before the battle?"

"Because we all have our demons, and we must face them alone."

"We should face them together," Roan said immediately. When had he started believing that? Sometime between getting infected with the plague, nearly being devoured by dragons, mauled by an ore cat, and almost falling to his death in Raider's Pass. *Aye, somewhere in there I have changed.*

"You surprise me," she said.

"I surprise myself. But I want to know the truth about my mark. Yours too. All of them."

"Good," she said. "Because I'm coming with you."

Roan raised one of his arms, shaking his chains. "Only one problem," he said.

Gwen glanced around, and Roan followed her gaze. Several torches winked orange in the darkness, but none close by. They were alone. She withdrew a key from somewhere beneath her armor.

She unlocked the chains and removed his manacles, helping him to his feet.

"What about Gareth?" Roan asked.

"He is king of the east now. You've done all you can for him."

He is alive. He is safe. I have no choice.

Silently, they moved away from camp.

May we meet again, Roan thought.

Despite leaving Gareth behind, for the first time in Roan's life he felt as if he was doing the very thing he was meant to be doing at the very precise moment he was meant to be doing it.

Chapter Thirty-Seven

The Northern Kingdom | Gearhärt

Annise Gäric

Annise sat by her brother's bedside, hunched over, exhausted but unable to sleep while Arch's life hung in the balance. She was back in *The Laughing Mamoothen*, Netta's female-only establishment that was once more making an exception for several men, including her brother. Arch's chest rose and fell, rose and fell. Several times his eyes fluttered, but did not open.

Please, she begged the frozen gods of the north. *Don't take him too early.*

His wound was grievous, and if not for Sir Dietrich he'd surely be dead.

I would be too, she reminded herself. She owed the knight a life debt, one she doubted she'd ever be able to repay. *The way he'd moved . . .*

Supernatural, was the word that sprang to mind. Her lost brother, Bane, had authority over death, and yet Sir Dietrich had defied him. None but one who was skinmarked could've defeated him, and even then it wouldn't have been easy, though it had seemed that her brother had begun to weaken toward the end of the battle, his body trembling.

Sir Dietrich, she mused. She remembered when her uncle had his men strip the knight naked and shine a torch over his skin. There were so many scars, interlaced like vines dangling from a wooly tree. One scar in particular had stood out on his back, a rippling burn mark, larger than all the others. Would Sir Dietrich really have gone so far as to have himself severely burned in order to hide his mark? And if the answer was yes, why? He could've had a good life in the service of the crown. The finest food. The most lavish quarters. He would've stood side by side with the Ice Lord, second only to the king.

But he gave up all that for a hard life as a knight in a frozen land torn apart by war.

Thrice Sir Dietrich had come to check on Arch, and thrice she'd told him to go away. She still didn't know why, only that she wanted to be alone with her brother. Zelda had tried to talk to her, too, but Annise had begged off, requesting a few days to consider what would come next. Zelda told her not to wait too long, for she had a duty to the kingdom.

I don't want this duty, Annise thought now, as she had a dozen times before. This time, however, it was harder to tell whether the words rang of truth.

Annise flinched when someone cleared their throat.

"Frozen hell," she muttered, seeing the giant man in the doorway. "Have you heard of knocking?"

"I didn't want to disturb your brother's sleep," Tarin said, stepping inside. Before they'd left Raider's Pass, he'd replaced his helmet. To her knowledge, he hadn't removed it since. She wondered whether he ever would again. His breastplate was dented in, the shape of a smallish fist where her brother had punched him. She still couldn't believe how much force had been behind the hit. Tarin was a mountain, but he'd flown backwards like a pebble.

"He's unconscious. If a battle broke out in this very room he'd sleep right through it."

"I'm sorry," Tarin said. "I wish there was something I could do, but outside of battle I am of no use."

Images flashed through Annise's mind: Tarin knocking over the famed warrior, Beorn Stonesledge, he who was ironmarked, swatting him aside with almost predatory ease; Tarin smashing King Ironclad's head with his Morningstar; the dark look in Tarin's eyes when he was strangling the farmer, Killorn, what seemed like an eternity ago.

Yes, Tarin had mastered the art of violence long ago, either due to circumstance, experience, or simply because of the black blood flowing through his veins.

Annise blinked and forced herself to replace the disturbing images with others: Tarin wrapping his arm around her, his warmth flowing through her; the twinkle in his eyes when he first looked at her with undisguised awe and called her the Bear-Slayer; the way he always defended her against her own self-deprecating quips, like she was worth more than the sum of her external parts.

"You are a good man," Annise said finally, realizing the knight had been staring at her for a long time, his head cocked to the side.

Tarin's eyes narrowed behind his faceplate. "Your mother said that to me once."

The mention of her mother made Annise choke slightly. Perhaps it was because Arch was now fighting for his life that she felt suddenly emotional. "She was right," she said. "No matter what the rest of the kingdom says."

Tarin shook his head, but he wasn't disagreeing. "Sounds like good advice. Maybe you should listen to it yourself."

Annise smirked at the knight's cleverness. He'd caught her in her own words. A swell of something magnanimous and heavy filled her belly, her chest, her throat. Her mouth watered with feeling for this knight who hid behind plate and metal and dark mesh.

"Take off your mask," she said.

Tarin didn't move, frozen in place.

"I am the queen," she said, feeling slightly bad for using her position so frivolously. "I command it."

"You have seen my face once, and you would dare to look upon it again?" Tarin asked. She could see the confusion in his shadowy eyes.

"You question the courage of the woman who played Snow Wars with an ice bear and emerged victorious?" Annise said, trying to keep the mood light.

Tarin chuckled, but still didn't move to take off his helmet. "I'm willing to barter. I will show you my face if you will look in that mirror." He pointed to a looking glass hanging over a dressing table. Annise had been avoiding it ever since Arch was given this room for his recovery.

"Why?" Annise asked.

"Because I want you to see what I see."

"Aye? What's that? A pear with arms?"

"No," Tarin said, his eyes serious. "Someone beautiful and strong and determined."

She wanted to laugh at the fact that he'd not only used the word *beautiful* to describe her, but that he'd said it first in his list of compliments. But she couldn't because there was no jest in his voice.

Frozen hell, man, she thought. *We must both be blind or stupid. Or both.*

But still . . . she wanted him to remove his mask, and she could take a quick peek at her archenemy—the mirror. "Fine. I'll look."

Like it was nothing, she stood and stomped over to the looking glass, standing directly in front of it. She froze.

It was her, all right: muscled arms, broad shoulders, wide, dimpled chin. But there was something different there, too, something she'd never seen before. Steel in her eyes. Determination in the set of her jaw.

It was the face of a queen.

She turned away, as if she saw nothing but Princess Annise from Castle Hill. "There. Satisfied? Your turn," she said.

Tarin nodded. "You're a terrible actress," he said. And then he removed his helmet and placed it on the dressing table.

Annise tried not to stare, but it was impossible. She could see his veins through his skin, bulging from his flesh, black blood streaming through them. She could see the ivory of the bones in his jaw, thick and strong.

There were so many things about his appearance that should scare a normal person, give them nightmares, make them run away screaming. But Annise was no normal person, and the thing she noticed above all else were his eyes.

His eyes were the same, conveying the entirety of his facial expression in a single glance. She could see the self-hatred, the fear, and something else that couldn't be hidden behind his own self-loathing.

The thing he felt for her.

She could see the love.

And beneath whatever the witch had done to him while sparing his life, he was a handsome man, every bit as attractive as Sir Dietrich with his rugged manliness and scars. She lunged at Tarin and he caught her in his strong arms. Her lips found his and for a moment the kiss was one-sided, making her wonder if she'd misinterpreted everything.

But then, slowly, firmly, his lips moved against hers. She cupped her hands around his cheeks, letting her fingers roam his skin, which was unnaturally smooth, save for the ridges caused by the protruding veins. None of that mattered now. All that mattered was that they were here together.

When Tarin had gone, the massive hunk of man fumbling to replace his helmet like a young boy, Annise smiled at herself in the mirror. Her reflection returned her smile, and there was something about the way it lit up her face that wasn't so bad.

Arch would recover, she knew, as she turned to watch him sleep. But he wouldn't be king.

No. Not until Queen Annise, the Bear-Slayer, is dead.

She left the room, finally ready to speak to her aunt about the future of the kingdom.

Chapter Thirty-Eight

The Western Kingdom | The Crimean Sea

Grey Arris

The sea-worn ship bucked and writhed beneath his feet, causing Grey's stomach to lurch once more. He hung over the wobbly railing, spewing out the little that was left in his empty stomach. It was only the first day of a voyage that would take several weeks, and yet he already felt like death. His stump was clearly infected, and his stomach hated the sea.

"You all right, lad?" one of the crewmembers asked, clapping a hand on his back.

Grey spit into the blue waters of the ocean and nodded thinly.

"Cap'n Smithers said ya can take the day off, 'til ya find yer sea legs."

Grey let out a heavy sigh of relief. Hopefully a good rest while his body grew accustomed to the rise and swell of the sea would do the trick. "Thank you," he said. "But what if I don't find my sea legs?"

"Then we'll throw ya to the sea monsters," the man said, laughing.

As Grey stumbled below decks, he wished he hadn't asked.

Being below decks did little for his nausea, which rose and fell in pattern with the sea. He tried to sleep on the salt-stained sheets in his bunk, but he couldn't stop thinking about two people:

Rhea and Shae. Not necessarily in that order. Even as the ship sailed away from the west, Grey had the urge to ask the captain to turn it around. He could go back to Knight's End, plead with her to help him find his sister. After all, the furia were hers to command now—she could force them to bring Shae back. Rhea owed him that much, especially now that her father was dead and she was queen. More than that, he desperately wanted to see her again, to somehow reconcile the mistakes they'd both made, pour water on the angry flames that had seemed to erupt out of nowhere between them.

An impossible idea. Regardless of what had transpired between them, she was a queen and he was . . .

A thief? A pathetic, lost boy without a hand? A jape with no punchline?

Tears pricked his dry eyes, stinging. A tear fell, then another, so foreign to his face they might've been strange blue rain in cloudless skies. For the first time in nine years, for the first time since his parents' deaths, he wept.

And when he was finished, he wiped the tears and snot from his face, gritted his teeth, and clenched his fists. It was the same reaction he'd had the last time he'd cried. Refusal to go quietly into the night. Refusal to give up on his sister or himself.

No, he thought fiercely, biting back another swell of nausea. *I'm a brother. I'm Shae's brother, and I won't abandon her to the furia.*

As those determined thoughts rattled around in his brain, he swore he could see the infection in his stump grow, poisoning his blood, sucking the life from his soul.

He only hoped he would live long enough to find Shae.

Chapter Thirty-Nine

The Western Kingdom | Knight's End

Rhea Loren

The Fury was bound by her own archaic laws, a fact that Rhea couldn't help but to relish. Her sins had been forgiven by the king, just before he'd died. Therefore, in the eyes of Wrath, she was once more eligible to inherit the throne. An absurd rule—why should a king have the power to forgive sins?—but one that was benefitting her now.

As the Fury dripped holy water on Rhea's head, the crimson-haired warrior said, "By Wrath's authority, I anoint you Queen Rhea Loren, ruler of the west and holy symbol for the realm." As the golden crown was placed atop her head, the water snaked its way into Rhea's scars, funneling down toward her chin, where it cascaded to her feet.

She didn't need to hide her face. Never would she hide it again. If she couldn't be Rhea the Beautiful, she would be Rhea the Beloved, Rhea the Holy, Rhea the Fierce.

Either that or Rhea the Feared. She hadn't decided yet.

Rhea smiled, as the masses who'd gathered to witness her coronation cheered. For her. "Today is a Day of Forgiveness," she announced. "Today, all sins shall be forgiven." As the crowd pushed forward, she bent down and extended her arm. They pressed their lips against the same blue diamond ring she'd kissed to earn her own forgiveness. They looked at the scar on her face not with judgment or disgust, but with *adoration*.

After the rest of the Lorens learned that Jove had been murdered right in front of Rhea's eyes, a story had been hastily concocted to explain the 'W' on her face. The lie was necessary if the people were to respect her. It was said that she loved Wrath so much, was so dedicated to his righteous cause, that she'd used a holy knife to etch his symbol into her own skin.

"What righteousness!" the people were heard to have said. "Her holiness rises above us all." Already, the most devout servants of Wrath were following her lead, carving his symbol onto their own faces. She could see several such worshippers in the crowd, their cheeks rent with ragged blood-clotted lines.

Rhea rose from her crouch, stepping purposely in front of the Fury, blocking the holy warrior as she faced the people. Her people. She smiled. She waved. She soaked in their admiration.

A few days earlier she'd pretended to be in shock as the guards had carried her away from Jove's corpse. She'd refused to eat or speak or leave her room. When her cousins had finally managed to drag the story from her lips—how a demon had appeared in the throne room a moment after she'd kissed King Jove's holy ring; how the evil creature had killed the king in cold blood, slashed Rhea's stomach, and then vanished; how she'd tried to put pressure on her cousin's wound, his blood coating her dress—they'd believed her. Only Ennis seemed unsure, his gaze suspicious, especially when he learned the killing stroke had been dealt using a blade of shattered glass. But he wisely had voiced no concern regarding the truth of her tale.

Even her twin siblings had hugged her, sobbed into her chest, begging her forgiveness for the way they'd treated her. She knew they weren't being sincere, only playing to the future queen. She'd sobbed along with them, speaking the words they expected, resisting the urge to wring their little necks.

The healers said she'd been lucky the wound to her stomach was only skin-deep. It would heal. Some herbal ointment and a few bandages would do the trick. It might not even scar, not that it mattered—scars meant little to Rhea now.

Not one of her cousins challenged her new claim to the throne. After two dead kings in as many days, she could see the fear in their eyes. Rumors of monsters and demons were being repeated over and over again throughout the city, not only in temples but in shops, cafes and homes. The people were scared, and she would take full advantage.

The people cheered and cheered and cheered some more, showering the dais with handfuls of fragrant rose petals. She picked one up and breathed it in. It was the smell of defiance, of victory. Whatever evil had killed her father, it had *not* killed her. Her cousin had thrust her aside like a petulant child, using his righteous dog, the Fury, to scar her, to maim her. But he had *not* had the stomach or foresight to finish her off. That had proved to be a fatal mistake.

Then she'd been a weak, naïve little girl.

Now she was strong and spiteful and angry at the world that had failed her. She would not fail herself. She would not fail the west.

♌

Later on, when she was back inside the castle and the self-declared Day of Forgiveness was coming to a close, Rhea sat in front of her mirror—which had been replaced, upon her request—brushing the knots out of her hair. Although her reflection in the looking glass continued to shock her, she forced herself to stare at what she'd become.

A monster, she thought.

For once, the thought did not bring her sadness. No, not anymore. Now it brought her anger. But not only anger. Satisfaction, too. For this monster had become a queen.

She pulled her brush through her lustrous golden hair, humming softly to herself. Yes, today she had been the righteous, holy queen that Knight's End deserved, giving the realm hope for a better future.

With a sudden jerk of her hand, she slammed the hairbrush down on the dressing table, shattering its wooden handle, sending it spinning across the shiny floor. She hissed at her horrifying reflection, her heart racing at how . . . *unhinged* she looked.

Staring at herself, she resisted the urge to shatter the mirror once more, this time with her fist. She longed to feel physical pain, a distraction from her inner turmoil.

"Tomorrow the Four Kingdoms will burn," she growled.

And then she gave into the temptation, thrusting her fist forward, smashing the glass, relishing the tinkle of the broken shards as they rained down upon her dressing table. The tight flesh of her knuckles was broken, smeared with warm blood. She raised her hand to her lips and licked the blood off.

Yes, she thought. *I am unhinged. And I like it.*

She spun around to face the Fury who had carved her face like a butcher. The strong woman was bound to a chair, a dirty rag stuffed into her mouth. She'd had several of her most trusted guards abduct the red-cloaked warrior shortly after the coronation.

The Fury tried to scream at her through the gag, but it came out as nothing more than a muffled growl. Her face turned as red as her cloak as she struggled against the ropes, which chafed against her muscular body.

Rhea smiled wickedly, idly resting her hand on a silver platter that contained several freshly sharpened knives, gleaming under the light of the wall sconces. "Is something the matter?" Rhea asked, cocking her head to the side. "Surely a Fury would want to follow the holy lead of the queen. Am I mistaken?"

The Fury stopped moving, her cheeks paling.

"No?" Rhea said. "No matter. You will thank me later." She kicked out, her bare foot catching the Fury in the chest. The chair rocked backwards, landing with a rough thud on the hard floor.

After selecting the longest, sharpest knife from the tray, Rhea sauntered over, taking her time, relishing the moment. After a brief hesitation, she knelt down and tightened her grip on the blade's handle.

And then she began to carve, ripping the rag from the Fury's mouth so she could hear her screams.

ço   ૭

Get a free short story from the bestselling Fatemarked high-fantasy series by signing up for David's email list at https://www.subscribepage.com/b2v6v3

If you enjoyed this book, please consider leaving a review on Amazon, Goodreads, or Audible. Reviews are monumentally important when others are deciding to give the series a try.

Truthmarked Sneak Peek

The Western Kingdom, Knight's End

Rhea Loren

"The red-barbed funnel is the most poisonous spider in the world, did you know that?" Rhea asked.

The red-haired woman was huddled in the corner, her head down. Her hair was tangled and matted, covering her face. She didn't respond. But Rhea didn't care, it was meant to be more of a rhetorical question, a part of her ongoing monologue.

The spider crawled along her palm, repeatedly dashing its mouth against her skin, trying to sting her with the red barbs inside its mouth. The barbs containing the deadliest poison in the world.

Rhea laughed, letting the spider crawl across to her other palm. "So deadly, and yet it cannot use its poison against humans. See?" The spider tried again and again, never giving up its attack. Crawling and striking. Crawling and striking. "Its mouth is too small. Isn't that amusing?"

Again, there was no response from the woman who used to be one of the Three, the Furies that led the *furia*, the righteous warriors of Wrath and servants to the crown. The woman who now appeared as broken as a china plate smashed on the ground.

"See how it strikes again and again, desperate to end me?" She placed her palm against the side of a table, and the spider crawled onto it. "And yet I am the one who holds its life in my hands."

Her fist slammed down with a thud that made the Fury flinch in the corner. When Rhea raised her hand, the spider was crushed, a mushed body and tangle of broken legs. She noticed the Fury's dark eyes staring out at her between a gap in her wall of crimson hair.

"Do you see where I'm going with this? You are powerful, oh yes, a strong warrior, fit to serve a queen. Probably strong enough to *kill* a queen. But you won't, will you? Because if you try, I will crush you." Rhea slammed her fist down again and again, and with each hammer blow the table shook and the Fury flinched.

She stopped abruptly, letting silence fall like a scythe. She stood. Approached the woman, who she had taken to death's doorstep and back again. Reached down, enjoying the way the Fury trembled in anticipation of the blow she thought would come.

But Rhea didn't strike her. Not this time. Instead, she peeled back the hair on one side, tucking it behind the woman's ear. Then she did the same on the other side, until she could see her entire face.

A ragged W was carved in her skin, from temple to chin to temple, and for a moment Rhea admired her handiwork. It was a near perfect match for her own facial scars. At the time her own face was cut, she'd thought it was the end of her life, when, in reality, it had been the beginning. It had opened her eyes to a world beyond beauty, beyond wealth, a world that existed only on *power*, and those who had it.

It had only been a few fortnights ago, but it seemed an eternity since the W on her own face stood for Whore, though that wasn't public knowledge. No, the people of Knight's End, her loyal and adoring subjects, thought the mark stood for Wrath, a symbol of her righteousness and devotion to their deity.

The Fury closed her eyes as Rhea ran the fingernail of her thumb along the scab, which was finally beginning to heal. She traced the W from end to end and then back again, relishing the *feel* of it.

When she was finished, she said, "Whom do you serve?"

The woman's lips moved, but Rhea couldn't make out her words.

"Repeat. Louder."

"I serve the queen," the woman said through cracked lips.

"Be. More. Specific."

"I serve the queen, Rhea Loren, first of her name, Wrath's humble servant."

"Yes. You do. And you will do great things. You have been forgiven of your sins. Now kiss the ring." She held out her left hand and the ring that adorned it, its thick gold band studded with an enormous blue diamond, the only one of its kind, at least as far as Rhea knew. It was the ring of kings, a family heirloom passed down for generations.

She'd plucked it from her dead cousin's fingers herself after she'd killed him.

The woman's eyes flashed open, the surprise obvious in her expression. Rhea knew she expected more pain, more torture—not mercy. Which is exactly why she chose now to offer the woman a second chance—because she knew she would take it.

The Fury kissed her ring, the one Rhea had once kissed while her cousin, Jove, the king at the time, had worn it. She'd killed him a moment later.

Rhea knew it was only the beginning.

◈

Not only had the bootmaker given her shelter when she was at her weakest, but he had given her a beautiful pair of boots, the finest Rhea had ever seen.

Now Jordan Vaughn stood before her throne, looking uncomfortable as he shifted his weight from foot to foot. His storm gray eyes darted from the Fury to Rhea and back to the Fury.

"Do you know why you are here?" Rhea asked.

"I, uh, well, no. Not ezzactly. I was hopin' yer boots dinnit need repairs so soon?"

Rhea was surprised when a very real smile creased her face. This gray-eyed old man had showed her kindness when she wasn't certain she deserved it, and she owed him. "No, good sir, the boots remain as perfect as the day you gave them to me." She lifted her purity dress slightly to show him that she was wearing them, and he blushed.

"Good. I—that's good."

"I sent for you for a far more auspicious purpose. I could use your services."

His eyes widened. "'Nuther pair of boots?"

"How about five thousand?"

His jaw dropped and he began licking his lips back and forth. Then his face fell. "I'd have to decline," he said.

"Why?"

"I handcraft all o' me boots. An order of that size would take years. Mebbe me whole life."

"I thought you might say that. What if you created the pattern, and I provided a team of expert leather cutters and seamstresses to manufacture the boots. Would that be fair? I would pay you three Goldens per pair."

"Three Goldens per . . ." The thought trailed away from the aging bootmaker, and he shook his head. "Aye. I accept, that's more gold than I've ever dreamed of. But why are you doin' this?"

Rhea stood up, floating down the steps toward him. She touched his cheek briefly with her palm and she felt him trembling. Fear, excitement, anxiety . . . it was all running through him, just beneath his skin. "Because you showed me great kindness once. And I need boots for my army. Your boots will help protect the Wrath-loving people of our great kingdom."

"Thank you, Queen Rhea," he said. "From the bottom of me heart, thank you."

She watched him go, surprised at how warm she felt all of a sudden.

The Northern Kingdom, Gearhärt

Annise Gäric

Annise Gäric never expected to be a queen. *Frozen hell, I never wanted to be a queen*, she thought, sitting by Arch's bedside. No, she'd planned to live out her time as a princess, until her father, Wolfric Gäric, the Dread King of the North, died of old age, and her brother, Archer, as the eldest male heir, took the throne.

However, she was quickly learning that the more you expected something, the less likely it was to happen. Her father had been murdered by the brother she'd thought died long ago, the brother who was now known as Kings' Bane. And then she'd had a name day, leaving her as the queen until Arch turned eighteen, which was still almost two long years away.

Originally, she'd planned to relinquish all rights to the crown to her brother, regardless of his age. But then something had happened. She'd changed. And Arch had been injured in battle.

She'd held vigil by his bedside for days, taking her meals there, sleeping on a lumpy cot brought in by the owner of the tavern they were staying in, *The Laughing Mamoothen*, a formidable broad-faced woman named Netta who also happened to make the best mamoothen stew in all of the Four Kingdom's, at least by Annise's reckoning.

Now, as she stared at her brother's handsome, peaceful face, she wondered whether, when he awoke, he would hate her for stealing his throne. She also wondered if today would be the day he finally opened his eyes. The healer said some people came out of such a condition in mere days. Others took longer, sometimes months, requiring liquid meals and water to be dribbled down their throats to sustain them. Annise didn't want to think about the third group of people, the ones who never woke up.

There was a knock on the door, but Annise didn't look up. It was probably Lady Zelda, her eccentric aunt, once more requesting a queenly decision on strategy. The truth was, Annise wasn't ready to make a decision—not with Archer like this. And yet, she couldn't delay much longer, for the more her uncle, Lord Griswold, sat upon the ice throne and played king, the more the northerners would assume the crown was his.

Annise sighed when there was a second knock. "If you don't have a hot bowl of mamoothen stew, go away!" she shouted.

The door opened slowly, but not all the way. Just a crack. A white piece of cloth fluttered through the opening. "Don't throw anything," a voice called through.

Sir Dietrich. Though he was the best swordsman Annise had ever known and he had saved both hers and Arch's lives during the battle at Raider's Pass, twice they'd argued in the last two days. And yes, she might've thrown a boot at him, which explained his odd request.

"Are you ready to talk about the burn scar on your back?" Annise asked.

"We've already talked about that." More white flag waving. Well, white *shirt* waving.

"Shut the door," Annise said. Dietrich had given her a story about his scar, but Annise was certain it was a lie, or at least only a fraction of the truth.

"Frozen hell, woman," the knight said, pushing the door open the rest of the way and dropping the white shirt. He crossed his arms over his face, presumably to protect himself from projectiles. He wasn't wearing his armor, merely a white cloth shirt tied up the front and sturdy-looking trousers secured with a leather belt. A long sword dangled from a scabbard.

"One—don't call me 'woman.' I am your queen. Two—I'm not going to throw anything at you, so you can stop acting like an unflowered maiden. And three—you don't have any mamoothen stew for me. That perturbs me greatly."

Sir Dietrich's strong arms dropped away from his head, revealing his scarred, but handsome face, and two bright periwinkle eyes that always seemed to contain a hint of mischievousness.

Annise launched the boot she was hiding behind her leg. Dietrich's arms came up, but they were too slow, and also too high, protecting his face. Unfortunately for him, she had aimed for his crotch, and she had excellent aim on account of all the games of Ice Wars she'd played as a child.

He doubled over, groaning and clutching his midsection.

"*Now* are you ready to talk?"

His only response was a groan. He staggered out, his face green. It looked like his breakfast might make a reappearance.

Annise sighed again. What use was being a queen if you couldn't get information out of your subjects? She wondered if her boot-throwing antics could be considered torture, and whether she might eventually earn the title Dread Queen of the North, following in her father's footsteps. She laughed at the notion.

Arch stirred in his sleep, his head rolling from side to side.

Annise froze, watching. Hoping. *Please.*

He continued sleeping, his chest rising and falling with mighty exhalations. *At least he looks peaceful*, Annise thought.

A shadow fell over her as a massive shape filled the doorway. She couldn't hold back a smile as she looked up. Couldn't prevent the loss of breath or the giddy sensation in her chest. But she could hide them. She was a queen, after all, and every queen had to be a master of their emotions. Or at least so Zelda told her, though her aunt was as spontaneous and unpredictable as a winter storm.

"To frozen hell with that," Annise muttered, leaping to her feet and throwing herself at Tarin, who looked confused by both her words and her sudden movement.

Still, he caught her in his strong arms, holding her close. And then he did what would've seemed impossible a mere fortnight ago: He allowed her to lift his black mask, revealing those beautiful dark eyes she'd stared at for days on end while wondering what the rest of him looked like. She pulled down the mesh shield that blocked the lower half of his face. The face which, despite its ghostly pallor and black, bulging veins, no longer seemed so foreign to her. No, she had memorized the lines of his strong jaw, the shape of his masculine nose, the feel of his thick brows.

The taste of his lips, which she tasted again now, pressing her mouth against them so hard she could barely breathe. In this moment, he was her breath. He was the beat of her heart and the blood in her veins. He was her knight in black armor, the only one who seemed to truly understand her.

And when their lips separated it was too soon, was always too soon, and Annise felt as if a part of her had been removed, like a severed limb.

How is this possible? she'd wondered to herself on numerous occasions. *How is he possible?* He was her best friend from childhood, a boy who she'd been told was dead from a horrible bone disease, now reborn as a man. Though Tarin Sheary considered the witch's dark magic that had saved his life a curse—the source of his unusual appearance, superhuman size and strength—Annise would only ever think of it as a blessing, a second chance.

"You know, Sir Dietrich might never be able to have children because of your boot," he said. She could feel the rumble of his voice as it rose from his chest, which was pressed tightly against hers.

"Pity," she said, cupping his cheek in her palm.

"He saved your life. Perhaps he deserves a little patience."

"I appreciate what he did, and have thanked him for his courage numerous times. But until he tells the truth, I will not see him."

A look of amusement crossed Tarin's broad face. "I think I've come up with your royal nickname," he said.

Annise didn't think she was going to like it, but she said, "Go on."

"The Stubborn Queen."

She tried to hit him, but he grabbed her hand and held it back and then kissed her again, softer this time, exploring her lips, her tongue. She explored back.

This time, when they broke apart, his eyes bore into hers, and she detected a question in that look. "What?" she asked.

"How?" he said.

"How what?"

"Just . . . how?" he repeated.

She thought she understood what he meant. "I've asked myself the same question a million times. Remember, I'm not the one who returned from the dead."

"To me you did." His voice had grown gravellier, more serious, sending electricity to every part of her.

"Why, Tarin," she said, "I would've never taken you for a romantic."

His eyes never leaving hers, he carried her backwards, setting her on the edge of her cot, his giant hands roaming down her sides and around her hips.

He kissed her once more, quick, stabbing kisses broken up by words. "The reason"—kiss—"Sir Dietrich"—kiss—"came to see"—kiss—"you . . ."

"Stop talking," she said, clutching the back of his helmet, ripping it off, pulling him closer. "Keep kissing."

He did, and for the next few minutes they fought the urge to do more, an urge they'd been fighting for the last fortnight due to the lack of privacy that came with staying in a busy tavern. Oh, and the fact that her brother was sleeping in the bed next to them and could awaken at any moment.

"There's someone to see you," Tarin finally managed to get out. He was breathing heavily, and so was Annise.

"Lady Zelda?" Annise said, gulping down air.

"No. A stranger. An unusual fellow. Calls himself Sir Christoff Metz."

Annise frowned. "And why should I talk to this Sir Metz fellow?"

"He claims he has information on your uncle's army," Tarin said.

Acknowledgments

Whew. It's been a long road to publishing Fatemarked, both for myself and my family. Doing justice to a high fantasy novel requires full immersion in the world, which meant sometimes my family had to deal with me "disappearing" into the world of the Four Kingdoms for long stretches of time. Endless thanks and hugs to my lovely wife, Adele, for letting me escape into my writing cave to craft this book and series I couldn't have done it without you.

A special thanks to Andrea Hurst's team of expert readers, particularly Jordan Nettles and Leslie Murray, you helped make Fatemarked the best it could be.

To my cover artist, map designer, and crafter of sigils, Piero, WOW. You bring my world of words to life with the most beautiful hand-drawn images I could possibly imagine. I can't wait to see your future depictions of my characters!

Thank you to my beta readers, Laurie Love, Elizabeth Love, Karen Benson, Jenny MacRunnel, Kerri Hughes, Terri Thomas, Rachel Schade, Sheree Whitelock, Abalee Cook, Daniel Elison, and Anthony Briggs Jr. You challenged me at every turn, and my world is a million percent better because of it. May you each be fatemarked.

A leaping high five to my friend and fellow fantasy writer, Marc Edelheit, for all your support and advice during this journey.

You are a truly generous person. To those who haven't read Stiger's Tigers, GET IT NOW.

To the giants of high fantasy who came before me, namely, JRR Tolkien, George RR Martin, Brandon Sanderson, and Robert Jordan, thank you for inspiring me to be a better writer.

Most importantly, to the thousands of readers who decided to read one or more of my books . . . YOU are the heroes in my story. Your support allows me to do what I love for a living, and your enthusiasm keeps me going!

Kickstarter Backers

Our eternal thanks go out to the following people (and to those who chose not to be recognized publicly), for being patrons of the arts and making the hardcover editions of this book possible.

— A, B —

MC Abajian • Thérèse Abrams • Shawnie Adams, Oceanside CA • Myla Aguilar • Faizaan Alam • Dana Aldridge • Seth Alexander • Cody L. Allen • J.A. Andrews • Jerome Anello • Brianna & Aerith Arana • Mike Armstrong • Ivan Patricio Tamayo Arteaga • Dyrk Ashton • Jon Auerbach • Padraig Ayre • Amanda B. • Charles Scott Bach • Mrinal Singh Balaji • Ben P. Balestra • Dan Barnes • Michael Jonathan Basaldella • Andrew Bayuk • Kristopher & Mackenzie Beaver • Brandon Bender, Mandan ND • Karen Benson • For my son Bentley, may your love of reading take you on many unforgettable adventures. • D. Berger • Greg Bergerson • Rachael Besser & Rafi Spitzer • Nathan Biewer • Jedidiah Blake II • Howard Blakeslee • Billie Bock • Tom Bohac • A.J. Bohne IV • Bonk • John H. Bookwalter Jr. • Alexander Joseph Borns • Jason Bowden • Travis Bowen • Michael

Boye • Tom Branham • Curtis Brown • Kristopher Brown • Scott Bullock • Laura Bumbulis • Jenny Busby • S. Busby

— C, D —

Justin C' de Baca • Brian Carroll • Jose H. Castaneda Jr. • Jonathan Cervantes • Joshua C. Chadd, fellow author • Dennis Clarke • Chuck Coatsworth • Steve Cobb • Lewis A. Colau • Sean Conley • Kay Cook • Emma Coombes • Michelle N. Cooper • Jonathan Cormier • Stephen Costanzo • Phyllis J. Cotner-Fellous • Larry J. Couch • Timothy Frank Couch III • Kevin & Cody Cronic • Tim Cross • James R. Crowley • Shaun Cutting • Kyra Dagny-Heath • Kevin "Big O" Daniels • Graham Dauncey • Anna Davis, Centralia WA • Richard Davis • Rocky Davis • Julian Delgado • Scott Dell'Osso • Eugene Anthony Deziel • Stephen Dittmann • Donna • JL Dougherty • Stephen Dye

— E, F, G —

Mary & Suzan Eaton • Ryan T. C. Eckerson • Mark T. Eckstein • Alex & Evie Edwards, keep reading! • Larry Marshall Elliott • Autumn Engdahl • Troy D. Erickson • Jolinda Erolin • Brian Josue Pedroza Esparza • Lynne Everett • Rob Falla • FanFiAddict • Jeremy Feath • Michael Feeney • George Ismael Feliu, author • Rui Ferreira • Shawn Finn • Sylvia L. Foil • Devon Fountaine • Mrs. Fournier • Jessica Fox • G. Miles Frankum • Scott Frederick • Kevin Frey • Samuel Frick • Darren Fry • Marc Garcia • Cedric Gasser • Brian Gaudet • Laura Gaudet • Jessica Gendron • Ashley George • Tashkent Ghosh • Ashley Gibson • Ginger Gilbreath • Lenny Godinho • Josue Ruben Gomez • goosebag • Peter J. M. Gorham • Marie Goursolas • Aaron Granofsky • For Will Grant, for reading on those early mornings as a new dad. • Dion F. Graybeal • Maxime Gregoire

— H, I, J, K —

Phillip H. • Dominik Halper • David Hammer • C.S. Hammermeister • Kristian Handberg • Sydnie Barksdale Harman • B. Harris • Megan Haskell • Travis Hayden • B Heathen • Kenneth Hess • Patrick High • Bryan Hill • T. Hise • Daniel Hogue • David Holzborn • Phil Hucles • Kyle Humphreys • John Iadanza • John Idlor • Eleazar Jarman • Jiazheng • H.I.M. Jimenez • Joshua Johansen • Collin M. Johnson • Fred W. Johnson • Jolsba • Peter Alan Jones • Krys Joseph • James M. Joyce • Kala Judd • Cheryl Karoly • Anthony Kimball • Sarah Kingdred • Michael Kirschenman • S.A. Klopfenstein • Adrian Klovholt • Zachary A. Kosan • Koteric • Paul Krause • Debyi Kucera & Shirley Urie • Alex Kuczwara • Kimberly Kunker

— L, M —

Tom Lancaster • Samantha Landström • André Laude • Sandra K. Lee • Wade Leibeck • Nicholas Liffert • Tima & Tom Lima • J. Lim J. K. • Sarah L. Linser • Nicolas Lobotsky • B. Lovrek • Jesse' Lowery • Karen M. • Kevin M. • Richard Mandolfo • Nick Mandujano III • Scott Mangan • Michael Markins • John Markley • Craig Martens • Jason & Sunisa Martinko • Christina Masters • Mathias • Lisa Maughan • Robin Mayenfels • Lysane Maynard • Donald Dean McBride Jr. • Nate, Sarah, Owen & Kate McBride • Gerald P. McDaniel • Colin McDermott • Joshua McGinnis • Tom McHugh • Courtney McWaters • Pablo Salas Mercado • Miggel • Seana Millard • Michael B. Mitchell • James Molnar

— N, O, P, Q, R —

Joseph Nahas • Brett Nance • Neil • John Nicholson • Øyvind Nordli • Caitlin Northcutt • Dr. Charles E. Norton III • Louie Nuñez • Steve Ognenovski • Michael John Olson • Alexander Ourique •

Rob P. • Daniel J. Pack • Dudley Pajela • Matt Paluch • Emmanouil Paris • Rebecca J. Parker • Katie Pawlik • N. Scott Pearson • Bonnie Phlieger • Jennifer L. Pierce • Mackenzie D. Pierson • Justin Planck • Jacob Platt • Andrew Pleydell • Carl Plunkett • Jake Polk • Pookster • Ian Porter • Lawrence Preijers • David A. Quist • Tim & Julia Raley • Marcos Ramirez • Mikhaïl Ransquin • A. Razor • Steve Reckelhoff • Stephen & Tana Reeve • Daniel Reichmann • Alex Reynolds • Jason Rhine • Anthony Rinella • Jason Rippentrop • Smooth Rivera • William J. Robbins • Yankton Robins • Dylan Rosier • Mary Lynn Ross • Matthea W. Ross • Cheryl Ruckel • Patrick Ryan • Trevor W. Rycroft

— S, T —

David Saelee • CJ Sailey • George Salway • Eric Sands • Seamus Sands, Northern Ireland • Trey Saunders • Doni Savvides • Josh Sayers • Jack N. Scriber • In loving memory of my mom, Margery Seid • Colin Shoemaker • Nicholas J. Short • The Shumate Family • Derek Siddoway • SirCobalt • six60_thebeacon • K. E. Sizemore • Kristian Skog • Ella Sloat • Vince Smeraldo • Alison Tierney Smith • Jacob Smith • Randy Smith • Tanner Smithkins • Snowy • Tommy Snyder • Henrik Sörensen • Tyler Spencer • Charlie Spivey • Mike Stamp • Scott Stiffel • Sean Stockton • Joshua Storm • Kayla Strickland • Jennifer Strohschein • Strongarm • Jenn Stumme • Michael J. Sullivan, author • David Swisher • Greg Tausch • Jeff Taylor • The Tedder-Kings • Cade Thedford • Donald Thompson • Vicky A. Thompson • Travis Triggs • Alex Tuel • Tasha Turner • Shannon Tusler • Mitchell Tyler

— U, V, W, X, Y, Z —

Roberta Upton • Jalle Van Goidsenhoven • Matthijs van Soest • Judy Vandagriff • Eric Vilbert • Waverly Villaire • Greg Vochis • Karissa

W. • Esper Wadih • Madge Watson • Sara Webb • Crystal Weber • Mark Wehling • Pieter Willems • Brittany Williams • Joseph Williams • Kyle Williams • Larry Williams • Holden J. Wiseman • John Woosley • Wraithmarked Creative • Alex Wrigglesworth • Kyle A. Yawn • Jeffrey Yeh • Angel R. York • Robert Zangari • Lord Zuzur, NC

Author Q&A

If you want to learn a bit more about David, his writing, and his other books stay tuned for an exclusive author question and answer session.

When did you first know you wanted to be a writer?

Strangely, it took until I was tenty-nine to figure out what I wanted to be when I grew up. I was working as, of all things, an auditor (yawns) in Sydney, when my soon-to-be wife, Adele, encouraged me to stop talking about writing a novel and "just write one." Easier said than done!

Being the stubborn fool that I am, I fired back, "I don't have any Harry Potter level ideas!"

Being the wise woman that she is, she said, "Just choose the best idea you have and get started."

Surprisingly, I took her advice. I took another corporate job that required fewer hours, and I used my extra free time to write. On the ferry to and from work each day (a full hour round trip). During my hour lunch break. On the weekends. The writing hours began piling up, as did the words. One sentence grew into one chapter grew into a whole book and then my first trilogy.

But to answer the question, I knew I wanted to be a writer when I wrote that first, life-changing sentence. It was like a door had been opened into a part of my mind I never knew existed, a part that I wanted to, no...needed to explore. The rest, as they say, is history.

Are you a full-time author?

Yes! If you'd have told me 11 years ago that I would be writing full-time AND supporting my family doing it, I'd have laughed at the absurdity of such a claim. That said, I think I always did believe I could do it, that I could get to this point, if only I put in enough work (which I most certainly have). Still, none of it would've been possible without my loyal, supportive readers!

What did you do before becoming writer?

As mentioned earlier, I was an auditor (yawns again). I graduated from Penn State with a degree in accounting, and shortly thereafter became a CPA. I landed a job with a "Big Four" accounting firm and audited financial services companies (mutual funds, hedge funds, private equity funds, etc.).

In truth, I never really enjoyed anything about my actual work, but it was a job that paid the bills. And while I wish I had discovered my love for writing sooner, I won't go so far as to say I regret working in public accounting, for three reasons: First and foremost, my job brought me to Australia, where I met my wife. Who then encouraged me to start writing. See where I'm going with this? Life is weird sometimes. If I didn't become a CPA, I might've never become a fantasy author. Second, I met a lot of cool people who I enjoyed working with (even if I didn't enjoy the work itself). And third, I gained general business/finance skills that I still use as an Indie author.

What is the next project you'll be working on?

This is always a good question, because one thing I discovered when I became a writer is that creativity breeds creativity. From the moment I put metaphorical pen to metaphorical paper, I unlocked entire worlds of ideas. This means I have a HUGE list of potential books just waiting to be written. Whenever I finish a project, I usually take a good look at the list and pick out the ideas that I feel the strongest about. I keep narrowing the list until I find the one that "speaks to me."

However, right now my focus is on one world. It all started with Fatemarked, which is set on a single continent known as the Four Kingdoms within a much larger world just waiting to be explored. Kingfall reveals more of that world in the form of another continent separated from the Four Kingdoms by a large landmass and a massive ocean. My next project will further uncover this world and the strange and varied humans and creatures that inhabit it. Without giving too much away, let's just say my next series involves an escaped prisoner, a young woman in search of the truth, and a man with nothing left to live for.

Do you have any interest in writing in any other genre?

I think 'yes' is the answer most authors would give, and it's the same for me. As an artist, it's important to challenge myself, to push the boundaries of what I think I'm capable of. I started my career writing primarily SciFi dystopian novels (The Dwellers Saga, The Country Saga, and The Slip Trilogy). Since then, I've also written a witch apocalypse series (Salem's Revenge), a SciFi fairytale retelling (titled Strings, I retell the story of Pinocchio in a darker, more suspenseful way). I even wrote a six-book children's superhero series (The Adventures of Nikki Powergloves), before finally landing on my favorite of all the genres: epic fantasy.

Why did it take me so long to write in my favorite of all the genres, you might ask?

Easy. Self-doubt and imposter syndrome, hooray! Unfortunately, most authors experience this to one degree or another over the course of their careers, that feeling that you aren't really good enough, talented enough, and that your previous success was just a meeting of luck and perseverance, something that can't be recreated. (There was also that fear that my favorite author of all time, JRR Tolkien, would roll over in his grave if I dared to dabble in his genre.)

However, what I learned when I finally delved into epic fantasy, was that I have so much more to offer to the genre than I thought possible. Feedback from readers in the forms of e-mails, reviews and direct messages on social media proved that my epic fantasy series' (Fatemarked and Kingfall) have made a difference in people's lives, just like Tolkien's books (The Hobbit and The Lord of the Rings) have made a huge difference in my life. *warm fuzzies all over*

So why not another genre? Why not urban fantasy or LitRPG or even mystery? For now, those genres are a distant possibility, but I have years of writing ahead of me, so who knows what the future will hold once I feel I've stowed away in epic fantasy long enough? I can't wait to find out.

What authors did you read the most as a child?

Tolkien! I was a very avid reader from a very young age, devouring books by the shelf-ful (I'm a writer so I get to make up words) from the second I learned to read. Thankfully, my parents fed me well, entire plates of pages and binding and print. They bought me *The Hobbit* and then the boxed set of *The Lord of the Rings*. In a few years, I'd read each of them a dozen times, until the bindings were breaking and the covers falling off.

I also read every Hardy Boys book I could get my hands on, which stoked a love of mysteries I still have today. From there I headed toward Dean Koontz, who swiftly became one of my favorite authors, his creativity knowing no bounds (his Frankenstein retelling is INCREDIBLE).

In my 20s, I discovered Neal Shusterman (*Unwind* and *Bruiser* are a couple of my favorites!) and Patrick Ness (*The Knife of Never Letting Go*). Everything came full circle, returning to epic fantasy when I started reading Brandon Sanderson's Stormlight Archives and Michael J. Sullivan's Riyria series, cementing epic fantasy as my favorite genre.

How the heck did you end up in Hawaii?

Good question! My parents are probably wondering the same thing, considering I was born in El Paso, Texas and grew up in Pittsburgh, Pennsylvania (go Steelers and Penguins!). Well, as I said before, my auditing gig took me to Sydney, Australia. After my wife encouraged me to start writing, I churned out about six books in a couple of years while still working full-time. I'm generally a responsible person, so I figured I had the best of both worlds, a steady income and a hobby that allowed me to express myself and earn some extra money on the side.

My wife, who is more adventurous, made a kink in my carefully laid plans when she suggested we quit our day jobs (she was also an accountant) and go traveling for a while (a while meaning TWO years). I was shocked. Could people really do that? We had savings, but could we really spend it on travel rather than saving for retirement? We didn't know how much, if anything, my writing would earn us in the future. And what would we do afterwards? It was all a bit much, so I rejected it out of hand as nothing more than a fantasy.

My wife is persistent. After the seed was planted, she watered it, gave it plenty of sunlight, and pruned it when necessary. When I had bad days at work, the seed began to grow into a very real plant. When I had really bad days at work, she pounced. Planning to leave in two years moved up to one year moved up to three months! Were we really doing this? Before I chickened out, I gave my notice at work, shocking everyone in my office as well. Adele did the same, and soon we were budgeting for two years on the road and figuring out where we were going to go and where we were going to stay and for how long.

Those two years were some of the best of my life, traveling around the U.S. first (Hawaii, Texas, Pennsylvania, Florida), then Mexico, the Caribbean, Morocco, Europe (Spain, France, Greece, Italy, England, Estonia) and Asia (Thailand, Indonesia) before returning to Australia to figure out what was next for us. During our journey, I wrote the books and Adele edited them, making us a real team as we simultaneously explored the world.

And at the end of it all, sales from my books (I released eight books over the two years) were paying for the entire cost of travel. We realized we could live anywhere in the world. So we decided to look each other in the eyes and say the name of the first place that popped into our heads as somewhere we'd like to live. We both said, "Hawaii" which happened to be the first place we'd visited during our trip. Within a couple months we were touching down in Honolulu, finding a place to stay, getting a car, and enjoying the sun and sand on a daily basis (after my writing was done, of course). Eight years, two kids, two cats and a mortgage later, we plan to stay here forever.

What are some of your favorite books, and why?

I mentioned some of them earlier, but I'll add a few more and explain why:

The Hobbit and *Lord of the Rings* by JRR Tolkien- I learned what it meant to be immersed in a world so deeply that it felt real, like the characters were people I knew and cared about. I mean, Frodo, Sam, Bilbo, Tom Bombadil, Gandalf, Aragorn, need I say more?

Bruiser by Neal Shusterman- utterly creative, beautifully written and heart-wrenching at times, this book gave me all the feels.

Bastion by Phil Tucker- gods, where do I start? This book is all about finding oneself, never giving up, and friendship. All wrapped up in an incredibly inventive world that will capture your imagination.

The Knife of Never Letting Go by Patrick Ness. This book (and series) has more imagination within its pages than I'll ever have in my entire life.

A Game of Thrones by George RR Martin. The depth and breadth of the world surpasses all others.

What other indie authors should I be checking out?

There are so many! Phil Tucker is at the top of my list (*Bastion* and Chronicles of the Black Gate). Ben Galley (*Chasing Graves*) is an incredible wordsmith. Dyrk Ashton's Paternus series is unique and just so much fun. J.A. Andrews' writing in The Keeper Chronicles is nothing short of beautiful. T.L. Greylock's newest series written with Bryce O'Connor, *Shadows of Ivory*, is another wonderful Indie novel. Folks who enjoy Fatemarked and Kingfall also tend to really love A.C. Cobble's books. I've read *Benjamin Ashwood*, and it is excellent! And, of course, you can never go wrong with any book by Michael J. Sullivan, who has built an indie publishing machine, which I continue to try to aspire towards reaching myself!

About the Author

David Estes was born in El Paso, Texas but moved to Pittsburgh, Pennsylvania when he was very young. He grew up in Pittsburgh and then went to Penn State for college. Eventually he moved to Sydney, Australia where he met his wife and soul mate, Adele, who he's now happily married to.

A reader all his life, David began writing science fiction and fantasy novels in 2010, and has published more than forty books. In June of 2012, David became a fulltime writer and is now living in Hawaii with Adele, their energetic sons, Beau and Brody, and their naughty cats, Bailey and Luna.